TONI
BLAKE

the
giving
heart

HQN™

ISBN-13: 978-1-335-50505-7

Recycling programs
for this product may
not exist in your area.

The Giving Heart

To Lindsey
for giving

the giving heart

PART 1

How dear the woods are! You beautiful trees!
I love every one of you as a friend.
                              Lucy Maud Montgomery

                              Anne of Avonlea

CHAPTER ONE

SNOW BEGAN FALLING on Summer Island the first Monday of December. It shouldn't have surprised her—despite the name, winters here came early and often lasted into spring. But she hadn't checked the forecast, and as she stood peering out the big picture window of the Summerbrook Inn while thick, heavy flakes dropped from the sky, Lila wondered if she'd made a mistake in coming.

She'd never been good at looking ahead in life, even in the smallest of ways, like knowing if she should take a jacket when she left home—or in this case, a parka and mittens. Or in bigger ways—like failing to see the signs of imminent danger, the kind that were so easy to recognize in hindsight but you just didn't put the pieces together before it was too late. She tugged a furry robe that belonged to her sister, Meg, tighter around her, hugging herself to ward off a chill—whether real, from the cold and snow outside, or imaginary.

She'd always seen the trait as a sign of optimism—not worrying about the weather, or not expecting doom to strike. She liked being a live-in-the-moment woman. But since arriving two days ago at the family inn—run by Meg since their grandmother's death when Lila was only a teenager—she'd realized that coming to house-sit for her sister hadn't delivered the peace of mind she'd hoped for when she'd made the offer. Leaving Chicago for the blustery month of December had seemed appealing for more reasons than one—but it turned out weather and doom had followed her north.

North. *Why did I think the weather would be better in northern Michigan than in Chicago?* She'd been flustered and emotional at the time, but still. *This is why developing a weather-checking habit would be wise. If you'd checked the weather—and given this trip at least a modicum of thought—you'd have a parka, and a furry robe, and flannel PJs, and a pair of cozy slippers.* More things she'd had to borrow from Meg's closet: below Meg's purple flannel pajamas, decorated with white snowflakes, Lila wore Meg's fleece-lined slippers with cat faces on the top.

Taking her cell phone from the robe's deep pocket, she pulled up a weather app. *No time like the present to build a habit that will make you a more responsible person.*

Her immediate future looked snowy. Light snow was expected on and off 'til nightfall, and tomorrow it would become heavier and more measurable. Each day in the extended forecast featured a snowflake. She chose not to dig any deeper beyond that, not sure she wanted the answers. *This is why I don't check the weather.* Maybe she'd rather not know when bad things were coming. In case they didn't. Maybe pure optimism could wish bad things away.

Though that had been easier to believe two weeks ago.

As it was, doom and danger had found her, and now so had snow. She should probably venture out to Koester's Market today, stock up on some simple foods, and hunker down for the storm. Because even if she was a little sorry she'd come, it was too late to leave—she'd promised Meg to feed the cat and take care of the big Victorian house their great-grandparents had built just after World War II while Meg and her boyfriend, Seth, spent time with his grandpa in Pennsylvania between Thanksgiving and Christmas.

She'd promised. And she'd never been a very good sister. And she wanted to start being one now.

And even if she threw Meg over and hopped the next ferry back to the mainland, where would she go? Back to Chicago? No, she'd left for a reason—and had no desire to return to the scene of the crime so soon. Or to her parents' house in Ann Arbor? They'd all gathered there for Thanksgiving just last week, yet through no fault of her family's, she'd suffered the strong desire to be alone.

Well, Summer Island in winter was good for alone time. And given that no motor vehicles were permitted on the tiny island near the point where Michigan's Upper and Lower Peninsulas met, she'd at least have the solitude. Maybe she'd curl up in the overstuffed easy chair in the little room they'd always called the nook and read some of the many books in the house. Maybe she'd meditate by watching the snow silently blanket the lawn and the trees that cocooned the inn. Maybe she'd even get together with Meg's friends here, one of whom—Suzanne Quinlan—had kindly stopped by yesterday to welcome her. And maybe, somehow, through all that, she'd figure out how to start letting go of the doom that had sent her haring away from Chicago as quickly as she could pack a suitcase—minus a robe, slippers, and parka.

And if nothing else, maybe she'd finally get some sleep. Somehow. A large yawn reminded her that sleep had been difficult to come by the last couple of weeks. She'd been sure that would change when she reached the winter solitude of the inn, but no such luck—at least not yet.

That was when a loud *clank* jarred her from her thoughts, followed by an ominous rumbling noise.

Her spine went rigid at the grating sounds. What were they from? Some kind of...big truck? Heavy machinery?

But no, not possible here. This was Summer Island, land of no vehicles. And it was winter. If you discounted some whipping winds, no place could—or *should,* anyway—be quieter.

Yet the clanking and rumbling sliced through the otherwise silent snowfall until Lila convinced herself she wasn't hearing things and began trying to track its source. She stalked through the house, peering out windows, and startling the calico cat from a bookshelf in the library. "Sorry, Miss Kitty." Across the street, nothing but choppy Lake Michigan and the South Point Lighthouse. To the east, the pastel shops and businesses lining Harbor Street, most of them closed for the season, their roofs all covered with a dusting of snow. Out the west-facing windows of the nook and sunroom, only the inn's sprawling yard and gardens could be seen, and the thick woods that stretched beyond. Even while all but the evergreens stood bare of foliage just now, the woods to the west marked the spot where quaint Harbor Street narrowed to a wide bicycle trail and gave way to untouched hillsides and shorelines.

Rumble, rumble, rumble, clank, clank, clank.

And then a sharp, sudden *crack, crash*.

Was that…the sound of falling trees?

Heart beating fearfully, Lila rushed to look north out the kitchen window near the back door—and saw a bulldozer. A bulldozer! Ripping down the trees across the brook that gave the inn its name!

Her heart froze in her chest. How could this be? *It can't be. That's all. This can't happen.*

She couldn't make sense of it—and she wouldn't have believed it if she hadn't seen it with her own eyes—but indeed a big yellow bulldozer violently mowed down the woods behind the house as she stared in horror. Every awful cracking noise as another tree broke and fell pierced her like a gunshot to her soul. What the hell was going on?

Quit watching. Do something.

Without another thought, she shoved through the back door, crossing the snow-covered patio, and trudging across the lawn, barely registering the cold and wetness seeping up through the bottoms of the cat face slippers. Heart pounding like a hammer against her chest, she glanced down at the stream, running a little more heavily than in some seasons. As a kid, she'd picked her away across easily on dry rocks that stuck up above the water. Right now, she spotted only one and it was risky—but she had to get across that creek, now, so she boldly made the leap, touched down on the flat ridge of the rock, and catapulted herself to the other side. She slipped on landing, her feet flying out from under her, but caught herself on her hands—stingingly cold in the snow—and soon marched forward again, up the hill, between the trees, toward that horrible rumbling, clanking, tree-murdering machine.

She ran, to the best of her ability in the wet slippers, through the slick snow beginning to coat the ground between pines and oaks that had stood here her entire life. Wet, heavy snowflakes landed on her hair, shoulders, face, making her feel as if she were out in a cold drizzle. Nearing the loud bulldozer, she could see that the older man operating it—signature yellow hardhat perched on his head, gray hair peeking out from underneath—hadn't noticed the woman running toward him in purple pajamas and a fluffy open robe fluttering in the wind. He looked serious, focused on his work—his tree-slaughtering. But Lila would be damned if one more tree was killed on her watch, so she didn't hesitate to run right into the path of the dozer's destructive bucket—which, she realized, actually bore something like teeth.

Now the driver noticed her. The dozer came to a squeaking halt in the snow, the man staring down at her as if he feared he was imagining things. She intended to make clear that she was very real.

His bushy gray brow furrowing, he turned off the machine—presumably only to enable conversation, but having the silence restored eased a little of the alarm inside her. He leaned out over the panel of levers before him to eye her critically. He'd probably never had a woman in pajamas throw herself in the path of his bulldozer before. But she'd never had anyone come mowing down the trees behind her family's inn, either.

"Miss," he began in a slow and uncertain tone, "pardon my French, but just what the hell do you think you're doing?" He sounded more perplexed than angry.

"I'm stopping this travesty, that's what," she called

up to him. "And I was about to ask you the same question."

The man blinked, looked tired.

She didn't care.

"Well, I'm clearing this land."

She remained incredulous and shook her head. "But why? Why would you do that?"

He blinked again, a couple of times.

She stood her ground, adamant.

"Well, they're fixing to build some houses up here, miss—that's why."

Now it was Lila who blinked. Houses? Here? Behind the inn? She shook her head. This didn't make sense. It had to be a mistake. "This land belongs to Harvey Vanderkamp," she informed him. It had belonged to Mr. Vanderkamp her whole life. He was a goat farmer. Occasionally brought Meg down some goat's milk. A quiet but friendly neighbor up the hill from the inn.

"Sorry to tell you, miss, but Mr. Vanderkamp died."

Her face fell, any shred of hope she'd harbored dropping away along with it. "He did?"

The older man nodded. "Land was sold to a developer."

God. This was awful. Really awful. The woods behind the inn had always just…been here. A thing you didn't question. A thing you never thought would change. And houses, here, right behind the inn—they would ruin the view. The idyllic sense of seclusion. The inn's lovely, quiet, private backyard would be… someone else's backyard now, too.

Lila tried to think fast. Because developer or no developer, she refused to let this happen. "I'm still not moving," she said. Simple as that.

Mr. Bushy Brows was back to blinking. "You have to, miss. I have to clear this hillside."

She tried to do that thing she wasn't great at—thinking ahead. "It's winter. It's snowing. Why not just stop this now and give me some time to get it worked out with whoever bought the land?"

The man sighed. She almost felt bad for him. But she felt worse for *her* if she couldn't stop this from taking place. *You had one job—take care of the inn.* And she'd never done much to take care of Meg in any other way, even when Meg had needed it. She was *not* going to tell her sister that the one time she'd deigned to leave this place for more than a few days in fifteen years that Lila had allowed someone to come along and mow down the picturesque forest behind it.

"That's not how things work, miss," the gray-haired man said.

"It's how they're working now."

"I'm just trying to do my job."

"And I'm just trying to save my sister's inn." She pointed to the big yellow Victorian down the hill.

More blinking. "We're not going to hurt your house, miss."

"If you mow down all these trees, you're hurting the house."

Still in his seat on the bulldozer, the agitated operator extracted an outdated cell phone from a pocket, flipped it open, and dialed a number. Lila tried not to look as cold as she felt as he explained to someone on the other end that a woman wearing pajamas was blocking his bulldozer. He had to say it twice. "No, you heard me right. A woman in pajamas is blocking the dozer."

When he disconnected, he told her, "That was my boss. He lives right up on West Bluff."

Hmm. Figured. Rich people territory. And at the moment, rich men who thought they owned the world and everyone in it were on her blacklist.

"He's coming right down."

She nodded. And tried like hell not to feel the cold permeating her bones. But her fleecy slippers were soaked through and her hair hung wet with snow. She wanted so badly to be back inside the inn, where it was warm and cozy. But she couldn't leave. She couldn't. Even if she looked like a crazy person.

Five long, cold minutes later a tall, broad-shouldered man wearing a winter coat with blue jeans and some weird, worn, leathery sort of cowboy hat on his head came walking down from the direction of West Bluff. Despite herself, and for the first time ever in her life, she found herself envying work boots like the ones he had on because they appeared so sturdy and dry. She braced herself for a fight.

When she looked up at him, two things struck her simultaneously. First, he was ridiculously handsome—with dark hair peeking out from beneath that dumb hat, and dark stubble on his chiseled jaw to match. And second, his warm brown eyes wore that same confused, cautious look as the man on the bulldozer's as he said, "I'm Beck Grainger. And…there seems to be some sort of problem here?"

Lila drew back. *This* was Beck Grainger? Who Meg had spoken of so fondly? And even Suzanne, too, during their short visit yesterday, had mentioned him as a friend. Meg had told her he'd been interested in dating

Suzanne and she'd declined, but they both still thought he was a great guy.

"Well, I'm Lila Sloan," she said. "And yes, there's a problem. I'm not letting you destroy Meg's property value like this."

Beck Grainger's dark eyebrows shot up beneath his leathery brim. "You're Meg's sister?"

She gave a terse, crisp nod.

The handsome man sighed, shifting his weight from one work boot to the other. "Look, no one is trying to destroy anyone's property value. And I assumed Meg knew about this. It's not a secret. It was brought publicly before the town council and zoned for residential use back in the spring."

Ugh. None of this was good news. But Lila was certain Meg didn't know. Her sister had been dealing with a lot this past year and perhaps hadn't been paying attention to island business. They'd actually discussed these very woods over the Thanksgiving table last week, recalling how they'd played here as children when their grandmother was still alive and running the place. Meg said that a couple of years ago she'd crossed the stream to plant some shade-loving trillium and blue cranesbill among the trees, and that the small blooms had added color visible from the patio each of the last two summers. Meg loved and valued these trees. And Lila brimmed with anger that no one had made Meg aware of this—but that was neither here nor there. "I can assure you she doesn't know."

The handsome man's brow narrowed skeptically. "Well, if it's a problem for her, why didn't she just pick up the phone and call me?"

"Because she's away right now—traveling. And

even if she were here, she wouldn't have known you were the person to call. And maybe she would have done something sensible—because Meg is definitely sensible—like contact someone on the town council. But I, being less sensible and more rash, took a more direct approach. Meg left me in charge of the inn while she's away—and I can't let you do this. I just can't."

The tilt of Beck Grainger's handsome head told her he was going to try reasoning with her. "You know, it's not gonna be that bad. Luxury homes. With big yards. They'll fit into the landscape." He even ended the sentence with a wink. Was he serious? Given what Lila had been through recently, he was definitely barking up the wrong tree with an elitist suggestion that rich people made better neighbors.

"I don't care what you're building—you're doing it at the expense of my sister's inn. People stay here because of the ambiance and atmosphere. They stay here to listen to crickets in the trees and see fireflies blinking in the woods. We played in these trees as kids. They've been growing here since…well, since before Summer Island was even Summer Island. I can't let you tear them down."

Again, the tree-murderer was shifting his weight, clearly trying to figure out how to get the crazy woman to go home. And maybe she should. Hell, maybe she *was* crazy. She was standing in pajamas in the snow in front of a bulldozer, after all, a place she couldn't have imagined herself even an hour ago. But if she had to go back inside the inn and hear the hideous sounds of these trees being destroyed, if she had to face Meg with the news that she'd let some rich developer ruin the inn's picturesque setting, she didn't think she could handle it. And she was still in no frame of mind to let some entitled, wealthy man run roughshod over her.

"Listen," he said, "I'm sorry Meg didn't know. Sincerely. We're friends."

"Some friend," she muttered.

He went on. "But it's freezing out here and you're soaking wet."

"Thanks for that newsflash," she murmured again.

Which he continued to ignore. Since she probably appeared to be insane. "I understand your compulsion to run out here and try to change the situation, but standing in front of this bulldozer isn't really gonna fix anything, so I'm afraid you're just getting wet and cold for nothing."

She simply glared at him. "You're not as nice as Suzanne said you were."

His eyebrows rose. "You know Suzanne?"

"Yes." Suzanne, whom he'd previously expressed romantic interest in. Maybe she should have mentioned Suzanne sooner. "She claimed you were a good guy—but she may change her opinion when she finds out what you're doing to Meg's inn. People here love Meg, you know. You may not have any friends left if you go through with this."

At this, however, he just let out a sigh. "Well, guess that's the chance I'll have to take." Another shift back to the other boot—which reminded Lila her own feet were in that painful place between freezing but not quite numb. "Look, this is just business, nothing personal—and I'm afraid it's a done deal. It's not something that can be stopped."

"Done how?" She didn't even know what she was asking—but she would grasp at any straw.

"This land is valuable and plans are already in place."

This gave her an idea. "I could buy it. Or we. Meg and me. The land."

But Beck Grainger simply cast her the sad look one bestows on a delusional child. "The land has already been bought. Zoning's in place, and permits have been obtained. Plat maps have been drawn and lots marked off by surveyors. Sewers and utilities will be going in by spring. And don't take this the wrong way, but I doubt you'd want to pay me the amount I'd have to ask to make up for the loss incurred by not building homes here. I'm sorry, Ms. Sloan, but this is happening, with or without your blessing."

At a loss, Lila leaned her head back, peering up through the trees at a white sky, only to be smacked in the face by more big, wet snowflakes. Her voice came out more softly than it had so far—with an honest question. "You do this work in winter?"

"When we can," he answered, holding on to the same no-nonsense tone he'd used for the entire conversation. "Permits just came through a few days ago after a lengthy process. Thought we could get a good start on clearing the land today, but the snow's coming down heavier than expected. The town council requested we halt work during the tourist season, so that means doing it anytime it's reasonably dry and not subzero. After today we're probably stalled until the weather gets a little better, but we'll keep moving forward whenever we're able."

"Like…gets a little better in the spring?" she asked, hoping to buy some time.

But he shook his head. "Like gets a little better by next week, hopefully. It'll be a day by day decision."

Another honest question from her. "What happened to there being no motorized vehicles on Summer Island? Isn't this…against the law? Or something?" She didn't really *know* the laws, but it seemed worth asking.

He only shrugged. "They make exceptions in the name of progress and practicality."

That irked her—and also reminded her that the island authorities also possessed a few snowmobiles for wintertime emergencies, and a small SUV-sized ambulance. Summer Island talked a good game of simple living, touting streets filled with bicycles most of the year, but apparently simplicity came with limits.

"I'm not leaving here," she proclaimed, no matter how bad her feet hurt from the cold, no matter how wet and clammy she was beginning to feel—despite Beck Grainger somehow looking perfectly warm and dry next to her, "until you give me the key to that bulldozer."

He blinked. "Are you kidding?"

"Not at all."

"You might freeze to death," he pointed out matter-of-factly.

"Then you'll have that on your head."

"It's not my fault you're irrational."

"It's not my fault you're unreasonable."

He sighed, glanced heavenward, then drew his gaze back down. "Fine," he bit off. Then glanced up to the man still on the bulldozer, who'd been quietly observing the entire exchange. "Jim, give the lady the key."

"Seriously?" Jim asked.

"Yep. I can't have her getting hypothermia and somehow blaming me."

When Lila stepped toward Jim, she realized that her feet had become painful nubs that didn't work quite right anymore. She tried her damnedest to hide the discomfort as Jim passed the key down into her nearly numb hand.

Then she turned and started down the hill on her nubs.

"Taking that key isn't going to stop this from happening, you know," Beck Grainger called after her.

"It's going to stop it for today," she called back, still moving forward, hoping she didn't add insult to injury by slipping and sliding her way down the hill on her ass.

She kept her footing, painful though each step was, and even when one foot landed in the frigid water of the brook, she just kept going, driven by knowing warmth lay only footsteps away and she had at least stopped the tree destruction for right now. Suddenly, she became grateful for the snow, grateful it would fall for days to come.

Because turned out doom really *had* followed her to Summer Island. She'd let an entirely different kind of it drive her here, and now Beck Grainger was heaping still more onto her.

CHAPTER TWO

BECK COULDN'T BELIEVE he'd given her the damn key.
Twenty-four hours later, in fact, the whole bizarre incident remained on his mind even as he shoveled the
front walk of his house on West Bluff Drive. Normally, the front yard afforded an expansive view of
Lake Michigan and the mainland to the south, but right
now, everything was white—from the sky down. Snow
continued to fall as he worked, but he found shoveling
a lot easier if you kept up with it, removing it every
few inches.

Of course, by the time he'd willingly surrendered
the key, he'd determined that maybe he needed to handle this situation with some care. Try to show some
empathy. He valued Meg Sloan's friendship and Suzanne Quinlan's esteem and didn't wish to lose either.
He'd only moved to Summer Island last spring and
was just starting to become a part of the small community here, after all.

And hell, with any luck Meg and Suzanne would be
mature and sensible enough to understand that sometimes things changed, places evolved—nothing stayed
the same forever. Maybe they'd see the value in it,
same as the town council had, and as he did himself.
Nice homes meant expansion, and he'd seen before
how much a little expansion could improve a com-

munity. Beck liked adding to the world in that way. Maybe Meg's cute but angry purple-pajama-clad sister had just overreacted, and once she told Meg about it, the innkeeper would give the project her blessing.

And if not, and if worse came to worst—hell, he'd have to get another key. Lila Sloan probably had no idea that, unlike cars and houses, most large equipment took universal keys—she probably thought taking the one now in her possession would require having a whole different dozer ferried over to continue the work. That said, on the mainland getting another key would be easy—whereas here, it was no small feat. But it could be done with a ferry ride to St. Simon and a short drive.

Normally, for a job this size, he'd be using more than just one dozer and would maybe even have an extra key or two on hand. But Summer Island would only make so many concessions to the practical business of building, so Beck's equipment resources were currently pretty slim. He thought the island should make more given the tax revenue involved—and he knew good and well that was the main impetus to them approving his development—but he'd take what he could get.

Before he went to the trouble of chasing down another key, though, he'd at least take a shot at getting the first one back. He didn't know how yet. But, in spite of the ire she'd spewed at him, he couldn't deny the strange—under the circumstances—urge to see Meg's little sister again.

Which was more than a little surprising to him.

He'd harbored an attraction to Suzanne, the flower shop owner in town, since the day he'd met her last spring—but it had gone pointedly unrequited. As in she'd completely shot him down, eventually taking an it's-not-you-it's-me approach that had dulled the sting only a little but had at least left them being able to say hi if they passed on the street.

So now he felt an inkling of interest in an irate woman who'd hated him on sight? *Yeah, that'll go well. You really know how to pick 'em, Grainger.*

But maybe Lila Sloan's intense determination and loyalty appealed to him despite himself. While it wasn't exactly convenient given the problem between them, he liked people who didn't let anything stand in their way. He saw *himself* as that kind of a person, in fact. But at the same time, he wondered what she was like without the pajama-clad raving involved, and when she wasn't angry. *Would be easier to find out if you weren't the* source *of that anger.*

Still, maybe he could navigate these waters to a good outcome for all involved—and if he got to see Lila Sloan under improved conditions, all the better. Of course, maybe he wouldn't even like her—it was hard to say given their limited interaction so far. But maybe he would. And maybe she'd hate him anyway. Or maybe she wouldn't. He only knew she'd stayed on his mind.

Glancing across the street, he noticed the unshoveled walk at his neighbors', the Waltons. George and Marie—who were probably in their seventies—had left the island at the end of summer but come back just a few days ago. According to George, whom he'd run into on the street one day, they were taking care of a young grandchild while the kid's mom recovered from back surgery, and they'd all be back home for the winter in northern Ohio by Christmas.

After finishing his own shoveling, he headed across

the street, figuring he'd help George out a little. He was halfway through the job when one of the double doors opened on the front of the big island house and out came a tiny kid, bundled up and carrying a plastic snow shovel of his own. Beck could barely see the little boy's eyes between his hat and the bright red scarf looped numerous times around his neck.

"Well, who might you be?" he asked the child. "I'm Beck."

"My name's Cade Walton. My grandma said I could come out and help you shovel. Oh, and she also said thanks."

"Well, I appreciate the help," Beck told him. "It's a big job." It actually wasn't a big job at all. Fifteen minutes at most.

"My dad said I should bring my shovel on the trip, that it would probably snow," announced the little boy. Not shy, this one. Which Beck appreciated. He never knew how to communicate with shy children. This kid seemed easier than most.

"Good thinking on your dad's part," he replied. "And it's a nice-looking shovel." It was red plastic, with a blue plastic handle.

"I'll get a bigger one like yours when I'm older," Cade informed him. "But I'm just a little boy right now, so this one is the right size for me."

Beck grinned. Clearly the kid remembered and repeated everything the adults in his world told him. "How old are you?"

Cade stopped shoveling and held up a mittened hand. Beck was pretty sure underneath he was displaying a set of fingers that answered the question, but the mitten kept them hidden. So it helped when Cade said, "Five." Then he started shoveling again. "Until next June. Then I'll be six. And then I'll go to school."

Ah, to be five again. Beck could barely remember it, but it brought back a general sense of…ease. He hadn't started knocking heads with his father yet. He hadn't realized they were poor yet. At five, life had been mostly about cartoons and tricycles and grilled cheese sandwiches. Yep, to be five.

But he wouldn't want to be ten again. Or fifteen. Or even twenty for that matter. So he didn't stay wistful for long—instead he shoveled the walk, and when he saw that Cade didn't actually know how to *use* the snow shovel, he stopped to give the little guy a lesson. "See, you push it forward and it scoops the snow out of the way. Later, when you're a grown-up," he said with a wink, "your back will thank you for pushing instead of lifting."

He watched as Cade did his best to mimic Beck's motions, sliding the shovel forward on the walk. "Like this?" he asked hopefully, stopping to look up, wide-eyed. Was the kid trying to impress him? Make him proud? It tugged at Beck's heart a little.

"Absolutely," he was quick to answer. "Good job."

And the big smile that peeked out over the top of Cade's scarf confirmed Beck's suspicions.

They worked in silence a few minutes, Cade focusing on the push-and-scoop method of snow removal, until he announced, "My grandma said maybe after it quits snowing I can build a snowman in the front yard."

"That sounds like fun," Beck told him.

Cade flashed wide crystal blue eyes. "You could help me if you want."

Hmm—the kid really liked him for some reason.

"Tell you what," he said. "Whenever you're ready, just come knock on my door, or have your grandpa give me a call. He has my number."

Cade's mouth had disappeared behind the scarf again, but Beck could tell by his eyes that the little boy was smiling. "Okay, Becker, I will."

Beck laughed and told him, "It's just Beck."

"Whatever," Cade said, and Beck laughed harder. Ah, to be five again, without a care in the world.

"You're a pretty funny kid," Beck told his new little friend. "I bet your grandfolks are happy to have you visiting."

"That's what they tell me," Cade replied matter-of-factly, making Beck chuckle once more. "But Grammy Marie says I get bored easy."

"Most kids do," Beck informed him. "And up here, in winter, even some grown-ups." It was a pretty intense level of isolation.

The two worked in companionable silence for only another minute or so before Cade could apparently stand the quiet no longer. "Tonight we're going to put up the Christmas tree," he told Beck—and the way his eyes lit took Beck back in time. Christmas trees and snowmen—the simple joys of life, even better when you were a little kid, because they came without things like responsibilities, conflict, or problems. "Have you put yours up yet?"

Beck shook his head. He wasn't bothering with a tree this year—it was only him in the big house across the way, after all, and he'd be at his sister's in Kentucky for the actual holiday. But he kept his answer simple. "No, not yet."

"Grammy Marie says a pretty, lit-up Christmas

tree makes her soul happy. Or her spirit happy. Or her Christmas spirit happy." The kid scrunched up his face, then shook his head. "Something like that."

That was when the sound of jingling bells drew their eyes up toward the street, and Cade declared with great wonder, "Horses!"

In summer, the mail on Summer Island came by horse and wagon—and when it snowed, the wagon was traded for a good old-fashioned sleigh. Though mail could be picked up at the post office anytime, delivery only happened once a week—and today was the day. The sight of the two large horses and the sleigh drawn behind them was Christmas-card-worthy, so Beck hoped it wouldn't dash his new friend's awe when he informed him, "That's the mailman."

He shouldn't have worried though—Cade's eyes only grew even bigger and rounder. "The mailman comes like Santa does?"

Beck smiled. "Sort of, I guess. But only here on the island."

"How come?"

"Cars and trucks aren't allowed here," he explained, "so people have to travel in old-fashioned ways."

Cade looked critical. "Are you calling Santa old-fashioned?"

Beck leaned his head back in a laugh. "No—no, sir. I would never do that. Might get myself on Santa's naughty list."

"I'm on the nice list," Cade informed him smartly, obviously still wanting to impress.

"Know that for a fact, do ya?"

The little boy nodded knowingly.

"Well, that's good. I wasn't always on it myself."

Beck realized immediately it was the wrong thing to say, as Cade suddenly appeared wary. "Why not?"

Hell, how to answer? *Keep it simple.* "Well, I just didn't always do everything the way my parents wanted me to. But don't worry—I'm back on the nice list now." Even if Lila Sloan might not see it that way.

When the mailman glided to a halt, his two big, brown horses clopping their way through the snow, Beck and Cade abandoned their shovels and walked out to meet him. Seeing Cade's awe, the mailman kindly let Beck lift Cade up to pet his Clydesdales.

"This one yours?" he asked of Cade. Beck had said hello to the guy before but didn't know him beyond that.

"Oh—no," Beck answered, lowering Cade back to the ground. He pointed to the Walton house. "George and Marie are his grandparents."

Then the mailman hefted a sizable box from the mail sleigh and said, "Want this on your porch?"

Beck lifted his eyebrows. He hadn't been expecting anything. "That's for me?"

The guy nodded, then glanced down at the box. "From an Emma Sturwold."

For a second, Beck wondered what the hell his sister could have mailed to him—but then he remembered. She'd told him she was going through Dad's office. And that she'd send him anything she thought he might want.

"I don't want anything."

"Maybe you will."

"I won't."

But clearly, she'd ignored his wishes on that.

Cade looked from the horses up to Beck, eyes big

and round once more. "Do you think somebody sent you a present?"

Beck tried to keep the low chuckle that escaped him from sounding too cynical. "No, probably not," he replied, leaving it at that.

Though on the inside, he quietly added this to the list of things not exactly going his way. *Let's see—I have one woman on this island who just isn't into me, another I'm a little intrigued by but who hates me, a halted land development, and now some mysterious anti-present from my recently deceased dad.* This December just kept getting better and better.

SUZANNE QUINLAN HAD known a lot of snow fell on Summer Island when she'd decided to move here almost three years ago. And mostly she didn't mind it. She'd been seeking a quieter life with fewer complications, in which she could keep mostly to herself when she wanted. And winters here certainly gave her that. It was the getting around in it that could be challenging.

Her flower shop, Petal Pushers—currently jampacked with Christmas trees, wreaths, and boughs of holly to decorate the homes of the year-round faithful—rested directly across Harbor Street from Dahlia's Café. But battling the wind made the usually short walk there a lot longer as the choppy Lake Michigan straits heaved tumultuously in the distance. Despite that, though, as she pressed forward through ankle-deep snow in warm boots and a puffy knee-length parka with the hood drawn tight, she looked forward to lunch with Dahlia—as well as with Meg's younger sister, Lila, who would be joining them.

The café opened only from noon to three this time of

year, but was a convenient place to meet since most of the island's businesses closed down completely through the winter months other than on select occasions. And when Lila had texted her asking to discuss a problem at the inn, Suzanne had suggested involving Dahlia, too. Suzanne's and Meg's dear, older friend, Dahlia Delaney, had lived here much longer than Suzanne, making her a staple in the community and possibly better equipped to deal with any inn problems in Meg's absence.

And while no one wanted problems, of course—for anyone, about anything—something about the lunch had already given Suzanne a fresh sense of purpose. The truth was that she'd been out of sorts lately, with Meg away, and the early dose of winter bringing on a seclusion that had left even her with too much time to think—and too much time to…feel.

Something inside her was shifting, leaving her restless and with a case of…was it island fever? Cabin fever? Basically the same thing, she supposed, but this wasn't exactly *that*. It was more the sense something was missing from her life. Well, something more than usual—something had been missing since Cal died. But as a frigid gust of wind swept past, she couldn't deny that the particular emptiness besetting her now felt new, different.

Life was so much simpler when you were content with your circumstances. But whatever the problem was with the inn, perhaps she could help, and perhaps it would give her something to do besides indulge in all that thinking and feeling.

"Come in, come in," Dahlia said, greeting Suzanne at the quaint café's front door the same as if it were her home. Every other pastel building on the street stood quiet and still in the snowfall, and Suzanne suspected she and Lila would be the only lunch guests on this wintry day.

Suzanne estimated Dahlia, a unique woman with her own sense of flair, to be in her sixties—though she'd never asked because it was clear that to Dahlia age was just a number. Today she wore a large, slouchy winter hat of red-and-white candy cane stripes over her short, silver hair and a thick, red cable-knit sweater. Summer usually brought out a variety of hippie-style sunglasses that made the red-framed ones she wore today seem tame in comparison, yet they remained a bolder choice than most would make and accented her seasonal style.

"Looking all Christmas-fied," Suzanne merrily observed.

"'Tis the season, and the season's short," Dahlia said with a wink.

Suzanne herself had chosen a fuzzy white sweater for the get-together, draped with a glittery snowflake scarf. "I'm doing more of a weather homage," she declared, striking a pose as she shed her big coat. While it would only be a party of three, island winters held few enough social outings that it was fun to make fashion choices with some care.

Normally, the third member of the trio would be Meg—but Suzanne welcomed getting to know her friend's sister better. Somehow even that delivered a small sense of purpose, too. And though she missed having her bestie here for the holiday season, she remained pleased about Meg's new relationship with Seth, and glad to see her enjoying all that such a change brought with it—in this case some time away from the everyday.

As the café's door opened behind them, they both looked up to see Lila, bundled in—if Suzanne wasn't mistaken—one of Meg's parkas, with a too-thin-for-the-weather fashion scarf wrapped around the lower half of her face. When they both looked a bit taken aback, she greeted them with, "This is a stickup."

Which made Dahlia laugh and reply, "Oh, I like you already." She stepped forward. "Hello—I'm Dahlia, and you seem like a breath of fresh air." She pushed the door tightly closed behind her new guest. "Not that we need any fresher, colder air at the moment. But I'm so pleased to finally meet our dear Meg's little sis."

"I'm Lila," she introduced herself while pulling down her scarf, "and guilty as charged." Her slightly self-effacing smile threw Suzanne a little—she'd expected someone more carefree than Lila seemed, both on their previous meeting and today. "I'm the sister who hasn't been around much, and I'm embarrassed never to have met either of you before now. But glad to finally change that."

Suzanne knew from Meg that Lila had quit visiting the island with any regularity after their grandmother's death. The sisters talked on the phone once every month or two, according to Meg, but typically only saw each other on holidays. And perhaps Suzanne hadn't expected to like Lila. Meg often described her as frivolous and "the fun one," in which Suzanne had heard the unspoken words *irresponsible* and *selfish*—but so far she found Lila easy enough to be with. Though the slightly younger woman had also instantly struck her as…tired.

In summertime, Dahlia's deck was an island hot spot, jutting out over the shoreline with a backdrop of masts and sails from the marina—but now the three women settled around a table in a room boasting a fireplace and a lake cottage vibe. Two Christmas stockings hung from the mantel, flanking a roaring blaze in the hearth—one bore Dahlia's name, the other that of her nephew, Zack.

Meg's ex, Zack Sheppard, lived in the apartment above the café and wasn't Suzanne's favorite person. "Where's Zack?" she wondered out loud. A fisherman by trade, he was on the water from spring until fall, but was island-bound in winter.

Dahlia waved a hand down through the air. "Sulking, most likely. He's spent a lot of time alone since coming back into port. He's at loose ends without Meg."

The breakup had happened less than six months ago, around the time Seth had entered the picture, and Suzanne thought Zack deserved every loose end he got, but kept the sentiment inside. He hadn't treated Meg well, in her opinion, but Dahlia loved him and had been saddened by the split.

On a day like this, Dahlia chose to be a one-woman operation and had whipped up their lunch herself—finger sandwiches and a hot quiche, fresh from the oven. The scent of pine emanating from the live tree in one corner, strung with white lights, served as the perfect complement to the scene, reminding Suzanne that on Summer Island, even a winter of discontent could hold certain charms.

"This is all so lovely," Lila said, using fancy tongs to move two egg salad triangle sandwiches onto her plate. "And I apologize if I yawn a lot." She shook her head self-consciously. "Trouble sleeping lately. But hopefully a nice lunch will perk me up."

Holiday small talk commenced:

"Harbor Street looks so pretty lit up."

"The tree is lovely."

"Is your shopping done?" But once they began to eat, Dahlia said, "Well, as much as I'd love to chat mindlessly with you both all afternoon, I hear this meeting was called for a reason."

Suzanne waited with bated breath, ready to focus on something productive—as Lila took the cue. "Ladies, I came to Summer Island with a mind toward hibernating for a few weeks, and also trying to get some sleep—" she paused to yawn "—but circumstances have forced me to alter that plan. I've reached out to two women I don't even know because I'm desperate."

CHAPTER THREE

IT HAD TAKEN everything within Lila to so boldly call this lunch and go to her sister's friends for help, but it was all she could think of. And now she sat before them at the quaintest little café she'd ever been to, thinking it far too cute a spot to indulge in tragedy—and yet having no choice but to relay in detail the unpleasant story of what had unfolded yesterday morning. "That's when I realized someone was bulldozing down the trees behind the inn. I ran across the creek and stopped it by planting myself in front of the bulldozer—and it turns out the person responsible is Beck Grainger. I refused to move until he gave me the key—but that can only stop this travesty for so long, and I'm not sure what I'm going to do."

When she finished, Suzanne just blinked—looking utterly confused and dismayed. "None of this makes any sense. Beck is mowing down the trees behind the inn? Beck? Because… I've just never known him to be anything but kind and respectful."

Yes, so Meg had clearly thought, too, but now Lila had unfortunately discovered this other side to the man they all liked so much. "Can you imagine?" she went on. "Houses behind the Summerbrook Inn? Instead of all those big, old trees that have always stood over the place." She shook her head and sighed, letting her gaze drop sadly. "Our family never owned the land—but somehow it felt like ours anyway, you know?"

Suzanne cringed, clearly taking in the gravity of the situation. "This will crush Meg. And could very well affect her business." She gave her head a doubtful tilt. "At the very least, it'll make the inn feel much less secluded and idyllic, and—" she sneered "—possibly a little more suburban."

"Exactly," Lila said, glad Meg's friend understood why this mattered so much.

"I once stood in front of a bulldozer myself," Dahlia offered wistfully. "The year was 1975 and a group of us were trying to stop the building of a highway through sacred Native American burial grounds in Montana."

Lila sat up straighter, her heavy eyelids lifting hopefully. "Did it work?"

Dahlia's glance lowered to her quiche. "No." Then she looked back up. "Yet I still heartily applaud the move, dear."

"I just can't believe Beck is doing this," Suzanne said once more, shaking her head in continued confusion.

"Yes—our Beck?" Dahlia asked, sounding as puzzled by that part as Suzanne. "On our little island?"

"So neither of you knew about this zoning change either?" Lila asked, switching her gaze back and forth between them.

They both shook their heads—and Dahlia said, "I admit to not attending enough town council meetings the last few years. They're very dry affairs, hard to sit through."

"And I never even started," Suzanne confessed on a regretful sigh. "But apparently I should have. I guess this is the kind of thing that happens when you're not paying attention."

"I plan to give Tom Bixby a piece of my mind," Dahlia announced. "Tom's a longtime member of the town council." Then she shook her head once more, her tone softening as she put her hand over Lila's on the table. "But honey, if Beck has the permits and the zoning, I'm not sure there's a way to stop him, much as it saddens me."

Lila's heart fell like a stone to the pit of her stomach. She couldn't accept that. Couldn't even acknowledge it, in fact. So she glanced to Suzanne. "I told him he wasn't nearly as nice as you said."

Suzanne looked as if she were still trying to wrap her mind around this strange new reality. "The woods behind the inn—gone? Beck Grainger the culprit?" she mused. "I just don't get it."

"Maybe he...*isn't* so nice," Dahlia cautiously suggested. "I've been fond of him since his arrival here, but I guess the truth is that none of us knows him very well."

Yet something about that suggestion started Suzanne shaking her head. "No. No, he *is* a good guy. I just feel that to my core. Only...maybe he's a little more hard-nosed when it comes to business or something."

"Well, that hard-nosed man is going to ruin the inn's grounds if I don't figure out some way to stop him," Lila told them—even as she prepared to make another bold move, letting Suzanne's belief in Beck Grainger draw her eyes directly to the other woman's. "I...don't suppose you'd want to try to work some magic and win him over. Since he likes you and all."

Suzanne's spine jerked straight as she sat up taller,

blinked, and said, "You can't be serious. Me? Work magic?"

Lila bit her lip, bummed that Suzanne seemed so instantly resistant. Just like this meeting, it was all she could think of—even if she knew it was pushy. "When I mentioned your name," she explained, "he seemed interested to hear I knew you—and…well, interested, period. If he still has a thing for you, maybe you could have some influence over him."

But when Suzanne hesitated, looking almost unaccountably wary, Lila knew she'd pushed too far, expected too much of someone she'd just met, no matter how nice. Which left…zero ideas for how to fix this. "Meg is going to kill me," she murmured, overcome with a fresh wave of exhaustion—whether from the situation or lack of sleep, she wasn't sure. Maybe both.

"Why would you say that?" Dahlia asked. "It's not your fault."

Suzanne quickly nodded her agreement. They both seemed shocked.

Yet Lila just looked back and forth between them, stating the situation as simply as she could. "I promised to take care of the inn."

"You agreed to house-sit, not stop a major construction development in the works long before you got here," Suzanne reasoned.

This, however, did nothing to console Lila. She shook her head grimly and heard herself confess an ugly truth—one she'd never before spoken out loud even while she carried it in her heart. "I've never been a good sister. Never been around a lot. Even when she was sick, when we were younger."

Meg had gone through leukemia in her early twenties—it was what had ultimately brought her to live here. Recuperation had eventually led to running the inn when their grandmother died unexpectedly. And Lila had been largely absent for all of it.

Still, her self-criticism about the situation seemed to catch Suzanne off guard. "Wait. You were—what—a teenager at the time?"

Lila nodded. "I was still in high school."

Dahlia jumped in, too. "Well, what could you have really done, honey?"

Lila scrunched up her nose. She could have done a lot—and she knew it. "Just…supported her. Spent time with her. Showed her I cared. But instead… I kind of ran from it. I wasn't there for her."

"Because it scared you," Suzanne told her knowingly, reminding Lila of something Meg had mentioned—that back before opening her flower shop, Suzanne had been a nurse in Indiana. And now Lila became the recipient of her comforting bedside manner. "Don't beat yourself up. You were young, and it was overwhelming."

Even so, Lila tilted her head, unwilling to absolve herself that easily. "Maybe, but… I guess as I've gotten older, I've realized that still doesn't make it all right. Not to have been there for her. And even since then… I've just kind of gone my own way and done my own thing. And now I really want to be a better sister. And coming here to give her some time off the island seemed like a nice way to start. But if the whole ambiance of the place goes up in smoke while I'm here… I just can't be okay with that." She stopped, blew out a sigh, let her head droop. Calling on Meg's friends for help had given her a measure of hope—two or three heads were better than one, and she'd been sure they'd come up with some constructive way to approach this. But hope had already pretty much fled the scene, and with it, any chance that she could protect the trees and be the sister Meg deserved.

Suzanne's mind raced as she tried to take all this in. She liked Lila and hated hearing—feeling—her despair, over the trees behind the inn, and over the revelation that this was really about more than just trees. And she *loved* Meg and didn't want anything to hurt the inn. But now she had to share with Lila something Meg probably had not. "About Beck—Lila, if you were suggesting I woo him into submission, afraid I'm, um… not exactly a skilled seductress. Or even an unskilled one. I'm not…into dating. At all. Which Beck already knows, by the way." She'd wanted to help, to have purpose—but not like *this*.

"Oh…" Lila sounded understandably perplexed.

Leaving Suzanne compelled to try to explain what she'd just said—and why she would have no sway over Beck Grainger. She took a deep breath, blew it back out, forcing words that still came with difficulty. "My husband died. Kind of tragically. It was five years ago, and I know I should probably welcome something new, but so far…" She shook her head, left it at that.

"Oh God, I'm sorry."

Suzanne sensed Lila wanting to ask more about the loss, but holding her tongue. For which Suzanne was grateful, because she didn't like dredging up those memories.

Now she shrugged, trying to somehow be light about something that wasn't light at all. And to make it even *less* light… "For what it's worth, after a while,

I did *try* dating—but it didn't go well. One of the guys was married." She stopped to stick her finger in her mouth in a gagging motion. "And the other, it turned out, had a whole harem of women. Total player. So I decided the brave new world of thirty- and fortysomething dating just wasn't for me. And I lead a very full, contented life. I have my shop, and my little cottage on Mill Street, and my friends, and a beautiful island to call home. I have all I need."

Of course, that had all been truer a few months ago, even a few weeks ago—before this nebulous "something missing" had come trundling into her awareness. And part of Suzanne couldn't believe she was just spewing all this out—telling Lila way more than was necessary here. But the understanding expression on her face said that perhaps Meg's sister had gone through some losers in her life, as well. "I understand," Lila replied. "Some men can really do a number on you."

"If you let them," Dahlia chimed in, her tone both airy and mysterious. She punctuated the statement by popping the last bite of a miniature ham salad sandwich into her mouth. When both women cast her a look, she went on. "Now, don't get me wrong—I don't mean to discount what anyone has been through. But I don't like to paint the whole gender with a broad brush—and we have to look out for our own hearts. Which sometimes means using our heads."

"Which is exactly what I'm doing by not dating," Suzanne pointed out. "I know I'm softhearted and form attachments easily, so…" She held up her hands in a stopping motion. "Pffft. I'm better off just not going down that road."

"But if you did," Dahlia said slyly, "wouldn't Beck be someone you'd like to go down it with?"

Suzanne blinked, sighed. How had this conversation turned back to putting her on the spot? In an even more pointed way this time. And about Beck Grainger, of all people.

"No," she insisted emphatically.

You're lying. You're so lying. You think about him sometimes.

And—oh. God. She'd been so dense. Because that was it. That was it. The something missing.

It had come on with the cold weather. There had been moments she'd see him on Harbor Street, they'd exchange a wave, and she'd think it might be nice to cuddle with him next to a fire. But then she would push the thought away. Because of that attachment problem. And not wanting to acknowledge that she desired anything more than she had. She'd completely declined his advances, after all. "And besides, now he's destroying the land behind Meg's inn, so that's a pretty big black mark against him."

Suzanne watched as her words sent Lila's shoulders drooping in defeat once more. It reminded them all what was at stake here. This wasn't the first time an unwanted land development changed someone's way of life, of course. But things like that didn't happen *here*, on Summer Island. And to someone they all loved, no less.

"But I'll try to talk to Beck anyway," Suzanne heard herself say quietly without planning. Because her heart broke for Lila. And for Meg, too.

"Really? You will?" Lila lifted her head with a bright smile. Her hazel eyes sparkled against the hunter green sweater she wore, and Suzanne realized it was the first time she'd seen Meg's sister actually look happy. It was also the first time she'd seen the resemblance to Meg. Different hair—streaks of blond made Lila's hair lighter than Meg's medium brown, and hers hung more shoulder length and tousled than Meg's longer locks—but otherwise it was suddenly easy to tell they were sisters.

"I will," Suzanne promised, glad to make Lila feel better, at least for the moment. And knowing Lila had no idea what a big thing it was for Suzanne to agree to, despite the personal information she'd just shared.

Because Suzanne still thought Beck was too handsome and too rugged and too intimidating for her. Intimidating only because he seemed so…comfortable in his own skin. She wished she carried herself through life with so much smooth confidence and ease. He was everything she was *not* prepared to deal with.

And yet at the same time, hearing from Lila that he still seemed interested had sent an unexpected ripple through her core. And she realized that if she suddenly thought he *wasn't* interested anymore she'd be a little devastated. He was like an invisible life preserver she carried around with her, letting his distant affection silently buoy her these past months. And if she thought it had disappeared, well…maybe she'd sink.

"That's amazing—thank you!" Lila said, positively beaming now. She even reached for a second slice of the ham and cheese quiche between them on the table, the news seeming to increase her appetite.

And much as Suzanne hated to say this, it probably needed to be said. "Though…you know it probably won't make a difference. I mean, yes, he wanted to go out with me back in the summer, but I really don't know him well. No matter how much he likes me, business and pleasure are two different things."

"But you never know," Lila said, clearly grabbing onto a hope that Suzanne already found unrealistic, even if she'd brought it on herself. "It's at least worth a try. I mean, even if it only slows down the process a little more, it'll help. Anything that might change the situation is worth it."

Suzanne nodded, tried to believe that, and wondered what she'd unwittingly gotten herself into. Because she *didn't* know him well. But she was going to ask him to stop a major land development project because he was attracted to her? And all the while she'd be standing there trying not to gape at his ridiculous handsomeness, trying not to care too much or feel like anything personal was at stake. Even if he was the something missing, that didn't mean she was ready to pursue it, ready to welcome that something into her life. "It's still probably best not to get your hopes up," she told Lila. "Because it really might be a silly idea."

"But it's the only idea we have," Lila pointed out.

And Suzanne couldn't argue *that*.

"Listen," Lila said, "if either of you happens to talk to Meg, don't mention this to her, okay? I don't want to ruin her time away."

They both agreed.

"Meanwhile," Dahlia said, "now that you're no longer hibernating, you'll have to socialize with us more while you're here."

"Yes," Suzanne chimed in, still wanting to make Lila feel at home, and also happy to switch to an easier topic. "There are weekly knitting bees at the Knitting Nook." She pointed in the general direction of the town's yarn shop.

"I don't knit," Lila was quick to say.

But Suzanne shrugged off the concern. "Neither do I. No one cares. There are easy chairs, and coffee from the coffee and tea shop next door. It's a nice way to get together, especially in winter, and not really as boring as it sounds."

"And the big tree-lighting is coming up next week— you won't want to miss that," Dahlia said, lifting one finger in the air.

"That's right," Suzanne added. Social gatherings, town events—so much easier to talk about. "We've already had to postpone it due to the weather—but fingers crossed it'll happen next Tuesday, so long as the tree is up and decorated in time."

"And if not," Dahlia said, "we'll just postpone it again. You learn to roll with the punches here in winter."

Suzanne had never heard a truer statement—and she supposed she'd learned to do that well enough these last couple of years. If only she were so skilled at rolling with the punches of her life.

Some people would say she had. She'd suffered in a lasting way from losing Cal, but in other ways she'd moved on. She'd left nursing, she'd started a business, she'd even moved that business north to the island. She was making her way in the world.

But then why is it so hard for you to even talk to a handsome man? And why has it stayed on your mind even now that the conversation has shifted to other things? And why are you wondering right now what it might be like to hold hands with him, kiss him?

If romance is the something missing, why don't you want to let it in?

CHAPTER FOUR

LILA SAT IN the nook, the fluffy Miss Kitty at her side, studying her iPad. "What do you think—these?" she asked the cat.

The calico cat appeared as bored as she usually did, but the slippers Lila had just found on Amazon looked at least somewhat like the ones she'd ruined out in the snow yesterday, so she hit the Buy Now button, with a plan to wrap them up as a Christmas gift. *Merry Christmas, Meg. These are to replace the ones I ruined while letting some big lug in a stupid hat destroy your business and our family legacy.*

She'd run the originals through the washing machine, but they just weren't the same anymore. *Kind of like the inn won't be the same once there's a subdivision behind it.* No matter what Beck Grainger said— luxury homes or not—it would be a subdivision. And back on the mainland, Lila had nothing against a nice subdivision. Her parents lived in a nice subdivision in Ann Arbor, where she and Meg had grown up and where they still celebrated holidays. She had friends who lived in nice subdivisions in the suburbs in Chicago. But a subdivision on Summer Island? Behind the Summerbrook Inn? Ugh.

When the cell phone resting on the arm of the easy chair trilled, she looked down to see Meg calling. And part of her didn't want to answer. Because she had no intention of telling her sister what was going on here. And that meant lying by omission.

But not answering now would only mean having to explain why later, which would result in a more *direct* lie—so after all this analysis raced through her mind at lightning speed, she scooped up the phone and swiped to answer. "Hey." She tried to sound more cheerful than she felt.

"Hey yourself," her sister said—sounding truly happy. Happier maybe than Lila had ever heard her. It warmed a cold spot in her heart—because if anyone deserved happiness it was Meg. And she seemed to have found it in Seth. "How are things going?"

Lila tensed slightly. "Oh, you know, as usual. Snow is falling, cat is purring. And she hasn't tried to escape or anything."

Meg laughed lightly on the other end. "Miss Kitty isn't the escape artist type. She's pretty content with her life." As Meg seemed to be, which inspired just a bit of envy in Lila. Some recent heart-to-hearts had revealed that Meg had actually grown restless with her island existence for a little while—but enter Seth and, that quick, Meg seemed ready to live the rest of her life here. *Will you still feel that way if we can't stop Beck Grainger?*

And will I ever know that kind of contentment myself? At thirty-five, Lila had been on a grand search for…something—for as long as she could remember. Maybe that was part of the reason saving the land behind the inn felt so crucial to her. Maybe she'd *never* find real happiness—but she at least wanted it for her sister.

"How's Pennsylvania?" she asked.

"Great," Meg replied. "Last night we helped Seth's grandpa put up his Christmas tree, and we're about to attempt cookies from Seth's late grandma's recipe."

"Sounds fun," Lila said. Along with everything else, she envied how much joy Meg took from simple things.

"Have you ventured out?" Meg asked. "Or is the snow keeping you at home?"

"I went to the market. And I had lunch with Suzanne and Dahlia today, at Dahlia's restaurant."

At this, Meg let out a small gasp of joy. "Oh, I'm so glad. I was hoping you would connect with them. Aren't they great?"

"Yeah, they really are. I think I'll probably get together with them at least another time or two while I'm here." Of course, she left out that it had actually been an emergency meeting called by *her*, which had accomplished little. But she truly did like Meg's friends.

"Good," Meg said. "I'll feel better about you using your work hiatus this way if you're not stuck in the house alone the whole time."

Work hiatus. That was what Lila had told Meg and their parents. Because the truth was too ugly and hard to explain. And who knew if they'd even believe her anyway. "I don't mind," she said softly. "That's why I offered."

"Well, I still appreciate it—so very much. Seth's grandpa is thrilled to have us here. We're trying to talk him into coming to Ann Arbor for Christmas."

They were all meeting up back at Mom and Dad's in a few weeks. Suzanne was scheduled to feed Miss Kitty for the brief time between Lila's departure and

Meg's return. "That sounds like a nice idea," Lila told
Meg.

"Oh, hey," Meg said, "did you remember to put away
the stuff on the patio before it snowed?"

Oh crap. It had been a simple request. Move the café
table and chairs into the shed along with a box of lawn
tools Meg had been using for fall gardening. Meg had
realized only after leaving for Ann Arbor that she and
Seth had forgotten to store them and asked Lila to do
it upon her arrival. Easy-peasy.

Only… "I forgot." *Because I'm irresponsible and
can't be counted on for anything.* Everything she'd been
telling herself—and others—about what a bad sister
she was clearly remained true. She couldn't remember even one little task. "I'm so sorry, Meg—I totally
meant to. I'll do it as soon as we hang up. And I'll dry
everything off once I get it all in the shed, I promise."

"Lila, it's all right. Not a big deal." Meg's tone was
at once consoling and…well, unsurprised. *She's used
to me letting her down. And even still, she's being nice
about it.* Meg always did the right, nice thing. The un-
selfish thing. She was Lila's polar opposite.

"No, it is," Lila insisted. "And I should be more
responsible. I'm taking care of the rest of the house,
though—I promise." *Even if the hillside behind it is a
different story.*

Yet Meg just laughed. "I'm sure you are. And no
worries, really."

They hung up, leaving Lila torn—freshly pleased
she was able to do this for Meg, and freshly disappointed in herself for not taking care of the place the
way Meg would, or their grandmother before her. She
knew not putting the stuff away for winter was a lit-

tle thing—Meg had forgotten it herself, after all—but she'd wanted so badly to do everything right here, wanted to make up for mistakes from the past as best she could.

After finalizing her cat shoe order, she set her tablet aside, then headed for a linen closet, grabbing up the most worn-out towels she could find. As she bundled up in Meg's parka and boots to head outside, old guilt haunted her—memories of her dad encouraging her to call Meg, back when Meg had been going through chemo. It had been Meg who lived in Chicago then, and their mom had gone there to help her through it. Lila had always found a reason not to. Not to call, not to visit with Dad on weekends. Maybe she'd been afraid, as Suzanne had suggested. Or maybe just selfish. It had been more fun to think about cheerleading and high school dances than the horror her sister had been enduring. And when Meg had come here to Summer Island afterward, to recover under the care of their grandma, her parents had urged her to go up with them for a week in the summer, and on a few additional weekends—but she hadn't done that, either.

She had no idea what had made her open up to Meg's friends about that at lunch today. Or…maybe she did. They were kind, and she was desperate and depressed and exhausted. It had felt like a safe space.

And maybe such unexpected comfort had been a balm to her. And what she'd actually come here seeking—comfort. None of her spaces in Chicago felt safe anymore—and she feared they might not for a very long time, if ever.

As she toted the small table, then the chairs, to the gardening shed just across the creek from the hillside of trees that made the yard feel somehow sheltered and protected—even now, with everything covered in snow—part of her knew it was futile to wage war with Beck Grainger and his ugly hat.

But the ace up her sleeve was that Beck Grainger didn't know what he was up against in her. That she was a woman with little to risk right now. A woman who'd lost control over her life—and was on a mission to get some of it back. She had nothing left to fight for—except the trees behind the house.

She had the key to a bulldozer and the weather on her side. And she had his affinity for Meg's best friend—which indeed might not change things, but it couldn't hurt for Suzanne to let him know she didn't support his plans. Lila understood that none of those things would save the trees for long—but they were each little stopgaps that bought a bit more time. The real thing Beck Grainger should fear was that she had nothing else to do but watch the snow fall and keep working to find a way to stop him.

As she wiped down the tables and chair, then the gardening tools, she knew the safe money was on him. But every now and then a dark horse came from behind and won the race. She'd come here beaten and down—and now, unbeknownst to him, he'd given her something to stand up and do battle for.

Coming back inside, she shed now-wet boots and mittens, placing them and the towels near the fireplace to dry. She held out her hands, letting the heat warm them, and a few minutes later went to the kitchen—to the pantry, thinking about chamomile tea. She'd never actually drunk any, but it was supposed to help you sleep, right? And it seemed exactly like the type of thing her very thorough innkeeper sister would keep on hand for guests.

She was determined to get some sleep tonight, once and for all. She'd been so sure the peace and quiet here would make that happen. And then she'd even tried sleeping in different guestrooms. She'd started in one of the twin beds in the blue room, where she'd always stayed as a girl. When sleep hadn't come there, she'd tried Meg's lovely turret room, which had been her grandmother's when Lila was young. Tonight she might try the yellow room, or the lilac room. Mellow tones of lavender sounded relaxing.

Looking through the pantry, she discovered a selection of teas—and aha! Chamomile was among them. "Come to mama," she murmured, plucking up a tea bag.

Tonight she would sleep. And tomorrow she would conquer the world. Starting with Beck Grainger.

THE DAY AFTER he'd met Cade, snow still fell on Summer Island, and Beck was still shoveling it. And it didn't surprise him when his new little friend joined him again. "Figured you could use the help," Cade told him, once more sounding like a miniature adult, and of course Beck assured him that his assistance would make the work much lighter.

After parting with the little boy, Beck made himself a grilled cheese for lunch, pairing it with some chips—having just remembered the simple goodness of such a meal—and then he tackled a few unwelcome business calls to explain that clearing the land for Bluffside Drive was on hold. Due to weather. He'd left out the protest of a cute-but-crazy woman in pajamas or the fact that he no longer had a key to the bulldozer. And it was true that the weather would prevent progress for the immediate future—but hopefully a little time would clear the way, in more than one respect.

He spent some time staring out the window into the falling snow—irritated that he'd spent months of good weather making plans and getting permits, and now that the plans were in place, the weather was not. Of course, he'd known weather would be a factor when he decided to move here to develop some of the untouched land.

His development wouldn't change the feel or charm of Summer Island—even if the cute pajama lady acted like he was the devil incarnate, that wasn't his goal. Luxury homes made sense here. There weren't enough of them—and when one went on the market, it typically sold fast. That kept prices high—but not as high as on neighboring Mackinac Island, which made such a commodity a little more affordable here for someone seeking solitude in a picturesque setting.

He'd been lucky to get his *own* home here—he'd missed out on one that had sold on East Overlook by just a few days the summer before last, and nothing else had come available for months. Even people who only summered here tended to hold on to their property for a long while. So when an island real estate agent let him know 135 West Bluff Drive was going on the market this past spring, he'd headed over from the mainland quickly, toured the large cedar shake home, and put in a bid for the asking price that very day, not wanting to risk losing it.

Set back in the trees, the home was too large for him, but he liked it anyway. He liked space, he liked nice surroundings, and he could afford it. And maybe Emma and Mike would bring the kids up in the summers. This past summer had been hectic, with Dad having just died—but they'd probably welcome some free vacations and he'd enjoy giving them that. And maybe…maybe one day he'd have a family of his own.

Not that it looked promising at this point. Thirty-nine, divorced, living on a quiet, isolated island with low population, and he couldn't get Suzanne Quinlan to look at him. He was pretty sure Lila Sloan wasn't going to be beating his door down for a date anytime soon, either. But as his father had been fond of saying, sometimes God worked in mysterious ways. And as hard as Beck had toiled to leave most of his upbringing far behind him, some of it was ground in too deep. That particular belief, about God and mysterious ways, though, didn't seem like a bad one to have held on to.

When he'd killed about as much time as he could, he turned reluctantly to the box now adorning his dining room table. He didn't want to open it. And hell, maybe he shouldn't—nothing to say he couldn't just stick it up in the attic and let it rot there.

But opening it would prevent tenseness with Emma at Christmas. And he saw no need to mar the gathering in the house she shared with her husband and their kids, Tara and Grant, in Kentucky, not far from where Beck and Emma had grown up. She'd gone to the trouble of sending it, so whatever it was, he'd take a glance—and *then* shove it in the attic.

Grabbing a steak knife from a butcher block on the long, granite kitchen counter, he sliced through the packing tape, then folded back the four lids. Inside, another box. A much *nicer* box. Wooden—cedar to be exact. Lifting it from the cushioning of packing peanuts, he found that the top and sides bore carvings—and looking closer at the top, he made out a relief of the Nativity scene. If the box had come from anyone else, perhaps he'd have only seen a hut-like structure with people beneath it—but knowing this had belonged to his father, it was the manger for sure.

Also floating within the packing material, he discovered a blue envelope bearing his name in his sister's handwriting. It wasn't sealed—he extracted the matching blue sheet of stationery and opened it.

Beck,
This was in Dad's office, with a note saying it
was for you. I'd have waited and given it to you
at Christmas, but I know how you still feel about
him, and I didn't want Christmas to be sad for
you. It will be hard enough for Mom and the
kids—the first year without him. No reason to
make it hard on you, too. I know you said you
didn't want anything of his—but under the cir-
cumstances, I couldn't not give it to you. Love you.
                    Em

He let out a long sigh, indeed unable to fault his sister, and even appreciating her forethought in not making the holidays any more awkward by handing him some big box to take home. Even if it must have cost her a mint in postage—which he'd insist on repaying since she and Mike didn't need any extra expenses. Clearly he wasn't the only one strategizing to make Christmas as drama free as possible.

What the hell had the old man set aside for him on

his deathbed? Bracing himself, Beck went to lift the lid—only to find that the box possessed a lock.

Which made one thing finally clear.

Walking back into the large, open kitchen and living area, where a wall of windows in back overlooked woods and—currently—the still-falling snow, he headed toward the little row of hooks where he kept keys. It was old-fashioned, but they'd had one in the house where he'd been raised, and it was another of those little things that had stuck: keys are kept on hooks in the kitchen, and that way they don't get lost.

From it, he drew a tiny, ornate silver key which had arrived inexplicably in his mailbox well over a year ago, before he'd moved here. Return address: his parents'. Handwriting: his dad's, albeit looking more scrawled and shaky than it used to. He'd noticed that, but hadn't taken the time to wonder why. Inside the envelope, no note of any kind, just the key, wrapped in a tiny piece of flowered cloth, likely a scrap from Mom's quilting basket.

He hadn't picked up the phone to ask what the key was for—maybe sending it without a note had been a ploy to orchestrate such a call, or maybe it was only his dad being mysterious, just like God. But he'd brought it with him on the move, figuring sooner or later he'd find out what it opened, and the answer had just arrived on the postal sleigh.

Though as he walked back to the box and slipped the key into the tiny lock—*whoa*. A blizzard of unanticipated memories washed over him. Keys, locks. Magic.

Despite himself, a small smile stole over him at the memory of Johnny's Toys in Latonia, a northern Kentucky suburb of Cincinnati. Every year, the store had mailed gold keys to members of its "birthday club." When Beck's birthday came, Dad would drive him to the store, where he'd use the treasured key to unlock the door to the castle—a full fairy-tale castle inside a toy shop—where he was allowed to pick a toy, or game, or action figure from the shelves.

It was a damn good memory, so good that it surprised him. Most of his memories weren't about things he got but more about things he'd lost. Yet when they went to Johnny's, every year like clockwork—same for Em on her birthday—he knew whatever he picked was really his, his to keep, and the whole thing had been...special.

"Damn, Dad," he murmured into the quiet air. Because he'd almost forgotten—about *any* good times— and through the mystical, magical turn of this key, his father had brought them back, even if unwittingly, even from the grave. *You did have your gifts. Even if most of 'em weren't for me.*

He realized his heart beat a little harder than usual as he lifted the lid—but more from that remembered anticipation, that return to childhood, than from wondering what was inside.

And good thing, because otherwise he might have been disappointed to find merely a pile of papers. Folded sheets of loose-leaf notebook paper like he'd used in school, folded pieces of fancier stationery, one small spiral notebook, some paper in envelopes, some not. The box was a good six inches deep and filled to the top.

Beck reached down and drew out the first set of several sheets of stationery, folded in half, and opened them. His eyes fell on a Bible verse written in his father's hand, John 3:16. *For God so loved the world that he gave his only begotten Son...*

He quit reading. He already knew the damn verse—he'd had it and many others ground into his head at an early age. His father had always seen signs in Bible verses—claimed that when he had a question in life, or needed to learn something, the right, perfect Bible verse appeared before him. Divine guidance, literally.

Below the verse on the page, more of his father's precise handwriting in black ink—a sermon.

Hell, his dad had sent him a box of sermons? Still trying to save his soul from the other side, even if it wasn't especially lost in Beck's opinion. And the sermon was, as always, about giving. Giving, giving, giving. Give unto others. Give until it hurts. Give all your worldly possessions. The story of his life. His childhood anyway.

Talk about a disappointment.

But then, not really. He hadn't expected the box to contain anything wonderful, after all—or at least not until that unlikely memory of the toy store had colored his vision for a moment. Well, moment over—back to reality. Back to now.

According to the weather app on his phone, the snow was expected to slack off tonight, ebbing into intermittent snow showers tomorrow. Might be a good day to try making some peace with Lila Sloan—and his new buddy, Cade, had given him an idea of how to at least take a stab at it, one that would lead him to see Suzanne in the bargain.

He probably should have completely given up on Suzanne Quinlan by now, but for some reason he still held out a little hope. She was pretty, wry, forthright, feminine, and even if she had shot him down from the start, she'd slowly started being nicer to him since summer. Maybe something good would happen between them yet.

Christmas was a time of miracles, after all. One more ground-in belief he hadn't quite surrendered.

CHAPTER FIVE

THE VERY FACT that the snow had stopped drew people out onto Harbor Street the following morning. Sure, that meant trudging through eight inches or so of fresh powder, but for a year-rounder, that was child's play. Suzanne decided to grab something to drink at the Cozy Coffee and Tea Shop before heading to Petal Pushers—she suspected this might be a big day for tree and wreath shoppers who hadn't gotten their Christmas decorations hauled home before the storm, and she might need the caffeine a big cup of coffee would provide.

All of Harbor Street seemed aflutter with holiday cheer. Clark Hayes, who owned the Huron House Hotel, stood up on a ladder—its legs planted deep in the snow—draping strings of lights across the building's front awning. And Jolene, a waitress at the Skipper's Wheel, currently hung a wreath on the restaurant's front door. To the east, against the backdrop of a bright blue sky, a crew of men worked to erect a giant Christmas tree in the middle of the street between Lakeview Park and the marina. On an island with no cars, the street could be used for any purpose desired in wintertime. She'd volunteered to help with the decorations as time permitted in the coming days—another form of purpose, and one that would provide far more of a distraction than the one Lila had assigned her.

As she stepped into the coffee shop, she found the mood as festive inside as out. A tree glowed in one corner, a fire roared in a hearth, and Nat King Cole sang from hidden speakers about tiny tots finding it hard to sleep tonight.

Dahlia waved from a table near the fire, bringing a smile to Suzanne's face. It was nice living someplace where unexpected meetings with friends happened often. She slid into a chair across from Dahlia, slipped out of her parka, and ordered a double mocha latte when the owner, Josh, came by with an order pad.

"Can't stay long," Dahlia told her. "Audrey Fisher's bunco club is having a holiday luncheon at the café. And I suspect we'll have a few more customers today anyway, during the break in the snow. I even called in a couple of cooks and waiters."

"I can't stay, either," Suzanne informed her. "Nothing as exciting as a luncheon, but I think the weather will draw out the tree shoppers today, too."

"Speaking of which, did you notice the tree going up in front of the park?"

Suzanne nodded. "Meet me later this afternoon to hang some ornaments?"

"Absolutely." Dahlia glanced back in the general direction of the large tree. "I volunteered Zack to spearhead the effort this year. He was spitting nails at me about it, but it'll be good for him. He's got to get over this Meg funk sooner or later, and I'm voting for sooner."

"Good luck with that," Suzanne offered up dryly. She'd seldom met a man more stubborn or set in his

ways. "Probably giving hell to the other poor guys trying to get that tree up."

"No doubt," Dahlia agreed. "I'm hoping it will give
him a little holiday cheer, but could be it's a lost cause."
Then she shrugged. "I do what I can for the boy."

The boy was in his early forties and—in Suzanne's
opinion—indeed a lost cause. But she never went so far
as to say so, knowing how much Dahlia cared for him.

"Have you given any thought to this Beck situation?" Dahlia asked—and Suzanne flinched. How did
Dahlia know he was on her mind so much lately? The
woman was known to have hidden powers, but this
was ridiculous.

"Well, I don't know what I'm going to do—if anything. Because I'm not sure if my feelings for him have
really changed—or if I'm just looking to fill some unexpected gap in my life. Feelings can sneak up on you
and even be hard to interpret at times—or at least that's
been my finding, particularly when dealing with matters of attraction and affection. And as you said yourself, we don't really know him all that well, so who's to
say we'd really have anything in common or truly hit
it off? And I'm well aware that both you and Meg, and
probably this entire island, think we'd make a lovely
couple, but romance really just isn't as simple as that."

When she finally ceased rambling, Dahlia simply
blinked, then spoke evenly—as her eyes dripped sarcasm. "I *meant* the situation with the land behind the
inn. Since you promised Lila you'd talk to him about
it."

Oh. That.

Suzanne sighed and tried not to let her nervousness
show. As if she hadn't already completely blown her

cover. "Um, I'm hoping to just bump into him some- where soon and find a way to bring it up."

Dahlia took a sip from the big green mug before her. "Yes, because if you actually contacted him, he might get the crazy idea you like him or something."

Another sigh. "Correct."

Josh dropped off Suzanne's drink then, along with the bill. And only after he'd rushed off to another table did Dahlia tilt her head to ask, "What *is* the problem between you and Beck anyway? Not that I mean to pry."

"But you're going to anyway."

Dahlia simply shrugged. And Suzanne couldn't re- ally blame her—she'd done this to herself, stuck her foot in her mouth. "Well, the other day you blatantly denied having any romantic interest in the man. But you tipped your hand just now, girlfriend. So what's up? And don't try to just talk your way out of it—I want a real answer."

Suzanne looked at her wrist—then wished she had actually worn a watch. Darn it. "Time flies—Christmas trees to sell. And you have a luncheon to throw."

"Not so fast," Dahlia said, calm as ever and not re- motely frazzled by Suzanne's threat of leaving. "I'm serious. What is it between you and him? Or *not* be- tween you and him? I'm your friend—talk to me."

Suzanne blew out one more sigh—this one heavy with emotion as she tried to construct an answer. She was open about most things with her close friends— but when it came to romance and all her reasons for not wanting it, she kept things mostly on the surface. "Well, what I actually said was that I wasn't sure how I felt. And by all accounts, it's safe to say I've been pretty flighty on the whole subject since he first showed up here, so why ask about it now?"

"Perhaps matters of the heart are just on my mind," Dahlia replied, catching her off guard. "And the fact that life is short."

"Which is why I'm living mine exactly as I choose." Suzanne finished with a succinct nod.

Still, Dahlia tilted her head, looking truly puzzled. "That's the part I don't get. Why you choose to be alone when a lovely man—and I mean that in every way because he's about the most handsome specimen I've ever seen on this island—wants to get to know you better? I realize you had a rough time when Cal died, and afterward, too. But time has passed, and they say it heals all wounds."

Suzanne attempted a smile at the thoughtful suggestion. But her wounds ran pretty deep.

Even so, she tried to be a little more honest than usual on this topic and explain to her friend as best she could. "Finding someone you connect with, really connect with, on every level—it's not as easy as the whole world likes to think. And it can be a lot of work—and heartache—trying to make that happen only to find out it won't. The experiences I had after Cal just…left me tired. And made me feel foolish and even more broken. But maybe in the end, what it really comes down to is… I'm not sure I believe perfect love can happen twice. I had my perfect love—and now he's gone."

"It doesn't have to be perfect to be worth having," Dahlia said without missing a beat. "In fact, imperfect romance can be ever so fun in its own way."

Suzanne narrowed her gaze on her older friend.

"For a woman who says such wise-sounding things, I haven't exactly seen *you* out dating up a storm."

At this, however, Dahlia let a sly little smile steal over her face. "Maybe I have secrets."

Was Dahlia bluffing? Suzanne simply eyed her friend.

And was about to ask more when Dahlia said, "And on that note, I really do have to go." She stood up, pulling on a large purple woolen wrap, laden with colorful costume jewelry broaches, probably collected over a lifetime. "But if you run into Beck, while you're busy doing what you can for Meg, consider doing something for yourself, too. Coffee's on me." She scooped up the bill currently facedown on the table and headed to the counter, leaving Suzanne to look after her.

People got so wistful at Christmastime. Always looking for something to make the season feel special, give it meaning. The whole world wanted everyone to be in love at Christmas, acting as if it couldn't possibly be a pleasant holiday otherwise—it was almost as bad as Valentine's Day in that way. Well, whether or not Dahlia had a real secret, Suzanne hoped it would be the last time she'd push Suzanne toward Beck. Suzanne had already endured enough of that—even if done lovingly—from Meg last summer. And if she moved toward Beck…well, it had to be because she was ready—not because her friends were feeling all sappy and sentimental about Christmas.

But the man did stay on her mind.

SUZANNE'S INSTINCTS HAD been spot-on—it was a big day in the tree and wreath business. Every person staying on the island through the holidays who hadn't already put up a tree ventured to Petal Pushers to buy one while skies were clear. She worked through lunch, and only when a snow shower hit around one o'clock did the crowds disperse, so she stopped to eat the sandwich she'd packed, then straightened the table of poinsettias near the front door, which had also gotten rather picked over the last few hours.

The morning blue sky had transformed to white, and a check of the weather app on her phone suggested it would stay that way. The reprieve had been brief— more dry weather tomorrow, but until then snow showers would increase in intensity through the afternoon and evening. She could probably lock up and head home if she wanted to—and looked like trimming the big tree in front of the park would have to wait.

When the bell on the front door jingled, she glanced up to see—speak of the land-developing devil—Beck Grainger. And her heart nearly stopped. Just from the sight of him.

Or was it that Dahlia had made her think too hard about him? *No, quit lying to yourself, once and for all—he was already on your mind.* Or maybe it was because of the mission for Meg and Lila. *But no, just stop it—you were thinking about him before that, too. You* like *to think about him. Thinking about him feels warm, cozy.*

"Heard this is the hot spot for Christmas trees," he greeted her with a smile.

She met his gaze. Or tried to. God, his brown eyes did sparkle. It was hard to look at him directly, hard to hold eye contact.

She gave up, stared at his mouth instead. Which was also attractive to her.

Coat. Safe to look at his coat. Well, better anyway. Even if her heart still beat too hard. "You want 'em, we got 'em," she said, trying to be just as jovial. "Spruce, Scotch pine, fir—both Douglas and balsam. Just take your pick." Then she pointed over her shoulder, toward the back door of the shop—and used the opportunity to divert her gaze. "The bigger ones are out back. You'll probably want at least a ten-footer for your place, right?" She hadn't been inside his house, but even just from the outside knew it was spacious, as were all the homes on West Bluff.

"Actually, it's not for me," he said. "And maybe you can recommend the right size. I'm taking it to the Summerbrook Inn."

At this, she swung her gaze back toward him—too surprised to remember that looking at him was difficult. "Really? A tree? For the inn?" She tilted her head. "Why?"

He scrunched up his nose, appearing just a little guilty, a little hesitant. "Then you haven't heard?"

She let her eyebrows lift. "No, I heard," she told him knowingly. "But still, what does a Christmas tree have to do with it?"

He winced, lightly scratched at his darkly stubbled cheek, and appeared uncertain. "It's...sort of a peace offering. For Meg's sister. You probably know Lila."

She nodded. "Yes." And she supposed this was her chance to do what she'd promised. If only she hadn't reverted back to finding it so hard to meet those amazing eyes, a brown so warm they could almost melt all the ice in her heart.

Why on earth could she not just look at the man the same as she looked at anyone else? Was it because she was fed up with love or…was she so ridiculously attracted to him that she simply didn't know how to deal with that? Could the two be so easily confused? And yet, her heart beat faster in his presence. It always had with him. Always.

He gritted his teeth lightly. "She's pretty worked up about the situation. And I noticed there's no tree in the front window, or any other Christmas decorations I can see, so I thought a neighborly gesture might…help." Then he shifted his weight from one foot to the other. "Any chance you think she's overreacting and that Meg will be okay with the change behind the property?"

Oh boy. The "change behind the property" was putting it lightly, so now it was *her* nose that scrunched. "Um, no." She wanted to say more, *should* say more—to keep her promise—but no words would come. *This is why you can't date. Handsome men paralyze you.* Though this case was extreme. And in that moment a startling and horrifying truth struck her—no man had ever had this effect on her. Ever. Not even Cal, the love of her life.

Uh-oh.

She realized she was gaping at him now—well, at the front of his coat anyway—her mouth hanging open. Hopefully he'd chalk it up to the situation with the inn. She needed to move things along here somehow. "But if you're serious about taking Lila a tree, an eight-footer would be nice in the parlor, and I have a pretty Douglas fir that size right out front."

She stepped past him, opening the door. A burst of cold air blew in as she pointed to the nearest tree in the row of them currently lining the front of the lavender building. When he leaned past her to look, she caught the scent of him. Something leathery and musky and masculine, it seemed to ricochet through her body.

And when he turned to say, "That sounds fine— I'll take it," it put their faces close. Maybe closer than they'd ever been. A liquid, ice-melting awareness flowed through her.

"It's starting to snow," she said, apropos of nothing, realizing that wet heavy flakes had just begun dotting his shoulders, face, hair. It gave her a reason to duck rapidly back inside and put some distance between them by circling the small counter to the register.

As he let the door close and pulled a wallet from his back pocket, she wondered if he'd felt it, too— that awareness. If he'd felt *her* feeling it. Or if he just attributed her odd behavior to the fact that she *often* acted weird around him. *What on earth does he even see in me?*

"You're not wearing a hat," she said. Another genius, random remark.

But he didn't act like it was an odd thing to say. "It was sunny out when I left the house. I'm still not used to—you know—not being able to throw something in the car you might need later." He ended that statement with a little wink—which, good Lord, reached right down into her solar plexus.

She attempted an answer. "Yeah, it takes a while. And for you, not like you can just run back home and get it." She suspected it was at least a fifteen-minute walk up to West Bluff from here, maybe longer through the snow. And a glance out the window revealed that it was coming down heavier now. "Things are different here."

He looked up when she added the last words. And could tell he got the deeper meaning behind them.

It was her opening, so she needed to pull herself together and make her play for Meg's inn. "Beck, I have no idea how land deals work, and I'm sure there's a lot of money involved. But taking out the trees on the hill behind the inn is a pretty big move for this place. Things don't change here in big ways overnight. Even having been on the island only a couple of years myself, I'm aware of how much people appreciate the… sameness of the place. And it's why most of them are here." It pleased her to have gotten all that out despite being a little breathless.

He gave a solemn nod. "Don't worry, I understand that. Thing is, though, anytime *anything* is built in this world, there's usually somebody who doesn't like the idea or feels it hurts their way of life. But for any progress to happen—anywhere—you have to look to the greater good change brings."

That all sounded very nice—and even heartfelt. But it didn't help anything, and she hoped she could spit out a measured response despite how painfully hard her heart still beat. "I suppose if this were happening on the other side of the island, I wouldn't care so much. But it's right up the street behind my best friend's business."

He let out a long sigh before pasting on a small smile. "And here I was hoping you'd be on my side."

Something in her deflated—upon realizing that… she wished she could. Support him. For no other reason than…just wanting to. Because it would build a little bond between them. And the very desire for that stymied her all over again—she wanted a bond with Beck Grainger.

"It's not that... I mean..." She stopped, sighed. Again, so short of breath and inarticulate with him. She usually said exactly what she meant, with everyone. *Take a second. Think clearly.* "The thing is, I *have* to be on Lila's side on this. Because I get the value of those woods for Meg and the inn and their whole family. It breaks my heart to think of them being gone, for lots of reasons." Her heart hurt, her chest went tight—*but keep going. Say what you mean. Just say it.* "Though if this were something where I *could* take your side, I *would*. I mean, because..." She stopped, pursed her lips, tried to gulp in some air without being obvious about it.

"Because why?"

Say it. "Because I think maybe I finally have a crush on you. Or maybe I have had all along and was too confused to know it. Because I like you."

Whoa. That was saying it, all right. Putting it right there on the table. She couldn't breathe. She watched his coat, light brown with darker buttons. She zeroed in on a button, studying it closely.

"That's good to know," he said. She took in the warm little smile on his face only peripherally.

But it slowly gave her the courage to lift her gaze.

"Because I like you, too," he went on. "But I think you already know that."

Yikes. She had no idea how to respond to that last part, and what came out was, "Still?"

"Still," he said. "I mean, if you...wanted to get together, I'd love to take you to dinner." He looked absently around, offered up another small smile. "Though

I guess Dahlia's or the Pink Pelican is about as close to fine dining as I can come until spring."

Of course Dahlia's or the Pink Pelican—the bar at the Huron House Hotel—sounded just fine by her, but this change of heart was still new, and her declaration felt sudden, and certainly unplanned. She needed to slow things down here. And also try to quit acting like a basket case. So she just nodded. "That's…good to know, too. Because, you know… I don't know… maybe."

"Maybe what?"

Somehow now she'd focused on his hands—big, strong hands—where they held his wallet, ready to pay for the tree. But this drew her eyes back up. To his. For only a second. A really good second, though. "Just…maybe." Eyes down. And then a new thought occurred to her—one he'd just inspired. Eyes back up. "Maybe…spring."

Then she rang up the tree and told him how much, thinking it would have been a better strategy to declare her feelings *after* he'd paid. *You are so bad at this.*

But as he passed her a credit card, their fingers brushed, and she felt the tiny touch *everywhere*—and as her entire body processed the lovely sensation, she swiped the card and wondered if he'd experienced it, too.

Returning the card to him, she switched the subject back to the original, practical one. "I…hope you don't think taking Lila a Christmas tree is going to fix things."

He appeared pleasantly pragmatic, even if an inkling of the guilt she'd seen earlier crept back into his expression. "I know it won't. It's just…a gesture. To show her I'm not the bad guy. To try to make amends."

She gave her head a knowing tilt. "I wouldn't hold my breath if I were you."

And for the first time ever, Beck Grainger cast her a downright flirtatious look that moved through her like liquid heat and made her forget all about winter. "Sometimes holding your breath and being patient pays off. After all, if I'm lucky, I might get you to go out with me next spring."

Then he pushed his way through the door and back out into the snow.

AFTER THE LAST few days, he was already tired of the snow. But as Beck dragged the big fir tree up Harbor Street, colored Christmas lights lining storefronts and snow falling all around him, suddenly Summer Island felt a little closer to being an idyllic winter wonderland. His conversation with Suzanne had unexpectedly brightened his mood.

Of course, he wasn't getting ahead of himself. Calling Suzanne a slow mover was an understatement. If it had taken her this long to even admit she might like him a little, it wasn't as if they would go out tomorrow. And she had baggage—her husband had died and it was enough to keep her from dating, apparently for a pretty damn long time.

So the upshot was that they might eventually have dinner. *Spring*, she'd said. And *maybe*. Perhaps it would finally happen—when the snow melted and the flowers began to bloom. But a long winter lay ahead before that came to pass. So maybe the thing he shouldn't hold his breath about was a date with Suzanne.

Even so, she had a crush on him? And she'd actually told him about it? It *was* a Christmas miracle!

And hell, who knew, despite her doubts, maybe he'd get another miracle with this tree. He knew it was a pretty unorthodox idea. But he also knew things did work differently here. And he suspected a personal gesture like this, not to mention one that ushers in the holiday spirit, might just bring about the peace he sought. Christmas miracle number two, coming right up!

After maneuvering the long tree up the Summerbrook Inn's snowy front walk—maybe he'd even offer to shovel it if this went well—he dragged it up the big Victorian's front steps and onto the covered porch, grateful to get out of the wet snow.

Clearing his throat, he rang the bell—and waited, until Lila Sloan opened the door wearing dark leggings and a big, cable-knit sweater. He smiled. "Merry Christmas."

She just blinked, appearing a little repulsed by the very sight of him. "What the hell is this?" She motioned vaguely toward the tree behind him.

"I brought you a Christmas tree."

She narrowed her gaze on him, continuing to eye him like something repugnant the cat dragged up. "Are you serious?"

He nodded. "Yes."

"You, Beck Grainger," she said, "can go to hell." Then slammed the door in his face.

CHAPTER SIX

LILA STARED AT the door she'd just slammed, in disbelief. That man had brought her...a tree? Why on earth
would he do such a weird thing? And did he not see
the horrible irony in it? Even having shut the door between them, she felt waylaid and flummoxed. It was
almost—not quite, but almost—as shocking as the bulldozer had been.

That was when he rang the bell again. And then
knocked on the door—as if she hadn't just heard the
ringing, as if she wasn't standing right on the opposite
side, clearly visible through thin curtains that covered
the front door's half window. It made her head pound—
despite the chamomile, she still hadn't slept much, a
few hours at most.

Part of her had a good mind to just walk away, ignore him, and leave him out there ringing and knocking for however long it took him to get the message
and go away. But another part of her wanted to give
him a piece of her mind.

The second part won. She yanked the door back
open. "Why the hell would you bring me a Christmas
tree?" Exhaustion made her extra irritable.

"I noticed you didn't have one. And I was hoping it
might give us a chance to—"

"If you think *this* tree is going to make up for all

the trees you plan to murder," she broke in, pointing vaguely down at the one behind him, "you're out of your mind."

"You have a thing against Christmas trees?" he asked her.

She eyed him warily. "No, I don't have a thing against Christmas trees. I just have a thing against *you* being audacious enough to bring me one."

"So you don't hold it against Suzanne that she *sells* Christmas trees?"

She drew back slightly. What was he talking about? "No, of course not."

"So the murder of every Christmas tree that ever stood in a house for a couple of weeks each December is okay with you."

Oh. Trick question. The nerve of him. Now she stared him down like a foe. "Christmas trees are grown for that purpose. And even the ones that aren't don't take out an entire hillside of trees. *Those* trees—" she pointed over her shoulder "—have…decorated my life. And Meg's life. And our mother's life. And her parents' lives. And the lives of every person who's ever stayed at the inn. It's two different things. So don't go trying to play your little murdered Christmas tree card with *me*, mister."

"I was just making a point," he said evenly.

"A dumb one," she informed him.

"Tomato, tomahto," he replied.

"I still don't want your stupid tree. Or you, here— period." The fact that he was still handsome and still had amazing eyes remained completely overshadowed by the fact that he intended to put up a subdivision in Meg's backyard. Which was to say—she noticed, again. The handsomeness, and the eyes. But attractive or not, he was the enemy. "Unless," she went on, "you've brought this tree as a way of saying you've changed your mind and aren't going to cut down the ones behind the inn, I have nothing to say to you."

The man on her front porch looked all too reasonable as he replied, "I think you know that's not the case." He *always* looked calm and reasonable, she realized—even out in the snow the other day when she'd been raising hell in Meg's pajamas. It made her resent him all the more given that calm was the last thing *she* felt. She'd been walking around bleary-eyed and frustrated from fatigue—but Beck Grainger's crazy Christmas tree delivery had woken her right up.

"I'd really like to put up this tree for you, though," he went on, "and I'll even help you with the lights if you want—and we could talk more about the situation. I'd like to make you understand that it's not going to be so bad, answer any questions you may have, and show you that I don't mean the inn any harm and that we can be friendly neighbors as this work takes place over the coming years. It's important to me to make that happen."

"Years?" She balked. She'd been planning to tell him what he could do with all his calm, mild-mannered peacemaking gestures, but this new revelation took precedence over that.

"Yes," he said—tone still even and deep as ever, "it'll be several years at least. New communities don't go up overnight."

Whoa. This was…this was even worse than she'd thought. Not only was the wooded serenity of the backyard being taken away, Meg was going to have to put up with construction for *years*?

The news actually left Lila light-headed—she reached to steady herself by pressing her palm to the wide-open door, but the world still spun and she realized she needed to sit down, so she backed her way toward the wide mahogany staircase and plopped down on one of the lower steps.

"Are you all right?"

She'd bent forward, lowering her head, trying to get her equilibrium back. Her eyes took in her feet, in gray socks sporting red snowflakes—and *his* feet, covered in brown work boots currently trailing wetness onto the hardwood in the foyer.

"I will be," she assured him—both because she didn't want to appear weak and because that was what nice Midwestern people pleasers did: they rushed to assure others they were okay, and to make everything all right. She'd exercised no people-pleasing tendencies toward Beck Grainger so far, given that she had no reason to put this man at ease—but the quick assertion had simply snuck out from habit. Though just as quickly it struck her as preposterous. "But no, I'm not. And maybe I never will be again."

If he thought that was dramatic, he ignored it, and said, "Can I get you a glass of water or something?"

The truth was, she'd probably gotten a little dehydrated. It was past lunchtime and she hadn't yet eaten and she never drank enough water and knew she should drink more. But she hadn't been thinking about things like her general health lately, other than the lost sleep she couldn't seem to regain. She'd been too busy trying to recover from the loss of everything she held dear in Chicago—and then the loss of what Meg held dear here.

But she didn't especially want him traipsing through the house any more than he already was, friend of Meg's or not. "No," she said, then lifted her head. "Well, yes." Because looking up had made her dizzy. "Kitchen's that way." She pointed before lowering her head back down. And hated that she was suddenly dependent on this jerk to help her feel better.

A moment later, she accepted a bottle of water that he'd found in the fridge and guzzled some of it down. A few more big drinks and she started feeling steadier. She resisted the urge to thank him, aware that he still stood nearby even though she purposefully didn't look at him.

Upon realizing he'd closed the door at some point, she battled a sudden gut reaction of panic, but then reminded herself it was okay—it was snowing out and for all his faults, the guy didn't mean her harm. Well, not the kind of harm that came from being behind a closed door with someone anyway. *This is okay, this is okay.*

Only it *wasn't* okay. In the big picture way. And even as she got her balance and wits back, she had no idea what to do or say.

"Better?" he asked.

She nodded. "Yes. Much." Still not saying thank you. Instead, she finally lifted her gaze to him to ask, again, "Years?" Then blew out a depressed sigh.

"Only in the off-season if that helps," he told her. "I think I told you the town requested that, and I agreed to honor it."

"Well, I suppose that's…something," she admitted, but remained just as downcast. "And I'm sure the

summer guests will enjoy looking out on a construction site for years to come."

"We'll do everything we can to keep it as pleasant
as possible," he assured her. Though she didn't feel assured of much. Other than the fact that pieces of her
world both big and small kept dropping out from under
her lately and at this point she had no idea what was
going to plummet next.

"Listen," he said gently, "can I bring the tree inside?
Set it up? Put some lights on it for you?"

The idea still struck her as ludicrous and not serving much purpose. "I'm going home to Ann Arbor before Christmas even comes. No one will be here for
the holiday." And ugh, maybe she shouldn't have told
him that—it meant no one would be around to throw
themselves in front of bulldozers, either.

But if she'd just paved the way for tree murder, he
didn't let it show. "I'm not, either."

Oh good! Not that he couldn't get driver Jim or
someone else to do his dirty work, but maybe the period directly around the holiday was a free no-work
zone.

"Still," he went on, "you might enjoy it for however
long you're here." Oh, he was still talking about the
dumb Christmas tree. "What do you say?"

Exhausted, in so many respects, she spoke the God's
honest truth. "I really have no interest in this tree either way. So if you put it up, it's for you, to assuage
your guilt or whatever—not for me. Do whatever you
want." She shooed him—and the whole idea—away
with a sweep of her hand.

Oddly, however, this brought a smile to his handsome, unshaven face, rough with stubble. "Well, who

knows—maybe you'll be surprised and actually enjoy having it around."

She sneered slightly. "It'll probably just make me think of *you*—which I *won't* enjoy."

It surprised her when this made him laugh. Did the man not know how to properly take an insult?

"Tell you what," he said, opening the door to begin hauling the big tree inside. "If you point me toward the ornaments and lights, I'll even decorate it for you."

She tossed him a dry, sideways glance. "You plan to stay that long?"

He answered by lifting his gaze from the tree to look out the open door toward the street and Lake Michigan beyond. "It's snowing harder."

Oh. He wanted to wait out the snow shower here. Great. "And you aren't even smart enough to wear a hat." She shook her head at the simple ineptitude. Summer Island in winter equals hat on head—everyone knew that.

But he only grinned quietly to himself, focused again on getting the tree inside, apparently finding her insults humorous, despite that she wasn't joking.

"And your taste in hats," she informed him, "is abysmal, by the way. That one you wore the other day, that leathery cowboy-type monstrosity—it should be retired, right into the garbage can."

He looked at her over the tree lying on its side, appearing surprised. "Really? I always thought it was… kinda cool. Kinda Indiana Jones or something."

She kept her expression bland and grim as she said, "Um, no."

And she really, really did not want Beck Grainger, Tree Killer, hanging out in her parlor all afternoon, and she thought about telling him so—telling him to just leave the tree and she'd do the rest, whether or not she really would being up to her to decide. But the snow indeed fell heavily, turning everything out the window white, and winds had begun to swirl.

She'd heard about people losing their way in blinding snowstorms and dying only a few feet from their camp or their door. Of course, she was pretty sure the stories had taken place out West in pioneer times, or on Mount Everest, but still…enemy or not, if she asked him to leave and anything crazy happened to him, she'd feel terrible.

On the other hand, his untimely death might save those trees.

Okay, stop—you can't will the guy to his grave to save the trees. Even if it was tempting in a way. Tempting to just somehow wipe one of her troubles off the big, messy whiteboard of her life. Wiping something away sounded nice. Because if she didn't wipe something off soon, there'd be no room to add anything new.

Finally standing up from her spot on the stairs, she padded quietly to the wide opening that led to the room her grandmother—and Meg after her—had always called the parlor. She watched quietly as Beck began trying to stand the tree upright in front of the picture window that faced Harbor Street. She couldn't deny it was a nice tree.

The man holding it had shed his coat and wore a plaid flannel shirt open over a navy tee and blue jeans. His thick, dark hair, damp from the snow when he'd arrived, had begun to dry. She took him in, trying to see not only the tree-slaying land developer who seemed bent on thwarting her stay here, but the man Meg considered a friend, the man Dahlia and Suzanne were fond of, as well. There was a part of her that wanted to see the good in him—since she supposed, like it or not, he'd been quite decent to her in every way other than not relenting about the trees.

"Don't imagine you have a tree stand," he said, looking up at her. "Didn't think about that part."

"I'm sure there's one in the attic," she answered a bit glumly. "I'll go look."

"Can I help?"

"No need," she replied. *No need to let you get any closer and risk me thinking of you as more human.* She feared she might almost like him if that happened. And she didn't *want* to like him.

"Are you sure?" he asked, sounding sincerely concerned. "You were just dizzy, you know."

"I'm fine now—coming back to myself." *Back to my usual self. Back to my stronger self.* Back to the self who wasn't going to let a man manipulate her or talk her into seeing things his way. Because how could she ever like someone who would do what he was planning to do to the Summerbrook Inn? Simple—she couldn't.

OKAY, NO SECOND Christmas miracle. Not yet anyway.

It actually made very little sense to Beck that he should stand here holding this pine tree while she went climbing up into an attic by herself—especially since there would probably be decorations to haul down, too—but he decided to give her some space.

Weirdly perhaps, he considered what had happened so far a win. He didn't like that she hadn't felt well, but it had forced her to start…okay, not being nice, not by a long shot—but to at least start tolerating his presence. And beginning to accept the inevitable. He could hear that in her voice. She was starting to wrap her head around the fact that the development couldn't be stopped. That was a step in the right direction— and would hopefully keep her and her purple pajamas from showing up in front of his bulldozer whenever it got going again.

He'd seen the bulldozer key in the kitchen, lying on the counter next to a set of old-fashioned canisters. And he could have easily taken it, quietly slipping it in a pocket and never saying a word—but it would have been underhanded. Not that it was exactly aboveboard for her to halt his work in the first place by putting her safety at risk. But given the circumstances, he wanted her to *choose* to give him the key. With each passing day since the bulldozer incident, it grew more important to him to keep peace with Meg and Lila, to make them understand that times change and sometimes you just have to roll with it and be flexible.

As he stood holding the tree upright, thinking indeed Suzanne had made a nice choice for the space, sounds echoed from above, perhaps the lowering of an attic door.

Despite himself, he still couldn't deny that Meg's little sister was cute—even when she was trying to be mean. She wasn't much like Meg—a quieter, more mature, more polite woman by any account. But the fact that Lila *loved* Meg so much, and felt so driven to protect the old family home, tugged at his heart a little. He didn't delight in destroying the trees. Hell, if he'd realized how much drama it would cause, maybe he'd have taken it into account when parsing out lots with the surveyor. But it was too late for that now.

Now all he could do was continue his peacekeeping

efforts here, hoping it led to some good—like a voluntary surrender of that key—while he waited for the snow to stop so he could go home and relax. No matter how he sliced it, the day would be one he looked back on gladly in a few hours when he'd changed into some sweats and started a fire, then watched some college basketball on the big screen TV in his living room. He'd have done his best to make a nice gesture toward Lila, laying the seeds for a better relationship going forward—and he even felt cautiously optimistic that something good might eventually happen with Suzanne, too.

LILA SCOURED THE dark attic, lit only with a dim bulb operated by a pull string, trying to determine where Christmas stuff might be. She hadn't been up here since she was a girl, her primary recollection that of having made it a play place, a hide-and-go-seek place, running hither and thither even while no one else in the attic at the time cared, too busy with whatever they'd climbed the drop-down ladder looking for.

Except maybe Gran. Gran had always made her feel…relevant. And loved. She tried to grab onto a memory flitting around the edges of her brain. In it, she crouched behind a trunk or table up here, thinking herself sly—only to have Gran sneak quietly up and scare the wits out of her with a loud "Gotcha!" that came with a hug. She'd been maybe six or eight at the time.

Now she scanned the space. Boxes, crates, an old trunk, a set of old snowshoes, and even a pair of antique wooden cross-country skis that would probably be hanging decoratively on a wall somewhere if the inn wasn't in the business of branding itself as a summer destination. Searching wooden shelves, she spotted old cookware—pots and pans—and bowls made of what Gran had called circus glass, passed down through her family. Other shelves held old lamps and picture frames. And then, on a bottom one—aha—a tree stand.

She picked it up, and—heavier than she'd expected, it slipped from her fingers and hit the planked floor with a loud *thud*, barely missing her sock-covered toes. "Oooh," she screeched. Lifting it back up more carefully then, she moved it toward the opening in the floor that led to the inn's second floor hallway and set it down, thinking of starting a pile, since she might as well locate the ornaments while she was up here.

Returning to the shelves, she peeked in an unlabeled box to find—oh, her knitting looms! She'd totally forgotten about them! And to think they'd just been sitting here since…well, who knew since when? She probably hadn't used them since high school.

Gran had bought them for her one summer when, around the age of twelve or so, she'd complained of that angsty sort of boredom only an adolescent girl can truly express. Resentful of having to spend summers stuck on an island far away from her friends. Missing malls and movie theaters and swimming pools.

At first, she'd been just as bored with the looms as she was with Summer Island in general, but Gran had bribed her in that way only Gran could. "You'll have a special talent that none of your friends do—one that not even Meg has." Meg had always been so smart and accomplished and together, whereas Lila had been—or at least felt—the opposite. Gran had introduced her to the joys of yarn and built in her a love of playing with and combining colors and textures, even taking her to the mainland one day on a special trip, just the two of them, to a place Lila remembered being called The Yarn Barn, actually *in* a big red barn. She'd wanted to think it was dorky but had actually found it almost as fun as walking into a shopping mall.

Later, after Lila had produced a few winter hats, Gran had made an observation. "I think it sometimes just takes a little more to hold your interest than it does Meg. Something like this requires just enough focus to keep your thoughts in one place." And at the same time, she'd learned that loom knitting went much faster than the traditional knitting her mother dabbled in, so she didn't get bored trying to complete a project. She'd soon been whipping out cozy hats in only an hour or two.

"Um, you okay up here?"

Startled, she flinched, dropping the round loom in her hand back into the open box with a small clatter and spinning to see Beck Grainger's handsome head poking up through the attic door.

CHAPTER SEVEN

"YES—FINE," SHE bit off, just short of snapping at him.

"I heard a big clunk—and then nothing—so thought I should check."

"I dropped the tree stand," she said, pointing at it. "And then figured I'd look for ornaments while I'm here—but so far, no luck."

As Beck climbed the rest of the way up into the smaller, more isolated-feeling space, her back went rigid, her chest tightening. Again, she had to remind herself—he wasn't a personal threat to her, and it was okay for him to be in the attic with her.

And while she watched him begin to look around the opposite end from where she'd searched so far, her heart beat a little faster. But not in the frightened way—instead in a...surprised way. *For a guy who is heartlessly doing something that hurts my sister's livelihood and my family traditions, I feel...safe with him.*

It seemed a backward emotion, maybe even a foolish one. But a calmness hung about him that it was difficult not to like. She'd always liked it in Meg, too, actually—no wonder her sister respected and appreciated this man.

"Pay dirt," he said then, peeking over his shoulder at her with a smile. "Found a whole box of lights. We can take the whole thing down and just hope some of them work."

Noticing the word *Christmas* scrawled in black marker on a box next to where he stood, she walked toward it. Stepping up beside him, she opened it—and gasped. "Oh gosh—look! Meg and I made these ornaments as kids." She'd forgotten about those, too. She'd forgotten a lot of things—things before Meg got cancer.

Some of them were glittery and juvenile—clearly the work of children. But others stood the test of time a little better: candy canes and bells made from salt dough, angels from painted pine cones, green strips of fabric tied creatively to a twig to create a tree, and snowflakes cut meticulously from thick, sparkly paper.

"You can tell which are Meg's and which are mine," she said matter-of-factly, holding up two dough candy canes, nearly identical except that one was perfectly shaped and neatly painted and the other was slightly misshapen and messier. "Mine are the sloppy ones."

"Well, she was older than you," Beck pointed out— and Lila looked up, because it was a revelation. She'd spent her whole young life comparing herself to Meg, but it had never occurred to her that of course Meg would be better at most things merely because Lila was so much younger—five years to be exact. "And I kinda like this one." He pointed to the messy candy cane with a small grin. "It's got character."

Lila lowered her eyes, unsettled by the rush of warmth through her chest brought on by his simple kindness.

"What's in here?" he asked then, reaching for another box behind the ones they'd already opened. Peering inside, they saw mostly bubble wrap and tissue paper—until he plucked out a handful of white paper and unwrapped a glass ornament in the shape of a reindeer.

The find drew another gasp from Lila. "Oh my God—I remember that! Gran's antique glass ornaments. They're from when she was growing up here, back in the forties and fifties. And some of them are even older. There's a glass pear ornament somewhere that's been passed down through the family since the early 1900s."

Beck took a reverent step back. "Okay, suddenly I feel a little nervous around this box."

She laughed lightly. "You? You're not the one who dropped the tree stand and can't paint decent stripes on a candy cane." Then she glanced down at the box. "I'd like to use them, though. I haven't seen them in ages—it'll be nice."

"We'll just be careful," he promised with a short nod. "And they seem well wrapped, so we've got that much going for us."

As Beck rewrapped the glass reindeer and placed it gently back in the box, his flannel-covered arm brushed Lila's, setting off a fresh burst of warmth inside her. Maybe it was just hot up here in the closed space or something—but she still took a step back.

And caught herself. *Stop it. What are you doing? Becoming friends with him? That was all part of his evil plan. You can let him put up this stupid tree, but you can't be his friend.*

Of course, as they worked together to carefully transport the Christmas boxes and tree stand down the stairs, she tried to figure out what they *were*, what they *could* be. If she was going to let him put up a

Christmas tree in the parlor, and she was presumably going to communicate with him during that time, what were they to each other? She wasn't sure. Nor did she know how she'd gotten herself into this weird situation.

Maybe the best thing to do was just try to roll with it. For the rest of the day. *Be...cordial, but quit being so damn nice. Even when you're finding old ornaments that bring back your childhood, and memories of Gran, and everything that...well, that make the trees behind this house matter. Just get through the day—but remember who he is and what he's doing.* A Christmas tree didn't change that.

As she handed the last box down to him, she glanced over at the nearby shelves—at the box containing the looms—and said, "Wait a sec." And a moment later, passed that one to him, as well.

"I don't know what this is, but it doesn't look Christmasy," he commented with a glance down into the lidless box. It held five round looms of different sizes, the largest about the circumference of a basketball, all sturdy plastic, in varying colors. Underneath them all, she'd spied a few random skeins of old yarn.

"Just something my grandmother gave me that I want to bring downstairs," she said, and left it at that. *That's how you stop being too friendly. You don't chit-chat and volunteer information. Well done.*

Downstairs, she held the stand while he maneuvered the big tree into it. Then watched as he started untangling strings of lights and plugging them into the wall—some lit up and some didn't. Her stomach growled, reminding her—lunch. Which presented a whole new quandary with the presence of the persistent man currently moving around the inn like he owned the place.

Roll with it. "I haven't eaten lunch—have you?"

He looked up from the lights, a string of colored ones, most of them blinking, stretched between his large hands. "Actually, no."

She blew out a breath, having hoped for a different answer. And kept being honest with him. "I really don't want to be too friendly with you under the circumstances—but I also don't want to be an asshole. So would you like some soup and a grilled cheese?"

As usual, he threw her off—this time by responding to her grudging offer with a big, wide smile, same as if she'd offered the lunch with total cheer. "A woman after my own heart."

She regarded him dryly through tired eyes. "I'm not sure what that even means in this situation, but I doubt it. In fact, so far I suspect our hearts operate very differently."

Again, a light laugh from him. She seemed to amuse him to no end. "I just was thinking about the simple pleasures of grilled cheese recently, that's all." Then he glanced out the window into the heavy snow, blowing about in the cold wind. "And it sounds like the perfect choice for today."

"So I take that as a yes," she said dryly. Remembering who he was now. And who *she* was. And that he would not win her over with an afternoon of niceness.

"Yes, that sounds great," he told her, obviously trying to give her a very clear answer, "and I appreciate it. Need help?"

"No," she answered, her tone matter-of-fact. Not nice, not mean—just betraying no emotion. Just taking—

keeping—control of this situation. Well, if she forgot about the fact that he'd somehow wheedled his way into her house to put up a Christmas tree she didn't want. "You just stay here and work on the tree. The sooner that's done, the sooner you can take yourself back up to West Bluff." Then she started toward the kitchen.

"Hopefully the snow will stop by then."

"Yes, hopefully," she tossed over her shoulder. "Because I'd hate for you to get lost in the storm and die." Even though she knew she wouldn't really send him out into that. *He* didn't need to know.

As she prepared the hot lunch, she found herself wishing he weren't so handsome, because she was growing more aware of that. *That's what happens when you let your guard down. That's why you need to just keep reminding yourself what he's doing to the inn.*

She set up TV trays in the parlor—because she refused to sit with him at Meg's kitchen table. In fact, she wasn't even sure, when she told Meg about the trees, how she would explain this: letting him inside, putting up a tree with him, feeding him lunch. It was cavorting with the enemy. *Damn, he's good. He totally manipulated me.*

The revelation brought fresh ire rising to her chest. *Another* manipulative man had just ruined her life. And Beck Grainger didn't come close to reaching the monster level of Simon Alexis—but how had she gone from one such situation straight into another? It made her all the more determined not to let Beck win. Maybe he was winning the day—the tree, the lunch—but this tree-killing, house-building business wasn't over yet, not by a long shot. And while part of her had started thinking it inevitable, not knowing how to fight it, just

the mere knowledge that she was being subtly manipulated right now built in her a brand new compulsion to
find a solution. She wasn't giving up yet.

They made small talk while they ate. "You whip up
a good grilled cheese."

"Are there enough lights that work?"

"I didn't know it was supposed to snow this much—
did you?"

Another way Summer Island had gone modern: Lila
had noticed everyone constantly checking the weather
on their phones. Maybe in summer that might slack off,
but right now people wanted to know about snow and
ice and cold, in order to best plan their lives around
it. And even while she had started out thinking such a
habit might make her more responsible, it had quickly
become merely practical. Every simple walk from one
place to another revolved around what was going on
outside. So after spooning the last bite of vegetable
soup into her mouth, she swiped a napkin across her
face, glanced out at the snow once more, and reached
for her phone—and the weather outlook.

"Doesn't look like it's stopping anytime soon," Beck
said, peering out the window past the undecorated tree.

Lila barely heard him, though, because—oh God.
She blinked, then focused on the phone screen to make
sure she was reading the forecast correctly. "Um, no,"
she told him slowly, trying to wrap her head around it
as she spoke. "It, um, says...it'll keep falling heavily
until...almost midnight."

"Huh," he replied.

She thought of making him go—right then. *She*
could decorate the tree. And if he left before it got dark
in a few hours, he'd have a much easier time making

it home. And yet…it was pretty much blizzard conditions out there. And unlike on the mainland, it wasn't a matter of hopping in the car and driving down roads hopefully already plowed and salted. He'd have a long uphill walk in deep, blowing snow. Without even a hat on his head, for God's sake.

So instead, she stood up, walked to the hearth, carefully lowered a couple of fresh logs onto the fire, and said, "I need a stiff drink."

"Huh?" This time it was a question and he sounded baffled.

"A drink," she said, enunciating as if he were hard of hearing. "I'm thinking of hot chocolate with some Baileys in it." She glanced up, continued dourly. "And I suppose it would be rude not to offer you some, as well."

He looked as pleasant and amused as ever. Damn him. "I'd gratefully accept that."

"But don't get drunk and mess up my tree," she warned him with a shake of her finger.

"I thought you didn't even *want* the tree," he reminded her.

"Well, if I'm stuck with it, I want it to look decent. And be careful with the ornaments. Remember, a lot of them are irreplaceable antiques."

"Aye aye, Cap'n."

"That wasn't funny. And didn't even make sense. We're not in a boat or in any sort of seafaring situation." She didn't bother looking to see his reaction before she headed toward the kitchen to start heating the milk and measuring out the Hershey's cocoa.

Meg wasn't a huge drinker, but just like the tea in the pantry, Lila knew her sister kept a reasonably well-stocked liquor cabinet—or in the inn's case a shelf in a small china cabinet—in order to have anything her guests might want on hand, including Baileys Irish Cream, the perfect little additive to a nice cup of cocoa on a cold winter's afternoon. Especially a stressful one. Which would soon turn into a cold winter's night. Sure to be equally stressful.

IT TOOK A while to decorate such a big tree. The lights were a project unto themselves. Then came a disagreement over garland—Lila wanted the old but classic sparkly silver stuff they'd located in another box, cradling some snowman figurines that she'd now placed on the mantel. Beck, on the other hand, had the insane idea that they were going to pop popcorn and string it. And maybe even toddle down to Koester's Market for some cranberries for stringing, as well. As if there weren't a blizzard raging outside. As if Koester's would even be open during the storm. Clearly the man was still a newcomer here and didn't understand the way the island operated.

"We have the time to string the popcorn," he pointed out, clearly trying to reason with her. "Since the snow isn't stopping for a while. And my mom used to do it for our tree—it was nice, natural. And would look good with the handmade ornaments."

Lila won, though. "No—we're going sparkly. End of discussion. Here." Then she shoved a rope of silver garland into his hand.

By the time they'd moved on to hanging the ornaments, both were on their second mug of spiked hot chocolate.

"You make some damn tasty cocoa, girl," he told

her. *Girl.* Maybe he was getting a little drunk. Probably. Since she was, too. But that had sort of been the idea—numb the the pain of the torturously weird sitch until it was finally over.

"Yeah," she said. "Between that and grilled cheese, I'm a real gourmet."

"You should learn to take a compliment," he told her, pointing at her with a salt dough candy cane.

"Careful," she said. "That's my messy childhood you're holding in your hand. Don't break it."

"Aye aye… Cap'n."

"You're just trying to get on my nerves now," she said, reaching to hang a glass Santa on one of the higher branches. She didn't bother looking at him to add, "And trust me, you really don't have to work at it. You manage it effortlessly."

Another typical Beck laugh punctuated the air. And she felt a little sad inside. To have to be mean to him. It was growing less satisfying. Since she guessed, deep down, she liked him and saw why everyone else did, too. And then there was that handsome thing he had going—another good reason not to look at him. She didn't want to keep noticing that, soaking it in. She'd thought maybe the Baileys would distract her from his rugged good looks, but in retrospect, it had been very flawed logic.

"You're a piece of work," he told her.

Okay, *this* drew a look from her. After all, she was the one who handed out the judgy comments here. "What does *that* mean?"

He focused on hanging a pointy blue glass star as he said, "You're cute. And funny. But so damn angry. What are you so angry about?"

She let her eyes go wide. *"Hello."* Then pointed toward the rear of the house. "Trees. Bulldozer. Did the alcohol really go to your head that fast?"

But her reply left him unfazed as he met her eyes. "No, I mean what else? Because there's something else."

Lila's chest tightened. He could see that? Tell that? It was horrifying to learn she was so transparent. Or was he just weirdly perceptive? Her family hadn't even noticed at Thanksgiving that anything might be amiss with her, and she regarded herself as a master of deception.

She followed the compulsion to deny it anyway. He knew nothing about her, after all. Turning her attention back to decorating, she plucked up a pine cone with the tips painted white and a loop of yarn attached to hang it with. "Wrongo bongo. My only problem is you—and knowing I have to ruin Meg's holidays by telling her about the trees."

She could see from her peripheral vision that he still eyed her suspiciously, though. "Sure there's nothing else?"

"Yes," she stated unequivocally. Eyeing him back, to be more convincing. Some people had trouble making eye contact in uncomfortable situations. But for Lila, right now, the act was like holding up a protective shield. Proving she meant what she said. Just daring him to cross her. "I don't know what you think you know—but just drink your hot chocolate and decorate the tree, or I'm kicking you out, blizzard or not."

A small smile came from her tree-trimming tree-slayer. "I'd better work slow, or you'll kick me out into the snow anyway."

"It might be an easier walk before dark." She grinned, winked.

And he caught her off guard with, "Whoa, you smiled. I didn't know you could do that."

"It was an accident. Don't get used to it." She reached for her mug on a nearby end table and took a fortifying sip.

"You have a nice one," he told her.

Confused and wary, she shot him a look. "A nice what?"

"Smile. You should do it more often."

"I reserve it for people not ruining my family's legacy," she quipped.

And he just laughed.

And when her gaze then happened to zero in on the area of the tree where he'd been working, she said, "Oh my God—you can't put all the glass ones together in a clump like that. You have to mix in the others to even things out. Is this your first time decorating a tree?"

She stepped up to move the blue star—just as he reached for it, as well, bringing their hands together, his over hers, on the antique ornament. She felt the touch in her panties—a rush, a warmth, desire. Oh boy.

She didn't draw her hand away. And neither did he.

She dared glance over and their eyes met, locked. More warmth cascaded through her as they stood frozen in place, tree-trimming statues.

"Maybe you don't hate me as much as you're acting like," he had the audacity to say.

"Oh, I do. I really do. Trust me."

"Then why haven't you pulled your hand away?"

She sucked in her breath. God, he was just…asking like that? Putting it out there, that plainly?

She tried to think fast. "Because it's an antique and I don't want to jostle it?" Ugh, it had come out as a question.

Which he answered with, "No." So sure. So bold.

Fine then. She'd just go back to being honest with him. She glanced toward their two cocoa mugs, one red, one green, sitting side by side on one of the TV trays. "I blame the Baileys," she said. "Why haven't you?"

"Same," he replied. "And…"

Her heart beat double time in her chest. "And…?"

"Like I said, you're cute. Saucy. Funny as hell." The whole time, they both stood frozen, holding their ground, hands touching, his lightly covering hers on the blue glass star. "You definitely stand up for what you want, that's for sure."

"Damn straight, Indiana Jones," she told him.

That was when his hand closed more fully around hers on the ornament, warm, firm, a touch unmistakably sexual, as their eyes stayed fixed on one another. Her heartbeat pounded in her ears. Her body swirled with liquid heat. And then he did that thing—that thing where the other person leans in, just a little, their eyelids heavy, their head starting to tilt. Body language for: *I'm going to kiss you, so if you don't want me to, you should back away.*

She didn't back away.

CHAPTER EIGHT

THE KISS WAS small, light, warm—a test kiss. And damn—for a kiss so small and tentative, it was the best thing Beck had felt in a long while. Despite the weather outside, it moved through him like heat lightning on a Kentucky summer night.

Given that she kept trying to dislike him so much, though, he had to make sure he wasn't the only one welcoming that heat—so he drew back a little, met her pretty gaze. Her hazel eyes shone on him, big and round, maybe a little stunned, her rosy lips parted. Surprised—but wanting. Just like him.

So he bent, leaned, lowered another soft kiss to her waiting lips. Heard her quick intake of breath. Maybe at first she'd been surprised it was happening, but now she was clearly only *surprised* at how good it felt, and how fast.

When she drew her hand away from beneath his on the ornament, he'd thought maybe she was stopping this—but no. Instead, she lifted the same hand to touch his cheek. And the next kiss was deeper, longer, more consuming. No more test kissing—this was turning into the real deal. His hands went to her waist—slender beneath the big sweater she wore—and she released a little gasp as he pulled her closer.

She kissed him back now with all the passion rising up inside him, as well. The kind that slowly makes you stop thinking, measuring, until you just give yourself over to it.

It was the kind of kissing Beck hadn't had the opportunity to indulge in for longer than he cared to admit. Summer Island had been isolating, and on the few occasions last summer when he'd almost connected with attractive female tourists looking for vacation fun, he'd realized that at thirty-nine, he'd apparently moved past wanting a meaningless, one-night connection—no matter how the rigid part of his anatomy between his legs had protested the decisions.

This, now, seemed like it had all the ingredients to be exactly that—a quick, nonlasting connection. Except for one thing. He liked her. And one more thing. Nothing was telling him to stop. Even if it seemed like an awful idea in ways. She was angry with him. She seemed angry in general. She was Meg's little sister. Maybe it would spell even more drama.

But she felt too good in his arms. Her lips too soft beneath his hungry mouth. Every little sigh and gasp that left her made him harder. And soon that hardness pressed hotly against the sweet crux of her thighs through their blue jeans as they made out next to the Christmas tree, her palms now at his chest, beginning to knead him through his T-shirt same as if she were a cat, his own hands molded around her hips, learning her curves.

"This changes nothing," she told him breathlessly between kisses.

His reply came in a rasp. "What do you mean?"

She peered up at him, bit her lip, looking sensual and defiant all at once. "If you think sex is going to make me give you back the key to that bulldozer, or just look the other way about the whole situation, you're barking up the wrong tree."

"I'm not barking up that tree," he assured her, voice deep and low.

"What tree are you barking up?" More kneading fingers at his chest. The slight scrape of feminine nails. He liked it.

And he tried to think of an answer, but it was difficult. Due to the fingernails, and the way their bodies pressed together below. "Pretty much just the this-feels-good-and-I-want-to-be-inside-you tree."

Another little gasp. This one she tried to squelch, he could tell—but what he'd just said had excited her even more. "That's…a good tree."

"Let's make a deal," he managed to say—mostly just wanting to get back to kissing, and maybe taking off her clothes. He hadn't been sure where this was going until she'd mentioned sex, but now the path seemed much clearer. He didn't want anything to mess that up.

"What deal?" She looked wary—perhaps understandably.

"Something easy, I promise," he assured her. "For right now, let's not say one more word about trees—good, bad, Christmas, ones you bark up, or otherwise. Fair?"

"Fair. Now shut up and kiss me."

Lila knew this was insane. She knew it lacked logic. She knew the alcohol was blurring her good senses and heightening her desire.

But she also knew Beck's logic was sound, too—this felt good. And she simply hadn't anticipated that, with anyone, so soon. The simplicity of attraction, chemistry, wanting to connect physically with a man. It was hitting her like a ton of bricks when she'd least expected it.

And if she was honest with herself, she'd harbored a fear: that after Simon she'd be scarred now, afraid, that she'd never want to have sex again. And surprise—she did!

So it made sense to take advantage of that. This was getting-back-on-the-horse sex. This was finding-the-joy-in-life-again sex. This was reclaiming-your-womanhood sex. This was even reclaiming-your-power sex! What had happened with Simon Alexis in Chicago would not bury her.

And further, in a simpler way, this was…a gift. Beck had no way of knowing what an enormous and wonderful gift he was giving her right now.

She was pretty sure most people who knew her thought she was promiscuous, but in fact, she wasn't. If ever she was going to be, however, this seemed like a good time for it. And with that thought in mind, she pushed his open flannel shirt from his shoulders.

He released her from his grasp only long enough to shrug free of it, then yank his tee off over his head. And—oh. Nice. A nice, broad, firm chest. Not the showy kind that said I-work-out. Instead a more authentic sort that said I'm-a-strong-rugged-guy-who-lives-an-active-life. She sensed that in his shoulders, his arms. She wasn't sure exactly what all a developer did, but she felt in her bones that he built things, too—swung a hammer, did heavy lifting. That natural strength drew her to him even more. He was the exact opposite of Simon—who worked out.

But stop thinking of Simon. Stop thinking of any-

thing. Except maybe Beck's chest. Arms. Mouth. The dark stubble on his chin, so alluringly rough beneath her fingertips. They were kissing again, touching— she was exploring all the skin and muscle he'd just revealed. And also thinking about the very hardest part of him, which had pressed so deliciously and unmistakably against her a few minutes ago.

His hands went under her sweater, making her breasts ache. It seemed to her a crime that a man could never know how the sweet, hungry ache in a woman's sensitive breasts felt. But when his hand tenderly grazed its way up her side to frame the outer curve, then he stroked his thumb across the nipple hidden within her bra, she hoped the sigh of pleasure that left her gave him some small glimpse into the consuming sensation of bliss that had just passed so powerfully through her.

He began to push her sweater upward, murmuring, "Help me with this." She did, and soon it lay on the floor near an empty ornament box. When she shivered from the cold, he took her hand and pulled her toward the fireplace, grabbing up a throw blanket from the back of the sofa along the way. The heat from the fire warmed her skin instantly—and somehow also fueled her onward.

"I want this," she heard herself say, unplanned. Maybe it was to assure him—or maybe to assure herself, she didn't know. But she even said it again, this time looking right up into his big brown eyes. "I want this."

Spreading the chenille throw on the floor, he lay her back on it, her body stretching out in front of the hearth. He peeled away her jeans, then her bra. He laved her breasts with kisses that reached to her core and nearly made her come, just from that.

Next, he pushed his jeans off, too, and his underwear. He dug a condom from his wallet as she waited.

And then heaven was attained right there on the floor of the Summerbrook Inn while a blizzard roiled outside. And in the missionary position, too. She'd never especially been a fan, but somehow Beck made her one. She liked the bigness of him hovering over her, moving, thrusting deep. She liked rising to meet his body with hers. She liked that something so simple could feel so good.

She didn't *keep* it simple, though. For truly she *was* restless and not easily pleased. Soon she pushed against his chest, instigated a roll, got on top. Felt the beauty of her own nakedness and his, too, as she moved on him. Took in the details of his hard, planed body, felt how solid and large he was inside her, gave a fleeting thought to that thing about a man's hands correlating to his penis size being true. But mostly she just followed the rhythm of her body, the rhythm of her heart— which blocked out everything bad as she connected with him. And soon she was biting her lip, finding her bliss, calling out her pleasure when she toppled into the abyss of orgasm.

SLEEP. SUCH A MYSTERY. Where do we go when it happens? What is our brain doing? How is it possible that we can turn off so completely and yet our bodies keep working—our lungs keep breathing, our heart keeps pumping blood, our mind dreams. As Lila awoke, though, mostly her thoughts were that of comfort—

the sweet comfort of deep sleep. She felt rested for the first time in weeks.

But opening her eyes changed things—left her disoriented. She began to take in certain details. The cracking and flicker of the blaze in the hearth. Firelight and the Christmas tree illuminating the room—the other lights had been turned off and fresh wood laid on the fire.

Oh, I'm at the inn.

Lying on the floor.

And nothing is normal.

And she wasn't lying there alone—a man's warm body spooned her from behind, his palm curving over her bare hip beneath a chenille blanket. He'd apparently gotten up, fixed the fire and the lights, then come back.

What time is it? She shifted her gaze, searching for the cable box near the TV. Whoa. Two-seventeen. In the morning. She wasn't sure what time the sex had occurred exactly, but it hadn't even been dark out yet. And it got dark early this time of year—five or so. Had she really been lying here asleep on a hard floor for eight or nine hours? She hadn't slept soundly in weeks, but now, like this, she had? It made no sense.

Yet that wasn't what mattered here. What mattered was…oh no. She'd slept with the enemy.

She drew in her breath at the horror of what she'd done. Memories began to seep back in. Alcohol. And surrender. Even if it had given her a little of her feminine power back—oh God. Why? Why had she had to do it with *this* man? Of all the men on the planet, she'd slept with the one who was planning to take from her—and her sister and whole family—something she held dear?

And she couldn't even blame him. Oh, she could blame him for tearing down the trees, and she could blame him for foisting his stupid Christmas tree on her. But she couldn't blame him for the sex.

It was her fault she'd started being nice. Her fault they'd started drinking. Her fault they'd started touching. Her fault they hadn't stopped.

How would she ever explain to Meg that she'd had sex—on the floor of the inn, no less—with the man determined to do the place harm?

Well, she just wouldn't. She wouldn't tell her things had gone this far. Or even close to this far. And maybe she'd just take down the stupid Christmas tree before she left for Ann Arbor—she'd make it so no trace of Beck Grainger remained in this house. Because he shouldn't be here. He shouldn't. That simple.

That didn't take back what she'd done with him, though. What she'd done with him that…well, if she was honest, made her just want to stay this way. She wanted to put this moment in a jar or a box and keep it separate from everything else that made it an impossible situation. Because it felt so incredibly warm and nice. And safe. Again, safe.

Steeling herself, she silently turned to peek over her shoulder at him. But damn it—he'd felt her stir and opened his eyes. His quick, small smile warmed her as much as the fire. "Getting stiff from the floor? Want to move to the couch, or a bed? Or stay here? I'm good either way."

She drew in her breath. And did what she had to.

"You have to go."

Those sparkling brown eyes of his opened wider, his body tensing next to hers. "What?"

She drew her gaze from his and turned back around, because this was harder than she wanted it to be. But only part of this was her fault—the rest was his. *Remember that. And that he manipulated you.* Not into the sex, but the rest of it. "You have to go. I'm sure the storm is over, and the snow should make it easy to see in the dark."

She felt more than saw his puzzlement. "You're serious."

"This was a huge mistake. Which I blame on alcohol and exhaustion and temporary poor judgment. But my judgment has cleared now, and I need for you to leave and forget this ever happened."

She thought he'd argue, waited for it. But instead, she suffered an unmistakable sense of loss, along with a dull sadness, as the warmth of his body withdrew from hers—he pulled away from her and got up. And she stared into the fire, trying not to feel. Anything.

Your life wasn't already enough of a shambles? There wasn't enough drama for you? Enough problems? So you did this?

But stop. Stop thinking. Toughen up. Be the woman who stood in front of a bulldozer.

And so she did. She stared blindly into the flames, waiting as he dressed quietly behind her. It was a miserable sort of moment—fraught with tension and various kinds of pain. But *this* would be the one she'd put in a box—though unlike that nicer one from just a minute or two earlier, this one she'd close up and shove very far away, to a far corner of the proverbial attic in her mind, and hopefully forget it ever existed.

You shouldn't feel mean to make him go. Yet somehow she did.

"Has the snow stopped?" The words left her unplanned. But maybe she just had to make sure she
wasn't being a *totally* horrible person.

She sensed him crossing the room to look out the
window. Finally, "Yeah."

She nodded. At the fire, since she couldn't look at
him. "Good." Spoken softly. Then, even more quietly,
she said, "Goodbye."

In her peripheral vision, she saw him pulling on his
coat. But no hat. *Quit being so concerned. He's a big
boy—he can walk home in the cold without a damn hat.*

"Goodbye," he returned.

A moment later, she heard the door open, and felt
the burst of winter chill enter the house even from that
far away. She waited for it to close, for him to be gone.
But instead, he said, "I can leave if you want. But forgetting this ever happened? Sorry to tell you, but that
part—impossible."

CHAPTER NINE

LILA OPENED THE front door and peered out on a serene winter morning. Subfreezing temperatures sent chunks of ice teeming past the South Point Lighthouse beneath a winter white overcast sky. Snow blanketed the ground—from a glance at the mailbox post, she estimated an accumulation of at least ten or more fresh inches. She only prayed that would be enough to keep bulldozing work from continuing—or from whatever it would take to get another bulldozer onto the scene. Since at least she had the key to the one already there. And hoped blindly it was the only one.

She tried to ignore the large footprints leading down the front walk from the porch through the deep snow and turning left onto Harbor Street. Then she closed the door, ate a little cereal for breakfast, and did the next logical thing. She decided to loom knit.

Meg had told her she often felt Gran's spirit still in and around the inn. And if Gran were here now, Lila knew with near certainty that her grandma would advise her to make something on the knitting looms she'd brought down from the attic yesterday. For the same reasons Gran had thought it would be a good idea when Lila was a teenager—as a distraction. Because she refused to think about Beck Grainger and what had happened here yesterday. It was indeed the perfect time for some looming.

If only she could remember how.

After a shower, she dressed in fleece-lined leggings and another big, cozy sweater, then planted herself on the couch in the parlor with loom and yarn. The original looming instructions and pattern book she'd used as a girl weren't in the box, but thank God for the internet. A little googling on her tablet easily led her to patterns for hats, scarves, and other useful things—and she soon found her way to an easy beginners' pattern for a simple winter hat.

From the several skeins of old yarn residing in the box with the various looms, she pulled out an icy winter blue with just a hint of sparkle to it—a chunky yarn that, if memory served, would be easy to work with until she got the hang of it again. She even recalled selecting this very yarn at the Yarn Barn—apparently right before she lost interest in loom knitting. As a "scattered person," as Gran had once gently albeit aptly called her, her life was littered with the leftovers and remains of hobbies and projects she'd been consumed with—until suddenly she wasn't anymore, giving up one thing to move on to the next.

The wintry yarn reminded her of the ensemble Suzanne had worn to the café the other day—and though she had no real idea what Suzanne's personal taste or style was from their two brief meetings so far, she decided to make a hat for Meg's friend. For being nice to her, welcoming her. And because she thought the color would contrast nicely with Suzanne's dark curly hair and draw out her rather crystalline blue eyes, which Lila had noticed over lunch. And for trying to help with

Beck—which maybe she'd already done and it hadn't worked given that the Christmas tree had surely come from Petal Pushers. But she appreciated it regardless.

Tying a slip knot around a circular loom's anchor peg, she wrapped the thick yarn around all the pegs twice, then used the knitting hook to methodically lift the back loop of yarn over the front one on each peg, creating the first row in the e-wrap stitch, the simplest stitch in loom knitting. Lila remembered learning lots of stitches with Gran's help, but that mostly she'd used the basic e-wrap and the u-wrap knit stitch because they were simple, and therefore easier to remember and harder to mess up.

Projects on the loom indeed went quickly, so it wasn't long before she was folding rows over to create a thick brim, then proceeding on to construct the crown. The crackle of the fire kept her company—and loath as she was to admit it, even to herself, she found the Christmas tree cheerful. Yes, it reminded her of Beck and everything that was so wrong about this situation—but in a bigger way, it felt like stepping back into her childhood.

Every ornament made by her and Meg came with a memory, many which included Gran—and hikes up into the woods behind the house to collect pine cones or acorns or twigs. The glass ornaments took her back in time, as well. As a little girl, she'd thought them so old-fashioned as to be ugly and boring, but now she saw in them history, family, warmth, and tradition.

When did I start appreciating tradition? She tilted her head, eyeing the tree, wondering. Maybe what happened with Simon had made her grateful to have someplace old and safe to run to. Or maybe it had come with the bulldozer and the impending loss of the woods. Regardless, though, the antique glass bulbs made her think of her parents and Gran, and Gran's parents before her. The family hadn't celebrated many Christmases on the island since Gran's passing—and she liked to think if Meg was right about Gran's spirit being here, she'd be happy to see the old ornaments decorating a tree, and the front parlor of the inn looking Christmasy again.

Damn you, Beck Grainger, for being right about me enjoying the tree.

But stop it. Knit. Knit, knit, knit.

Soon she found herself trying to determine if she had knitted enough rows for the crown, deciding she had, and following instructions to remove the knitting from the loom using a long tail of yarn and a plastic sewing needle—which she thankfully found in a zipped baggie in the box. Once the hat was knitted off the loom, she carefully pulled and tightened the yarn like a drawstring, which suddenly created a pretty decent-looking hat! She smiled at her creation, followed the internet instructions for finishing the project with a hidden knot and some weaving in of yarn tails, then headed toward the mirror in the foyer, pulling the hat onto her head.

It looked good. Good enough to give to Suzanne as a Christmas gift before she left the island later this month. Mission accomplished.

Returning to the parlor, she glanced at the mantel clock. It was—oh dear—ten a.m. How would she possibly fill the rest of her quiet day? It hadn't been a question before yesterday—exhaustion notwithstanding, the quiet days had felt relatively peaceful, easy.

But just a glimpse at the spot by the hearth where she and Beck had done the deed brought it back, too close. Especially now that she no longer had loom stitches to concentrate on. Maybe she needed to make more hats.

Because she simply refused to think about him. Even if having to refuse to think about him meant, technically, that she was still thinking about him. She just needed to keep busy, keep her mind on other things.

She started by tidying up the kitchen—putting some dishes in the dishwasher, wiping down the table and counters, scrubbing a dirty griddle from yesterday's grilled cheese by hand in the sink. After that, she gathered up the ornament boxes and extra lights from the parlor floor, toting them all back up to the attic. Returning to the parlor, she straightened it, as well, even breaking out the vacuum cleaner for pine needles and bits of garland that had fallen while decorating. That was when she spotted that clump of glass ornaments on the tree, the blue star in the center of them and still needing to be moved to create a sense of balance.

And it was as she gently plucked the blue star off the branch that her chest tightened. Because this was... useless. You couldn't not think about something—or someone—who had already permeated your world. She'd sent Beck away, but he was still here.

He was in the yellow bulldozer peeking monstrously up through the snow when she glanced out the kitchen window. He was in the dirty cocoa mugs she'd found in the sink. He was in the chenille throw she'd just shoved in the washing machine to clean the scents of sex away. And he was in this tree, and now in all these ornaments and lights, and he was in front of the fireplace, filling her, thrusting into her, moving her, taking her so far away from the trees on that hillside for a little while that they had ceased to matter, or even exist.

But now they mattered again.

And what she'd done with him—ugh, that mattered, too. So much more than she'd intended it to. So much more than she'd expected it to.

Lila had never seen herself as a woman who got attached to a man that quickly. But then, despite how people saw her, she'd never been a woman who slept with a guy on the first date—or in this case, anti-date—either.

Why on earth had she done it? Besides desire and alcohol, that is. Why had she had sex with the last person she should be having it with?

Unwitting attraction. Plus telling herself it would be empowering.

Without the alcohol in the mix, they seemed like pretty bad answers. Especially since she felt ridiculously far from empowered right now. Instead, she felt like she'd just done one more bad thing as a sister. Meg would never have to know, but the upshot was: sleeping with the guy who was ruining her sister's property value just didn't seem like the prudent, ethical move here.

Except for when she recalled the moment she woke up. That sweet, safe, tranquil moment. How warm his body had been behind hers. How rested she'd felt. How at peace.

Before she'd blown it all to hell by telling him to leave.

You didn't blow anything to hell. You just ended something that had to end because it never should have started. And it's over now, and that's that.

So what now, genius?

She looked back at her box of looms and spied a skein of variegated purple-and-pink worsted weight yarn. She didn't know Dahlia well, but she thought the colorful yarn had the older lady's name written all over it. One more hat, coming up.

Knitting bee tonight at the Knitting Nook at 7. Hope you'll join! Dahlia and I will both be there, and like I said, I don't knit either. The text from Suzanne felt like just what the doctor ordered. Lila was out of yarn, out of distractions, and out of patience. So she bundled up in one of Meg's parkas and a pair of her mittens, packed her looms and knitting hook in a shopping bag she found tucked away in a closet, and went trudging up Harbor street in Meg's practical black snow boots.

The blazing lights of the Knitting Nook on the otherwise dark street welcomed her as she stepped up on the porch. The door opened before she could reach for the handle, held by a friendly looking young woman in a ponytail and fleece hoodie. "Hi, I'm Allie. You must be Lila," she said with a smile. "Welcome to the Knitting Nook."

Lila stepped inside, saying hello without bothering to ask how Allie knew who she was. On Summer Island in winter, everybody knew everybody. She only hoped everybody didn't know everything everybody had been doing.

But she pushed that troubling thought aside as Allie pointed to a gathering of snow boots on a rubber mat just inside the door and said merrily, "This is a socks-only zone this time of year."

Feeling girlishly pleased that she'd worn socks with

reindeer faces on them, she shed the boots and soaked up the ambiance. Christmas music played, a tree with white lights twinkled in one corner, and women in seasonal garb sprinkled the yarn-filled room. Not exactly the type of holiday party she was accustomed to, but it would do.

"Josh has coffee, tea, and cocoa next door—and…" Allie paused, glancing down into Lila's shopping bag. "Oh, you're a loom knitter! Nice."

"Well, I just took it back up—literally this morning— after a twenty-year hiatus. So I'm a little rusty."

"Not to worry," Allie assured her. "You'll be back in the saddle in no time. Though I don't believe we have any other loom knitters here. Traditional knitters and crocheters, yes, but not sure anyone will be able to help if you run into trouble."

Lila had run into much worse trouble than loom knitting could dish up, so she only shrugged. "That's why God made the internet."

Allie laughed in reply, then added, "But we have yarn—lots of lots of yarn." And she wasn't exaggerating. Every yarn imaginable lined rustic wooden shelving along every wall, making it a veritable color feast for the eyes. It almost reminded her of the Yarn Barn of her youth. "And we have several knitting totes and carriers that would hold your looms if you want to ditch the paper bag."

Lila let her eyes widen as a light gasp escaped her. "Oh—yes, I'd love to see what you have." Working from a cardboard box hadn't been nearly as pleasant as from the pretty foldable carrier Gran had given her as a girl—which was either long gone or more deeply buried in the attic than she cared to dig for.

Half an hour later, Lila had bought the perfect carrier for her looms and yarn and tools in a lovely flowered print that she'd have never selected in Chicago, but apparently Summer Island brought out in her an appreciation of the old-fashioned and quaint. Even in winter, all that picturesque pastel on Harbor Street had a way of soothing her soul.

She'd also bought some yarn, thinking of gifts for the family. And when Dahlia and Suzanne found her seated in an easy chair in one corner of the room, she was sipping coffee from a big blue mug with snowflakes painted on it, and starting a hat from a lavender alpaca blend for Meg.

"Well, don't you just look all moved in and cozy here," Dahlia said with a grin.

"I'm jealous," Suzanne announced as both women dragged up nearby chairs to form a semi-circle with Lila's. "You have a yarn project. I thought you didn't knit. I thought I had a non-knitting buddy."

Lila smiled. "I found looms in the attic and remembered our grandma taught me when I was a teenager. It's pretty easy, though." She pulled out one of the other looms. "Here, I can show you how."

From the chair to Lila's right, Suzanne scowled at the loom as if it might bite her. "I'm handy with plants and flowers—not yarn."

"Oh, give it a try," Dahlia said from Lila's left. "I've been knitting the same blanket for three years. It's mostly just for show. Doesn't really matter if you can do it or not."

"It really *is* easy," Lila promised. "I wouldn't be able to do it if it wasn't."

"The confidence in this corner is overwhelming,"

Allie stepped up to say. "Come on, ladies—act like the capable, talented women you are."

Dahlia sat up a little straighter. "You're so right." Then she looked to Suzanne and Lila. "Normally, we are the picture of confidence, but we get self-deprecating over arts and crafts? I won't have it." Then she held a knitting needle in the air. "I hereby declare I'm going to finish this blanket this winter. And you, Suzanne, are going to learn to use one of those looms. And you, Lila, are going to be a great teacher and make lots of gorgeous things yourself. Thank you, Allie, for getting our heads back on straight."

Allie just shrugged. "I've always found making things—creating something that wasn't there before—to be kind of…empowering. Because you're…adding something to the world."

As the other ladies left to get drinks and let Suzanne select a skein of yarn, Lila thought about that. Even if Dahlia had kindly included her in the *we* who were "normally confident" without knowing her well enough to be sure, making hats for her new friends today *had* felt good. Indeed, like giving a little something back to the world in some small way. Maybe loom knitting *could* be empowering. Which didn't sound like nearly as fun a way to find empowerment as having sex with Beck Grainger, but it was a hell of a lot simpler.

"WHAT'S YOUR SECRET?" Suzanne asked.

"Who—me?" Lila answered, sounding slightly alarmed.

Suzanne laughed lightly, shook her head. "No. Her." She looked to Dahlia. "She recently hinted to me about a secret and I want to know what it is." Harry Connick was crooning a jazzy rendition of "Jingle Bells" in the background, the mood was festive with hot chocolate drinkers and knitters all around them, and Suzanne decided to ask because Dahlia's sly statement had stayed on her mind ever since she'd made it.

Her older friend took on the same expression now as then. Dahlia was a woman of the world—she'd been places, done things. Suzanne didn't actually know much about her past, but she knew that much about Dahlia instinctively. She was a woman of timeless simple wisdom. And if she had a secret, it was probably a good one.

When she didn't answer, though, Suzanne said, "You've become one of my closest friends, but you don't share much about yourself. In ways, I barely know you at all." She voiced it as a challenge of sorts.

A slow, mischievous smile unfurled on Dahlia's face, and her eyes sparkled like Christmas lights behind her tiny, round John Lennon glasses. "All right, fair enough," she said. "I do have a secret." Then she leaned forward, closer to both of them, and said in a hushed tone, "I've taken a lover."

Suzanne's eyes bolted open wide. From their earlier conversation, she'd thought maybe Dahlia would say she had a date, or some man she harbored a distant interest in. And maybe she'd even thought Dahlia's secret would inspire her, make her braver with Beck. But this news was shocking to say the least. And somehow it made her feel the opposite of brave. "A lover?" She feared it had come out in the same way one might say, *a spider*?

But Dahlia appeared undaunted. "Yes, a lover." She looked back and forth between the two women. "Is that not how we phrase things these days? Should I say I'm hooking up with someone? Or hittin' that?"

She grinned, and a giant gulping laugh erupted from Lila's throat. Who then replied, "I think 'taken a lover' sounds ever so much more sophisticated."

"Yes," Suzanne agreed, still stunned. And hoping she didn't look horrified. Why did she *feel* a little horrified? She wanted her friend to be happy, after all, and Dahlia seemed happy. And Dahlia probably didn't get as easily attached to men as Suzanne did. "So…who? I mean, more." Incredulousness had her fumbling and bumbling to communicate the same way she commonly did when she got nervous with Beck.

"His name is Pierre Desjardins," Dahlia began. "He came to the island in the fall, from the Provence region of France. He's staying at the Bayberry B&B until Christmas, when he'll connect with his daughter and grandchildren in Toronto. He's debonair, suave, and rather handsome for a man of seventy."

Suzanne was still trying to wrap her head around this. "But…how…how did this…you know…"

Dahlia laughed. "Oh, the usual way, I suppose. Mr. Desjardins—which is how I addressed him for quite some time—became a frequent diner at the café. We would chat, and somehow that became flirting. Around Halloween he confessed he'd been eating in the diner every day in hopes of gathering the courage to express his feelings for me. I invited him to my place for dinner, one thing led to another, and now I call him Pierre and he spends the night with me a few evenings each week."

"Wow," Lila said, looking more fascinated than horrified, which Suzanne tried to emulate.

"Is it...serious?" she asked.

Dahlia swept a dismissive hand down through the air. "Oh—no. Not at all. It's a fling. A winter's diversion. A pleasant way to pass a snowy evening."

Lila tilted her head, appearing inquisitive. "And it's not serious for him, either?"

At this, Dahlia paused, peered off in the distance at something neither of the others could see, and answered softly, "I can't really say. He seems...a sentimental sort. He'd planned to leave two weeks ago, in fact, but stayed on—postponed meeting with his family."

"That *sounds* kind of serious," Suzanne pointed out.

Yet Dahlia merely shrugged in her calm, simple manner. "Perhaps. Perhaps not. But either way, it's about to run its course, and life will go on as it did before."

She sounded equally acceptant and cheerful, prodding Suzanne to ask, "If he wanted something more, would *you*? Something...lasting?"

Dahlia answered with a trill of laughter that filled the air with absolute frivolity. "No, my dear, I would not."

It stung Suzanne in a way, a way she couldn't define. "Why?"

Her friend smiled, the lines at the corners of her eyes crinkling, the rich character in her face striking Suzanne as beautiful and reminding her age really *was* just a number. "I've had three husbands, ladies, and that's more than enough for anyone."

She winked, and Suzanne soaked that in, as well. She hadn't known.

"What happened to them all?" Lila asked, making

Suzanne appreciate not having to be the one to pose this question, too.

And in response, Dahlia appeared wistful, again staring off into that distant nothingness likely connected with memory and emotion. "I was…too much for them," she finally said, though the words held more pride than regret. "Some men can't handle an independent, freethinking woman. And some women—by which I mean me—aren't content to live with one man, day in and day out for a lifetime. Each of them eventually drove me batty. They'd all tell you I broke their hearts, but I suspect they're happier without *me*, too." She ended on a merry sort of shrug, adding, "And the middle one left me with my last name. Delaney was my favorite name, and he was my favorite husband, so I went back to it later."

Suzanne felt as if she'd been sucked down by an icy tidal wave rolling in from Lake Michigan right there in the Knitting Nook, struck almost painfully by what a full, rich, varied, wild life Dahlia had led. And never even felt the need to talk about.

She'd lived so much. And was *still* living.

And Meg was living, too—with Seth. She'd made changes in her life, acted boldly, determined what she wanted and gone for it.

What am I doing?

"It's hard for me to imagine that," Lila mused thoughtfully. "Having three complete marriages, three relationships that fully…deep and developed. And… recovering enough after the loss to go on to another, and another."

Suzanne glanced over at Meg's sister—who had practically taken the words right out of her mouth. Or at least out of her heart. It comforted her to know she wasn't the only one on the planet who had a hard time bouncing from relationship to relationship like they were flavors of ice cream.

"Life is complicated," Dahlia said. "I'm making it all sound much simpler than it was. But the upshot is... I had to spend some time forgiving each of my husbands for not being what I needed. And I had to forgive *myself* for being too independent to be fulfilled by one man. I know I hurt them and I truly regret that. But life goes on and I've always resolved to keep living mine, in whatever way feels best to me at any given time. Ultimately, I do better on my own than with a lifelong companion."

"And you...don't feel any attachment to Mr. Desjardins?" Lila asked curiously. "From, you know, the intimacy."

Dahlia appeared to think it over. "Some women get attached through sex, some don't. I've learned not to."

"I would *hate* not to," Suzanne heard herself say without planning, and with more passion than she wanted to feel on the subject. But it was true. "Because...it's this ultimate union. The closest two people can get to one another. I *want* to feel something profound from it."

She hoped, even as the words left her, that Dahlia wouldn't take it as a judgment—and her friend's wise smile said she didn't. "Sex can be different things to different people."

"Hence the problem with it," Lila mused aloud. "To one person it's fun, to the other it's serious business."

Suzanne blew out a sigh. "Which, not to be a broken record, is why I just don't go there. Because I'll be the one who thinks it's serious. And when you're in the serious camp, it sucks when the other person is just having fun."

Through all this, however, Dahlia continued looking as easy, breezy, and carefree as she had from the start of the conversation. Contented. Like a cat in a windowsill. Or a woman stretched out on a lounge chair on a perfect sunny summer day. "None of us sets out to hurt anyone," she offered thoughtfully. "It just happens sometimes."

But Suzanne smirked. "Oh, I don't know," she countered, "I've known a few men who seemed completely comfortable doling out hurt."

And Lila added, "And I've known men who…well, whether or not they set out to hurt me, they wanted to… have power over me, just because they thought they could." A glance to Meg's sister told Suzanne the words had been hard to say and that they held a story. But maybe not a story for right now. Right now felt heavy enough already—and she wasn't even certain why.

"Don't get me wrong," Dahlia replied. "Some men are beasts. Some *people*—regardless of gender—are beasts. I don't mean to give hall passes to everyone. But most of us are doing the best we can and sometimes the things we want simply conflict. So it seems to me that it can be worth taking a chance. That you might come out with more than you lose."

The words caused Suzanne's heart to deflate, making her sink a little deeper into her chair—the loom and yarn in her lap long since abandoned. Damn Dahlia and her wisdom. Something about it—something about this whole conversation—had dug deep into her soul, and now, *now*, she understood why she'd felt so unhappy about Dahlia's affair.

Because if even Dahlia—in her sixties with her silver hair—had a lover, shouldn't Suzanne be out there living life the same way? Living, loving, romancing, riding the waves of it all rather than letting them pull her under? Meg had Seth now, after all, too. Both her best friends had love lives. And Dahlia's had come as…well, as an utter surprise. She should have been delighted for her older friend. But instead the news had left her feeling somehow infantile, backward, left behind.

And like…like she wanted something fun and exciting, too.

Sooner than spring.

Maybe sooner than Christmas.

Which couldn't have been more shocking to her.

"Why do you look so very fraught, Suzanne?" Dahlia asked then. "Don't worry—I'm not going to press you toward Beck. Just because I have a lover doesn't mean you have to take one, too."

Suzanne blew out a breath. "But that's just it. Maybe I…want one." She bit her lip. "Maybe. I'm not sure. It's just that…" She looked back and forth between the other two women. "Okay, I'm just going to say this. And I'm sorry Meg isn't here to hear it, too. I think maybe I'm changing my mind and I want something with Beck, after all."

CHAPTER TEN

LILA'S JAW DROPPED. But she worked to clamp her mouth shut and look normal as Dahlia cheerfully announced, "I knew it! I knew it all along!"

Suzanne had sounded so very *not* into him when they'd had lunch. It had never occurred to Lila that sleeping with him might be stepping on Suzanne's toes. It had been a terrible idea for many *other* reasons, but this one she'd thought was free and clear. Oh boy.

Everything in her world blurred a little as she tried to wrap her mind around this while Dahlia asked Suzanne what she planned to do about the situation and Suzanne said she wasn't sure but that she thought maybe she was finally ready to take action. "And believe it or not, I recently even admitted to him that maybe I *would* go out with him. But in a way he had no reason to take very seriously given how flighty I've been. Maybe it's time I give him something to take seriously. Sooner rather than later."

And possibly the worst part for Lila was the fact that she felt…jealous. And sad. To lose him to the woman he *really* wanted.

Which makes no freaking sense at all. Have you gone completely off the deep end?

Maybe she had. Maybe this was the thing that tipped

the scales so far that she no longer knew up from down or right from wrong.

Because she'd sent him away.

Because she knew she couldn't be with him and never should have in the first place.

Because he was the tree-slaying enemy.

So jealousy was…well, the absolute worst reaction she could have. Because she shouldn't care. She shouldn't want him. She should loathe him. She should be wishing Suzanne Godspeed with him right now— not feeling the same way she had in the tenth grade when she'd found out her best friend, Erika, had made out with the boy she liked on the basketball bus ride home from an away game.

Though, technically, Suzanne is the one who should be feeling that way. Only she didn't know what had happened between Lila and Beck. *God, please don't tell her,* Lila willed him. Not that she'd done anything wrong. Or had she? The waters just kept getting more and more murky.

And all that aside, there remained the awful, gnawing pain. Of jealousy. And wanting something you couldn't have. She'd been trying so hard not to feel that. Loom, loom, loom—every time she'd felt it, she'd picked up a loom because it required her to pay at least a modicum of attention to creating the e-wrap stitches and occasionally stopping to count rows. The way things were going, she might have to learn some more complex stitches or start using multiple colors in order to require a deeper focus.

"But what about Meg?" Suzanne was saying now. "Given the situation with the land behind the inn, I'm not sure she'll be as happy about this as she would have a few weeks ago."

"Oh, honey, Meg will understand," Dahlia said with her usual sweep of a hand, brushing away the concern as she seemed to do with so many things.

But will she? Lila wasn't sure. *I certainly didn't think she would when it was me connecting with him.*

"What do you think, Lila?" Suzanne asked as if on cue.

Lila had said nothing since Suzanne's grand announcement, and now she could only narrow her brow and say, "Well, it's a complicated situation."

"I know, right?" Suzanne said. "If, say, Seth had been doing something to hurt *my* business or home before he'd met Meg, I'm not sure I'd be crazy about her getting romantic with him." She let out a sigh. Yet then held her hands up in front of her to say, "But wait. I'm really putting the cart ahead of the horse here, worrying about something before it's even happened. I guess it makes more sense to just…see where things go with Beck, and deal with the situation from there. True?"

"Sure," Lila said quickly, trying not to look suspicious. And still suffering a sensation that bordered between numb and tortured.

"But enough about me," Suzanne said to Lila. "Did *you* get anywhere with Beck?"

"Wh-wh-what?"

"Yesterday," Suzanne clarified with a smile. "When he brought you that Christmas tree. I tried to talk to him about the woods and Meg myself, but got nowhere. And I tried to tell him taking you a tree wasn't going to fix anything, but he seemed set on it. I figured if nothing else, it would give you a chance to state your case some more—and that maybe it would go better when you weren't standing in front of a bulldozer."

"Stop. Back up," Dahlia halted her knitting needles to say. Then tilted her head as she glanced over at Lila. "He brought you a tree?"

Lila nodded. And tried to think how to respond. Since most of the truth was unmentionable. She kept it simple. "Yes. And I felt kind of sick, and he got me a bottle of water and next thing I know, he's decorating a Christmas tree in the parlor. But it certainly didn't make me feel any better about the development. And nothing I said seemed to matter to him, either. We're definitely at an impasse."

"I called Tom Bixby on the town council," Dahlia announced. "Tom was sympathetic—he didn't vote to approve the project or the zoning change. He said it was all hotly debated, but that ultimately the council approved it in a four to three vote. All while the rest of us had our heads in the sand, I suppose." She sighed, looked sad. "You learn not to expect the unexpected here—and I guess it made us complacent, assuming it was safe to just go with the flow and think everything would always stay the same."

That was why Lila had come here. Because it *was* a place where things usually stayed predictably the same. And because she'd wanted to bury her head in the sand for a while. Best laid plans.

IF YOU LOOKED up, it was a beautiful day. Bright white cottony clouds, lit by the sun, drifted leisurely across a deep azure sky. It was only when Beck drew his gaze down to all the snow thickly blanketing the ground that he felt winter surrounding and consuming him. *Better get used to it, though.* Dahlia Delaney had once told him the first winter on the island was the hardest, and after that they went more swiftly, one blending into another and another—so he'd take her word for it and hope it was true.

Standing on his front porch, he glanced in the general direction of the Bluffside development, thinking of the bulldozer stuck there on the hillside, and admitted to himself that the land likely wouldn't be cleared until spring now. Construction could take place in the cold if it wasn't snowing—he'd already witnessed other winter maintenance work starting on the island in the last couple of months—but a steep snow-covered incline wasn't the safest place for dozing. Even in dry weather, an incline presented challenges. So he'd need to take steps to get the dozer cleared of snow and covered with some tarps to protect it from snow and ice damage.

Stepping back inside, he made a few business calls—including one about tarps. He thought about calling the Summerbrook Inn, trying to again make peace with Lila—but that hadn't gone so well the last time he'd tried. Or had it?

Sex was definitely good—sex with Lila specifically, outstanding.

But getting thrown out into the cold—literally: less than good. Referred to as the enemy: also less than good.

Which was all a damn crying shame—because if she wasn't so stubborn, he thought they might really click. More than just sexually. But also *very much* sexually. When the sex had unexpectedly occurred, he'd thought maybe some of the stubbornness was dying away. Actually, he'd thought that when she'd relented and let him put up the tree, and then even made him lunch and helped him hang ornaments. He'd really believed the situation was changing—even if the sex part had come as a surprise, albeit a very hot and welcome one.

If he was honest with himself, every moment he'd spent with her had stayed on his mind, permeated his thoughts, ever since. He grown painfully aware of his desire for her as he'd decorated the tree. *I want to kiss her so damn bad.* And when their hands had touched on the ornament, he'd realized: *She wants that, too. She doesn't* want *to want it—but she does anyway.*

The rest had been…easy. Like their bodies just fit together. They touched and kissed the same way. No one ever acknowledged that, but he'd always found that some people just kissed differently than others—and the same was true with sex. Maybe it was about age, about getting a little older, being well into adulthood—as time went on, you just knew what you liked, did what came naturally. And sometimes that matched with the other person, but sometimes, when it was a new connection, there were hiccups, awkwardness, adjustment. With Lila, though—none of that. It had been the perfect mating dance. They might not be able to get along otherwise, but in bed, that quickly, they'd been in sublime harmony.

Though in the end, maybe all that sexual harmony didn't matter. Since getting thrown out in the middle of the night kind of trumped any headway he'd made.

He also considered putting on his weatherproof work boots and making the trek down into town for some lunch at Dahlia's Café. But Dahlia was Meg's good friend, and all things considered, he feared he might be persona non grata on Harbor Street by this point. When he'd bought the land and petitioned for a zoning change, he'd had no idea the can of social worms he was opening.

But your job isn't to be a social butterfly. You came here to develop and improve some land, and earn some money. He hadn't headed north to make friends—in fact, by the time he'd moved to Summer Island, he'd been pretty fed up with people in general. Work, land, building—all things that were solid, straightforward, so much simpler than people. The fact that he'd found the people here pleasant and welcoming had come as an unexpected perk. But maybe he needed to get his priorities straight and quit caring about that.

What he hadn't factored into his move to a tiny island in northern Michigan was just how the hell he'd fill his hours during the quiet winters. At the time, isolation had sounded good, easier than dealing with difficult relationships—but days without work to sustain him were already starting to feel long.

After eating some lunch, he looked to the wooden box still sitting on his dining room table, which he'd been ignoring since opening it up to discover sermons inside. If his father had thought Beck would suddenly want to sit around and read years' worth of religious advice, it was only a testament to how much his dad had never understood or respected him.

And yet, maybe he should be the bigger man here and honor his father's memory enough to at least take a longer look. If his father had meant for him to have them…well, it was probably just a form of preaching from the grave, trying to get through to Beck in death what he'd failed to in life. If so, and if his dad was watching him through the bars of the Pearly Gates, the old man would be sorely disappointed. But boredom and curiosity were just enough to make Beck open the wooden lid once more and pull out a set of the folded papers.

My son, Beck, and I could never see eye to eye. When he was a little boy, it was easier. Children, in their innocence, can have such loving, generous hearts, and Beck was no different. But children grow, sometimes away from us.

I have long admired many practices of the group most commonly known as the Shakers, among those practices that of turning away from the world, by which I mean living separate and apart from the worldliness that can make us selfish or greedy, or confuse our priorities. For the world can indeed infest and confuse our minds, leading us from the ways that are pure and just. I often had the fanciful notions to wonder who my boy would have grown up to be if he hadn't been influenced by the pursuit of the almighty dollar.

But Beck, he loved things. Material possessions. He wanted the latest sports shoes, or video game. Later it was cars and a fancy house.

Now, don't get me wrong. I love my son. And desiring material things doesn't make anyone a bad person. But too much want, my friends, begets greed.

And so today I want to talk to you about gifts and giving. The gift that is giving. The Book of Acts tells us that it is more blessed to give than

*to receive. And the further truth is—the more we
give in life, the more we receive in return.*

BECK SKIMMED A little more. More about giving, giving,
giving. The man had been obsessed with the concept of
giving. He'd literally given the clothes off his back to
more than one person in need, and occasionally thrown
in some of Beck's and his sister's in the bargain. He'd
kept them poor. Almost intentionally, it had seemed.

The upside? It had inspired in Beck a strong work
ethic. Not that his father had ever noticed or valued that.
He'd started mowing yards at the age of twelve. He'd
worked after-school jobs and full-time ones in the summer. He'd gotten into building—hired on by a church
member who ran a small construction outfit—during
his sixteenth summer. And he'd saved his money to buy
nice things—for himself and his family. Most parents
would have been proud—but not Kenneth Grainger.

The man had possessed the ability to lift a congregation so high they could almost touch the clouds. But
when it came to fatherly love—well, the older Beck had
gotten, the less there'd been. Until eventually there'd
been none at all—other than attending Thanksgiving
and Christmas dinners for the sake of his mother and
sister, he'd been estranged from his dad for nearly ten
years, right up until the old man had died last winter.

The breaking point had come when Beck learned
from his mom that his father was using him as a cau-
tionary tale in sermons, casting him in the role of devil
incarnate for making a good living. Truth was—he'd
made such a good living that some people would call
him rich. The big difference between him and his dad

was: earning that much money made Beck proud—but it made his father ashamed.

Well, he'd seen enough of what lay in the box. He didn't need to read any more of his father's sermons to find out what a disappointment he was to the man—he already knew. It only pissed him off that even on his deathbed it had been a top priority for his dad to make sure Beck didn't forget it.

It almost startled him when his cell phone rang—but after a flinch, he yanked it from his pocket and looked down to see George Walton calling.

"Hello?"

"Hi, Becker—this is Cade!"

Beck couldn't help but laugh—the funny kid was a welcome intrusion to his too-quiet afternoon. "Hey, Cade buddy, what's up?"

"I was calling to see if you want to build a snow-man."

Hell—cold, snow, and a cute little kid. How could he resist? And it sounded like a lot better way to spend the day than getting insulted from six feet under. "Sure," he said. "Sounds fun."

On the other end of the line, the little boy cheered. Then Beck heard a muted, "He said yes!"

He couldn't help thinking it was as if he'd been asked out on a date. And given the way things were going with the women on this island, it sounded like a pretty good offer. "I'll bundle up and meet you outside with my best snowman-building equipment."

The boy sounded utterly awed as he said, "You have snowman-building equipment?"

Beck had been mainly thinking of less-than-exotic tools like a bucket and shovel, but replied, "Sure do.

We'll build the best snowman Summer Island has ever seen."

"Cool!" Cade said.

An hour later, a pretty majestic snowman was well underway in the Waltons' front yard, and despite himself, "Becker" was having a good time with the little kid from across the street.

"That's going to be a nice one," Marie Walton called as she came out onto the front porch with a shopping bag in hand. "I put some finishing touches in here for later—a carrot and a scarf and such. And when you're done, there's hot chocolate on the stove."

Soon enough, Cade was peeking in the bag and declaring gleefully, "Looks like Grammy has snowman-building stuff, too!"

Beck lifted Cade up, instructing him where to poke the carrot nose deep into the big snowman's head. They then pressed in some walnuts for eyes and a mouth, also courtesy of the little boy's grandma. Cade watched as Beck tied an old blue scarf around the snowman's neck, the tails draping down on one side, and they added more walnuts as buttons down the front of an imaginary coat.

"Think he needs a broom? Lean it right up against him there," Beck instructed his young friend.

Cade placed the old broom Beck had brought along as carefully as if he were building a house of cards.

After which Beck concluded, "All right—he's done. Good work, buddy!" He held his hand out for a high five. As high as a kindergartner could give one, anyway.

But rather than slapping Beck's hand with his mitten, Cade appeared seriously troubled. "Wait. He's not finished. He doesn't have a hat."

Beck weighed various options. Tromp across the street and into his house and try to track down an old ball cap. Bother Marie for one—which meant make a nice old lady go digging through the closets for something that might end up blowing away. Explain to Cade that maybe the snowman didn't *need* a hat. Or... "Here, he can have mine." He reached up and took off his Indiana Jones hat, plopping it on the snowman's head.

Cade just looked at him. "Won't you be cold?"

He shrugged. "I'm fine." Then he stood back to admire it. "Cool hat, though—right?"

Cade hesitated and said, "I guess. I mean, in a funny sort of way."

Beck drew back slightly. He'd been sure the kid would see the coolness even if Lila Sloan hadn't. "Funny? You don't think it looks kinda like something Indiana Jones would wear?"

"Who's Indiana Jones?"

"Never mind." Beck sighed, then patted the kid's head. "Ready to go get some hot chocolate from your grandma?"

Cade nodded, then his little eyes lit up in a way Beck was becoming accustomed to. "I bet after that it'll be almost time to take a bath and go to the tree-lighting party down in town."

"Oh, guess that *is* tonight, isn't it?" Beck had known, but wasn't particularly interested. Usually he made an appearance at town events—it was how he'd gotten to know people—but this one he planned to skip given all the drama of the past few days.

"Yep! Are you going, too?" Cade asked.

"Nope."

Cade's expression darkened. You'd think Beck had just announced Santa had run out of toys. "Why not?"

Um, let me count the reasons. It's cold. Snowy. There's a Kentucky basketball game on ESPN. Lila Sloan might start throwing ornaments at me. "I, uh, just thought I'd enjoy a nice, quiet evening at home."

"You have to go!" Cade insisted.

"Why is that?" Beck inquired very reasonably.

Cade gaped at him, like it was obvious, like he should know. "Christmas trees make your soul happy, remember?"

Oh yeah, he remembered, all right. It had been that cockamamie notion that had led him to take Lila Sloan a tree. Which he still wasn't sure if he regretted or not. It had been an event of extreme highs and lows, after all.

"And your soul doesn't seem very happy right now."

Beck took that in. It showed? Enough that a five-year-old could see it?

"And I'll be there!" Cade went on. "So you'll get to see *me* again!"

Beck couldn't help but laugh. And then relent. "Well, when you put it that way, sounds like I'd be crazy to pass it up."

Cade's whole countenance brightened. "So you'll go?"

Beck blew out a sigh. "Yeah, sure, I'll go."

That kid had a way of finding his soft spot, making him do exactly what he wanted.

And hell, maybe the tree-lighting would distract him from his troubles. Or maybe not—but the truth was, if trouble in the form of Lila Sloan showed up, he'd be glad, despite himself. She was a loose cannon for sure, but the idea of seeing her again made him feel like a teenager hoping to run into the girl he had a crush on. He'd just have to look out for flying ornaments.

PART 2

The tree which moves some to tears of joy is in the eyes of others only a green thing which stands in the way.

William Blake

CHAPTER ELEVEN

IT WAS RARE that a cold, snow-covered winter night on Summer Island held such promise. But as Suzanne meandered up Harbor Street toward the tree-lighting ceremony, the crisp air veritably sang with it. Christmas was coming, lights twinkled in shop windows and stretched across awnings, and the whole island felt merry. Perhaps more so because of heavy snows having caused the event to be delayed—it was already December 10. And while this was only her third holiday season here, she'd quickly learned that until the big tree in front of Lakeview Park sparkled with thousands of tiny bulbs, it wasn't truly yet Christmastime.

That same fresh sense of promise fluttered in her heart, as well. Beck would probably make an appearance. And she was looking forward to seeing him. Maybe she'd *always* liked seeing him but could only just now admit it to herself. Terrible when one's own mind keeps secrets—but a flurry of relief washed over her at having finally figured out her true feelings, and with her readiness to be brave.

People were beginning to gather around the enormous spruce in the snow when she approached, and the Summer Island School choir stood in two lines singing carols. Trent Fordham, who operated the bicycle livery in summer, stood with Josh Callen, owner of the coffee shop, fiddling with massive cords near an electrical box nearby. And she spotted Zack Sheppard on a ladder near the tree, apparently taking a break from sulking tonight to bark orders over the choir at the two men on the ground. "Not the tan cord—the green one!"

Despite herself, she was almost happy to see him— she didn't hate him or anything, and she knew it would ease Dahlia's mind if he was starting to get over Meg at least a little.

Just down the street from the main event, The Cozy Tea and Coffee Shop was lit up and open for business. She ducked in from the cold to find the place buzzing as she bought a hot chocolate with a swirl of whipped cream and chocolate sprinkles on top.

Pushing through the old-fashioned wooden screen door to leave, she nearly collided with a tall, silver-haired man in a tan wool coat and dark woolen flat cap like the ones worn by old-timey golfers and current day hipsters working too hard to earn that title. Unlike most golfers and hipsters, this man wore it well—or maybe he'd have worn *any* hat well by virtue of being strikingly handsome with high cheekbones and a cleft in his chin. *"Excusez-moi, mademoiselle,"* he said with perfect French pronunciation—and Suzanne nearly gasped. *Mr. Desjardins, I presume.*

She simply smiled in response, then caught sight of Dahlia standing nearby as she stepped down off the porch into the snow-covered street. "My, my," Suzanne said in sly greeting. "You were right—he's the cat's meow."

Dahlia laughed. "I suppose he is, at that." And un-like during their conversation at the Knitting Nook, now Suzanne could see in her friend the girlish glow of romance. Maybe Dahlia cared about Mr. Desjardins more than she'd let on? Suzanne chose not to press it, however—at least not right now—though the thought made her happy.

"Have you seen Beck? I'm hoping to run into him tonight," she told Dahlia. Ready to be brave, brave, brave—no more holding back.

"Not yet," her friend said. "But I can't tell you how pleased I am that you've come to your senses about him. I mean, I wish this conflict over the land behind the inn wasn't happening—but everything else about the man is tall, dark, and yummy."

Dahlia had just echoed her own sentiments. And among other reasons she'd shied away from his attention last summer was his being so handsome that he felt out of her league. His good looks had only added to the things about him that intimidated her. But if he found her attractive, who was she to question it?

"Oh!" Dahlia said, latching onto the arm of Suzanne's coat with a glove-covered hand. "Dreamy land mogul at nine o'clock and approaching swiftly."

Suzanne glanced up Harbor Street to see the object of her affections indeed striding briskly through the snow toward the center of town. Then wished she had a plan. Why hadn't she thought of one? She wasn't good enough at this stuff to wing it. "What do I do? What do I say?" she asked Dahlia.

Dahlia dropped her gaze to the mug of cocoa between Suzanne's mittens—then grabbed it away from her.

"Hey!" Suzanne protested.

"Ask him if he'd like to get some hot chocolate with you."

"Oh." She began to nod, getting with the program. "Okay, that's good. Got it."

And it was fortunate Dahlia thought fast, because Beck certainly *walked* fast at the moment—he was already about to pass by without having noticed them standing there. "Beck," she called.

He looked over. Smiled softly, lifted his hand in a quick wave. "Hey, Suzanne. Dahlia." He'd slowed down, but hadn't stopped moving.

Still, she pressed forward, pointing toward the coffee shop—and only then realized that when wearing a mitten, it might look more like a traffic-directing motion. "Chilly night out. I was about to get some hot chocolate. Care to join?" Okay, traffic directions aside, it came out smooth, building her confidence.

Until he paused only to point his own finger farther down the street and say, "Thanks, I would—but I need to talk to Lila."

Suzanne glanced ahead to see that indeed Meg's sister stood by herself near the tree, peering up at it in the dusky air as night descended full and deep and cold over the island. "Did you make peace with her?" she asked on a lark.

On the move again, he said, "Still working on it, but wish me luck." He ended with a grin and was gone—and Suzanne and Dahlia stood looking silently after him as he headed toward Lila in the distance. She wasn't sure if they'd gone quiet from shock—or if there was simply nothing else to say about him brushing off her invitation like it wasn't the most courageous thing she'd done in…years, actually, when she thought about it. Her heart sank.

She couldn't make out Lila's expression from such a distance—but she thought Beck looked…well, maybe like she *wished* he'd looked when she'd asked him to the coffee shop. Though maybe she was misconstruing the situation. It was getting dark and he stood far away now—so maybe she was seeing something that wasn't there. "Am I reading this wrong," she said to Dahlia, "or…does he suddenly seem more interested in talking to Lila than in talking to me?"

Dahlia replied gently but certainly. "You're not reading it wrong."

She drew her gaze from the couple up the way to her friend. "You think something is happening there? That I've waited too long?"

Dahlia sighed, then looped her arm through Suzanne's as she handed back her drink. "Maybe, maybe not. Maybe there's a big, unexpected land negotiation going on. Time will tell. For now, don't be discouraged, my dear. He's had his cap set for you since he landed on this rock. Now let's find Pierre and watch them light the tree."

BECK HAD TRUDGED on from Suzanne and Dahlia feeling like a jerk. Maybe he should have stopped. But all things considered, that would have made him feel like a jerk, too. Given that Suzanne might want to go out to dinner with him sometime in the spring, and that he'd slept with Lila a few nights ago, having hot chocolate with Suzanne would have felt pretty smarmy. Talk about being between a rock and a hard place. He suddenly theorized that whoever had first coined that phrase had probably been a guy caught between an honest attraction to two very different women.

And hell—maybe walking away from hot chocolate with the one who liked him in order to pursue the one who didn't made no sense. But all he could do was follow his gut, and his gut had led him marching up to the feisty lady with tousled hair, currently peering up at the island Christmas tree with the wonder of a child.

"Don't suppose you decided you're sorry you threw me out into the snow," he said by way of greeting.

She turned matter-of-fact hazel eyes on him. "Don't suppose you decided not to destroy the woods behind the inn."

He shook his head shortly. "No."

"Me neither."

The problem here, already, were those eyes of hers. Peering down into them instantly re-ignited an intense attraction. He might have blamed it on the Baileys, but the culprit was something much worse: chemistry. That pull that grabs at your chest—and other parts, too—making you just want more. All things considered, it was extremely inconvenient. But that didn't make it go away.

"Look, Lila," he said, deciding to just keep it real, "I don't want to be enemies. I actually want the opposite—I like you. I like how we connected."

He watched as she drew in her breath, pursed her lips. Trying not to feel. He could see that. "I like my trees," she countered.

But he was going to keep on with reality here. "There's more to life than trees."

In response, she turned back to the big Christmas tree they stood next to, towering at least twenty feet above them, all decked out in simple colored balls of red, blue, purple, and gold. "Trees are pretty amazing," she said. "Spring trees, with flowers and fragrance. Summer trees making things scenic and shady. Fall trees, adding color to the world. Christmas trees, bringing light and warmth to the holiday."

Oh boy, she was waxing poetic. And maybe he should just agree with her. But a continuing sense of reality and justice wouldn't quite let him. "This tree had to be cut down, you know," he pointed out. "Just like the one in your living room. I still don't get how you can say you like Christmas trees if you're all about saving trees' lives?"

She spun to face him. "As we already discussed, it's two different things. Christmas trees are raised on farms, for the purpose of being Christmas trees."

He merely shrugged. "Some. But not all. A tree this big…" He glanced up toward the star at the top. "Maybe it came from a tree farm, but more likely it was cut down in the woods somewhere on the island."

"Well, I'm sure all its friends weren't mowed down along with it," she snapped. "And at least it's going out in a blaze of glory, with purpose, bringing joy to the residents of Summer Island."

Lila knew she was just rambling combatively now, but he was forcing her to, antagonizing her. The truth was, this whole situation made it so she wasn't sure *how* she felt about Christmas trees anymore. But while she hadn't put one up in her apartment in Chicago this year, she was suddenly grateful, in light of everything, that she owned a lovely artificial one that didn't cost a perfectly healthy tree its life every winter.

"I wish you could see the woods behind the inn in

spring." She spoke more softly now. "Mixed into the pines, there are pink crabapples and white dogwoods. And purple redbuds. Meg and I called them purplies when we were kids," she recalled with a smile. "It's beautiful. And I just can't face never getting to see that again."

At this, however, he merely arched one dark, accusing brow in her direction. "Come up here a lot in the spring, do you?"

"No," she answered shortly. Darn him. "But I remember it fondly. And my grandmother would turn over in her grave if she knew what you were planning to do to that hillside."

At this, he simply sighed, the gesture giving away for the first time that maybe deep down he knew he was the bad guy here. "Wouldn't be the first person I've made turn over in their grave."

She opened her eyes wider, curious. "Oh?"

Then he shook his head, looked away. "Sorry. Just thinking about my dad."

"You made your dad turn over in his grave?" She raised her eyebrows.

"Long story." Another headshake.

And God knew she didn't want to care—but damn it all, she did. She drew in a breath, let it back out, and offered up slowly, "You could tell me—if you want."

He returned his gaze to hers. "I thought we were enemies."

She blew out a breath, then admitted the ugly truth. "It's hard, because I like you. Even if I threw you out into the snow."

"Likewise," he said, his expression as stalwart as she suspected her own to be. But then it relaxed—making him look more like the guy who'd put up a Christmas tree in her parlor. "How about, for tonight," he said kindly, "we quit talking about trees and just drink some hot chocolate and enjoy the evening?"

He'd made a similar suggestion right before they'd had sex. *Don't agree. Don't soften. Don't let him get you where he wants you. Or next thing you know, you'll be telling him it's okay to tear down the trees.* "All right," she heard herself say anyway. Because she *did* like him. And having an enjoyable night sounded *nice*. She could *use* a nice, simple night with a pleasant companion.

Then she remembered—with maybe just a hint of embarrassment—that she had indeed thrown him out into the snow. "I guess you made it home okay. In the snow and all."

"I'm a big boy. I can handle a little snow." Despite herself, she still liked the simple strength that emanated from him. Well, at least when it was about something other than the development behind the inn.

A thought which reminded her, once more, not to be *too* nice. "You're still not wearing your stupid hat."

"Well, you said it was stupid."

"Is that why you're not wearing it?" she asked with a slight tilt of her head.

"Actually," he confessed, "I loaned it to a snowman."

Full of surprises, this one. "You made a snowman?"

"I helped my neighbor," he said. "A little kid named Cade."

Aw crap, he was kind to children, too? What was next? Did he volunteer at homeless shelters? Give food to the poor? He kept making it harder and harder to dislike him.

"And as luck would have it," he said, letting out a good-hearted laugh, "here comes the little guy now."

Lila glanced down to see a small child running toward them in the snow. "Hey Becker! You're here! You came!"

"Told you I would."

"Becker?" she asked softly, eyebrows raised.

"Code name," he told her smoothly.

In spite of herself, a light trill of laughter escaped her.

Then Beck introduced them. "Cade, this is Lila. Lila, my buddy, Cade."

"Is she your wife?" Cade asked.

And Lila's spine went ramrod straight. *"No,"* she said. Then raised her eyes to Beck, mind suddenly racing right past the horrific suggestion to weird, bad, panic-inducing thoughts. "Please tell me you don't have a wife."

"No," he replied just as quickly as she had, looking offended.

Okay, whew. And *of course* he didn't—or he wouldn't have been pursuing Suzanne. Another thought that stung.

"Used to," he added, just as casually.

"Oh." Oh boy. She hadn't seen that coming. Though the man was probably close to forty, so it wasn't crazy or anything. Just new information to take in.

"That's a story for another time," he said to her.

"All right." She nodded. Still trying to digest it all. He wasn't married, thank God. Though why had she suddenly worried about that for no good reason? She supposed she just didn't want any more unpleasant surprises in her life. Or for anyone to get hurt here. At least beyond Meg and the trees. But he *had* been married. How long ago? Why did it end? Were there children? Was the ex still in the picture?

"Then is she your girlfriend?" Cade asked.

They both dropped their gazes to the little boy in front of them. *"No,"* she said again quickly, decisively.

"Then what *is* she?" Cade asked Beck.

Beck turned toward her. "What *are* you?"

She drew in her breath, pursed her lips, making a slight face. "We're…friends, I guess. Maybe. Sort of." She started out looking at Beck as she spoke, but ended up dropping her glance to Cade.

Cade nodded very seriously. "My Grammy says it's important to have friends and that Becker is a nice man. He's really good at snowman-building, too."

At this, "Becker" looked smug. Too smug for a man being called by the wrong name, but clearly he didn't see it that way.

She just rolled her eyes in response. Then spoke low enough for Cade not to hear. "Clearly Cade's Grammy doesn't know about your tree-slaying and inn-ruining."

"Ah ah ah," Beck reprimanded her, shaking his finger, "you promised. No more tree talk tonight."

"Whatever." She rolled her eyes again. "But I think *you* promised hot chocolate."

"Fair enough. We should be able to make it to the coffee shop and back before they light the tree." He lowered his gaze to the little boy. "You and your grandfolks want to go with us, Cade?"

The little kid's eyes lit up, same as if he'd been invited to Disneyland. "Wait and I'll go ask!"

"He really seems to like you," she observed aloud without planning it.

"Obviously a smart kid."

She blew out a derisive breath. "Or deluded. Looking through snowman-colored glasses."

He let out a laugh at that. And then—oh—looked at her like he wanted to kiss her.

And worse yet, she wanted to kiss him, too.

But she shouldn't—not here, in front of people. Not anywhere actually. So it was a good thing Cade came running back up just then. "They're gonna stay here, but I can go!" he reported, then held up a five-dollar bill, stretched out between two small striped mittens. "Grandpa gave me money!"

"You can keep that," he told the kid. "Hot chocolate's on me." Then he looked to her and spoke more quietly. "No Baileys this time, though."

"Definitely not," she agreed.

"Since we're just 'maybe sort of friends,'" he said, the words—and his expression—clearly challenging the claim.

In response, she lowered her chin, regarding him from beneath shaded lids. But, oh boy, that was a flirtatious look if ever she cast one. It snuck right out—a natural, and ridiculously flirtatious, response. They were *so* not just maybe sort of friends.

"What's Baileys?" Cade's little voice cut through her desire to ask.

"A…grown-up drink," Beck told him.

"Can I try some?"

"No," Beck said. "It makes you do crazy things. Now let's go or we'll miss the tree-lighting."

SUZANNE STOOD IN the shadows, next to Dahlia and Mr. Desjardins, but feeling rather alone as the Summer Island Christmas tree burst festively into light. At the same time, other, smaller trees in Lakeview Park lit up, too, their branches draped with tiny white bulbs that contrasted with the colored ones on the much larger evergreen in the street. Everyone *ooh*ed and *ahh*ed at the spectacular sight as the choir broke into "O Christmas Tree."

When the crowd began to disperse a few minutes later, Dahlia said to Suzanne, "The Pink Pelican's open tonight, serving dinner and drinks 'til ten. Join Pierre and me in knocking back a few? I think maybe you need it."

Suzanne forced a smile. Normally, she didn't mind playing third wheel with couples—since normally she chose not to be part of a couple herself. But suddenly she feared hanging out with Dahlia and her charming French lover would leave her even more lonesome. "Thanks, but I'm tired and ready to head home."

"Maybe it's nothing," Dahlia said. Despite the vagueness, they both knew what she was talking about. "He *has* to be nice to Lila—he's trying to preserve his friendship with Meg. Maybe that's all it is."

Maybe. But she'd watched Beck from a distance. He'd never come back. And in fact, "He spent the whole evening with her."

Dahlia shrugged, smiled in her wise way. "The whole evening was an hour. And besides, whatever the nature of their relationship is, Lila will be gone before Christmas. You'll be here long after, and so will he."

"That's a good point," Suzanne replied dryly, "if I want to be someone's second choice."

It surprised her when her older friend just laughed. "You're thinking too much, worrying too hard. It's

Christmas. Come have a drink with us. I hear the Pelican has some new holiday cocktails. There's something called a Grinch nog, which I think is spiked eggnog dyed green. And reindeer punch—which I'm told involves rum."

Suzanne took all that in, along with Dahlia's sensible, practical tone. Maybe she was right. Maybe it was nothing.

And either way, she hadn't come to this island to chase a man. She'd come here to live a contented life on her own. Maybe she just needed to get her head on straight and get back to that. It was the holiday season—she should enjoy a holly jolly couple of hours out with friends.

"All right," she conceded.

At this, Mr. Desjardins chimed in to say, "Very good. I will have ze company of two lovely ladies zis evening. I am a lucky man."

And Suzanne admitted to them both, "A Grinch nog might just hit the spot right now."

Or two. Or five.

Since apparently lying to herself no longer worked. Despite the inner pep talk, she didn't feel sensible, or contented, or merry. It was too late—her heart had left the gate and there was no going back.

CHAPTER TWELVE

Two weeks before Christmas, the Summer Island morning broke bright but cold. Despite beams of winter sun, the narrow stretch of Lake Michigan that separated the state's Upper and Lower Peninsulas teemed with jagged, angry-looking chunks of ice. It grew thicker closer to shore, the chunks and plates pushing against and piling up on one another to create what the locals called "shove ice." Lila thought it seemed early in the season for that—but she also knew that in winter, there *was* no normal and conditions changed constantly.

Standing on the front porch, even one of Meg's thick cardigan sweaters wrapped around her wasn't enough to ward off the biting cold. She stood there for a while anyway, though, somehow needing to soak in the quiet winter soul of the island, or maybe it was the soul of her grandmother she sought strength from just now—or maybe the two were one.

Despite the blessedly deep sleep she'd experienced the night she'd had sex with Beck, her sleepless nights had since returned. Though last night had been a little better. She'd gone to bed thinking about the time spent with Beck at the tree-lighting. Normally these days, no matter what she lay down thinking about, her mind ultimately returned to Simon Alexis and her ex-best friend, Whitney, and sometimes now also bulldozers and empty hillsides and letting Meg down, all of it keeping her tossing and turning all night—but last night she'd fallen asleep in an almost-reasonable amount of time. She'd awakened with the sun, and gratitude for sleep had been enough to lead her outside, thinking she should appreciate the morning.

She'd now made winter hats for Meg, Seth, her mom, her dad, Suzanne, and Dahlia. More than one for Meg actually—in different colors and weights of yarn. She'd made a couple for herself, too, but had quickly realized that making them for other people was somehow more gratifying.

Funny, she'd once been so proud to have a good enough job to afford to buy her family nice gifts—but most anything she'd ever bought them now paled in meaning next to the simple knitted hats laid out in a neat row on the back of the sofa. She wasn't even sure anyone would like them, or that they would fit. But she would enjoy giving them, and knew in her heart that at the very least, her family would appreciate the thought and effort she'd put into them. It had been a long time since she'd given handmade gifts—probably since her childhood.

In addition to the e-wrap and u-wrap stitches, she'd just added another to her repertoire—the figure eight stitch created a loose, pretty sort of stitch with worsted weight yarn, and in bulky yarn it resulted in a neat, stylized one.

I wonder if I can knit Meg enough hats to eventually make up for the loss of the trees. A silly thought, but probably why she suffered the compulsion to make more and more of them for her sister.

Unable to take the cold any longer, she ducked back

inside and headed for the kitchen to fill Miss Kitty's food and water bowls and brew herself a cup of hot tea. Turning on the faucet, a glance out the window drew her eyes up the hill toward the bulldozer. Where... something was different. It was covered up—with a tarp or something. Seemed like a good sign.

Even if, in her heart, she no longer held out much hope for the hillside.

Because even if that bulldozer sat there unmoving until spring, even if she continued to keep the key to it on mere desperate principle, she no longer believed she could really save the trees. She'd keep trying as best she could—but reality had begun setting in. Developers didn't stop their developments just because you asked them to. Even when they slept with you and honestly seemed to like you. Admitting that to herself made her chest tighten, her stomach knot. But she couldn't see a way around it.

Drinking her tea curled up in the easy chair in the nook, she stroked Miss Kitty's thick fur and thought through her day.

Maybe she'd call Allie Hobbs and ask if she'd open the Knitting Nook for a little while—despite the lack of regular business hours in the winter, Allie had given Lila her number and told her to call if she needed yarn or anything else.

Maybe she'd take a walk in the snow—maybe even on Gran's old snowshoes. She'd never actually imagined wanting to do anything like that, but that recent urge to reconnect with Gran's memory and the island still echoed through her.

Or maybe she'd call Whitney. Even though they'd had an awful falling-out over Simon. It still made her

feel a little sick to remember. She'd trusted Whitney
so much. They'd worked together at one of Chicago's
largest banks for seven years, and then two years ago,
Whitney had gotten a job at the Alexis Foundation
and soon after, on her recommendation, Lila had, too.
Whitney's betrayal had been one more thing to make
running away seem like a viable solution.

Though the longer she was here, the more she realized that coming to Summer Island hadn't solved anything. Other than giving Meg extra time away with
Seth, that is. That part was good. The rest she wasn't
so sure about.

The last potential activity for the day involved the
final skein of yarn she'd bought from the Knitting
Nook but not yet used. A dark, warm, serious-looking
maroon in a thick, soft alpaca blend. She had enough
charcoal gray left over from the hat she'd made for her
dad that she could probably get fancy and add a stripe
on the crown.

Whereas loom knitting was usually the perfect distraction from all her woes, today the idea came with a
problem. She found herself wanting to make *this* hat
for the one person she knew who actually seemed to
need a hat.

It also happened to be the same person who was
tearing down her trees.

And the same person who she now knew Suzanne
had romantic aspirations toward, making her feel, however unwittingly, like the "other woman."

By all accounts, he was the last person she should
make a hat for. After all, what kind of message did that
send? *Tear down my trees and I'll make you a hat?* By
that logic, it was a pretty preposterous notion.

And yet he stayed in her thoughts. She wondered what the story was with his father. And his wife. Ex-wife. Or...maybe she'd died, like Suzanne's husband? Ugh—that would be tragic. But regardless, she wanted the answers. She wanted to know who Beck Grainger really was beyond a callous destroyer of nature and a rather masterful lover.

That stayed on her mind, too. The sex. Images of it flashed in her head even now.

It was fortunate that last night after the tree-lighting, his little friend Cade had come bouncing up to grab onto his hand and announce, "You can walk home with us!"

Beck had flashed Lila a look somehow shy and decidedly sexy as hell at the same time as he answered, "I was just about to offer to walk Lila home, and her house is in a different direction."

However, Lila was nothing if not quick on the draw when it came to avoidance techniques, so she had taken Cade's arrival as a sign from the universe—and quickly said, "That's okay—I can make it on my own. You should walk with Cade and his grandparents. Have a nice evening." Partly she'd thought maybe it just made sense to accompany elderly people on a long walk through the snow. And partly she'd thought—*my skin is vibrating with how much I want him right now, and if he walks me home, I'm probably going to invite him in, and make this whole situation even more complicated than I've already made it.*

Sleeping with him once had felt like betraying Meg. Sleeping with him again would feel like betraying Suzanne. Even if none of this was Lila's fault. The same way that what happened with Simon wasn't her fault.

But she'd been blamed for it anyway. By Whitney, and by Simon himself. She hadn't done enough to protect herself from Simon Alexis—she had to do whatever she could to protect Meg, and the trees, and everyone and everything else that had anything at stake here.

I came here to keep a low profile, get away from the drama.

All things considered, that wasn't going well.

So coming home alone last night seemed like the most practical, successful move she'd made in a while.

She'd gone to the tree-lighting ceremony expecting—hoping—to run into Suzanne and Dahlia. They'd invited her, after all. But she never saw them. She only saw Beck.

Thinking back through her options for the day, she glanced down at the cat and voiced her thoughts, maybe just to fill the silence. "It's really too cold to go out if I don't have to—if I want to try snowshoeing, I can wait for a warmer day. And I'm not *completely* out of yarn. And Whitney's the one who got mad at me, so why would I call her, even if I miss her? If she wants to make up, she can do the calling."

She took a sip of tea. That left one option. Make a hat for Beck. Her nemesis. Who she should stay away from. Her lover. Who she wanted again—badly.

She took a deep breath, blew it out with a *whoosh*. "Okay, here's what I'll do," she said to Miss Kitty. "I'll make him a hat. Because I like making hats. And I like giving hats. And God knows the man *needs* a hat.

"But it's not an invitation-to-have-sex hat. It's just a hat. A nice, friendly hat. And maybe…maybe…okay this is a stretch, but…maybe the simple act of giving him a hat will…somehow change his mind about the trees.

"I know that makes no sense. I know it's not going to happen." The cat looked up at her. Probably thinking *Who the hell are you talking to? I'm a cat.* "But for some ridiculous reason, I just really want to make him a hat. Even though he's still the enemy. And this is the only way I can justify it. So I guess I'm going to make the tree-slayer a hat."

TWO DAYS AFTER the tree-lighting, Dahlia called and talked Suzanne into a "brisk winter morning's walk up to the Christmas tree" before she opened Petal Pushers, hoping to move a little more decorative greenery before the holiday selling season officially ended with the Harbor Street Christmas Walk this weekend. The event provided a last opportunity for shops and restaurants to do a little business before winter closed the island down almost completely until spring.

"We're the only people out here," she pointed out to her older friend as they trudged up the silent and rather frigid snow-covered street.

"Wimps. All of them," Dahlia said. "But I'm glad. I've always enjoyed quiet winter walks. And we'll get to have the Christmas tree to ourselves. I thought maybe I'd snap a picture or two and text them to Meg."

"That's a good idea," Suzanne agreed. Even if she suddenly felt more distant from Meg than she wanted to. Meg was off having a wonderful life—as she deserved—with her sexy new beau. And Meg's sister was *here* having a life, with—possibly—*her* handsome new beau. And the awkwardness she suddenly felt toward Lila now almost extended to Meg, as well.

But the notion of new beaus made her say to Dahlia, "Mr. Desjardins is a keeper." The silver-haired man had continued to charm Suzanne through their Pink Pelican dinner, largely by how smitten he seemed with Dahlia.

"He's sweet, I grant you," Dahlia replied with the same easy shrug from the last time they'd discussed him. "And a skilled lover, I confess. But he's a fling."

"I think you're being hasty not to value his affection more."

As they approached the large tree, still lovely even with its lights barely visible in the sunshine, Dahlia cast Suzanne a pointed look. "When it comes to men, you're either all in or all out, aren't you?"

She'd never realized that, but she supposed it was an astute and accurate observation. "I guess I've never known how to be any other way. Either I'm into someone—or I'm completely disinterested."

"Well, frankly," Dahlia said, "I'm grateful I don't feel that way. That sort of absoluteness sounds…as if it would be almost painful. Is it?" She glanced over again, appearing truly curious.

Suzanne blew out a sigh, thinking through it. "Sometimes. I mean, if the guy doesn't feel the same way, it's…devastating. But when he does? Pure elation."

Rather than reply to that, Dahlia posited, "It also sounds…full of risk."

To that, Suzanne raised her eyebrows beneath the hood of her parka. "Isn't that what love *is*, in a way? Risk? How do you love—really love—without risking? After all, I thought you weren't afraid of taking chances."

They stopped in front of the tree, and Dahlia pulled

out her phone, drew off the end of a flip-top psyche-
delic mitten, and began snapping pictures as she said,
"Maybe you're right. Maybe I *am* missing something
by not feeling romance as passionately as you do. But
I guess I just choose to feel *other* things passionately. I
love my nephew passionately. I love you and Meg rather
passionately. I love my business. I love this island. I
love the life I've led—both before and after coming
here." Done with the pictures, she repocketed her phone
and met Suzanne's gaze. "But I'm not sure I've ever
given myself completely over to loving a man."

Though spoken casually, it struck Suzanne as a huge
confession. She'd always seen Dahlia as so witty and
wise—the woman she wanted to be when she reached
that age. And yet, had she found the one thing about
Dahlia that *didn't* feel wise to her? Or…was *she* wrong?
Was Dahlia's way the wise one?

But no—no, she didn't believe that. She couldn't.
How did you ever really live—fully—if you kept your
heart guarded, if you never knew real love in all its
magical, alluring, excruciating, agonizing, inspiring,
uplifting, joyful, gut-wrenching, heart-pounding, heartbreaking glory?

And if Dahlia had never truly loved a man—if she'd
never truly surrendered her heart and been in it all the
way—well, no wonder her marriages had all ended in
divorce. Suzanne sometimes feared she didn't know
much about how to approach life, but she did know
what it was to love.

"Maybe," she suggested softly, "you should give
yourself over to loving Mr. Desjardins."

"Unlikely," Dahlia said—so very simply, as if Suzanne had recommended she try a new recipe or get a new haircut. "Like Lila, he'll be leaving."

Oh. So maybe that was the issue. Or just an excuse. "But what if he wasn't? What if he wanted to stay?"

Swiping a mittened hand down through the air, Dahlia blew off the notion. "I'm sure he doesn't. He has a life in France."

"But a daughter here—right?"

"In Toronto," Dahlia corrected her, her tone suggesting it might as well be the moon.

"Toronto's not all that far," Suzanne pointed out.

Dahlia answered simply by making a *pffft* sort of noise that effectively closed the topic. But at the same time, Suzanne sensed that she'd at least planted a seed, and she hoped maybe Dahlia would begin thinking about the situation in a new way. She suspected her friend had led a grand, adventurous life in many aspects, but to Suzanne, if she'd never truly loved a man, then it left her life incomplete. And if she let herself now, it would be a fine experience to add to the rest in her collection.

"I haven't kept in touch with Lila, texted her or anything," Suzanne said then as they started walking back toward their respective businesses. "I feel bad. Because it's not her fault if Beck is interested in her. In fact, it's probably my own, for beating around the bush so long." Sadness, and a little embarrassment, weighed on her—since, after all, she'd announced her intentions toward Beck in Lila's presence, never dreaming Lila would feel anything but contempt for him.

And maybe she didn't. Who knew. As Dahlia had pointed out, Beck and Lila had spent an hour in each other's presence the other night—so what? He'd been trying to make peace. Still, she wondered if it had worked—and if so, exactly how well.

"Don't feel bad," Dahlia said. "You have your reasons. Tell you what—I'll text her right now."

She pulled out her phone and again, flipped off the end of one mitten—and Suzanne leaned over to watch as she typed.

Suzanne and I are both sorry to have missed you at the tree-lighting. Wanted to check in and say hi. She hit Send.

A reply came quickly. Thanks for the hello—needless to say, it's pretty quiet here. I went, but sorry I didn't see you guys, either. Dahlia typed some more. We'll have to get together again before you leave. Meanwhile, come to the Christmas Walk on the 15th. Suz and I will both be working, but perhaps we can socialize a bit at the same time.

That sounds nice! I will!

Suzanne made no comment about everything that was going unsaid. Lila was right up the street at the Summerbrook Inn. They could easily connect with her for lunch, or dinner, or a morning walk like this one. They could connect with her right this minute, for that matter, hearing how much she seemed to welcome the communication. But the whole Beck question had erected an invisible wall between them.

"I'm letting the potential interest in her by a man I've never even gone out on a date with stand in the way of being her friend. That's awful," Suzanne said. "Maybe I should go down there right this instant, knock on the door, and invite her to lunch."

"It's a nice idea," Dahlia said, "but I think if you saw her right now, you'd behave oddly. For an otherwise smart, confident woman, you tend to behave oddly around anyone you don't feel comfortable with."

"My Achilles heel," Suzanne agreed. "But this isn't Lila's fault. And I promised Meg to be friendly to her. I'm a terrible person."

"You're a normal person," Dahlia said. "With terrible timing."

A few minutes later, Dahlia announced that she was going to open the café—again without staff— in case anyone stopped by for lunch. "Though I almost wouldn't mind if no one does. I suppose Pierre is wearing me out—I could use a quiet day to myself just relaxing."

"Maybe it's winter," Suzanne pondered aloud. "The snow, the cold. It can wear on you."

"Maybe. Or perhaps I'm just getting older," Dahlia said. "I live my life mostly ignoring that—but I suppose it does eventually sneak in and change things."

Suzanne didn't like thinking about that—about Dahlia getting old or being any less vibrant than she was now. She didn't like thinking about the passage of time, how swiftly life could go by. It suddenly *felt* swift. She suddenly felt her own thirty-eight years, and how it seemed like just yesterday that she'd been twenty-eight, and how she'd look back in ten more, from forty-eight, feeling as if they'd passed in only a day, as well.

Manning the counter at Petal Pushers, she'd soon sold another tree and two wreaths. Anything left by the Christmas Walk would be discounted in hopes of luring a last minute buy from someone who hadn't planned to decorate. And anything that didn't sell she would place in stands on Harbor Street and toss some lights on herself just so they wouldn't go completely to waste.

The solitude after the day's few customers had come and gone allowed her to keep thinking about Beck. And mistakes. And her heart. And time. And whether it was silly to suddenly feel so much for a man she didn't know well and had spent the last six months pushing away.

Maybe if you got to know him, you wouldn't even like him. Though the truth was—the *problem* was—the more she got to know him, the more she *did* like him. And the more she was drawn to him. And the more it hurt to think he no longer cared.

Late that afternoon, she remembered some remaining fir trees still stood behind the shop, near the greenhouses, and decided to drag them out front where they'd have a better chance of catching someone's eye now that her stock had dwindled. It would be her last act of the workday before closing up and heading back to the quiet warmth of her cottage.

Though lugging them around the building was hard, slow work, making her wish she'd gotten this idea a little earlier as dusk started to steal the daylight. And she was busy dragging the fifth of seven trees around the building when a deep voice said, "Need help?"

She looked up see the warm brown eyes of Beck Grainger.

CHAPTER THIRTEEN

"UM—YEAH, THAT would be nice." *Don't think too hard. Don't worry that you probably look like a wreck, sweaty from hard work even though it's cold out. Don't act weird.* But her skin fairly buzzed in his presence.

"Here, let me," he said, reaching to take the tree's trunk from her. Their hands touched, and even through gloves, she felt it. The little electrical connection. The nearness of everything about him that was rugged and masculine and warm.

"Thanks," she whispered. *It's okay that it came out whispery. You're winded from dragging trees. He won't realize he leaves you breathless now.* She tried to find her more normal voice as she motioned toward the tree rack up against the building. "Right there."

He handled the tree like it was a feather, leaning it into the rack and asking, "Are there more?"

"Yeah," she said. "Follow me."

Then tried not to slip on the packed snow as she walked, feeling floaty and happy with renewed hope.

Small talk ensued as he started to help with the last trees. About hoping they sold and it getting late in the season. About how cold it had gotten so early, and how much it had already snowed.

She tried to help by picking up the lighter end but he insisted on taking it alone. "No—I got it," he assured her. Then, "I can't believe you already hauled so many around by yourself. These things aren't light."

She shrugged. "It's part of the job. Just a part that makes me wish I had bigger muscles," she added on a laugh, following him around the building. Should she follow even though she was doing nothing to help? Was that weird? *No, it's a chance to talk more.*

"Seems like you need someone to do your heavy lifting," he tossed over his shoulder with a smile. Was that flirting? Or just a practical comment? She wasn't sure.

"It's not really a big enough operation to warrant hiring help. Though having some muscle power to call on would be nice."

"Well," he told her, leaning the tree against the rack, "if you ever need help, you can ask me. I'm happy to lend a hand."

Her heart warmed. Along with a few other sensitive parts of her body. It suddenly didn't feel so cold out here, after all. "That's...really nice of you, Beck. I'll keep it in mind."

"Especially this time of year," he went on as they returned to the back for the final tree. "My work's pretty much stalled until most of the snow melts, so I have plenty of time to kill." He started dragging the remaining tree, and she wondered what to say. About his work.

"I guess nothing has changed then? In terms of the trees behind the inn?"

He gave a short shake of his head as he walked, evergreen in tow. "Nope—with sincere apologies to Meg, they're gonna have to come down."

Even though any other answer would have surprised her, hearing it hurt her heart for Meg all over again. Which made her take another stab at changing it anyway. "And I guess there's nothing anyone could say—about nature, or neighbors, or anything else—that would make you reconsider?"

He glanced over his shoulder as they rounded the corner of the building onto Harbor Street, his expression still pleasant. "I understand and respect why you're asking. But it's beyond changing at this point."

Watching as he set the tree upright, she pressed onward, albeit in a slightly new direction. "I'm sure Lila's still not happy about that."

"Nope, definitely not."

"Did you, um, make peace with her the other night like you hoped? Or...not?"

"On that part I think I'm actually making some headway," he said—which she found difficult to interpret under the circumstances.

"Well..." She glanced toward the newly relocated trees. "Thank you for the help. I really appreciate it."

"No problem," he told her. And that was when she realized that somewhere between the time she'd started dragging trees and now, a glorious winter sunset had blazed into being, visible above the west end of Harbor Street.

"Look," she said, pointing. Large, dramatic swaths of purple and orange swept across the sky, the colors reflecting in the icy waters below, as well.

"Wow. Beautiful," he replied.

She forgot to feel the cold altogether now, even as darkness fell and turned the already-quiet street a little more intimate. "Um, would you want..." she began, motioning vaguely around them on the street "...to get dinner together somewhere? Or a drink? We could try the Pelican, but if they're closed, the Skipper's Wheel opens at mealtimes most all winter."

The handsome man next to her smiled. "Thanks, Suzanne—and normally I would, but I'm actually on my way to the inn. Lila kind of...summoned me." His expression hinted at sarcasm, and yet he didn't sound the least bit sorry to have been summoned. "Another time, though."

Keep the pleasant look on your face. Somehow. "Sure, yeah. Sounds good."

"Have a nice evening."

"You, too. Thanks again." She turned to shove her way through the door of Petal Pushers, feeling like an idiot. A heartbroken one. No matter what he said, she was pretty sure Beck had made peace with Lila.

REALLY? SUZANNE HAD to get interested *now*? It had been one thing when she'd mentioned spring, but he was pretty sure she'd just asked him out for tonight, as in right this minute.

Beck walked up the street, soaking in that breathtaking sunset, torn down the center of his soul. Maybe he'd been a little torn ever since that conversation about spring. But a big part of him hadn't taken it completely seriously, and had thought it might never go any further.

He'd been drawn to Suzanne from the start, an attraction at first sight when Dahlia had dragged him up to her on the café's back deck one sunny day late last spring. The truth was, if they'd been dating before he'd met Lila, he probably never would have even looked at Meg's sister in a romantic or sexual light. He wouldn't have let himself. Or maybe he'd be so attached to Suzanne by now that he wouldn't even have noticed how damn cute Lila was, period. He'd always been a one-woman man. Not because he tried to be—but because that's just how it worked for him. When he was in a relationship with a woman, she had all of him.

But things hadn't happened that way.

And maybe he was crazy to be pursuing Lila given that she'd be leaving soon, and that they had this big issue between them.

After all, Suzanne wasn't going anywhere. And Suzanne wasn't mad at him. And Suzanne didn't have a family business he was potentially damaging, however unwittingly. Things with Suzanne—despite her baggage—suddenly seemed a hell of a lot simpler.

She was a beautiful woman. He wasn't sure she realized it, but she was. Dark natural curls framed petite, feminine features, honest eyes, and an infectious smile.

He suspected she had a big heart. And he knew that heart had been broken.

And now, here she was, finally trying to open it, to him.

For the first time he could remember in a long while, he wished he could seek his dad's advice. Yeah, they'd knocked heads, hard. Hard enough that Beck eventually hadn't wanted him in his life. But Kenneth Grainger had been wise in many ways. He'd been moral to a fault. And Beck wondered what his dad would tell him to do right now if he could ask him.

Follow your heart.

He didn't know where the words came from. Out of nowhere, actually—just popped into his mind. The simplest advice in the world. And probably not from the ghost of his father—or Christmas past or any other spiritual being. They'd probably come to him because it was just what made sense.

And right now…well, right now his heart told him he'd agreed to drop by Lila's, so that was what he'd do.

They'd exchanged cell numbers at the tree-lighting, but he'd been surprised to get a text from her. I need you to stop by. I have something for you.

When?

How's five?

Maybe she was going to surrender the bulldozer key? Was that too big a thing to hope for?

Probably.

Or maybe she wanted to give him…her.

The longing between them the other night had been palpable. The desire to kiss her had burned in him like a blazing furnace despite the cold. He'd wanted to take her home and to bed almost more than he'd wanted to breathe. But when Cade had come running up to grab his hand, Lila had smiled knowingly and parted ways by telling him to have a nice evening. A nice evening of frustration was what he'd had.

But if he'd learned anything about Lila Sloan so far, it was that she had a penchant for being completely unpredictable. Not his favorite attribute, but at the moment he was a moth and the big Victorian house was a flame. He climbed the steps to the Summerbrook Inn's porch having no idea what to expect.

He rang the bell, figuring it just as likely she'd open

the door and punch him in the face as that she'd open the door and kiss him.

She opened the door and, looking grave, announced somberly, "I made you a hat." Then she held it out.

He flinched. A punch in the face would have been less of a surprise. From her outstretched fist hung a thick winter ski-cap-style hat of dark red with a gray stripe. He would never have guessed it hadn't come from a store or a catalog.

He lifted his gaze from the hat to the woman who held it, nonplussed. "You made this? Really?" He studied it again—it was a damn nice hat. Knitted or something? It looked warm, cozy. "How did you make it?"

"I knitted it on a round loom," she said, remaining just as stone-faced as when she'd answered the door. "It's a faster form of knitting by wrapping yarn around pegs in specific patterns and sequences."

"And why do you sound so serious and glum about it?" he asked.

"Because you don't particularly *deserve* a hat," she explained. "At least not from me."

The woman had been a mystery to him when he'd met her, and she remained a mystery now. He arched one brow, playing detective. "Then why did you make it?"

"Because the only other one you seem to own is ugly as sin and currently residing on a snowman's head. And despite that they sell a variety of lovely hats at the Knitting Nook, you don't seem smart enough to go buy one. So I felt it was my duty as a human being with hat-knitting skills to make you one." She finished on a succinct and conclusive nod.

And he held in his laugh—but a smile escaped him

anyway. Okay, no bulldozer key. But maybe this was better in a way. His father would have called it a gift of the heart. "It's really nice, Lila. Really great," he told her. "Thank you. Even if it pains you to give it to me."

"Put it on," she commanded, still speaking as solemnly as if at a funeral. "See if it fits. Fit can be tricky—there's some guesswork involved."

He tugged it obediently onto his head. It felt good, pleasantly snug. "How's it look?"

"Amazing," she told him, voice still dry. "I knew the colors would be good on you." Only then did she gently bite her lip, her expression finally softening, just a little, her voice along with it. "I've been making them for everyone, for Christmas gifts. But this is the first one I've given to anyone, the first one I've seen on any head except my own. It's kind of…"

"What?" he asked.

She hesitated, clearly seeking the right word—and eventually settling on, "Satisfying. I think I'm pretty good at this. I dabbled in it as a teenager, but the current hats are much better."

"You *are* good at it," he agreed. Not just to appease her, but because the hat on his head was truly impressive. "And I'm honored you would make this for me."

"Don't be," she insisted. "I told you—it was practical. I just don't want you to die in the cold because I'd feel guilty. A large percentage of body heat escapes through the head, you know."

He recalled hearing something about that back in his school days, but Lila's brand of pragmatism amused him and this time a small laugh snuck out. He grinned at her and said, "So are you gonna invite me in? Or—"

he pointed over his shoulder "—should I just take my hat and go?"

"I thought maybe it would be wise...not to," she told him. Back to the slightly softer Lila.

"Why?" he asked. "I don't bite."

"Lots of reasons," she said, pretty much blowing off the question. "And there are worse things than biting." He didn't know if she was referring to sex or land development, but he let it go when she kept talking. "Though unfortunately, I now find myself wondering if you're hungry."

"If that's a question, I could eat," he told her. Then raised his eyebrows, offering up another small smile. "Grilled cheese?"

She shook her head. "I have a sort of chicken and stuffing concoction simmering in Meg's Crock-Pot."

"Sounds good," he said, and just then caught the aroma wafting conveniently down the hall to greet him. "And smells good, too."

"I'm not much of a cook," she confided, "but the Crock-Pot does the work. And the recipe makes way more than I can eat, but desperate times—by which I mean Summer Island in winter—call for desperate measures. So I suppose it only makes sense to offer you some."

"Well, if that's an invitation to dinner, I accept. But, um, one problem."

"What's that?"

"Unless you're packing me a to-go plate, this means you're gonna have to let me in."

She sighed. "That's the unfortunate part." Then stepped aside to let him cross the threshold.

THEY MOVED AROUND the kitchen in relative ease, setting the table together, getting drinks from the fridge, Beck growing more grateful every minute that Lila seemed to be relaxing with him again. Until she started to take the lid off the slow cooker, only to stop and say, "Dinner's gonna cost you, Indiana Jones."

Did she have any idea that calling him that transported him back to the hot, tension-filled moment by the Christmas tree when he'd known they were about to dive on each other? He pulled himself back from it, refocusing on the moment at hand. "Cost me how?"

She tilted her head, looked curious and thoughtful. "You said some cryptic things the other night at the tree-lighting."

"Uh-oh." He had. Then wished he hadn't. And had been thankful when she'd moved on from them.

Sounded like now she'd come back. "Uh-oh is right, *Becker*. I want to know about your father. And your... marriage." Did she actually sound pained saying the last word? Did she truly care? It was the opposite of what he'd have expected, but again, Lila was the queen of unpredictability. "So you have to tell me over dinner. Or no chicken for you. Deal?"

He took in a breath, blew it back out. Unpleasant subjects, and ones he never talked about. But what the hell? He'd get through them quickly and be none the worse for wear. "Deal," he said. "If you care so much and want to know so bad."

"I didn't say I cared."

The denial made him smile.

"I'm just curious," she claimed. "Maybe I'll find out what makes you so Grinchy and hard-ass when it comes to your work—when you seem, otherwise, like an at least fairly nice guy."

He shot another smile in her direction—or maybe it was more of an amused smirk. But as he used a wide spatula to scoop a boneless chicken breast covered in a cream sauce and stuffing from the Crock-Pot and onto his plate, he said, "If I'm a Grinchy hard-ass about my work, it's because it's my work. Business. What you call Grinchy I just call doing my job and not getting emotional over it."

She shrugged, taking the spatula from his out-stretched hand. "You might get more emotional if it was *your* family's trees."

He was quick to assure her, however, that the answer to that was, "Probably not, actually."

"Ah, so you hate your family," she said like someone interrogating a criminal as they took seats across from each other at an antiqued, farmhouse-style kitchen table.

He only laughed at her amateur detective work. "No—afraid it's not that dramatic."

"Then start talking—tell me everything."

I'll tell you just enough. He thought about where to begin, how to say as little as possible without her realizing he was cutting corners. *But hell—just go for it, get it over with, then you can eat your chicken.* It smelled delicious and looked good, too, and he thought she might be as much a Crock-Pot gourmet as a loom-knitting savant. "Okay, the deal is—I was estranged from my dad for the last ten years of his life."

CHAPTER FOURTEEN

"WHOA." HER EYEBROWS shot up, and her fork stopped mid-bite. "That's not dramatic?"

He shrugged. "Okay, I lied. Fairly dramatic."

"What did he do to you? To make you…you know, estranged?"

Beck weighed the question. There was no short answer. He'd thought he could tell her succinctly, but he'd been wrong. Damn. *Okay, start. Say something. Just tell her.*

"He was a minister," he said.

"I didn't see that coming. You don't seem like a minister's kid."

"Maybe that was the problem," he said with a tilt of his head. Then went on, being honest. "But…it was a lot more than that. We valued different things."

She peered across the table at him with big hazel eyes. "I'm intrigued. Go on."

"A big part of his ministry," he said, pausing to take a bite, chew it, swallow, "was giving to the less fortunate. Which I admire, don't get me wrong. But he often gave at the expense of his family, his children. He sometimes gave away *our* things, even things we'd worked for—earned."

She blinked, looking taken aback. "Wow, that's intense." He supposed most people could remember being young, valuing certain possessions—be it toys or clothes or sports equipment or something else—and learning a work ethic in order to get those things. And he appreciated Lila acknowledging that what he'd just told her kind of sucked when you were only a kid.

"He was the most charitable man I ever met," he told her, "and he was trying to teach my sister and me to be charitable, too—but he took it too far. As in, 'You've got a roof over your head and a warm bed to sleep in, so you shouldn't mind giving your bike to a needy child for Christmas.'"

"Oh." She looked truly shocked. Which he continued to appreciate. "That's…awful."

"I lost more than one bicycle that way. And a video game system. Basketballs, footballs, a catcher's mitt. A boom box or two. You name it—if it was something a needier kid might want, it was fair game. And, for what it's worth, it's not like we were rolling in dough ourselves. We…got by. His job paid the bills. But we always lived in a small rectory house next to the church, drove a beat-up car, never took a vacation. So, all in all, his acts of charity always made me feel poor, and more like he was hurting *us* than helping someone else."

"I'm sorry," she whispered softly. Possibly the softest words she'd ever spoken to him.

His next words came without forethought. "Does that make me greedy?"

"No," she said quickly.

"Because sometimes on the news you see some kid who has decided to give all their Christmas presents to someone less fortunate. And I always think it's admirable as hell. Because I sure didn't have that kind of vision as a child."

"Well, it's an extraordinary act. That's why it made the news—it's rare," she pointed out. "I'm sure the rest of the kids out there are just being kids and liking their presents as much as you and I did. And…it's different when it's being *taken* from you. You never really had a chance to give if the choice was never yours."

He just looked at her. Damn. Talk about hidden depths. The unexpected insights went so far as to squelch that tiny voice inside him that feared his dad might actually have been right.

"And all this was enough to make you eventually cut ties with him?" she asked.

"There was more to it than that. He didn't…" Ah, shit. He'd walked right into this—suddenly seemed to be spilling his guts here. *Great job saying as little as possible.*

But again—hell, why not? Why not just put it out there? He was proud of the man he'd become, no matter what his father might think of his choices. Even if Lila Sloan might take his dad's side on this one. "He didn't like the professional paths I followed or the way I conducted business."

Her eyes narrowed. "Like cutting down the trees behind people's houses?"

He shot her a look, let it be his only response to the remark before going on. "I wanted to make enough money to be comfortable and have nice things. So I learned skills and worked hard. I started in construction, then became a foreman for a large home builder. From there, I got interested in land development and worked my way into a lucrative career where I've ended up doing better for myself than I ever set out to or knew I could. And if any or all of that is a crime, then I'm guilty."

Across the table, she paused her fork and knife to eye him curiously. "I'm still not sure I understand the estrangement part, though."

Yeah, it was complicated. Harder to explain than he'd realized. "He...wasn't proud of me. The opposite, in fact. He thought I was greedy, that I worshipped money more than God, just because I didn't give most of it away."

"Did you?"

"I guess I think the two acts can co-exist. God wasn't mad at me. My dad was."

"Fair enough," she said.

"And then one Christmas, I got fed up." He probably could have shut up and been done at this point, but he suddenly wanted to tell her the rest. "I was in my late twenties, making some money, enough to buy every-body some nice gifts for Christmas. I bought Dad a good leather coat—one I knew he'd like. And he *did* like it—but he wouldn't let himself *enjoy* it. He went on about how it was too much, too expensive. And then—by God—he gave it away."

"What?" Across from him, she blinked, jaw drop-ping.

Her surprise was gratifying and urged him on. "Yep. He gave it to a poor man on the street. I'd really wanted him to have that coat, Lila. It meant something to me to be able to give it to him. But it didn't mean any-thing to him.

"And that was the last straw for me. Between that and the constant criticism, I decided I didn't want him in my life." He stopped, shook his head. "Don't get me wrong—he was a good man. People who benefited from his kindness would probably say he was a *great* man. But he and I operated on two different levels—and he couldn't accept mine or stop judging me for it.

"After that, I only saw him at Thanksgiving and Christmas, and I kept contact to a minimum even for the few hours I spent around him on each holiday. And I was happier. Might sound cold, but it was the best thing I ever did for myself."

"It's not cold if it was…taking care of yourself," she reasoned. Which he found more charitable than anything his father had ever said to him. And again, unexpected. And again, wise.

"Thank you for…getting that," he said. "For getting the whole thing."

Rather than respond to the thanks, though, she took a bite and moved on. "And so you…also said you were married." She spoke lower now, reminding him how uncomfortable she seemed with that. He wondered why.

"Have *you* ever been? Married?" he asked.

"Me? *No.*" She said it as if he'd suggested something preposterous.

"You sound…against it," he observed.

But she shook her head. Wiped a napkin across her mouth. "Not at all. I've just never found anyone who… rocked my world in that way. Like in a forever, unconditional kind of way. Not even close."

"No?" He raised his eyebrows. "No great loves—nothing?"

"No," she answered, light and a little terse, as if perhaps embarrassed by it. "I mainly run into the kind of men who, say, mow down the trees behind my grand-mother's house without a care."

He narrowed his gaze on her, tried not to smile. "Ah. Ruffians."

"But about your wife," she said, shooting him a pointed look. "Don't think you can change the subject without me noticing."

His wife. He sighed. Where to begin. But this part he *would* keep simpler. "I married Chandra seven years ago. We were both thirty-two at the time. And our marriage was pretty much…one disaster after another. And you know how they say tragedies either bring you together or pull you apart? For us, it was the latter. Her mom passed away after a long illness. Her brother died in an accident. Then she wanted to get pregnant but found out she couldn't have kids. It was all hard on her—and I tried to be there for her as best I could. But—" he shook his head "—it wasn't enough. I couldn't fix anything. Wished like hell I could—but… well, over time she just shut me out. And then my dad was diagnosed with stage four bone cancer last year."

Across from him, Lila sat up straighter in her chair, went stiffer. "Oh." A tiny gasp. Even having heard his dad was deceased, she clearly hadn't seen that coming. No one ever did.

"Chandra wanted me to reconcile with him," he told her. "But I chose not to. And hell, maybe I should have—who can say? The but the fact is, he seemed fine with having me out of his life—and all things considered, I figured hearing from me might do him more harm than good. Anyway, the marriage was already shaky. I even think she might have been cheating on me. Regardless, my dad's illness was the last straw—

we separated and divorced quickly, and frankly, it was a relief. It ended a little over a year ago—but it feels much longer."

"Why is that?" Lila asked, head tilted inquisitively and looking pretty as hell.

He shrugged. "Like I said, it wasn't a great marriage from the start—fraught with problems. And not having kids, we don't keep in touch or anything, so it just… feels like it happened a long time ago. Maybe because my life is more peaceful without her."

"And did this sour you on the institution?" she inquired, eyebrows raised slightly.

He shook his head. "No. Truth is—she kind of pushed me into getting married—and I let it happen. Neither one of us was in it for the right reasons. I think she saw in me…what she thought I could give her, not who I was. And for me—well, guess I figured if I wasn't gonna be close to my *own* family it might be nice to have another one. But if I ever get married again, it'll be because my gut tells me it's right, because my gut tells me this woman is my other half, forever."

"Sounds like maybe no one's really rocked your world, either," she said, again sounding all-wise.

And even as he reluctantly agreed, "Maybe not," he found himself weighing things. Women. Her. Suzanne. He wasn't necessarily looking to have his world rocked right now—he just wanted to find a nice lady to date. But like it or not, the two women in question both made him feel things. Better things than Chandra had.

"And so the bone cancer is why your dad…died?" Lila asked cautiously.

He ate a bite of chicken before answering. He'd been talking so much his food was getting cold. "This past spring. It'll be the first Christmas without him. Gonna be hard for my mom and sister."

"Are you going home? For Christmas?"

He nodded. "They all live in northern Kentucky, just across the Ohio River from Cincinnati. I was born and raised there."

She smiled, making him realize he still hadn't seen enough of that and he liked it. "Kentucky," she mused. "Nothing about you says Kentucky."

He shrugged. "It's a beautiful state. Though the area where we lived was more suburban than you're probably picturing." He grinned. "Guess I'm still a pretty classic Kentuckian at heart, though. I mean, I know the most important things in life are the three *B*s."

She leaned forward curiously. "Three *B*s?"

"Bluegrass, bourbon, and basketball." He added a wink to say, "Though I'm especially partial to the latter. I'm a big University of Kentucky fan."

At this, however, her face went wooden. "Oh my God—no way."

A reaction he hadn't expected. "Why?"

"Because Michigan rules."

Beck just rolled his eyes. As if he and Lila didn't have enough roadblocks already. He usually had to do verbal battle with Duke and Louisville fans, but Michigan was another longtime rival to his beloved Wildcats. "Oh brother." Though…maybe it came as a nice surprise that she knew something about college basketball.

"And you live in Michigan now," she pointed out.

"But I bleed blue, baby." It was a common statement from Kentucky fans—having no professional sports teams of any kind, Kentuckians were loyal to their blue and white. It wasn't a school thing—it was a state thing.

She tilted her head and asked, "Why did you come here anyway?" And something in the question told him she'd moved on from basketball.

"I scouted around for the right location to buy some land I could develop in a lucrative manner. The search led me north, and I considered Mackinac, but most of the undeveloped land there is part of a park—untouchable. Summer Island turned out to make more sense, financially and otherwise."

"Well, that's definitely my loss," she replied pointedly. A common sort of response from her—but a little jarring to Beck after the last few kinder minutes. She clearly wanted to make sure he didn't forget. Maybe she wanted to make sure *she* didn't, either. She worked so hard to keep that little wall up between liking him and accepting the reality about the woods behind the big house where they sat sharing a meal right now.

So he answered in a different way than usual. "For what it's worth, Lila, I'm truly sorry about that. I can't do my job if I get attached to every rock and tree, and believe it or not, I really do try to improve the world through my work—but regardless of all that, I'm sorry it affects you and your family in a negative way."

"I don't think that's why you really came here, though." Clearly his apology had been a waste of time—she had her detective voice back on.

"What do you mean? It's the perfect place for a new development—ripe for growth."

"I think you came here to get away from things."

"Things?" He raised his eyebrows.

"Your dad's death. Your divorce. The past."

He supposed he knew all that already—so why did his chest tighten at the accusation? He ignored the reaction, tilted his head, and narrowed his gaze on her. "Well, how much do I owe you for the psychoanalysis, Dr. Lila?"

"Some trees would suffice," she quipped.

He gestured toward the room she always called the parlor and reminded her pleasantly, "I already brought you one."

"I prefer them still living, in the ground." She saved him from replying to that by shifting without segue, gesturing to an old-fashioned cake stand on the kitchen counter. "Dessert? I bought a pumpkin pie from Koester's deli."

"Sounds good," he said. And it really did. More than he could have anticipated. Sometimes it was the simple things in life. And right now it was just pie. With Lila. And the fact that she still wanted to share it with him even after reminding them both that she wasn't forgetting about the trees.

And despite everything wrong with this December, everything wrong between him and Lila and the inn, everything wrong with his life in general now that she'd forced him to ruminate on it in a way he usually avoided, he couldn't deny that…damn if he hadn't somehow started enjoying the holiday season more than he typically did. He'd never disliked Christmas, though his father had made it hard to love it as much as most kids did. He'd still liked it well enough in a low-key way. But certain interactions with Lila were making a few holiday traditions better. Better than usual. Better than they'd have been without her. If he'd come here to get away from things, maybe it had worked.

Together, they cut the pie and put it on plates. Beck liked being closer to her, same as when they'd dished up the food from the Crock-Pot side by side. He could smell her—some feminine, powdery scent—and that little skitter of electricity crackled through his veins. It happened more when they accidentally touched in small ways, like when he passed her the spatula, and again, now, when she'd handed him a dessert plate from a cabinet. But he stayed aware of it even when they didn't.

"Let's have dessert in the parlor," she suggested, and they made their way down the quiet hall and into the big front room, made more cheerful by the lit-up evergreen next to the window.

"How's the tree?" he asked, admiring it.

She cast a look in his direction that he almost read as shame. "Well, despite myself..."

"Yeah?" he prodded.

"I'm enjoying it," she confessed. "I don't like admitting that to you, but...thank you. Because it's made the room more merry. And brought back a lot of good family memories. It's made me...regret not coming here more. As an adult, I mean."

Plates and forks in hand, they both sat down at opposite ends of the sofa. It faced the fireplace—as usual, alight with warming flames—but they both faced *each other* as they ate their pie. "What made you stop?" he asked, thinking how fondly she spoke of time spent here in her girlhood.

"Meg got leukemia," she told him.

All the blood drained from his face. "I didn't know that." Meg was the picture of health and vitality. "Is she...okay?"

Lila was quick to nod and assure him. "Oh—yes. It happened a long time ago. When I was in high school. She recovered and has been fine ever since."

"Good. That's a relief." He cut into his pie, took a bite. "But…what does that have to do with you not visiting the island more?"

"Meg came to the inn after her treatment, to spend time with my grandma while she got better. And then after that, Gran died—quite unexpectedly. And I…"

She'd gone suddenly sullen. "You…?"

She peered past him for a moment, into the lights of the Christmas tree, but then drew her focus back to his face. "I couldn't handle any of it—Meg's cancer or my grandma dying—so I just kind of hid from it all down in Ann Arbor like a useless coward." Her eyes had dropped to her plate by the time she finished speaking.

And Beck wanted to hug her. For what she'd just said. For the sadness in her eyes right now. "Lila—my God. You were in a teenager. Don't be so hard on yourself."

She shrugged, lifted her gaze again. "That's what Dahlia and Suzanne said, too. Because apparently I can't stop talking about this lately." She gave a quick, self-deprecating eye roll. "But the upshot is… I wasn't there when Meg needed me." She scrunched up her nose. "I've always felt bad about it. I've always let it keep me away. I've only been here for a few short visits since she took over the inn fifteen years ago. I've always let the whole thing make us…not as close as we might have been. I've been trying to fix it, though." She sounded more like a little girl at the moment than the usually sassy woman he'd come to know.

"What made you come back now?" he asked gently.

"I wanted…to give Meg some time away. She never leaves, except just briefly around the holidays. She doesn't like to leave the house for long. Funny, since so many houses here sit empty all winter. But it has something to do with Gran, I think—her need to watch over the place. So I offered to watch over it *for* her."

Beck tried not to feel her words too much. Because, for once, she wasn't pointing out the whole tree issue—but he suddenly *felt* it, in his bones, way more than any other time it had come up. He instantly understood—in his gut—why it mattered to her so damn much. Because these people loved this house like it was a member of their family. And Lila had been in charge of caring for it on the day Beck's bulldozer had shown up. His stomach sank like a brick.

And yet—maybe because he didn't want to keep thinking about that, and maybe just because he'd been wondering about this from the start—he moved past that, yearning to understand something else about her. "What else?" he asked. "What else made you come?"

"That's all," she claimed. Blinking. Twice.

"I don't think so," he said softly.

She blinked again. Pursed her lips. Shifted back a little toward the more belligerent Lila. "What do you mean, you don't think so? Are you a mind reader now?"

Oh, sure, it had been fine when she was the one doing the psychoanalyzing. "More of a face reader," he said, "and yours doesn't hide as much as you think."

"I think my face does just fine," she said smugly, "given that no one else has ever said something like that to me."

"Then I'm just smarter than them. Or I can see something in you they can't."

"Oh?" she challenged. Both of them still held their plates and forks, but the half-eaten pumpkin pie lay all but forgotten.

"That anger I once asked you about," he said. "You're so sure *I* came here running from something— but Lila, honey, I think maybe that was the proverbial pot calling the kettle black."

Lila just looked at him. He'd used the endearment tenderly—with compassion. Why could he see it, her anger? She'd truly thought she hid it well. Or at least masked it behind an entirely *different* kind of anger— about the land and the inn. Given that, Beck should be the last person able to see that something else haunted her.

She hadn't told anyone. No one at all.

Well, except Whitney. Who hadn't believed her, and had then even blamed her.

Maybe that was part of what had kept her quiet about it all at Thanksgiving, too. What if her parents didn't believe her? What if Meg didn't believe her? What if Meg thought it was her fault—thought she hadn't done enough to stop it? What if Meg thought she *still* wasn't doing enough to *fix* it?

And so maybe…maybe she *could* tell him. If he pulled a Whitney and turned it back on her—well, that would be all she'd need to send him packing and con-clude he was the same jerk she'd assumed in the begin-ning. And maybe that would even be a *good* thing in a weird, backward sort of way since it would end the guilt she felt being nice to him—guilt about Meg, and newer guilt about Suzanne, and an even newer guilt that had something to do with…selfishness, the self-ish indulgence of being with him. Oh, what a tangled web she wove—and she hadn't even been doing anything deceitful, or technically wrong.

In fact, ever since she'd really started trying to do some good in the world, it had pretty much backfired in her face. When she'd tried to watch the inn and be a good sister to Meg, Beck and his stupid bulldozer had come along. Before that, when she'd tried to do a meaningful job that helped people, Simon Alexis had ruined *that*, and so much more.

All right—here went nothing.

"Do you know who Simon Alexis is?"

Beck squinted, tilted his head slightly. "Mega-rich guy in Chicago? Does a lot of philanthropic stuff?"

She nodded.

"Why?"

"Well, until a few weeks ago, he was my boss. Then he lured me to his house, held me down, and tried to force himself on me. And after I got away—he fired me."

CHAPTER FIFTEEN

FROM WHERE LILA sat, Beck's eyes appeared to blaze with rage. "He *what*? Oh my God, honey—are you okay? Did you press charges? Where is he now? Behind bars, I hope—and if not, he might wish he was if I ever get hold of him."

His reaction almost overwhelmed her—a rush of emotion came *whooshing* over her like a gust of wintry northern Michigan wind. She wanted to answer all his questions—even though the answers were kind of awful. She wanted to hug him—for caring, and even if he couldn't really beat Simon up for her, she kind of liked the sentiment. But mostly, she just wanted to express her profound gratitude.

"Thank you, Beck—so, so much," she said, setting her pie aside on the coffee table and spontaneously reaching for Miss Kitty, who was innocently padding past on the floor. She drew the docile cat up into her lap and hugged her close without quite knowing why.

Beck looked bewildered. "For what?"

"For believing me," she said simply. And then, like a breath she'd been holding for a very long time, a bunch of words came flooding out of her. "The only person I told didn't believe me. Because everyone thinks he's so wonderful. I thought he was wonderful, too. Really wonderful. But he's not. And no one wants to know that. No one wants to find out that a man who helps so many people in so many ways is just a great big Harvey Weinstein underneath it all. And that's why she didn't believe me."

"Who?"

"Whitney. My best friend. She works for him, too. Got me the job, in fact. And I know she just couldn't quite believe he could do something like that, but I couldn't believe it, either. Part of me still can't. Part of me still wants to find some way to explain it all away and turn him back into the man I thought he was.

"But at the same time, she's my best friend. And when I went to her after it happened, totally freaked out, she accused me of exaggerating the whole thing. Or it being my fault. She threw both of those at me. I couldn't believe she'd do that to me. It was—and still is—awful.

"So...to answer your question, no, I'm really *not* okay. And yes, I'm not even a nice enough person to have come here only to give Meg some time away. I came because I lost my job, and I lost my friend, and I lost my dignity. And no place is better for making you feel far away from the rest of the world than Summer Island."

In one sense, she felt sick. To go back there in her heart and mind—back to Simon's house, back to the utter shock and revulsion of it all. But another part of her felt free—free in a way she didn't even know existed until that moment. Because up until that night at Simon's house, she'd never felt particularly trapped in life. But what happened there had trapped her, caged her, leaving her helpless and alone. She'd been pushing it away ever since her arrival here—but it had stayed the whole time, lurking just beneath her skin. And now she'd finally spilled the ugly truth and someone believed her.

No, not just someone.

Beck. Beck believed her.

Now he simply looked at her, his eyes welling with an understanding she'd ached to feel for what seemed like an eternity despite it having been only a few weeks.

"I'm just so relieved you believe me," she whispered, still vaguely aware of holding the cat, running fingers through her calico fur, some nervous form of comfort seeking.

"Of course I believe you," he said softly. "There'd be no reason to lie about something like that. I'm just sorry your friend didn't see it that way."

She glanced past him then, her eyes fixing blankly on frosted panes in the window, not really seeing them, instead seeing… Simon. Not conventionally handsome, but charismatic as hell. Not particularly suave, but just charming and boyish enough that she'd never seen it coming. Any of it.

"On top of everything else, he's married. With kids," she added, her voice sounding tired and sad even to her own ears. "He was…everything I admired in a person. He used his money for good—so much good. The Alexis Foundation helps the homeless in Chicago, aids child advocacy, aids people recovering from natural disasters, helps get fresh water for people in Africa—and more. You name it, Simon supported it. And it was so fulfilling to be a part of that, to do work that actually put all the pieces in place to ensure needed money got into the right hands. It's…maybe the best thing I ever did. It helped me feel somehow like I was making up for a misspent youth. And so...there are no words to adequately describe my shock and horror to discover that underneath the philanthropist hid a monster."

At the other end of the couch, Beck asked gently, "What exactly happened, Lila? I mean, if you want to talk about it. If you don't, I understand."

She drew in her breath, her chest constricting. The details were...hard. She still wondered if she'd...made mistakes, done something wrong, been naive or careless. If she could have, should have, somehow done more to stop it. But the compassion in Beck's warm gaze made her think—*know*—he'd assure her she did nothing wrong. Which, deep down, she understood. But there were so many shades of gray that it could be hard to see the black and white of it—and maybe she needed some help with that. Or maybe she simply needed to get it off her chest.

"The week before Thanksgiving," she began, "there was a company happy hour after work one night. And it was...so normal, you know? Nothing weird or unusual. Simon is a gregarious man, the kind who feels free to throw an arm around your shoulder when he's telling a story, or to wink at you when he says something witty. Harmless stuff—I thought. And...if I'm being totally honest, it had the ability to make you feel special." Just having someone so revered and generous laugh at her jokes and pay attention to her was like having a dazzling light shining down on her—she'd felt a little awed just to be in Simon's orbit. "He was such a force in the world, and I admired him so much."

She stopped, bit her lip, remembering that kind of innocence. Which was a nicer word than *foolishness*.

She felt both—and a million other emotions—to her core.

"Girls like me are...taught to just...be nice, get along, be people pleasers," she tried to explain. She didn't know if a guy, in a guy's skin, who'd lived a guy's life, could ever really, truly understand the slightly different lens through which most women viewed the world. "And we want to see the best in men, and anyone really—and so we expect other people to be thinking the same rational, normal way we are. So...even when Simon asked me to follow him to his house so he could give me some contracts he'd printed out in his home office because he wasn't going to be at work the next day, I never dreamed..."

She thought back, still shaken by the eye-opening experience. "Some people say women ask for it. That if they go someplace alone like that with a man—even a man they trust implicitly—that they're asking for it, that they have to know what's going on and what his intentions are. But I didn't—I swear I didn't." He'd been her boss, her mentor. A guy she'd thought was making the world a better place. "And I assumed his wife and teenage sons were at home.

"Except when I got there, they weren't. When I asked about them, Simon told me they'd left early on the family Thanksgiving trip. And even then, I suspected nothing." She shook her head, feeling foolish again—and a little breathless, her heart beating too hard against her rib cage. She'd been caught up in the lavishness of the house—a palatial estate she'd driven past before but never been invited to. She'd been taking it in, trying to wrap her head around the lush surroundings, marveling that the man she worked with every day really lived this way. Her head had been in such a different place than Simon's.

"The next thing I knew," she told Beck, her voice coming out strained as her body suffered the memory, "he was starting to kiss me, with no warning. It was… so completely jarring I could barely process what was happening. Like—was it just some fond, friendly, I'll-see-you-after-the-holiday kiss? That sounds crazy, I know. But when you're in that situation, your head is spinning, trying to find some logical rationale that isn't…awful. Some way to keep him the man you admire, not one who is…the total opposite.

"But when it became totally clear to me that it was more than a friendly kiss, I pushed him away and said, 'Simon, what are you doing?' I couldn't even look him in the eye for some reason—I remember dropping my glance to the floor. Even then, it was difficult to…to challenge him, question him. I didn't want to have to call him on it—I didn't want to be in that position at all. And maybe that's hard to understand, but—this was my boss, and a very powerful man. I suddenly felt like David up against Goliath, like we'd *always* been David and Goliath but I'd just never realized it until that moment, and that powerful people hold all the cards and can crush you if they think you've challenged them. Or crossed them. Or denied them something.

"Anyway, he said to me, 'I'm kissing you.' Like that was normal, like we were dating or something. And… even then, I still wanted to absolve him somehow and not accept the truth. I told myself maybe he'd just had too much to drink, or that he'd taken some kind of medicine that was having an adverse affect on him. Stupid, I know."

"Not stupid," Beck said, voice low. "Nothing about you is stupid, Lila."

She pulled her gaze to his. To those warm, brown, consoling eyes. And she silently thanked him with her own. Then pressed her lips together tight, going back into that awful moment to try to finish the story.

"I..." She stopped, shook her head. "I just so desperately wanted to make it all less terrible than it was, keep him on the pedestal I'd placed him on. Because... when you put someone on a pedestal that high and they fall off, it's...it's world altering. It changes the way you see...everything."

She swallowed back a lump of emotion and forced herself to continue. "I was so scared, and so caught off guard by it—I remember staring at the floor, at different things in the room, anything but his face because I suddenly found him so intimidating and I just couldn't believe it was happening. I said something like, 'Simon, this isn't right.' And what I wanted to do was call him a cheater and a bastard, but I felt like I was tottering in such a precarious position—still somehow hoping I could just wish it away and turn things back to normal.

"But then he started acting as if *I* were the one not doing what I was supposed to. He said, 'You know we've been fighting a mutual attraction since we first met. It's been growing a long time and we both want this to happen.' He said I wouldn't have come to his house if I didn't want it. He said, 'Don't worry—it'll be our little secret.'

"I remember saying, 'No, Simon, no.' Maybe not as forcefully as I wanted to. And maybe I wish I'd come up with more words to say, something more concrete." She shook her head, remembering.

And Beck said softly, "'No' is pretty concrete."

And wow—whoa. "Oh. You're right. It is." All this time, she'd felt as if she should have done more to regain control of the situation. She'd worried she'd been too quiet, too meek amid her shock and confusion. But she had said no. She'd said no. More than once.

"He laughed," she remembered darkly, "in a mean, nasty sort of way, and called me a tease and a flirt. He kept insisting on things that weren't true, and said, 'Quit being a tease, Lila,' and then he pressed me down onto the couch, and pinned me there."

"When he kissed me that time, there was no more pedestal and no more confusion—I was trying to push him off me, and I couldn't. His hands were on my arms and his mouth was on mine and he was stronger than me and I couldn't budge him. And that—that—" She stopped, chest tight, struggling to breathe normally. "That was when I got *really* scared. Like panicky scared. And I guess it drew up some sort of strength I didn't know I had, because I shoved him as hard as I could and finally managed to push him back. But…" She'd dropped her gaze again, this time to the forgotten pie plate still in Beck's grip, because it would be hard to look *anyone* in the eye and say what came next.

Being under Simon that way, her skirt yanked up, an unmistakable hardness jammed between her legs over her underwear, had been the single worst sensation of Lila's thirty-five years. Even now, in this moment, she suffered the urge to curl up into a protective little ball and try to shut it out. But instead she went on.

"So I did what had to be done. I dug my fingernails into his face and I scratched—hard."

"Good girl," Beck murmured, appearing duly drawn into the intensity of it.

"He drew back just enough for me to knee him in the groin. And that sent him to the floor, so I grabbed my purse and ran out of the house shaking like a leaf."

"Thank God."

She gave a little nod of agreement—then added the kicker. "Of course, I could barely drive, was a wreck the whole night, and I tried to call Whitney but got her voice mail. I seriously considered calling in sick the next day. But since I knew he was going out of town to join his family and wouldn't be at the office, I pulled myself together and went—mainly thinking it would be the quickest, easiest way to talk to Whitney about it.

"So imagine my surprise when I was met at the front door by the HR director who had all my personal belongings in a box and told me I'd been terminated, effective immediately."

Beck's jaw dropped. "Oh. Hell."

She swallowed back painful memories: the deflating injustice of it, along with the embarrassment of having her co-workers observe it all from a distance. "I asked why. She said insubordination. I said, 'Did he mention the part where he attacked me?' And she said, 'I'm not supposed to discuss this with you, but according to Simon, it was the other way around.'

"I just looked at her, looked her in the eye. And I could see she didn't know where the truth lay, but that she didn't know what to do about it any more than I did. Then she told me he was offering me a generous severance package so long as I signed a non-disclosure agreement. I read it, my heart beating like crazy in my ears the whole time, and I was so upset I could barely grasp the words. But I grasped enough to know that while it purported to be about business, it was written in such a way that he was clearly buying my silence on what had happened.

"And… I'm ashamed to say I signed it." Heat filled her cheeks. "Because I was put on the spot, caught completely off guard. And I felt helpless. And I have rent to pay. And I knew no one would believe me anyway. And Whitney proved that when I promptly ignored the non-disclosure and told her everything later that day."

Lila had met Whitney after work for a drink. "I launched into what happened just assuming, you know, that she'd commiserate with me, be outraged for me, be shocked and appalled with me. But instead…she asked me questions." Lila could still hear her ex-best friend's voice. *Lila, are you sure you're remembering it right? How much did you have to drink before going over there?* Her heart hurt reliving that sobering moment when she'd understood Whitney wasn't going to be there for her.

"And then that turned into defending him." *That just doesn't sound like Simon to me. He couldn't have done that—that's not who he is.*

"And then into accusing *me*. Of trying to harm him." *Why would you say such horrible things, Lila? I thought I knew you!*

I thought I knew you, too. Both women had ended up crying, and Whitney had actually gone stalking out of the downtown bar—leaving Lila to pay the bill while she was busy falling apart.

"Her reaction," she told Beck, "let me know I'd made the right decision—horrible as it was and still is. Because if your best friend doesn't believe you, it's hard to think anyone else will.

"And you know what?" she continued, on a roll now. "There was another girl, named Mariah—she held my position before me, and after she'd quit, I heard rumors that she'd claimed Simon came on to her. But I didn't believe it. I didn't believe *her*. Because…he was Simon Alexis, all-around powerful do-gooder. I didn't *want* to believe her. I wanted to work for him. I wanted to do something meaningful like Whitney was. And if *I* didn't believe *her* then, well, of course I can't expect anyone to believe *me* now."

"But *I* believe you," Beck reminded her, and even though she already knew that, it was still nice to hear it again. To be reminded again. "And one thing I know, from experience, is that just because someone gives a lot to others doesn't mean everything about them is good. And this guy…" He stopped, appearing angry once more. "This guy is a piece of shit. He needs to be taught a lesson." And then his voice went back to being softer. "I'm so sorry you had to go through that, honey."

She lifted her gaze squarely to his, pressed her lips tight together, and told him one more thing she felt guilty about. "You don't think it's awful I didn't speak out?"

He just looked at her, let out a heavy sigh. "What I think is that it's tragic shit like this is still happening. Bad enough that it *ever* happened, but still? Now? Even with the whole #MeToo movement?" He shook his head. "I think the guy should be drawn and quartered, but…hell, I can't blame you for not wanting to go down that road. Because it seems like it can be a dark one."

It comforted her to know he realized that. Speaking out sounded so easy when you were on the outside of a situation, but from the inside, not so much. "I went on social media," she told him, "and looked up accusers of high-powered men—and no matter how credible they are, no matter how many of them there are, they still get attacked and blamed. Sometimes by men and sometimes by other women. Always by total strangers. Other people who don't want to let their heroes fall off the pedestal. And that…that just felt too ugly to me. I mean, I already had enough ugliness weighing me down. The attack. Whitney. Getting fired. I knew even as I was reading the agreement that I couldn't take any more. I just wanted to put it behind me. Somehow."

"No one can blame you for that, Lila. No one can say what's right for you. Only you can make that decision. Sometimes we just want to find the peace."

Oh. He got that—because of his dad. He knew about just wanting to leave the bad stuff and go someplace better—because of the way his father had hurt him. Very different situations, but ones that had clearly left them both seeking some serenity, instead of more theatrics or blame or criticism.

Despite his understanding, though, she heard herself say, "The thing is, I somehow thought signing that piece of paper and walking away would put it behind me—but it didn't. It's still with me—in so many ways. And I feel bad, guilty, about just running away, not trying to do something about it. In the same way I feel guilty about being a bad sister. Like I'm always just running away from the bad stuff." She stopped, shook her head, blew out a sigh. "I really *have* been trying… to give more. To Meg, to the world. But I keep failing."

"Hey," he said, pointing his fork at her, "you're not failing at anything. What you gave to your job and to helping people there isn't diminished by what happened. And look how much you care about this place, for Meg and your family."

At this, however, she only shrugged. Trying to feel it, but not really getting there.

"You seem to feel guilty a *lot*," he gently pointed out. "Over things you haven't done wrong."

She took that in, along with a deep breath, turning it over in her mind. Maybe he was right. "Goes back a long way, I guess. To Meg's cancer."

"Honey, you gotta let that go. Seriously."

"Easier said than done," she told him. Knowing something logically wasn't the same as feeling it. "And now I have to feel guilty about not protecting the inn while she's away."

Did another tiny hint of guilt flash through *his* eyes? She'd probably just imagined that, though, since he stayed pragmatic as ever. "Again, not your fault, nothing to feel guilty about." He tilted his head, giving her a long look that reached to her core. "I don't like knowing you feel guilty about things. Makes me sad."

She blinked, surprised, met his gaze. "Why?"

"Just not how I see you," he said.

"How do you see me?"

"Tough. Feisty."

Lila *whooshed* out another sigh. "Whitney always said I hid a lot with my sass."

"Why did you quit? Hiding all that? With me, I mean," he asked.

She shrugged. "You kept asking me why I was angry."

It surprised her when he let out a light laugh. "You don't strike me as a woman who does anything she doesn't want to, no matter how many times she's asked."

"Good point," she agreed matter-of-factly, "because I'm usually not."

"Then…" He leaned forward slightly. "Why?"

Lila narrowed her gaze on the man in front of her, taking him in, thinking about the question. She had no real, solid answers. All she had was… "This makes no sense, but something about you…makes me feel *safe*. Maybe it's because no matter how mean I am, you don't get offended, or mad, or go away."

"Because I like you," he told her. "Even when you're mean. Even when you're fighting me tooth and nail. Even when you're demanding the key to my bulldozer."

"I hate that you like me," she said.

He drew back slightly, clearly confused. "Why?"

"Because it makes it so damn easy to like you back."

The whole time they'd talked, their sock-covered feet had been near each other at the center of the sofa, and now Beck moved one warm foot gently over hers. The rush of sensation it created caught her so much by surprise that she gasped, arched her back, and said, *"Oh,"* the word coming out with an undeniably sexual lilt.

"Really?" Beck asked, dark and seductive eyes widening slightly. "Just from that?"

She bit her lip. "Never underestimate the power of playing footsie on a cold winter's night after a massive confession."

At this, he slid his cozily socked foot upward, over her ankle and up her calf. She slid her other foot over *his* other foot in a warm caress. Their gazes locked, issuing mutual invitations, and he reached for her hand.

He stroked his thumb over her skin as they both rose to their knees to move closer to each other, but even as his palm curved over her hip—he stopped, pulled back slightly. "Wait," he said. "Is this okay? I mean, last time I had no idea, but…after what you've been through…"

"It's okay," she was quick to assure him. "I wanted you then. And I want you again now." And to make sure he believed her about this, too, she lifted both hands to his face and kissed him like there was no tomorrow.

CHAPTER SIXTEEN

THE LAST TIME she'd kissed Beck, she'd been a little intoxicated, a little angry, a little confused—about so many things. Tonight, suddenly, she wasn't any of those things. Tonight she kissed him with clarity, a clarity that allowed pure joy and desire to rush through her veins.

And so it threw her when he drew back yet again. He appeared slightly tortured, and his voice sounded strained as he asked, "Are you sure? Because..."

Oh God, he was *that* concerned for her well-being! No wonder she was so drawn to this man.

And so she told him the whole truth about *this* part of it, too. "Beck, when we had sex the other night, it... made me feel whole again. Because I was afraid what had happened would ruin it for me—maybe forever. And then you came along and, much sooner than I ever could have imagined, it suddenly felt okay to be with someone that way. Because you made everything feel safe. Good. Right. And that's how it feels now, too. So will you please just shut up and kiss me before I change my mind and kick you out into the snow again."

She saw something in him relax as he finally said, "Okay—you convinced me. Get ready for some serious kissing, girl."

"I'm ready," she promised.

And oh—he wasn't kidding. Every commanding movement of his mouth over hers, every slide of his tongue between her lips, glided through her like liquid heat, settling in her core. Pressing her palms to his chest, she pushed him to his back on the couch.

And after that, it was all about instinct and rhythm and primal urges and two bodies in perfect concert with each other. His hands molded her breasts as she pressed the juncture of her thighs against the enticingly rigid length behind his zipper in a slow grind. They separated just long enough to peel off each other's clothes, then came together again.

"I want you inside me," she murmured against his lips.

And the position they were already in made the next obvious move to straddle him, sink onto him, let him fill her, let the sensation wash away thoughts of everything else but him. Pleasure, power, comfort, protection—Beck gave her all those things, almost in equal measure, as he moved inside her. And then he added...bliss.

It came quickly, breaking over her like a tumultuous Great Lakes storm. She hadn't felt this good with a man in...well, had she *ever* truly felt this remarkable with a guy? Had she ever found someone who was the whole package—strong, caring, funny, and oh-so-sexy and good in bed? *Stop. Thinking. Just be in the moment.*

And the moment—along with those that followed—were a fine place to be. Soon he was on top of her, driving deep, rocking her world in a different way, a way not about orgasm but simply about the connection, the unabated knowledge that their bodies had been made to fit together, to move and meet this way. She cried out at each deep plunge, vaguely aware of the fire, vaguely aware of the glow of the Christmas tree as darkness began to fall around them—inside the house and out—but mostly she focused on the man. And when he came, it left her nearly as replete as her own climax had.

The room went quiet, feeling suddenly cozier and more aglow with Christmas lights now that the sun had set—and as she snuggled against him on the couch, he reached around her to pull the same throw blanket over them as before. Then he asked, "Are you gonna make me leave again?"

She bit her lip, searched her heart. There was a lot going on in there to search, but the answer came simply. "No," she whispered.

"Even if I suggest moving to a bed," he said cautiously.

She let out a soft, self-deprecating laugh, remembering how last time that particular notion had indeed been the tipping point, the thing that had somehow brought her back to all the reasons this was a bad idea. Maybe it had been about…taking him deeper into Meg's home, into what was truly the heart of her family's legacy. Still, she said, "Even if."

"Just because… I like beds," he told her lightly. "I'm kind of a big guy, and…"

Oh—she supposed the couch *was* kind of cramped for someone considerably taller and broader than her. "We can go upstairs," she offered.

And after they rose from the couch, both of them grabbing up clothes, he tossed her a sideways glance to say, "I like this you."

"*This* me?" she questioned as they headed naked across the hardwood toward the staircase.

"This you who isn't yelling at me and doesn't seem…well, so mad anymore."

She looked back at him. "Maybe… I just needed to talk about things. Maybe I needed someone to believe me and make it…not my fault."

"So you haven't told Meg? About what happened?"

With another quick glance over her shoulder as they climbed the stairs, she shook her head.

"Why not?"

Drawing in a deep breath as they reached the second floor, she spoke aloud the awful thoughts just now becoming clear to her. "It was all so new and fresh at Thanksgiving. And…maybe I was afraid *she* wouldn't believe me, either. Or maybe that she'd believe me, but judge me for signing the non-disclosure, not doing something more."

He slanted a look in her direction. "I don't know Meg well, but…she's your sister. She loves you. I'm sure she'd be in your corner."

Lila nodded, albeit weakly. "I know you're right. Only… I guess I don't want it to seem like I just took the easiest way out. Since that's what I've always done. With everything."

Next to her, Beck simply shook his head. "You're so damn hard on yourself. Stop it. Come lie down with me. Point me to the right room."

A moment later, they crawled beneath the covers in the yellow room, where after a few false starts, she'd eventually settled. Her grandmother had always felt it was a cheerful room, and even if Lila hadn't slept any better there than in any of the others, cheerful had seemed a good enough reason to stay when she'd grown tired of moving and realized her poor sleep had nothing to do with her surroundings.

Snuggling up with Beck in bed, she listened to his even breathing and realized he'd fallen asleep almost instantly. It was a nice, solid, steady sound. A white noise that came with a delicious hint of masculinity.

I could stay like this. Cuddled with this man. Laughing with this man. Strengthened by this man. I could stay like this.

It seemed a dangerous line of thought, though. For many reasons. So it was a blessing in more ways than one when she soon felt herself drifting into slumber, as well.

WHEN SHE AWOKE to the sun shining in the window the next morning, Beck still beside her, she confessed one more truth to herself. He had indeed restored to her the gift of sleep. Simon had stolen it from her, stolen her peace, stolen her ability to truly relax and find real rest—but somehow Beck brought it back to her.

Not that they'd slept the whole time they'd been in bed. At one point she'd been awakened with kisses. Kisses that she'd eagerly returned—until they'd drifted from her mouth down over her neck, breasts, tummy, and below. They'd had sex twice more.

When he opened warm, sleepy eyes on her in the sunlit room, she smiled gently. "Morning," she said. "How'd you sleep?"

"Like a baby," he said. "You?"

"Same."

Under the covers, he ran fingertips gently up her arm. "Good."

All of this was good. She almost hated to end it. But

she was hungry. And God knew they'd done enough to work up an appetite. "Want breakfast?"

His eyes widened. "God, yes. I'm starving."

"Me, too."

"Waffles or pancakes?"

"Either sound great. What's easiest?"

"Pancakes probably. But…" She stopped, scrunched her nose slightly. "They're kind of Meg's specialty. She makes *amazing* pancakes. Mine are kind of average in comparison."

Next to her in bed, Beck's mouth straightened into a thin line, his brows pressing down on his eyes. "You should stop comparing yourself to your sister, honey. I've never had her pancakes, so you're safe on that count. And I'm sure yours will be amazing, too."

She eyed the man next to her appreciatively. She didn't mean to be self-deprecating when it came to Meg. And it wasn't Meg's fault or anyone else's—just a lifelong habit. But maybe one she *should* try to break. "You're a good man, Indiana Jones."

He grinned, then leaned over to drop a quick kiss on her nose. "Need help in the kitchen?"

She shook her head. "I've got it."

"In that case, mind if I take a quick shower?"

"Not at all," she told him, pointing to the bathroom. Every bedroom had been fitted with one when Gran had transformed the house into the Summerbrook Inn. "I'll be downstairs whipping up amazing pancakes when you're done."

Ten minutes later, she was moving around the kitchen, heating a griddle plus a separate skillet for brown-and-serve sausage links she'd found in the freezer, and mixing up pancake batter in Meg's robe.

This was the earliest she'd risen since arriving on the island—probably because she felt better rested than she had in weeks.

Sleep—a thing she'd never thought much about until she couldn't get any. She remained grateful to Beck for helping her attain some good slumber, for making her feel safe enough to surrender to that mysterious place we go each night. She bit her lip, stirring the batter with a big wooden spoon like Gran used to use. What was it about him? How could she feel so safe with a man intent on hurting—killing—something she cared about?

She stopped stirring, shut her eyes. She didn't want to think about that. She was so *tired* of thinking about it.

But not thinking about something didn't make it go away.

Still, just have a nice breakfast. Everything else about him is wonderful. And don't forget, he believes you about Simon! He believes you! That counted for a lot. Surely it made up—at least in some ways—for the one thing wrong with this situation.

When he entered the kitchen a few minutes later, fully dressed in the clothes he'd worn yesterday, the sausage sizzled and a batch of pancakes were ready to come off the griddle. "This all smells great! My stomach is growling. Sure I can't help?"

She glanced over her shoulder at the handsome man she now felt profoundly connected to. "Um, you can grab some drinks from the fridge since I forgot to put coffee on." She sneered her personal disappointment. "But there's OJ and milk." Then focused on flipping pancakes with a wide spatula.

"I'm a milk guy at breakfast anyway, so that works

for me. What's your pleasure?" She looked back over to see him at the fridge, door open, holding up half-gallon containers of both drinks.

"I'll take orange juice."

As she bustled around—getting the hot food onto plates, asking Beck to grab utensils from a drawer she pointed out with the big fork she used to transfer the sausage—she remembered a very recent time when she didn't even want him in Meg's kitchen. Now, this quickly, he fit here, rummaging in the drawers, taking a seat across from her at the old farmhouse table, digging into the hearty breakfast she'd prepared.

"You sold your pancakes short," he told her, shoveling a man-size bite into his mouth.

And she couldn't deny that they were pretty delicious. "Maybe you're right—guess I make a pretty yummy pancake."

"Damn straight you do."

There was so much to be happy about this morning. Good sex. Good sleep. Good pancakes. Good feelings about herself because being with him reminded her she was…well, just as good as anyone else, flaws and all.

And yet, if last night had brought clarity about how much she wanted to have sex with Beck again, the morning was delivering a clarity of a different kind. A kind she didn't want to feel, wanted to just keep ignoring. But trying to ignore what had happened with Simon and Whitney hadn't worked—and she was pretty sure ignoring the problem with Beck wouldn't, either. She really *couldn't* just keep taking the easy road in life— after a while, taking the easy way became, ironically, too hard to bear.

Even so, she tried to eat, tried to simply enjoy the

moment and stay with the good feelings. Because she was plain sick of all the doom and gloom around her lately—didn't she deserve to be happy for a while? At least for the length of a morning?

But then she realized she'd forgotten to carry the plate of sausage to the table, and when Beck offered to get it, standing up and heading toward the counter, her eyes landed on the bulldozer key near the back door. And she knew—she knew in her soul—that he saw it, too. And wasn't even surprised about seeing it.

She had no idea what that meant, so as he picked up the plate of sausage, she asked quietly, "Aren't you going to take that?"

He played dumb. "Take what?" Carried the plate to the table, sat back down.

"The key."

He forked two sausage links onto his plate. "No," he said evenly. "Not until you decide to give it to me." Then proceeded eating.

"Why?"

"Same reason I gave it to you in the first place. To let you have time to…accept the situation."

His simple words made all the blood drain from her face. Because her growing feelings for him made it painfully easy to forget what lay at the heart of the matter here—but he was reminding her. She sadly confessed, "I suppose I sort of have. Or I've at least run out of ways to try to stop it."

His response stayed just as composed and kind. "I still have no intention of pilfering that key away. You can give it to me when you're ready."

She stopped eating, lowered her fork, pressed her lips firmly together. She'd never be ready. Not to watch those trees fall—and certainly not to give her consent to it. "What happens if…if I *never* give it to you?"

He stopped eating, too, and narrowed his gaze on her. "Honestly?"

She nodded. "Yeah."

"Eventually the weather will clear and enough snow will melt that work can resume, and then I'll get another key for the bulldozer brought over from the mainland."

She drew in a deep breath, blew it back out. "Wouldn't it be easier…to just take the one hanging on the wall?"

He tilted his head. "You sound almost like you want me to."

"I don't want to keep causing you problems," she said. "But at the same time, I can't willingly give you my blessing to tear down the trees."

He met her gaze sadly, sighed. Then cut off another bite from his stack of pancakes. "I still don't want to take the key from you, Lila. You give it to me when you're ready—or not. I'll deal with the situation either way."

He was trying to sound kind, *be* kind. But she could also hear the businessman in him sneaking back out. The man who had a job to do, money to make, obligations to fulfill. She knew businesspeople had to do that, run their businesses. But she liked every other part of Beck better. Maybe his dad had, too.

She resumed eating, as well—but the air had thickened with tension, the silence felt heavy, and Beck clearly thought a change of subject might fix it. "So what's on your schedule for today?"

She blinked uncertainly, almost having forgotten

what it felt like to *have* a schedule. "I suppose I might loom knit some, maybe wrap some of the gifts I've been loom knitting, and then probably loom knit some more. And in between all that excitement, I'll probably look out at the snow and occasionally check my weather app. And if it doesn't snow today, I might get really crazy and walk down to Koester's for a few groceries. After that, I'll probably do some loom knitting."

"Turns out I've got some time on my hands, too," he said in a jocular way that told her he could relate. "I could, um, hang out and walk down to Koester's with you later. Maybe have lunch at Dahlia's or the Skipper's Wheel if either is open. Unless you have too much loom knitting to do to squeeze me in."

He wanted to keep spending time with her. She wanted that, too.

Only…when you really got down to it, what was the point? "There's a problem with that," she informed him sadly.

He raised his eyebrows. "I was right about the urgent loom knitting?" But his tone sounded just cautious enough that she knew he had some idea, joking or not, of what the problem really was.

"Even if I didn't throw you out last night, and even if I loved waking up with you this morning… I still can't get past the fact that you're going to tear down those trees." She'd said as much already, of course, but this time it came out more somberly, more gently.

Lowering her fork to the plate, she looked across the table into his eyes, longing to make him understand what was going on in her heart. "Surely now you get that this is…about more than trees. It's about letting a man take something from me that I don't want to give, feeling like I don't have any control over what's happening. But even if it were only about the trees, and the inn, and Meg, I'd still feel the same way. You make me want to let it stop mattering, but I can't. Because I forget for a while. I forget when you're listening to me, or being sweet to me, or making me laugh. And I forget when you're kissing me, and God knows I forget when you're naked with me. But there always comes a moment when I remember. And that moment is…crushing. That moment makes me feel like I'm betraying Meg. And my grandma. And…myself. Because I can't keep being selfish my whole life—I can't just keep doing what I want and saying the hell with everyone else."

"I don't want to make you feel that way, Lila. I don't want to make you feel any way but good."

She just looked at him. Words weren't necessary anymore. *Leave the trees alone.*

The silent answer, same as ever, came back through his eyes. *I can't.*

"If I could, I would," he told her, out loud.

"And if I could be with you without it being selfish, without it being…me just doing whatever I feel like, as usual, no matter who it hurts, *I* would. But as long as those trees are coming down, being with you is siding with the enemy, and letting Meg down. And I can't be the girl who lets down her sister anymore. Which makes this all just sort of…pointless."

She reheard her own words then—how serious they sounded. Like what had happened between them wasn't just sex, like it was serious and emotional. Maybe he felt the same way—she didn't know. But not knowing, it still embarrassed her, made her drop her focus back to her half-eaten pancakes. And it also reminded her that… "I guess it doesn't matter anyway since I'll be leaving at Christmas. But even if it's just for now—I can't see…past the trees."

She lifted her eyes back to him and their gazes locked again across the table. Her heart beat too hard. She'd ruined something here. Or he had—she wasn't sure anymore who was at fault. But maybe that didn't matter, either. Regardless, he pushed back his chair, stepped up to hers, and bent to kiss her forehead. A silent goodbye.

He lingered there, close to her—she could feel his warmth, his breath on her skin, for a heart-piercing moment—then he stood upright, turned, and walked away. A minute later, she heard the front door and knew he was gone.

CHAPTER SEVENTEEN

BECK SAT STARING out the floor-to-ceiling windows that lined the back of his West Bluff home. The view—in summer or winter—was simultaneously breathtaking and peaceful: Lake Michigan and the Upper Peninsula beyond viewed from Summer Island's highest ridge. It had a way of making you feel utterly secluded, hidden away in the idyllic north woods beauty.

When he'd bought the house with the aim of developing the land on the southern-facing slope adjacent to West Bluff Drive, it had been with the idea of giving more people a view just as stunning, and of bringing more prosperity to the island. He'd never imagined it would hurt anyone, and certainly not to the extent it seemed to hurt Lila.

What if you had known? If you'd realized it would hurt Meg and her family, would you have bought the land anyway? Gone ahead in the name of progress? He shook his head, truly unsure of the answer. Not that it mattered; he couldn't turn back the clock.

The idea of seclusion had appealed when he'd come here—and at certain moments still did. But the truth was: being alone had been better before meeting someone he thought he'd like sharing this all with.

That said, going to bed with Lila and then being sent packing afterward was getting old. No matter the reasons why, no matter whose fault, no matter which one of them couldn't or wouldn't bend on the issue. And sure, it had only happened twice, but he held little hope that a third time would end any differently. And as she'd pointed out, she'd be leaving soon anyway, so maybe the best thing he could do for himself was forget about it and move on.

Great idea, except that's impossible. Because the connection between them had been…real. And for her to have confided in him had *deepened* that connection. And it had torn him up inside—tore him up again now just thinking about it. No woman deserved to experience what she'd been through. He gave his head a light shake, unable to understand how any man, no matter how rich or powerful, could justify such behavior.

And hell—Simon Alexis aside, he didn't exactly enjoy making her feel like she was betraying her sister, either. He thought she was taking an extreme viewpoint, but given all she'd been through, he supposed he could almost understand her way of thinking.

Pondering how much nicer a day this would be if he were down on Harbor Street with Lila right now having lunch with the glow of Christmastime all around them, he walked to the kitchen in sock-clad feet and threw together a ham sandwich, grabbing a can of Coke from the fridge, as well.

Settling at his too-big dining room table—hell, why did a man who lived alone and never had guests need a dining room?—he ate, and thought. Christmas Eve was only a week and a half away. Lila would be gone and he'd quite possibly never see her again. And he'd be in Kentucky, visiting with his mom and sister, and watching his niece and nephew unwrap gifts on Christmas morning. Life would get back to normal. Whatever normal *was*. He'd kind of lost track.

But he supposed one thing was slowly becoming clear to him. Being alone wasn't all he'd hoped or anticipated. His dad's death, the divorce—isolating himself had sounded damn good after all that. But the joys of such solitude had run their course quickly. And if he was honest with himself, maybe he'd been hungering for companionship since soon after his arrival, starting the moment he'd met Suzanne and wanted to know her better. Now, spending time with Lila had deepened the urge not to go through life alone.

The whole time he ate, he found himself staring at the wooden Nativity box still sitting on the table, the papers he'd already looked at in a small stack beside it.

He didn't care to read more about what a rotten guy he was. But, same as before, some long-forgotten sense of duty niggled at him. *The man's dying wish was for me to read this stuff. Maybe I should give it one more go.*

Tossing a crumpled paper napkin atop his now-empty plate, he shoved it aside and reached to warily pull the cedar box closer.

Lifting the lid, he drew out the next group of folded pages and opened them up. He discovered another sermon, dated Easter several years ago, and titled "Ultimate Sacrifice." Beck perused it—words about God having sacrificed his only Son and what we should take from that in living our daily lives. The next sermon he drew from the box was about faith, and a third addressed miracles.

All in all, he mostly just found it a relief that they weren't about him and his shortcomings as a son or a person. And to his surprise, there was something warmly nostalgic about reading his father's more recent sermons. Having sat through hundreds of them in his youth, Beck could almost hear his father's powerful voice delivering the words—there'd been a certain cadence when he spoke that reverberated through the writing on the page. As a child, he'd admired his father's passion, and perhaps he still did. Perhaps the sermons were reminding him of that—and of a time when their relationship had been simpler, better. Just a father and a little boy.

On Sunday mornings, his dad had been a man in a suit in a pulpit, giving guidance to the masses. But on Sunday afternoons, he'd become a father who took his son fishing, or hiking. A smile stole over Beck along with an old memory: a pretend dinosaur hunt at a local park famous for the prehistoric bones and fossils discovered there. Life with his dad hadn't been all bad—no, not all bad by any means.

Beck began reading the next sermon, called "A Cheerful Giver"—yet he'd gotten only a few lines into it before realizing he'd indulged in those softer thoughts of his father too soon.

Turn with me in your Bibles to 2 Corinthians, chapter 9, verse 7. It reads: Every man according as he purposeth in his heart, so let him give; not grudgingly, or of necessity: for God loveth a cheerful giver.

I've talked to you before about my son, Beck, and ways in which we disagree. We approach life differently, my son and I, and it's caused me much heartache as he's become a grown man and gone his own way in the world. I tried to teach Beck to give, to those less fortunate, to our community, anywhere we can—to give just as the Lord instructs us to in His Word. But as he grew up, Beck seemed to resent giving just as much as I love giving.

Beck took a deep breath, blew it back out. Maybe this was a mistake—and maybe this would be the last damn sermon he read. Better to remember his father for dinosaur hunts than this.

But even so, his eyes continued down the page. Perhaps out of morbid curiosity to see just how much his father would denigrate his own son publicly.

Let me tell you a story about Beck that I love, though.

Okay, that was a surprise.

One Christmas some years back when he was a young man earning a good living, he gave me a wonderful leather coat for Christmas. And though he tried not to let it show, I could see the joy he took in it, and it was a fine coat indeed—certainly the finest I ever owned. And I was proud that my son wanted to honor me that way, and proud that he could finally see the merits and satisfaction in the act of generosity.

One cold winter's day soon thereafter, I encountered a homeless man named Robert on the street in downtown Cincinnati who had no coat

*of his own. My heart instantly told me to give
this man my coat—he needed it far worse than
I did, and it would carry my son's kind gesture
to a soul in need.*

Beck had heard all this before, but somehow, this
time, the words struck him in a new way. A homeless
man in winter with no coat? Suddenly, giving the man
the coat didn't seem like such a heartless thing to have
done. Maybe it just took time—and perspective—to
view it differently.

And then Beck nearly fell out of his chair—because
he reached a part of the story he didn't know.

*Just last week, a miraculous footnote to this event
took place. I received a phone call from Robert,
the same man to whom I'd given the coat so many
years ago. He'd remembered my name and that
I was a reverend, and he located me here at the
church through an internet search. And here's
what Robert told me when he called. That the
coat had given him more than warmth—that my
giving it to him had also restored his hope, his
belief that he could turn his situation around. He
wore that coat all winter as he started down the
road to seeking employment and having a home.
Before long, he found himself in a halfway house,
and with a job. And slowly but surely, he saved
enough money to get himself an apartment, and
his living situation continued to improve gradu-
ally over time.*

*Now, all these years later, that man owns a
small home, has a full-time job, and has just*

graduated from a technical college, where he learned a trade that can serve him for the rest of his life. He's gotten married, and he and his wife work tirelessly to aid the homeless. He still wears the coat, even though it's a bit on the tattered side now, he tells me, and he said when he pulled it from the closet on the first cold day this fall, he thought of me—and decided to track me down and thank me for the coat.

Sometimes, you see, a coat is more than a coat, and a gift is more than a gift. You never really know how far one gesture can reach or how much one simple kindness can give to a person. I was grateful to Beck for the gift of that coat. And I was grateful in a different way to be able to give it to our brother, Robert. Now, I'm even more grateful to Beck for his heartfelt gift—a gesture that has carried forward from me to Robert, and now from Robert to every person in his life, to his wife, to every needy soul who in any way benefits from his charitable heart. Look at the lengths one simple gift reached when given cheerfully, with love.

Beck felt a little numb. Nothing about that gift to his dad had been intended to reach so far. He'd just wanted his father to have a nice coat. And he'd been so angry—*stayed* so angry—at him for giving away the gift. But suddenly that seemed like a pretty narrow way of thinking. Suddenly he was pretty damn thankful his dad had given the coat to a man who needed it more.

He blew out a breath, still staring at the handwriting on the page. His first impulse? Tell Lila. Tell Lila there was more to the story, and how much good had come from what he'd thought was something bad.

Of course, he couldn't do that. Lila didn't want him in her life. And hell, maybe she shouldn't. *Read a story like that and it makes a man think. Maybe I am the bad guy and I don't even know it.*

Just then, the doorbell rang, making him flinch—it was the first time he'd ever actually *heard* his own doorbell. His heart expanded with hope: maybe it was Lila.

He rushed to the door and swung it open—to find Cade Walton standing on his porch dragging two saucer sleds behind him. "Wanna go sledding? Grammy said I should call first, but I said, 'Becker won't mind.' I even have a sled to lend you. In case you don't have one."

Beck just smiled down at the kid, again so bundled up that he was mostly a pair of little eyes peering out from between various cold weather garments. "I don't," he said. "Have a sled, that is. So lucky for me you brought an extra."

Even without being able to see Cade's grin, it came through in his gaze—and in small, frenetic leaps of joy. "You'll come? Yay!"

"Of course. Sounds fun. Step inside here while I find my boots and a coat, then we'll find some safe hills to go down."

WHIPPING A WINTER scarf over her shoulder, Suzanne said goodbye to Dahlia, with whom she'd just shared a cup of cocoa at the café, and exited onto Harbor Street. She'd just dropped her gaze to her snow boots, watching to make sure she didn't slip on the packed snow—

when a deep, masculine "Hello" drew her eyes up to Beck Grainger.

She blinked, utterly stunned. "Hi." Then her focus shifted to the miniature person at his side—a little boy. She realized Beck toted two circular sleds. "Um, who's this?"

"Oh—this is Cade. Cade, this nice lady is Suzanne. She sells Christmas trees across the street." He pointed toward Petal Pushers.

Suzanne tried to piece together possibilities in her head. "Is he…?" *Yours*. She didn't quite get that part of the question out.

But he heard it anyway. "Oh—no. He belongs to the Waltons."

Okay, that was sort of a relief. Not that he wasn't a cute kid, but it would have caught her off guard to find out Beck had such a big surprise up his sleeve. Still, she remained confused. "Are they his…"

Beck laughed. "Grandparents," he finished for her. "He and I hang out some. We just went sledding."

All right—now that she had the facts, the situation turned officially adorable and she reverted to her new-found state of smittenness. She smiled up at him, trying to forget every recent conversation with him that had left her a little embarrassed, and also trying to forget he might have something going with Lila Sloan. "That sounds like a lot of fun," she managed.

"It was," the little boy said from behind a scarf too big for his small body. "Now we want some hot chocolate."

Beck pointed vaguely toward the café. "We can head to the coffee shop if necessary, but I thought Dahlia might be open."

"She is," Suzanne assured him on a nod. "And always happy to have a customer—or two—this time of year."

"Then we're in luck," he said to them both.

And though she'd been mostly nursing her wounded pride and attempting to focus on other things, something in Beck's cheerful demeanor made her…not quite ready to give up on him yet. Dahlia was right—Lila wouldn't be here long. And Beck had been enamored of her since summer. "Are you…coming to the Christmas Walk tomorrow?"

He looked surprised. "That's tomorrow, huh?"

She nodded. "Second Saturday in December. Weather forecast is sunny and midthirties, so all the businesses on Harbor Street will be hawking their wares, me included. I'm headed to the shop to mark down my remaining trees and poinsettias. You should stop by."

His eyes narrowed slightly. "Maybe I will." Spoken with an intent that shored up a little of that newly restored hope when she'd least expected it.

"Good," she said with a brisk nod and quick smile. "Enjoy your hot cocoa." She left it at that, heading onward toward Petal Pushers without looking back, remembering that nothing's over until it's over.

CHAPTER EIGHTEEN

As BECK DESCENDED Mill Street toward town, he could already sense the festive atmosphere on the wider thoroughfare below. Sun shone down on the snow-covered island from a wintry blue sky, shoppers in thick coats and snow boots criss-crossed the street, and somewhere he heard the jingle of holiday bells. It was a beautiful day for the Summer Island Christmas Walk.

Wearing the hat Lila made for him, he couldn't deny it was much warmer and more appropriate for the weather than his old one. *But why are you wasting time thinking about Lila? Lila keeps sending you away.* If she couldn't look past the land development behind the inn, that left them at an impasse. Like it or not, Bluffside Drive was a done deal.

A glance to his left on Mill brought into view the Bayberry B&B and next to it, Suzanne's quaint cottage. Suzanne. Who had actually started to seem like a way less complicated prospect.

So maybe he should just do what Lila wanted—leave her alone. Maybe he should just do what Suzanne wanted—the opposite: spend some time with her, ask her out, see where that led.

Turning right onto Harbor Street, he discovered the western end less busy—understandably so as the businesses were fewer here and spaced a little farther apart.

He noticed a couple leaving Dahlia's as an older man entered, and a family lingered outside Petal Pushers perusing an arrangement of holiday wreaths Suzanne had set outside. Narrowing his sights on the shop's front door, he started toward it.

"Oomph."

Beck craned his neck toward the shore side of the street, from where the odd, gutteral sound had come— in time to see the movement of a snowbank, and he realized some of it had collapsed, like a tiny avalanche. Crossing toward it, he rushed past the bicycle livery— the building strung with pine boughs and colored lights, but closed for the season—and upon reaching the place where there now existed a huge gap in the snow, he peered down to see if someone had fallen.

Someone had. Lila.

"Oh God," she said, looking up at him, her face at a level just below his feet. "You? Really?"

She appeared to be fine, just standing in a deep hole, most of her covered in a dusting of white. "Nice to see you, too," he said. "Would you like me to just leave you here and go get someone else to rescue you?"

"That would be taking things too far."

"That's what I thought," he said. Stamping the snow he stood on to ensure it was solid, he bent to reach down a hand to her. "How the hell did this happen?"

"I thought I was on land, but apparently it was only a snowdrift. I was just standing there looking out at the lighthouse and it dropped out from under me." She looked uncharacteristically embarrassed but was clearly attempting to hide it.

Getting her up the embankment from so far below was awkward at best and involved some flailing on her part, until he stooped down far enough to say, "Try to get your arm around my neck."

Once she did, he anchored his own arm around her waist and dragged her up onto what he suspected was the sidewalk—down beneath the snow. Indeed, it had drifted heavily and created the illusion of land where, in fact, the slope dropped dramatically toward the shoreline.

"You okay?" he asked as their bodies slowly separated.

"Yeah," she said on a sigh as he began brushing snow off her coat and blue jeans.

Only, when he was done, it left them standing close to one another. And left him suffering the usual urge to get even closer. And left *her* looking wholly uncertain about all of it.

"You're welcome, by the way," he told her—mostly to break the weird tension.

Grudgingly, she replied, "Thank you."

He barely heard her, though, over the sounds of bells and horse hooves clopping lightly atop the snow. They both looked up to see a red horse-drawn sleigh gliding to a stop beside them. Most places, the sight would have caught him off guard, but here it was just one more Currier and Ives print come to life.

Anson Tate, proprietor of the horse-and-wagon tour company on the island, smiled down at them from the driver's seat. "Hey, you two—sleigh ride?"

"Yes," Beck said—at the precise moment Lila answered, "No."

Beck took her hand, gave her a persuasive look, and tugged her gently in the direction of the big red sleigh. "Come on, it'll be fun."

She got in, but only with an eye roll clearly meant to refute the idea of fun, and stayed just as grudging as she'd been about thanking him for his help. As Anson snapped thick leather reins lightly on the horses' furry backs and the sleigh moved forward, she spoke, keeping her voice low. "Why do you persist in trying to woo me when you know it ends badly every time?"

Beck considered the question. Even though he could argue whether this qualified as wooing given that the invitation hadn't come from him, it was still a fair one. "I don't know, Lila," he said, "maybe I'm just a glutton for punishment." Or maybe it was about what had just happened. He'd been on his way to see Suzanne, after all. His father had seen signs in Bible verses—maybe Beck saw signs in having Lila pop up, or in this case down, everywhere he went. Then he turned and looked squarely into her eyes, deciding maybe it was time to just cut the crap. "Or maybe I'm just really into you."

"Oh." The statement warmed Lila to her core. But she couldn't meet his gorgeous brown eyes after that— so she jerked her gaze forward, to the horses and the snow and the merriment of Harbor Street at Christmastime. She couldn't meet his eyes because it would make her feel his words even more profoundly. And she *couldn't* feel them—she couldn't let herself. Only madness that way lay, and she had more than her fair share of madness going on already. It had been one thing to acknowledge her own growing feelings for him, but to find out he felt the same way—she simply couldn't handle that right now.

Next to her, he said nothing more, instead reaching for a plaid blanket folded on the seat beside them, and spreading it over both their laps. A brisk and biting breeze nipped at their skin and the blanket made her feel cozy and warm. Taken care of. Safe.

She didn't want to be a woman who needed to feel taken care of. But sometimes, *sometimes*, it was just *nice*. And she *did* want to be a woman who felt safe— always. And an undeniable truth remained—Beck had been making her feel safe since the moment they met, since the moment he surrendered that bulldozer key when she'd asked for it. Even while taking something she valued dearly, even while unwittingly making her feel she was choosing between him and Meg, even with all that, he made her feel safe. How was that even possible?

SUZANNE HAD SOLD the last Christmas trees—even if at rock-bottom prices. And by day's end, most of the wreaths and remaining pine boughs had found good homes for the holiday, as well, and the poinsettias were gone except for a few white ones. Those she would donate to Dahlia for the café—maybe take one home for herself.

By most counts, it had been a lovely event—lovely weather, lovely customers, lovely caroling by the choir from the pretty white church at the opposite end of Harbor Street, and a lovely cup of hot chocolate she'd just treated herself to from the Cozy Tea and Coffee shop after closing up Petal Pushers. Dahlia's had closed, too, and darkness now descended over the island— days ended early in December—but the fudge shop, Knitting Nook, and coffee shop still bustled cheerfully with holiday business, along with a few gift shops and boutiques that opened their doors for this one and only occasion in the wintertime. Even so, a knot lay low in the pit of her stomach—no matter how much she tried to distract herself or wish it away.

Stepping back out into the snowy street lit mostly by Christmas lights now, she heard the bells on Anson's red sleigh and looked up to see it coast smoothly to a halt a few steps away. Dahlia and Mr. Desjardins stepped down, laughing, holding hands. Maybe it was the dim lighting, but for a moment Dahlia looked like a much younger lady, a fresh-faced girl in the prime of her life, a woman in love.

Only when Dahlia spotted her, too, and approached did Suzanne again see the vestiges of time in her friend's face. Releasing her companion's hand, Dahlia drew close to Suzanne. "Any Beck Grainger sightings?"

Last night, like a schoolgirl, Suzanne had texted Dahlia about her encounter with Beck outside the café. Now, once again, she felt silly. She attempted to shrug it off with a forced smile. "I thought I caught a glimpse of him out the window heading toward Petal Pushers a few hours ago. But then, next thing you know, he's in a sleigh with Lila." The last words felt like gravel in her throat and she winced a little as she spoke them.

"Perhaps Suzanne would join us at ze Pink Pelican for zomezing to eat?" the ever-suave Mr. Desjardins suggested from a few steps behind Dahlia. Today he wore an elegant wool coat of charcoal gray.

"Oh, that's sweet of you to include me," Suzanne replied over Dahlia's shoulder, "but it's been a long day." Then she looked back to Dahlia and lowered her voice. "He's a keeper." She raised her eyebrows for good measure.

Even in the glow of holiday lights, Dahlia appeared

flushed, almost girlish again, still smiling as she swiped a brightly mittened hand down through the air to say teasingly, "Oh, be quiet." But Suzanne couldn't help thinking that maybe she was getting through to her friend, making her appreciate her lover as...well, more than just a lover.

Though when he stepped up to join them, Dahlia blew out a big sigh, shoulders slumping slightly. "My goodness, all this fun and excitement today has worn me out! Much as I hate to turn down a winter visit to the Pelican, I think I may have to, as well."

Mr. Desjardins, ever the gentleman, looked completely undaunted. "Zen it will be my pleasure to escort my lovely lady home for a quiet evening."

She tossed him a sideways glance. "Fair warning, Pierre—I may fall fast asleep!"

"Zen I hope you will allow me ze honor of holding you in my arms as you drift off to dreamland, my fair flower."

Suzanne caught a light blush on Dahlia's cheeks as she said quietly, "He calls me that sometimes, his fair flower, because of my name."

"Shall we be off, flower?" he asked.

She gave a nod. "We shall."

"Goodnight, my dear Suzanne," Mr. Desjardins said in parting.

"Have a nice evening," Suzanne replied, and when Dahlia cast her a last glance as the two started to walk away, Suzanne mouthed the word: *Keeper.*

DARKNESS HAD FALLEN completely over Harbor Street, but moonlight on snow, accented with Christmas lights on storefronts, lit the way as Beck walked Lila home.

After the sleigh ride, they'd shared pumpkin bread and a funnel cake bought from street vendors set up near the large Christmas tree, both agreeing winter was, in fact, the perfect season for funnel cakes since the snow made it much less noticeable when you ended up wearing the powdered sugar topping. They'd perused some of the shops, each picking up a couple of small gifts for family members, then hit Molly's Fudge for the same purpose, though Beck treated them to a couple of slabs of chocolate-peanut butter fudge—one to share and another for Lila to take home, since she'd mentioned it was her favorite. After listening to carolers, and briefly joining in on a children's snowball fight in the park, they'd stopped into the Pink Pelican for a couple glasses of green Grinch nog and ended up grabbing burgers for an early dinner.

Now the shops were all closed, the Christmas Walk over. A certain finality struck Lila as she watched shopkeepers turning out their lights and locking their doors, knowing most of them wouldn't open again until spring. Their holiday lights would continue to make Harbor Street merry, but other than a restaurant or two, Koester's Market, and once-a-week knitting bees at the Knitting Nook, Harbor Street was officially closed for the season. It reminded her, too, how fast Christmas was coming.

Despite herself, she'd had a wonderful afternoon with the man next to her. And now, the usual inevitable emotions warred in her heart. It seemed that with Beck, she often didn't know exactly what she was going to do or say until she did or said it, and so it was completely without forethought, but ignited simply by how much she enjoyed his nearness, that as they ascended the steps to the inn's front porch, Lila bit her lip and asked, "Do you...want to come in?"

"I do," he said evenly, "but I'm not going to."

"Oh." She tried not to feel the sting or embarrassment of being turned down.

"You look disappointed."

She spared him only a sideways glance. "You claimed you were into me."

"I am," he assured her as they reached the door. "But you said it was pointless, remember? A guy's gotta protect his heart." He ended with a shrug.

She drew in a deep breath, let it back out. Her *own* heart beat a little too hard as she ventured, "Your heart is involved here?"

Another shrug from the handsome man now facing her on the porch. "Would I stay on this roller coaster of emotional abuse otherwise?"

A soft smile stole over her. But it lasted only briefly because of what the words meant. "Sounds like... maybe you're getting off it."

He looked down at her, dark eyes narrowed. Beck and Lila each held a shopping bag containing the day's purchases, but with his free hand, he reached out and grasped hers. Even through the mittens she wore, the touch rippled all through her. "I just don't want to have sex and get kicked out again," he told her. "Twice was enough."

She nodded matter-of-factly. "That's fair. And...it's only a week until Christmas, so... I guess it *is* pointless. Even if hearts are involved."

"Is yours?"

Given that the question made her heart soar with a rush of emotion—the answer was most decidedly yes.

However, she chose to ignore the inquiry and instead tell him, "But it would be nice to see you again. Before I go. I mean, if you want. It doesn't have to lead to sex. It could just be dinner. Or something." All unplanned and rambling. She sounded nervous, uncertain. And afterward knew she might as well have just said: *yes, my heart is involved.*

Even so, he let her off that particular hook and simply replied, "I hear the Skipper's Wheel stays open all winter as long as the weather's okay. Meet me there one night for dinner?"

CHAPTER NINETEEN

ALONG WITH OTHER purchases at the Christmas Walk, Lila had bought more yarn. It amazed her how quickly she went through it, but she'd added scarf making—both infinity and regular—to her looming skills, and she'd just started crafting potholders, too.

The potholders required 100 percent cotton yarn, which turned out to be a whole different animal compared to the much more common acrylic yarns. But acrylic would melt against hot pots or pans, and she'd grown determined to make a set of potholders for the inn's kitchen, so she was learning to work with the much thinner, less-stretchy cotton, and the more she knitted with it, the better she got at managing the tension and the tighter stitches.

Besides, potholders were necessary for another reason, too. She now had scarves and hats for everyone in her family, including Seth's grandpa, who may or may not end up being part of their Christmas celebration. And of course she had hats for Suzanne and Dahlia, as well, which she still planned to deliver before her departure. She'd tried to master mittens, but that was going to take more meticulous self-training at a time when she felt more patient—Gran had been right that she was easily distracted, and the fairly immediate gratification of loom knitting suited her personality.

But after finding a very doable pattern of fingerless hand warmers, she'd soon started producing them at the startling rate of a pair every hour or so. And given that she had no idea what she was going to do with all of them, it made sense to move on to something a person could really never have too many of: potholders. And fortunately, they took at least a little longer than the mod hand warmers.

The day after the Christmas Walk brought overcast skies with light snow on and off. And even more than last evening, when she glanced out the east-facing window in the inn's small library, she sensed the heavy solitude of the island's drift into true winter. Holiday decorations aside, Harbor Street looked like a ghost town.

So it was a good day for looming. She turned on Christmas music—in particular, old albums on a turntable, all located in the attic. Thus Bing Crosby and Andy Williams accompanied her knitting, which she ceased only when it was time to toss another log on the fire, go to the bathroom, or get something to eat.

A frozen lasagna from Koester's baked in the oven, and on knitting breaks, she nibbled on fudge from yesterday. Breaks were bad, though, because they gave her too much time to think. Funny, she'd come here for the peace and quiet, but what did peace and quiet give you but time for reflecting.

Right now, the fudge made her reflect on yesterday with Beck. If she didn't count the ridiculous humiliation of collapsing into a snowbank, it had been a near-perfect afternoon. Even without ending in sex. It had been like one big, long, perfect, unplanned but utterly romantic date.

The bad part was that it just confused her all the more, and left her increasingly torn over her upcoming departure. He claimed his heart was involved now, but what did that mean? And if his heart was so involved, then maybe...but wait, stop. She supposed it was time to quit asking questions and sending up inane wishes about the hillside behind the inn. And when she weighed all the factors, maybe it was just as well she was leaving and wouldn't ultimately have to make any decisions about the sweet, sexy tree-murderer.

Popping a last nibble of fudge into her mouth, then returning to her loom, she resumed wrapping and hooking off tiny loops of yarn that created the u-wrap stitch. She'd made several potholders for Meg already, but this one was unique—she'd fashioned a little gray cat face in the middle of a pale yellow potholder. She would have liked to go calico in honor of Miss Kitty, who currently lay curled up on the rug in front of the fireplace, but trying to replicate a multi-colored cat was just too complicated for this first attempt at creating a specific image with yarn.

Once the cat face was complete, her focus relaxed as she returned to creating a simple field of yellow for the remainder of the piece. Loop, hook, loop, hook. Bing Crosby dreamed of a white Christmas on Gran's old record player—while Lila dreamed of a Christmas that felt simpler and easier than this one, as simple as the repetitive looming stitches she created now.

But count your blessings. Gran had always been big on that: not fretting over anything too long, and if you caught yourself doing it, you were supposed to turn it around and think of things to be thankful for instead. And Lila had plenty to be thankful for.

Her family. Her sister's health. Her own health. The inn—even if what lay behind it would change, the inn was still here, still the special home that had been in the family for four generations so far.

Then she gasped. Because this meant someone needed to have a baby—to keep it in the family. Meg was turning forty, Lila was thirty-five, who knew if Meg would eventually marry Seth or even want to have kids by the time that happened, so...*yikes, that leaves me.*

Okay, don't think about that.

What else are you thankful for?

She looked around.

I'm thankful for this Christmas tree. It's brought me more joy than I could have anticipated when it showed up here unexpectedly.

Her eyes dropped to the coffee table. *I'm thankful for fudge.* Silly, but it was the little things in life sometimes, and Molly's chocolate-peanut butter was the bomb.

I'm thankful for...sleep. At first, she'd credited a couple of good nights' sleep to being in Beck's arms. But ever since that second night with him, she'd slept. Better and better. She was pretty sure it had to do with having told him about Simon, having gotten it off her chest, having someone validate what had happened to her.

But it still all felt as if it was about Beck—about ways he had improved her life since entering it. And she hadn't even yet gotten to being thankful for the good sex, the sweet kisses, the comfort of snuggling up with him in a big red sleigh yesterday afternoon, the warmth she felt whenever she was around him.

I'm thankful...for Beck. Hard to believe. A couple of weeks ago, the very notion would have seemed preposterous. But sometimes life was complicated.

Among the complications, Simon Alexis. Even having told Beck...well, something about knocking down that wall of silence had allowed her to let in more and more questions. Big ones.

How many women had he behaved so reprehensibly with? Had any actually welcomed the attention, coming from such a powerful man? Had any been so disillusioned as to believe they were special to him, that it held some meaning? Had he gone so far as to force himself on anyone? *Wait, stop—use the real word; quit softening it.* So had he raped anyone? Would he have raped *her* if she hadn't caused him bodily harm? Some women might not be strong enough—emotionally or physically—to fight back. Did his wife know? Did his sons? Would they become like him?

And smaller questions, too. How had he explained the scratches on his face to his family? What exactly had he told Kelly in HR when he'd fired Lila? How had her firing been explained at the office—what untrue things had been said about her? What twisted perception of the world did Simon hold that made his actions conscionable to him? Okay, that was a bigger one, but still...the upshot was, she'd never know the answers. She'd never quite completely have full clarity on what had happened to her and why.

She pulled in a breath, blew it back out. *Let it go. You have to.*

She kept looming. Focusing on that yellow yarn. But a large part of her had now returned to that ugly situation and what had followed. She'd not allowed herself to revisit many of the details up until sharing them with Beck—part of being good at running away from things was the ability to compartmentalize, and Lila was a pro at it. Only now, she'd opened that door and started letting it all back in. Along with how much the loss of Whitney's friendship and support had wounded her.

With a sigh, she set aside her loom and reached for her phone on the coffee table. She'd not looked at it much since arriving here other than checking the weather and sending occasional texts, mostly to Meg (*How's the inn?* Meg would ask. And Lila would reply with something vague and innocuous like, *Peaceful as ever.*) She'd come here to turn off the world for a while, and in many ways she'd succeeded.

Now, feeling wistful about her ex-bestie, she tapped on icons that would lead to Whitney's Twitter account to see what she was up to. Had life gone on as normal? Would there be a link to a new fruit smoothie? Whitney was obsessed with smoothies. Or would there be some pithy observation about Chicago traffic, or her latest Netflix binge, or what amazing charitable organization she was currently in contact with via her work at the Alexis Foundation? Or…no, it was Christmastime. So there would probably be links to low-cal holiday treats and—ugh—maybe pictures from the holiday office party. But regardless, Lila wanted to go there, find out—because if you can't bear to look at someone's tweets, you're still hiding. And given that she was leaving Summer Island in less than a week, it was time to stop that.

As she focused on the phone in her hand, though, she couldn't make sense of what she saw. No tweets directly from Whitney, but her page was filled with people tagging her—and saying bizarrely vicious things.

@whitneyventler, you should be ashamed of yourself! Casting aspersions on someone who does so much good for so many. What is wrong with you?

@whitneyventler is probably just looking for some kind of big payout. After all, who better to accuse of something than a rich guy.

@whitneyventler, what an evil slut you are!

Lila stopped, drew back slightly, took a breath. What the hell was happening?

Next, she searched Twitter for mentions of Whitney.

Can @whitneyventler prove her accusations? Anyone can toss an accusation out. I say innocent until proven guilty.

In the case of @whitneyventler vs. @SimonAlexis, I cry foul. She probably had a thing for him and he didn't reciprocate. At worst, she's a spurned lover.

Whatever happened between @whitneyventler and @SimonAlexis, it takes two to tango.

Who is this @whitneyventler chick anyway? Why should anyone believe her? Too many people are just looking for attention, or money, or fame, or whatever. Hang in there, @SimonAlexis! This too shall pass.

Lila's hands were shaking—which made it hard to close Twitter in order to google Simon's name. But when she did, numerous articles, dated yesterday and today, popped up front and center. She clicked on one from the Associated Press—and quickly learned that Whitney had come forward to a reporter at the *Chicago Sun-Times* accusing Simon Alexis of sexual misconduct.

Miss Ventler claims Mr. Alexis made unwanted advances toward her, cornering her in an office, forcefully kissing her and touching her inappropriately. She further claims that declining his advances led to her firing. A representative for Mr. Alexis states that the revered Chicago philanthropist rejects the accusations and falsehoods put forth by Miss Ventler and denies her version of events. According to Mr. Alexis, the rep says Miss Ventler approached his wife with these accusations before going to the press, making her feel threatened. He categorizes Miss Ventler as a "disgruntled ex-employee."

Lila went numb inside. Talk about having unanswered questions. Clearly she'd missed a lot after leaving Chicago. Of course, Whitney hadn't reached out to her, so how could she have known?

Some questions she did suddenly have answers to, though. Now Whitney knew she hadn't lied. And she felt all the more certain Mariah, her predecessor, hadn't lied, either. The only person lying here was Simon. And, of course, Lila had no idea what had happened between Whitney and Mrs. Alexis, but he was clearly trying to make Whitney look like some sort of crazy stalker type. Asshole.

This is why I didn't go to the press. I knew there would be denials. Name-calling. Attacks. She'd paid close enough attention to the #MeToo movement to see that the woman was always accused in return—if nothing else, of being stupid, or complicit, or inviting, or any number of other things.

Now Whitney had been brave, too. Braver than her. And was clearly paying for it.

And maybe from the outside, dealing with that in order to bring the truth out seemed easy—but Lila knew it wasn't. The victim was victimized all over again—one look at Whitney's Twitter feed made that scathingly clear. And Lila simply hadn't wanted to keep being treated like shit.

Chicago suddenly seemed more filled with blame and injustice than when she'd left it—and Summer Island all the more peaceful and inviting as a result.

THE FOLLOWING NIGHT a light snow fluttered through the darkness to coat the island with another layer of white. Lake effect snow meant snow early and often in surrounding areas, and for the hardy winter inhabitants of Summer Island always guaranteed that white Christmas Bing dreamed of.

Donning a parka and snow boots, Lila battled the elements, toting her knitting basket up Harbor Street to the Knitting Nook. When she'd stopped in during the Christmas Walk, Allie had informed her the last knitting bee before the holidays would take place tonight. Despite seeing both Dahlia and Suzanne from a distance during Saturday's shopping event, she hadn't talked to either in a while, and she felt the urge to connect with other women. She hoped things wouldn't be awkward with Suzanne, but had decided to just show up and hope for the best.

Unlike the last time she'd attended the knitting bee, she stepped into the cozy haven of yarn to find herself alone. But subdued holiday music playing low and shimmering white lights on the tree in the corner told her she didn't have the wrong night. Looking around at the shelves of yarn that nearly reached the ceiling, it was difficult not to feel surrounded in warmth, and it struck her as being like when a book lover steps into a library—if only the books were instead every shade and weight of yarn.

She was taking off her boots on the mat when she looked up to see Allie wearing a smile as she entered through the door that adjoined the coffee shop. "Hey, you made it."

Lila answered with a smile of her own, having taken a true liking to the other woman, along with her place of business. "I enjoy the vibe here," she told Allie. "Just being surrounded by all the yarn."

Allie tilted her head, casting a conspiratorial look. "I suspect we have a similar sensibility when it comes to yarn. You get me."

"I would even go so far as to say I envy you a little," Lila confessed. "I could be happy in a world of yarn." It was so soft, no hard edges, nothing ugly or mean.

"The last bee before Christmas can be quieter than most, so you're the first to arrive," Allie told her. "But don't worry—more people will show up soon."

"Even if they don't," Lila replied with a shrug, "I wouldn't mind just sitting here and knitting." Then she rolled her eyes. "Not that I need to keep knitting. I've made way more hats and gloves than I even know what to do with. But it passes the time on a snowy day."

Allie glanced toward a rack of knitted goods for sale that Lila had noticed on her previous visits. "If you really have more than you can use, I'm happy to take them on consignment. Mind you, it would have been better before the Christmas Walk as nothing else will sell 'til spring, but the option is there if you don't mind waiting awhile to get paid."

Lila bit her lip. The idea appealed to her. Even if it took some time, being able to earn a little money from her craft would make it all the more satisfying. "I might just take you up on that."

"Wonderful," Allie said. "So…does that mean you'll be here on the island awhile?"

"Oh—no, I'm leaving next week. But you could send the money through Meg." Or PayPal. But she wasn't sure if Summer Island was a PayPal kinda place.

"Darn. I was just about to offer you a job." Allie shifted her weight from one foot to the other. "I mean, I'm sure you're extremely overqualified, but if you were sticking around, maybe you'd like it. I generally hire high school or college girls, and they're great—but I wouldn't mind having someone a little more mature and experienced to help me manage the place long term."

Oh. Wow. What an…unexpectedly lovely idea. Not that many people had ever called her mature. But she'd managed Simon Alexis's foundation, so she would probably find managing a yarn shop a piece of cake in comparison. "Maybe I would. That's super nice of you. But I need to get back to the city." *To get my life in order. Somehow.* Even if she had no idea what came next.

True to Allie's promise, more people began to arrive, most looking chilled and happy to step into someplace warm and inviting. She was introduced to Allie's mom, and to Mrs. Bixby, an elderly lady whom she surmised might be Tom Bixby's mother. As a few more knitters came in, the mood turned festive, leaving Lila content enough to while away the evening with these island residents she didn't know—until she looked up from her loom to see Dahlia arrive.

"Well, if it isn't Lila Sloan," Meg's older friend said with her usual welcoming grin once she'd shed her coat and boots. She wore a kitschy, artsy scarf sporting purple and pink snowmen. "Nice to see you, my dear."

"You, too," Lila said, pleased when Dahlia sat down in an easy chair next to hers. As Dahlia drew her ongoing blanket project from a basket, Lila glanced back toward the door. "No Suzanne tonight?"

Dahlia shook her head, wrinkled up her nose just a bit. "Afraid she's not feeling very merry—wanted to stay home."

Oh crap. Like Lila didn't have enough to feel conflicted about. "Any idea why?"

Dahlia tilted her head, hesitating only briefly before she said, "I guess it's okay to say this since she confided in you about it the last time we were here. I think it's about her interest in Beck."

Lila's chest hollowed as heat rose to her face. "Oh." She dropped her gaze, unsure what to say, unsure what Dahlia knew.

Until Dahlia let her off the hook with "It's okay, Lila. I've seen the two of you in town."

Why did she feel as if she'd stolen Suzanne's man? Despite having done nothing wrong, she still suffered the need to defend herself. "I never planned—I mean, I never wanted—I mean, I tried to get rid of him, I really did."

Dahlia had abandoned her knitting in her lap to lift gently hushing hands. "Now, now—no worries. Nothing here is your fault. Suzanne just has bad timing, that's all. This isn't your problem."

"It isn't?" Lila asked, at once relieved but still steeped in guilt. "Because… I feel bad. I feel bad about…" She stopped, shook her head. "A lot of things."

"What other things?" Dahlia asked, brow knit as she leaned slightly forward, perhaps hearing the gravity of the last words.

And before Lila knew it, she'd told Dahlia everything. Of course, she'd already shared her guilt over Meg when they were young, and worrying about the trees being torn down on her watch, but now she added all her conflicted feelings about Beck—and how she'd originally been under the impression Suzanne had no interest in him. And how she felt like a criminal for liking him even while hating what he was doing to the inn and Meg. Then, without quite planning it, she even heard herself telling Dahlia about Simon, and Whitney, and how now Whitney had been courageous enough to do what Lila hadn't—and how awful she felt about what her ex-best friend was going through, even if Whitney *had* completely turned her back on Lila.

Dahlia listened patiently and said all the right, perfect things. She absolved Lila of all wrongdoing. About Beck. And about Simon. And about running away to Summer Island rather than staying in Chicago and speaking out. "You're not to blame—for anything you seem to feel bad about. Sometimes bad things happen,

Lila—that doesn't mean they're you're fault, or that you're able to fix them."

She took that in, thought it over. "Even though I didn't let people know the truth about Simon?" That one had been weighing on her even more heavily since learning about Whitney's actions. "I mean, isn't this one of those things where if you don't do the right thing, you've done the *wrong* thing? Like if you don't report a crime or stop a wrongdoing you're just allowing it to happen again to someone else?"

Dahlia blew out a thick sigh at Lila's heavy way of putting it. "It's a big question—and one not everybody would answer the same way. But this is one situation, dear, where I feel each woman is entitled to decide what's right for *her*."

Beck had said as much, too, but maybe hearing it from another woman—or having Beck's opinion seconded—justified her lack of action a little more.

"And in all honesty," Dahlia added, shaking her head, "why any woman would want to heap that kind of firestorm upon herself, I don't know."

"That's the thing," Lila said, having thought this through a lot lately, and certainly even more since yesterday. "No one *wants* to. No one wants something like this to happen to them. And no one wants to talk about it if it does. And certainly no one wants to talk about it in front of the whole world. And yet, some women find it within themselves to do it anyway—for the greater good."

"It does take courage," Dahlia agreed. "And I admire those that do. But I don't blame those who don't. Your choice is entirely valid. *Every* choice is valid.

We're all unique animals on this planet—there are no cookie-cutter answers for anything."

Just then, an older lady approached and introduced herself to Lila. "Hi—I'm Audrey Fisher. My husband and I run the Rosemont Inn. I hear you're Meg's sister. We all love Meg. It's a pleasure to meet you."

In one way, Lila wished she could continue the conversation with Dahlia, but when Audrey pulled up a chair, drew out her knitting, and started talking about her grandchildren, and her holiday plans, and saying she hoped to hire Seth to do some work on their inn come spring after seeing the renovations he did to Meg's kitchen… Lila rolled with it. Maybe enough had been said. Enough that she felt better than when she'd arrived anyway.

And at the end of the evening, as they all stowed their knitting projects and started putting their snow boots back on, she found a moment to grab Dahlia's hand and whisper, "Thank you. For listening."

"My pleasure. I hope it helped."

The truth was, every time she talked to someone about her troubles, it did help. Each person saw the world through their own unique lens, and the more people Lila confided in, the more she began to see through *their* lens, and realized that maybe *her* lens was a little clouded from things that had happened long ago.

She didn't return to the Summerbrook Inn free of her worries, but she felt a little lighter inside than when she'd arrived at the Knitting Nook. She still didn't know what her future held beyond spending the holidays with her family downstate, but maybe she was finally ready to stop running from her problems.

CHAPTER TWENTY

THE SKIPPER'S WHEEL occupied a Harbor Street storefront far deeper than wide, served all-day breakfast only, and sported a seafaring theme. Or, given the location, Lila surmised as she stepped inside, maybe it was actually more of a lake-faring theme. Either way, fishing nets, captain's wheels, and old-time black-and-white photos of fishing boats and fishermen graced the walls. Though right now some sparkly lights and garland were mixed in, round red mini-ornaments hung from the fishing net, and an advent calendar featuring a felt snowman wearing a boat captain's hat and smoking a pipe indicated that it was exactly a week until Christmas.

Moving back through the narrow space between the counter and a row of tables for two, she spotted Beck smiling at her from the only slightly more roomy area at the rear of the restaurant, lifting his hand in a wave. Though flagging her down wasn't necessary since just one other table was occupied—by an older couple—and the whole establishment was the size of a postage stamp. And while she knew the place stayed busy during tourist season, she didn't mind that it was quiet tonight. Despite herself, she was happy to see Beck, who had somehow started feeling as much like a friend as a lover.

"Hi there," he greeted her.

Unzipping Meg's parka, Lila slid into the old diner-style chair across from him. "Hey," she said with a soft smile.

He tilted his head. "You seem…different."

"Do I?" But she supposed she couldn't argue the point. Compared to most of the time she'd spent with him, she felt a lot…calmer inside. A change was truly coming over her. "I'm glad to see you," she added gently. Honestly. Tired of pushing so hard against things—fighting her feelings, fighting conditions she had no control over.

His dark eyes fairly glittered as he took that in. He lowered his chin, perhaps trying to decipher what was taking place here, before remarking, "I think that's the nicest greeting I've ever gotten from you."

She simply shrugged. "I guess I'm suddenly feeling nicer."

He eyed her skeptically, playfully. "Is this a trick? Should I expect it when I least expect it?"

A soft trill of laughter left her. "No—it's just me starting to…let go of some things, I guess."

Just then, a blonde waitress named Jolene approached, order pad in hand. Lila ordered a Belgian waffle and Beck went with bacon, eggs, and biscuits. When they were alone again, she said, "So there's a new development in the Simon Alexis story."

His eyebrows shot up. "I didn't expect that."

"Neither did I." Then she filled him in on the recent news that Whitney had sometime in the past few weeks become his next victim, and that she'd been brave enough to apparently tell his wife—and the *Chicago Sun-Times*.

"That's…wow. That's huge," he said, eyes going wide.

"I'm still trying to wrap my head around it, to tell you the truth. I mean, part of me feels vindicated, and part of me feels terrible since I know what it feels like to go through it, and part of me is still hurt that she turned her back on me. Part of me wonders if I should reach out to her, but part of me thinks *she* should be the one reaching out to *me*. Part of me admires her for calling him out, trying to stop him, and part of me feels ashamed *I* didn't do it.

"I mean, she's back in Chicago, bearing the brunt of this—being attacked online and who knows in what other areas of her life. Just like me, she lost her job—and I'm envisioning her trying to find one when her name is plastered all over the city in a way no one wants to have as their calling card. I'm sure these are dark days for her—same as they have been for me, but…even worse, you know?

"And I know blowing the whistle on a powerful man isn't something everyone is cut out for, and that no one would blame me for not doing it, but…well, I just keep thinking…maybe if I'd been the brave one, this wouldn't have happened to Whitney."

Across from her, Beck gave his head a slow tilt—pausing even longer when Jolene arrived with drinks. After she departed, he said, "Lila, honey, you have to forgive yourself for that. Nobody is at fault here but Simon—and well, maybe Whitney, too, for not being a better friend and believing you in the first place. I wish for both your sakes that she had."

"Oh, that's true," Lila mused. She hadn't thought of it from that perspective. She hated that Whitney had gone through something ugly with him—and if only she'd trusted Lila, maybe she could have avoided it. Or then again, with a man like Simon, maybe not.

"From where I sit, you haven't done a damn thing wrong," Beck went on. "Not with Simon, not with Whitney, not even with Meg when you were young. You beat yourself up too much, hold yourself to some impossible standard. You need to let all that go."

"That's pretty much what Dahlia told me at the knitting bee last night, too," she informed him.

"Well, Dahlia strikes me as a wise woman, so you should listen to her."

"I know you're both right—I really do. And I guess guilt can become…a habit. But I'm going to try, really try, to put it all behind me. I'm getting closer to that. Part of which is thanks to you."

The food came—and both agreed a hearty breakfast for supper was sometimes the perfect thing on a wintry night.

As Beck shoveled a forkful of eggs into his mouth, he regarded the woman across from him. So different than she'd seemed upon their first meeting, and it was hard to believe they'd gotten from there to here…wherever here was. A nebulous sort of place. A place she had called pointless—since she was leaving.

But he didn't see it that way—*couldn't* see it that way. He didn't sit around confiding in people about his past troubles, or much of anything else. He was a guy, and he mostly just dealt with his shit on his own, as best he could. Yet something had made him open up to her. And she'd opened up to him, too. And he didn't know *what* this was between them, but even if it only amounted to a couple weeks of attraction and lust and sex and communication, it wasn't pointless.

And maybe knowing that was what made him say, "Remember that story I told you about the coat my dad gave away?"

She nodded. And he went on to tell her about the box of sermons and letters from his dad. And how at first reading them had only left him feeling judged and persecuted all over again. "But the more of them I read, the more I actually…miss him. The more I realize that maybe I should have overlooked more, just sucked it up, put up with it, and been there more for my family rather than pulling away."

Across the table, Lila poured maple syrup onto her waffle, the scent turning the air around them sweet. "Isn't that exactly doing what you're telling me not to do?" she countered. "Beating yourself up? If the way he treated you was enough to make you back away, it must have hurt you a lot. You shouldn't *have* to put up with that in order to be a part of your family's life." Then her voice went softer. "But I'm really sorry if you miss him and have regrets about that. Regrets…are hard."

Simple but true words. He only nodded, feeling more connected with her than he wanted to.

Then she tilted her head, raising her gaze from her waffle to his eyes. "Only…what does any of that have to do with him giving the coat away?"

"Oh. Yeah." He'd gotten a little sidetracked—but now he told her the incredible outcome of his dad having gifted that coat to a stranger.

When he was through, her pretty hazel eyes shone wide. "Oh my God, Beck, that's…amazing."

"I almost didn't keep reading the papers in the box,"

he told her, "and if I hadn't, I'd never have known. I've spent the years since then assuming, frankly, that the coat had kept someone warm—but nothing more. I mean, you don't *expect* a coat to do more, you know? What are the chances the one guy he'd pick to give that coat to would let that one solitary gesture inspire him to get back up on his feet? And that he'd succeed? And that he'd also be the kind of guy to keep paying it forward?" He shook his head a bit, the news still feeling fresh to him and just as astonishing as when he'd read it.

She looked thoughtful as she chewed a bite of waffle, then mused, "They say God works in mysterious ways."

Beck couldn't help smiling. "My dad always said that."

She smiled back. "Sounds like he knew what he was talking about. Well, at least in some respects."

He knew she'd added that last part not wanting to imply his dad had been right about *him*. Which was sweet of her. Especially under certain circumstances. Unfortunately, he wasn't as sure about it himself anymore.

"Do you feel better now," she asked, "about the coat? Knowing it went on to serve such a big purpose?"

He nodded. "How could I not?" Then spilled a confession that had been weighing on him, the realization growing in him, the last few days.

"The thing is, though... I like to think I'm a good guy, but maybe I'm actually...not. That coat, my family, your trees—maybe I'm an ass who doesn't care about anything but my own damn agenda."

Lila nearly choked on her food. He was saying he

might be wrong? About the trees? She should care about more—care about the big picture of everything he was sharing with her—but it was hard not to latch onto the part that affected her personally. Because it could be a chance to agree, a chance to tell him he could change all that by surrendering the trees. She could work his newfound guilt to her advantage and save the woods behind the inn and have a happy ending to this story, after all.

Only…it wasn't the right thing to do.

The right thing to do was to be honest. The *hard, better* thing to do was to be honest.

And the honest truth was… "No."

"Huh?"

"No," she repeated. "I've seen how caring you are from the moment we met. You looked out for me when I was an idiot out in the snow in my pajamas. You've been kind and caring to Cade. You're a caring guy. You didn't even take the bulldozer key when you could have, despite it potentially curbing a lot of problems for you. In fact, you have a lot of nerve telling me I have to let go of my hang-ups when you're just as bad and need to do the same."

She couldn't read his expression—she only knew she found it surprisingly troubling to think of him feeling…the way *she* so often did. No one should be mired in guilt for doing their best to get through life, for doing what they thought was just.

"The difference is," he told her, "my hang-ups—as you so unpleasantly put it—are new, not just a pattern I got into. I think you judge yourself too harshly because you've gotten used to doing it, and comparing yourself to people who you think are nicer or braver or better than you in some way. When they're actually not. Whereas, me—I've never done that. I've always felt justified. I've always believed I was doing the right thing. Until right now. So I think my hang-up holds more water than yours."

Lila lowered her chin and cast him a chiding glance. "Look, Indiana Jones, don't be trying to trump my hang-up with yours. I have a long history of this—yours is mere child's play. Because, like I said, I've seen how kind you are. You've been kind to me when I was a total jerk to you."

At this, he shrugged. "Okay—true."

"Much as I may hate to admit it," she said a little more gently, "you're one of the good ones."

"Even though I'm going to tear down your trees?"

"Even though."

BECK WALKED LILA home holding her hand. The street lay still, silent, bathed in wintry white. With the lights lining the storefronts and a gentle snow beginning to fall, he thought it almost a shame more island residents didn't come out on such nights to enjoy it—but he also didn't mind feeling as if it was theirs alone. They didn't talk—they'd already reached that point where the silence was comfortable—and he liked that, too.

Despite temperatures below freezing, embers of desire smoldered inside him and his skin rippled with wanting her. Being with her was too damn easy—when she let it be. And as they neared the Summerbrook Inn at the westernmost end of Harbor Street, the tree he'd brought her shining through the window like a beacon of holiday warmth, he suspected she felt the same way, suffered the same longings. *Pointless my ass.*

Together, they ascended the steps to the porch, greeted by the outside light she'd left on. Their gazes met, and he didn't hesitate to ask her, "Can I kiss you goodnight?"

"Please," she murmured—and damn, he liked that, and didn't hesitate to lower his mouth over hers.

As he lifted his hands to her face, sinking deep into the kiss, it felt like…finding the place you belong. Where it's easy and exciting all at once. Where it's fun and profound. Sweet yet heavy.

Her hands pressed against his chest, through his coat and her mittens, but still the touch reached him potently, and he absently wondered if she could feel his heart beating double time for her. Mostly, though, he just kissed her. Kissed her like a man intoxicated with her. Kissed her like a man who would never see her again. Because maybe he wouldn't. *Likely* he wouldn't. After all, this had been their "see you before I go" dinner. It was, effectively, goodbye.

When their lips parted, she rose on tiptoes to whisper in his ear—as if there were anyone around to hear. "Doesn't have to be goodnight."

His hunger for her hardened at the sweet, sexy invitation, her breath warm on his neck, and temptation hung thick in the cold night air. Heat—more kinds than one—lay only a few steps away.

So it took a Herculean strength to say, "I want to. You know I want to. But…"

A small gasp of surprise left her. "But?" She peered up at him, eyes glimmering with yearning and confusion.

He took a deep breath, blew it back out, tried to crush down the ache in his groin. "It still wouldn't end well. Whether in an hour or tomorrow morning, at some point you'd tell me to leave and we'd both feel bad and it would be more complicated than either of us wants."

She bit her lip, looked up at him, appearing a little sad. "You're getting awfully good at turning me down."

"Not pointless anymore?" he asked.

She didn't reply—just lowered her eyes, clearly trying to hide just how very pointless it *wasn't*.

He used one bent finger to lift her chin, met her pretty gaze, let it own him a little too much, and then bent forward, his forehead lightly touching hers. They stayed that way a long moment, a long moment of rigidly mounting desire, of fighting down the temptation, of accepting the reality that she was really leaving and this was really ending and there wasn't a damn thing he could do to stop it.

"Thing is, Lila," he said, voice deep and low, trying like hell not to let her see how difficult this was, "much as I want to come in, knowing how things would end, I'd rather have this nice memory of kissing you good-bye in the snow."

And then he kissed her again, long and hard and deep. Her arms circled his neck as his closed around her waist and they clung to each other, just kissing, kissing, kissing. It reminded him of being sixteen, when it was all new and endlessly consuming—he had no idea how long they stood there continuing to kiss, only that he didn't *want* it to end, not any of it. He kissed her until her lips took on that puffy, slightly bee-stung look, until his own mouth felt used up and tired. He kissed her until he realized that no matter how long he kissed her it would never be enough—it wasn't a well that could be filled.

He could have said a million more things—he thought there were a million more conversations they could have. But at this juncture, one thing that did suddenly feel pointless was more words—since they would undoubtedly turn to what couldn't be. So after drawing back to share a long, quiet look, wherein he tried to memorize her bright eyes, slightly turned-up nose, heart-shaped lips, the curve of her cheek, the color of her hair, he simply lowered one more kiss to her forehead and walked away.

CHAPTER TWENTY-ONE

SITTING AT THE kitchen table, Lila made a list of things she needed to do before taking the ferry back to St. Simon in two days and then driving down to Ann Arbor.

1. *Finish wrapping gifts.*
2. *Pack suitcases.*
3. *Ask Suzanne and Dahlia to come over—give them gifts.* Even if that might be awkward. She only hoped Suzanne would come.
4. *Tell Suzanne when you're leaving so she can take over cat-sitting duties.* Also potentially awkward, but hopefully could be lumped with number 3.
5. *Clean kitchen.* She wasn't as naturally tidy as Meg and wanted to leave the place as spotless as it had been upon her arrival.
6. *Return bulldozer key to Beck. Or maybe not. Think through this.*
7. *Say goodbye to the trees.* She wasn't even sure what she meant by that, but she'd written it down, so she'd think through that, too.

SHEESH, IT HAD turned into quite a list, the items having gotten harder as she went.

She wasn't any more ready to leave Beck behind than she was to tell Meg the impending fate of the trees, but she had to face such things if she intended to take control of her life.

And she knew keeping that bulldozer key wouldn't prevent work from proceeding when the snow began to melt, so maybe she should indeed just give it back to him. But at the same time, surrender didn't sit well with her here—at least not about this, no matter how much she'd come to care about Beck. She'd surrendered so much already, back in Chicago.

So maybe she'd just leave that key for Meg to decide what to do with.

And she'd break the ugly news to her sister over the holiday. Or, well—maybe after, so as not to totally ruin it. Meg would probably give the key back—she was just a more accepting person than Lila, and faced things more gracefully.

Maybe when you boiled it down, that was ultimately the biggest difference between the two of them. Grace. In that moment, Lila aspired to approach life with more grace.

With that, she marked number 6 off the list, and let her gaze linger on number 7. Standing up, she crossed the kitchen to the window over the sink, then peered out across the brook at the hillside of trees that had caused...well, *everything* between her and Beck. *You could say they've kept you apart—but they also brought you together. Without them, unlikely you'd have met. Well, unless Suzanne had, by now, introduced him to you as her new boyfriend.* Lila cringed with jealousy at the notion and tried not to think about what might happen between Beck and Suzanne now.

You're horrible. You're leaving, and you refuse to be with him regardless, but you don't want him and

Suzanne to be happy here together? In a place, no less, where you know there's a very small dating pool? You're a despicable person. And even if she wasn't despicable for many of the things that had caused her guilt, she truly felt despicable not to wish them both romantic happiness, and it surely seemed like the most likely path to that would be the two of them, together, becoming a happy Summer Island couple. *This is not how one attains grace.*

Refocusing on the trees across the stream—many bare of leaves now but the evergreens still sporting snow-covered boughs—she wished she could see them in spring one last time. She hated how much she'd taken them—and this whole place—for granted her whole life. "Oh, Gran," she whispered, feeling as if her grandma were somehow there with her, looking out on the trees, and Lila wished she could have somehow protected them for her. A tear rolled unexpectedly down her cheek.

But she wiped it away, said out loud, "That won't do," and reminded herself that she'd done all she could for the trees—she'd done her very best, and now she had to let them go. With…grace. Real or imagined. *Fake it 'til you make it.*

And to do that, she headed upstairs, and to the attic. Pulling down the fold-up ladder, she started carefully up it, and this time she wouldn't have to search for what she'd come for—she knew exactly where they were. A moment later, she lifted the old snowshoes from where they hung on nails in the wall.

SHE'D NEVER SNOWSHOED. But how hard could it be?

Turned out somewhat hard, leaving her suddenly

thankful Harbor Street was so quiet as she stumbled and fumbled around the front yard trying to get accustomed to the damn things.

Fortunately the brook had frozen over and was covered with snow, so when she finally felt accomplished enough on the snowshoes to make her way to the hillside, crossing the water didn't complicate her journey.

A winter white sky served as a backdrop as she stood peering up from the foot of tall, bare trees at a complex web of branches above her. She reached out to touch the trunk of one. An oak? A poplar? Something else? She didn't know much about the most common trees—but she knew she was sorry these would soon die after gracing this hillside her whole life and longer.

She walked carefully, quietly, studying evergreens—some tall and old, many younger, smaller. Christmas-tree size. She appreciated how lovely they looked with the snow draped upon them, and how warm all the trees made even cooler days feel in summer. She thought of games of hide-and-go-seek played with Meg and their father. She remembered walks with Gran to the blackberry bushes along Mr. Vanderkamp's fence at the eastern edge of his property. "One cobbler for Mr. Vanderkamp," Gran would say, "because I fear the man is lonely and seldom gets any home cooking. And then one for us." She'd end on a wink—the plan both charitable and self-indulgent at once.

Soon snow began to fall and a cold breeze crept up on Lila—it was getting colder and she should probably go in and get to work on the rest of her list. The day after tomorrow would come fast and this vacation from the real world would be over. And maybe, in a way, it already was. She'd said goodbye to Beck, now she was saying goodbye to the trees. It was all coming to an end, both new things and old.

"Bye, trees," she whispered sadly, looking up and around at all of them. *I'm so sorry I couldn't fix this. So, so sorry.* Yes, she knew it wasn't her fault, but she was still sorry. A few tears fell, and she succumbed to them, for just a moment, before wiping them away with one of Meg's mittens lest they freeze on her skin.

Walking back across the small snow-covered stream, she reached the backyard and paused, peeking back one last time—and felt it. Grace. Just a little. She'd said goodbye to the trees with grace.

But the wind had suddenly turned more biting and bitter, so she gave up reminiscing, turned back toward the house, and started on the old wooden snowshoes back toward the front porch, trying to switch her mind from the emotion surrounding the trees to the more practical matters of getting ready to leave the Summerbrook Inn.

And while there were many things about departing that left her sad, she *was* looking forward to celebrating Christmas with her family. She'd felt like an empty hull of herself at Thanksgiving, so Christmas would be better. Christmas would be nice. The tree news notwithstanding. And, well, other stuff she knew she needed to tell her family about now, too.

But don't think about that. Think about hugging Meg hello, and showing her the pictures you took of Miss Kitty but forgot to text her despite your best intentions. Think about helping Mom in the kitchen, and telling everyone about all the old ornaments you came across. She'd decided to leave the tree up for Meg and Seth to come home to, hoping they wouldn't mind, thinking

Meg might like seeing the ornaments, too. *Think about ham and cinnamon apples and pumpkin pie and Mom's cookies. Think about everyone opening up their hats and scarves. Think about board games and Christmas movies and everything good about the holidays.*

She rounded the front corner of the big Victorian to see someone out on Harbor Street—realizing with a squinting closer look that it was Dahlia. Who had just spotted Lila, too, and began walking in her direction. Only when she got close enough to call, "What on earth are you doing, my dear?" did Lila remember she was taking small plodding steps with netted contraptions of wood strapped to her feet.

"Oh—I'm snowshoeing," she called back. "These belonged to my grandma."

The older lady tipped her head back with an approving smile. "That's a novel endeavor, and I always applaud novel endeavors." She patted mittened hands together lightly.

And Lila was just about to yell down an invitation for Dahlia and Suzanne to come over tomorrow afternoon—when Dahlia went on to say, "Good you used 'em now. I trust you've seen the forecast."

Lila blinked, the cold wind beginning to sting her face. Actually, she hadn't thought to check the weather in a while—too many other things on her mind. "No—why?"

"Oh my," Dahlia said, her ominous tone making Lila worry.

"What's wrong?"

Dahlia had grown close enough now for Lila to make out the pained look on her face. "I hate to be the bearer of bad news, but I'm afraid there's a blizzard blowing in hard. It came up fast—winter storm warning issued just about an hour ago, and the lake's starting to freeze already. Koester's is staying open another couple hours, so if you need anything, best get it now."

Lila's chest tightened. But she still hoped for the best as she asked, "How bad is it going to be?"

"Well, the ferry just canceled service—for the coming days and likely beyond. And even when the snow ends, the lake will be too icy. I'm so sorry to tell you this, Lila, but I'm afraid no one's getting off this island for Christmas."

PART 3

Between every two pine trees there is a door leading to a new way of life.

John Muir

CHAPTER TWENTY-TWO

LILA TEARFULLY TEXTED Meg one of the Miss Kitty pictures she'd accidentally been hoarding, along with the message: Miss K says hi, and we need to talk.

She was about to send another, asking if this was a good time, when the phone trilled and Meg's picture popped up. Lila sniffed back her tears—*quit being a baby, no one died or anything*—and answered.

"Miss Kitty needs to talk?" Meg asked. "Is she breaking up with me?"

The unexpected laugh left Lila feeling a tiny bit better—even if this sucked. "No, I think your relationship with the cat is safe. It's actually me who needs to talk to you."

"Are *we* breaking up?" Meg ventured, still sounding amused. But she wouldn't be amused in a minute. "Because that would kinda ruin Christmas. I can't wait to see you, by the way, and hear any juicy island gossip I might have missed."

Oh, Meg—you have no idea.

"We're heading to Ann Arbor tomorrow," her sister barreled on, clearly having missed the gravity in Lila's voice amid her holiday exuberance. "Seth's grandpa is coming with us, so we're excited about that! This is going to be such a great Christmas!"

Lila blew out a heavy breath and spoke dryly. "Maybe, maybe not."

"What do you mean?"

"Well, I'm afraid you guys will have to celebrate without me." Lila sniffed, trying not to whine. "There's a blizzard here and the ferries aren't running."

At this, Meg went silent. Then finally said, "You're kidding? Before Christmas? They almost *never* shut down before Christmas."

"Except for this year," Lila said quietly.

"But...it's okay. You can just come down in a couple days. I know you were planning to meet us at Mom and Dad's tomorrow night, but we've got a few more days before Christmas, so you'll get home by then."

Lila shook her head, even though Meg couldn't see it. "I don't think so, Meg. Dahlia said no one will get to leave until after Christmas."

"Oh no." On the other end, Meg expelled a big, sad breath. "Seriously?"

"I wouldn't kid about something like this. I can't stand the idea of not being with you guys for Christmas."

Meg sighed audibly. "I can't, either. This is...this is so awful."

Trying not to wallow in the disappointment, Lila told her, "Dahlia says I can spend Christmas with her and Suzanne. And Zack. And Mr. Desjardins. But it won't be the same." Okay, maybe a *little* wallowing.

"Who's Mr. Desjardins?" Meg asked.

"Dahlia's French lover," Lila replied.

"What?"

"You've, um, missed a few developments here."

"Clearly. Dahlia has a *lover*? A *French* lover? What else have I missed?"

Big mouth. Lila hesitated, then settled on saying, "Nothing that can't keep. I'm just…so sad. I was really looking forward to a family Christmas."

"Listen," Meg said, clearly flying into regrouping mode, "don't worry—we'll just have to postpone it. The ferries will get through again before the deepest freeze comes on—I'm sure of it."

"Still, you can't postpone Christmas," Lila reminded her.

"I admit, this is…this is…well, so disappointing that I don't even have the words to express it." Another sigh. "But…well, we just have to make the best of the situation."

Easy for Meg to say. She'd be with Seth, and Mom and Dad.

But then, no, if Meg were stuck here by herself, she *would* make the best of it, not let it get her down. *Grace.*

Then again, Dahlia and Suzanne were like family to Meg—so if she had to stay here for Christmas, she'd still have people she cared about to spend it with. Lila didn't have that comfort level with anyone on the island.

Well, maybe one person. Who just wanted to remember kissing her in the snow—they'd said their goodbyes already.

"Li—you there?" her sister asked.

She nodded again at the phone. Then did her own regrouping. "You're right, I just have to make the best of it." She wasn't even sure what she meant by that, but she'd figure it out.

BECK STARED BLANKLY at the text on his phone from George Walton.

> Don't know if you heard, but the ferries stopped running and word is that they won't be able to get through again until after Christmas.

What the hell? Was George serious? Did he have this right? Surely not. Beck tossed a glance toward the tall windows lining the rear of the house. Yeah, it was snowing and blowing like crazy, but Christmas was days away.

Rather than reply, he pulled up the ferry company's website, which he'd been told stayed updated daily in winter. And hell—sure enough, the ferry was closed, with an explanation in big red letters. They'd reopen as soon as possible but it was doubtful they'd run again before Christmas. Check back daily for updates.

He texted George again—trying to think outside the box. What about a helicopter? We could see about chartering one.

He'd never flown to the island, and there wasn't an airport here like on Mackinac—but he knew small aviation companies operated in the general vicinity. Already thought of that., George texted back. But they say it's weather dependent and unlikely.

Shit. He'd been planning to head down to Kentucky in a few days, arriving the night before Christmas Eve. And this year of all years, it felt important. Not only because it was the first Christmas without Dad but because he needed to mend some fences—apologize to Emma and Mom for being so absent from family affairs these past ten years. He needed to get to know his niece and nephew better—and felt thankful they were still young and he hadn't missed their whole childhoods. He didn't want to be an absentee uncle and he really hoped the whole family, or even just the kids if the adults couldn't get away, would want to come up in the summertime.

Not to mention, he'd figured the trip would be the perfect distraction from thinking about Lila.

A glance to the presents he'd amassed for the kids, sitting wrapped in a pile in one corner near the fireplace, made him feel even worse. The kids wouldn't get the presents on time. No gifts from Uncle Beck on Christmas.

Glumly, he dialed Emma's number—only to have it go to voice mail. He left a message explaining the situation, expressing his disappointment, and hoping she could hear how much he meant it. He ended by adding, "I've been reading some of the stuff in the box from Dad, Em, and…it's been good for me. So thank you for sending it. I'm going to miss seeing you guys more than I can say."

Then he exchanged a few texts with George. Thanks for letting me know about the ferry. Messing up my holiday plans big time. Same true for you?

George replied: Yes. Very disappointing for the whole family. We were leaving for Ohio tomorrow and hadn't planned to come back until spring.

That stinks. Hope you can get off the island before too long.

Me, too! And poor Cade—he's the most upset of all. Christmas is such a special time for the little ones—and he won't be home with his mom and dad for it.

Aw, damn—Cade. Poor guy. Texting back *that's too bad* seemed pretty empty, but he felt rotten for his buddy. It was crummy enough to have holiday plans ruined as an adult—as a little kid it would be infinitely more devastating. First world problem, of course—but he still hurt for the kid.

Another text came in from George. *Cade is asking if he can come over and see you. But if it's an inconvenient time, just say the word.*

Bundle him up and send him over., Beck texted back. *Maybe a visit will cheer us both up.*

Five minutes later, the front bell rang and Beck swung the door open to find the little boy wrapped up in the usual oversize scarf Marie was fond of looping numerous times around his neck. Even with only his eyes visible, though, his distress showed. "Becker, Becker, this is the worst thing that's ever happened to me in my whole life! What am I gonna do?"

Maybe Beck should have given a little more thought to how to appease a five-year-old whose Christmas was ruined. "Well, buddy—it stinks for sure. I don't get to go see my family, either."

"You have a family?" Cade asked, sounding astonished.

Beck reached down, grabbed onto the ends of the big scarf, and tugged, guiding Cade in so he could shut the door. Then he began to unwrap the scarf so he could see the boy's face. "Yeah—I have a sister, and a mom. And my sister has two kids, the littlest around your age."

"Oh." Cade then shrugged free of his parka and let it drop to the floor, looking as dejected as a child in this position could.

"Listen," Beck said, "it's a bummer, for sure, but we'll just have to make the best of it. I'm sure your Grandma Marie will whip up a nice Christmas dinner."

Cade nodded solemnly as they headed to two sofas that sat across from each other near the large stone hearth. "She's at Koester's right now. She said you can come over on Christmas, too, if you want."

The kindness touched him—he hadn't thought ahead yet to what he would do. And if he couldn't see his family, he wouldn't care much about the day—but on the other hand, he certainly wouldn't decline the Waltons' kindness, and it would be a lot more pleasant than just another winter day at home alone. "That's nice of her. And maybe you and I can watch some Christmas movies, or build a new snowman to keep our other one company. Maybe we'll find a game to play or a puzzle to do." Did kids these days even do puzzles? Beck had no idea.

"All that sounds fine, I guess," Cade said, not sounding as if it were fine at all, "but what am I gonna do about the really big problem here, Becker?"

Beck looked Cade in the eye, trying not to let it show that he had no idea what really big problem existed in addition to the one they were discussing. But eventually he gave up. "What really big problem would that be?"

Cade rolled his eyes impatiently. "Santa, of course."

"Santa?"

Cade blew out a breath. "He won't be able to find me! I'm not at home!"

Oh, *that* problem. The thinking kid's problem—since most five-year-olds, he suspected, would not have leaped ahead to this conclusion. But the answer seemed easy enough. "From what I hear, Cade, Santa's pretty magical. I'm sure he knows exactly where you are and will visit you here."

And then, damn, it hit him. George and Marie hadn't expected to be stuck here with their grandson on Christmas morning. They probably didn't have enough presents—if any at all—to make it appear Santa had come. And he didn't think Amazon was going to be making any quick deliveries up here in the next few days, either.

So maybe it was for the best that Cade didn't buy into it anyway. "No, he won't know where I am! I wrote to him and I told him where I lived! I told him I'd been real good this year, too, because I have! My dad helped me with the letter. We drove it to the post office and everything! He won't know I'm stuck on this stupid island in this stupid snowstorm." He concluded by sticking out his bottom lip in determined defeat.

Beck's mind raced. *How do I fix this for the kid? How do I even take a stab at it?* And while he was at it... "Um, what did you tell Santa you wanted, Cade?"

"A bicycle. With training wheels because I'm little," he added smartly. "And some Pokémon stuff. And a puppy."

A puppy. This just kept getting better and better. Beck blew out a breath.

"What am I gonna do, Becker? What am I gonna do?"

Maybe, rather than continuing to ask questions

about the really big problem, Beck should have instead been trying to distract the boy from it. But now that he hadn't, Cade looked near tears. And it broke Beck's heart—enough that he said something he feared he'd probably regret. "I'm not sure, buddy, but we'll figure it out. I promise!"

DAHLIA AND SUZANNE sat at the café, drinking coffee and watching the blizzard howl across Lake Michigan, the South Point Lighthouse barely visible just offshore. "When is this supposed to end?" Suzanne asked.

"Another day or two, I believe," Dahlia said, her tone blasé.

"You seem completely undaunted by it," Suzanne observed.

"It's winter on Summer Island. Just came in a little more fiercely than usual this year. You'll get used to it."

Of course it wasn't Suzanne's first winter here, but she considered herself a new enough resident to still be adjusting to the weather, and as Dahlia had said, this wasn't a typical December. And now people were stuck here who didn't want to be. And she wondered how that might change things for certain people. Or…maybe it wouldn't change anything at all—who could say?

"How's Mr. Desjardins?" she asked, remembering he'd planned to leave for Toronto.

"Looks like he'll be with us for the holiday," Dahlia replied.

Suzanne smiled, thinking fondly of the low-key, debonair Frenchman. "I bet he's delighted."

Dahlia shrugged. "Sorry not to see his daughter, but otherwise I suppose he seemed happy enough at the prospect of sharing the holiday with me."

Suzanne raised her eyebrows at her friend. "And are you happy about it, as well?"

"I'm fine with it." But still blasé. Maybe Dahlia was tired of Suzanne pushing the Mr. Desjardins agenda.

But she couldn't help herself, so announced, "Well, I for one am ecstatic. Not only because I find him delightful, but because, frankly, you and I and Zack seem like an odd configuration for Christmas. Given Zack's surliness and that I don't tolerate surly well, I welcome another pleasant personality around the dinner table."

At this, Dahlia chuckled softly. "Zack's first Christmas without Meg. And Pierre all smitten with me. And you all smitten with Beck. I've assembled quite the ragtag bunch of smitten kittens for the holiday—but I'm determined to make it merry for all involved. I want a nice Christmas. And afterward I may take a trip, once the ice clears."

Suzanne looked over at her. "A trip?"

Another easy shrug. "I've wintered here a good many years. Thinking maybe I'll head south for the rest of this one. You know, just take a break from the ice and snow this time around."

Suzanne blinked, trying to get to the bottom of this unexpected news. "With a certain Frenchman?"

Dahlia spoke coyly. "I've not yet completely decided on such details—time will tell."

Surely she was thinking of traveling with Mr. Desjardins. And surely he'd jet off to some tropical locale with her if she asked. In a way, this struck Suzanne as out of the blue and out of character for Dahlia. But on the other hand, her older friend was often full of surprises.

"Well, I look forward to hearing these details once

they're in place. And thank God Meg will be back after Christmas or I'd go stir-crazy without you."

Dahlia reached over, squeezed her hand. "It's nice to be valued." Her countenance—suddenly serious—caught Suzanne off guard, but she simply smiled. Because it *was* nice to be valued. She supposed that was all most of us really wanted.

"About Christmas," Dahlia said, "I should warn you—Lila will likely be joining us, as well. She's quite broken up not to be going home."

Suzanne took that in, turned it over in her head. "It only makes sense. I don't mind. I only mind that I've made things awkward with her. Which I hope I might be able to repair."

Dahlia nodded, her eyes kind. "You're a good woman, Suzanne Quinlan."

"It's nice to be valued," Suzanne quipped with a small smile. "So Lila…isn't spending the holiday with Beck?"

"Not that I know of," Dahlia said. "I invited her and she accepted. I would invite him, too, but that would cross the line into *much more* than awkward, I'm afraid."

"Agreed." Suzanne sighed. "I'm sorry if he has to spend the day alone, though."

"He's friendly with the Waltons," Dahlia reminded her, "and they're stuck, too. Perhaps he'll join their celebration."

"I hope so. I don't like to think of anyone being alone for Christmas."

A little while later, Suzanne bundled up and headed for home. But Beck remained on her mind. She still had no idea what existed between him and Lila. But if they were both stranded here for Christmas and not spending it together, that seemed...positive. For Suzanne anyway.

Of course, there were many unanswered questions, and all she had were a few puzzle pieces to try to fit together and form a whole picture. It didn't work. And she was tired of wondering where she stood with Beck Grainger.

And maybe, on one hand, she should let the fact that he'd spent the last couple of weeks with Lila instead of her provide her answer. But on the other hand, some of the puzzle pieces were that she'd inadvertently played hard to get for so long, and she *didn't* know what he and Lila were to one another, and try as she might, she hadn't been able to get the man off her mind ever since she'd suddenly decided she wanted him. No matter how many times she'd felt brushed aside in lieu of Lila.

Every time she'd seen him with Meg's younger sister had inflicted a deeper wound. But maybe...maybe she was hurting for nothing. Because Beck and Lila weren't spending Christmas together. And because maybe if Suzanne really put her cards on the table and let him know how she felt, things would change in her favor.

Not just flirting, not just saying "sometime soon"— but going for what she wanted. Cal had been fond of saying that if you didn't go after what you wanted, you never knew whether or not you could have had it. And she knew he would want her to be happy—and that the time had come. It was time to move on from her beloved late husband and find happiness again.

And maybe time was actually of the essence. She'd expected Lila to be leaving, after all, but now she wasn't. At least not yet. So while she'd originally been following Dahlia's advice to wait and see what happened after Lila's departure, maybe…maybe the time to make her intentions known was now. *Right* now. Before even one more long, wintry day passed. Before something could happen to push him and Lila any closer together. Before she could talk herself out of it. Before anything stopped her from finally being as bold and courageous as she felt in this moment.

Before she knew it, Suzanne had trudged through the snow and wind up Mill Street, past her cottage, and onward up the slope that wound around and led to West Bluff Drive. Blizzard be damned. Her heart be damned. Her good senses be damned.

But wait. Maybe this was…too much. Too sudden. Too crazy. Taking off a glove, she struggled to extract her cell phone from a pocket and dial Dahlia.

"Hi, Suzanne. Anything wrong?"

Given that they'd parted ways less than five minutes ago and that there was a blizzard on, it was a reasonable question.

"I don't think so," Suzanne said, still trying to puzzle it through. "I mean, I think something might be *right*. But I'm not sure."

"I need more to go on," Dahlia prodded her.

Yes, that made sense. So Suzanne didn't beat around the bush. "I'm marching up the hill right now, in a snowstorm, to tell Beck Grainger I care for him romantically."

"Wow," Dahlia replied, pretty much summing up how Suzanne felt about it, too. "This is unexpected."

"I'm calling you for advice. Am I crazy? Am I going to *look* crazy? Should I stop?"

On the other end, Dahlia took her time, then answered slowly. "Are you emotionally prepared for any outcome?"

"Yes," she said, almost surprised at how certain she felt. "Whatever happens, at least I'll know I took my shot and let him know how I really feel."

"Then press on, my love," Dahlia told her.

"Really?" Suzanne put her head down, walking against the wind. "I was sure you'd tell me to turn around and go home, think this through, come up with a better plan than just winging it."

"Then you were mistaken. If you want him, really want him, you should let him know."

"Even in the middle of a blizzard?"

"Even in the middle of a blizzard. Life is short."

CHAPTER TWENTY-THREE

SHE WASN'T SURE of the temperatures outside—but given the fierce winds, she suspected a wind chill in the teens. Marching uphill in the blizzard was one of the most unpleasant walks of Suzanne's life, but she forged on. There were plenty of reasons to turn back, but in her mind, she'd come too far, committed emotionally to what she was doing. She'd turned back with Beck too many times—if she turned back now, she feared she'd *keep* turning back, over and over. She had to push through this, make it happen.

She felt like a pilgrim on a strange crusade as she made her way up West Bluff Drive, the sole sign of life amid the large, stately homes lining her path. Anyone looking out a window might assume they were seeing a ghost. The Ghost of Christmas Crazy.

But you're not crazy. You're...determined. To move forward. At last. And that was a good thing. Even an amazing thing. In fact, it felt like...freedom in a way. To suddenly want another man so badly. To suddenly be ready to let someone new into her life. So despite having to keep her head down in the wind, on the inside, she stood up straight and tall as a sequoia and strode boldly in her snow boots toward Beck Grainger's big, woodsy-looking home of cedar shake and timber, the roof currently blanketed in white.

It was a relief to duck out of the wind up onto his covered front porch. Determination and boldness aside, she was also looking forward to a little warmth, so she didn't hesitate to ring the bell.

She waited, hearing no movement inside. Oh Lord. What if he wasn't home? What if he was down at the inn with Lila right now? What if she'd made this horrendous trek for nothing?

That was when the door swung open. The handsome man across the threshold squinted slightly at her. "Suzanne?"

She wasn't certain if his reaction was surprise, or trouble recognizing her, but under the circumstances either seemed fair. She was wrapped up tight, her head covered by a snug hood, her face half buried in a scarf. She suspected she was snow-covered, too. She nodded. "Yes."

He blinked, twice, still appearing taken aback. "Good God, come in." He took a step back to welcome her into the warmth and dryness of his home.

"Thanks," she said, moving inside as she reached up one glove to begin undoing the scarf. Her eyes fell to her boots, currently dropping clumps of wet snow onto his hardwood floor, but rather than apologize, she lifted her gaze to the home's interior, taking in thick wood beams, tall windows, and a massive stone fireplace worthy of a ski lodge.

Focus. Stay focused. But now that she stood here, face-to-face with the object of her affection, her chest tightened and her stomach churned.

"What on earth are you doing out in this weather?" he asked.

Just be cool. Be the woman he seemed so enamored of when you first met. Whoever that is.

She blew out a breath, tried to get her bearings. "I need to talk to you."

And he blinked again, clearly confused. He had no idea what was coming, that she was making a grand gesture to express her ardor for him. She'd sort of hoped maybe he would sense that, or at least seem more happy than puzzled. *But again—blizzard. So that's fair.*

"Can…can we go sit down?" she asked. "By the fire maybe?" Her goal was twofold—get more comfortable for this conversation, and get warm.

"Of course," he said. "Let me help with your coat." After freeing her from it, he hung it on a hook near the fireplace—only then allowing her to see exactly how wet and snow-covered the long parka was.

She shook her head. "I'm sorry. For the mess. Though I should probably take off my boots, too."

"No worries—but you must be freezing."

"Yeah, pretty cold," she confessed, laying her gloves on the long hearth and, a moment later, sitting her boots there, as well.

"Can I get you something hot to drink?" Then he made a slight face. "Not that I have much that's hot. Instant cocoa?" He raised dark eyebrows.

"Do you have any wine?"

"That's not hot."

"I know."

"Sure," he said on a short nod. "Red or white?"

"Whatever you lay your hand on first is great." This part wasn't about warmth; it was about liquid courage.

She warmed her hands and toes by the big fire roaring in the grate, struggling with what she was going to say. Her mind felt jumbled, though, and when he returned with two glasses of red wine, she was still stuck at winging it.

As they sat down on two sofas that faced each other, she took a gulp of the wine—then tried to get used to looking him in the eye. He had such great eyes. Eyes she wanted to drown in. But as was so often the case with Beck, she had trouble holding the gaze—too profoundly enamored, and now too profoundly nervous. Nervousness *often* got the best of her in his presence, but this took it to new levels.

He leaned forward slightly. "Whatever brought you out, Suzanne, it must be urgent. What's going on?"

She pushed out a shaky breath, her chest tight. Again, not the lead-in she'd been hoping for. *But just roll with it.* "It's urgent only because… I feel I haven't been clear with you. And now that *I'm* clear on things, I just…" She stopped, shook her head slightly. "I just don't want any uncertainty hanging between us. Not even for another day. Even if…" She sighed. "Even if it seems pretty extreme that I've come here like this."

"No," he said. "It's all right."

She swallowed another sip of wine, then peeked up at him from where her gaze had dropped to the coffee table that rested between them. She tried to read his expression, but found it difficult since she still couldn't maintain eye contact for long. She wanted to believe he didn't look uncomfortable. But hell—who *wouldn't* look uncomfortable? She'd *created* uncomfortable here. She just had to change it now—that was all. Everything would get more comfortable once she told him why she'd come.

"I'm just going to say this straight out," she told him with another swift glance.

"Okay," he replied.

She took a big drink from the wineglass in her hand, letting it instill the fearlessness she'd sought from it. *Here goes nothing. Here goes everything.*

"I know I pushed away your affection in the bluntest of ways when we first met. And I know that more recently I've indicated to you that my feelings were beginning to change and that I'd be interested in getting better acquainted." She raised her gaze, caught a glimpse of those brown eyes, shifted her focus to the stone of the fireplace. "But the truth is—I'm…more than interested in getting acquainted. In fact, I…have feelings for you. I realize we don't know each other well, but there it is—I have feelings for you. Ardent ones. Serious ones. And while I was content to just wait until the holidays passed and see if we crossed each other's paths, now I'm…not. Because it's almost Christmas. And there's a blizzard on. And I know that means you won't get home to see your relatives before the holiday. And because…because… Christmas just seems like the right time to…let someone know you care for them. And so—I care for you, Beck. I want more with you. And if you still think you might care for me, too—well, maybe the holiday would be a nice time to…move forward exploring that."

Okay then. She'd really just said all that. Made it plain. Cleared up any confusion that might have existed. She'd just said it—and now her heart beat like a drum and the simple act of breathing had grown even more difficult. She threw back another sip of wine, and discovered she hadn't the wherewithal to even *attempt* looking at him again.

But you need to. You need to look into his eyes. Let him see what's in yours.

And that was when it hit her what a horrible, ridiculous position she'd just put him in.

He'd had no warning this was coming.

For the first time, she took in more details about him: he wore a blue-and-white Kentucky Wildcats hoodie with gray sweatpants and white socks. His jaw sported the stubble that came from a few days of not shaving, and his thick, dark hair was messy. He'd been sitting here alone in his house, minding his own business, having an easy day while the snow fell outside—and she'd barged in professing her sudden and wild passion for him.

"I'm sorry," she murmured quickly.

"Huh?" he asked.

"I…" She shook her head. "I shouldn't have come. I should have handled this in some more subtle way. Only…" She stopped, lifted her head, then forced herself to look at that handsome, rugged face. "I kept trying to be subtle and it wasn't working. So I thought maybe being direct would get the job done."

His eyes shone on her with kindness.

Even though she'd barged into his privacy without warning. Even though she possessed all the romantic finesse of a tenth-grade girl wallowing in the throes of first love. Even though…she suddenly knew, before he even said a word.

She'd already said it all—she'd been subtle, made her moves, and he hadn't responded. *That* was his answer. She'd simply refused to see it.

"Thank you, for being direct," Beck said. Wishing he knew…well, more than he did. About the future, and his heart, and what he really wanted. "At least now I… well, I know where you stand, and I appreciate that."

"I…thought it might be refreshing. After the way things started between us."

He nodded. "I appreciate you coming. I appreciate you *caring enough* to come." Of course, he felt like he'd opened his front door and been hit by a Mack truck. And he felt awful—awful that she'd been so brave, put herself out there so boldly, and that he didn't know what to say to it.

He knew what he *wanted* to say. What it probably made *sense* to say.

Suzanne, I feel the same way. I'm glad you're ready to move on. I've been attracted to you and intrigued by you literally since the moment we met. You're a beautiful woman. You have a soft heart I'm drawn to. Yes, let's use these cold December days to spend time together, start a relationship. Let's be what I've hoped we could since the spring.

After all, he cared for her. True, they didn't know each other well, but he still cared. And pure logic made this easy. Suzanne was a sure bet. A lovely bet. She was a sweet, funny woman he could very possibly have an extremely happy existence with here.

The only problem was…he'd been using logic his whole life. To build a business and a lifestyle he wanted, to live more comfortably than his dad had chosen for himself and his family. But logic didn't work when it came to love. After all, marrying Chandra had seemed logical—and it had been a disastrous decision.

And the idea of moving forward with Suzanne,

while it sounded simple and pleasant and suddenly like the path of least resistance, brought him an entirely different kind of clarity than she'd intended to give him by coming here.

Taking a shot at love with Suzanne made all the sense in the world—except for one thing that he could no longer deny.

Lila, who would leave as soon as the ice melted, had his heart.

He'd been trying to move around that, push it down, stop feeling it, but she had his heart—that simple. And even if he had no future with Lila, and even if he hated this, he knew he had to, as gently as possible, break Suzanne's.

She'd been sitting quietly, waiting for him to respond, and now he stood up, stepped around the coffee table, and sat down on it to bring them closer, where he could take her hand in his. It was soft, delicate, and a part of him deeply regretted what he was about to do—because if Lila had never stood in front of that bulldozer, he'd be giving Suzanne an entirely different answer right now. Damn, but God *did* work in mysterious ways.

He squeezed her hand in his and tried to find the right, honest words. "I care for you, too, Suzanne, but… it wouldn't be right, or fair to you, to move forward. There's…somebody else." He knew those words stung, *more* than stung. Who hadn't, at some point in their life, been given that same heartbreaking news from someone they wanted to be with? But the words had needed to be said. Now *he* was the one who had to be clear. He didn't want to lead her on. He worried he had already—without meaning to.

He shook his head, lowered his gaze, swallowed back the awkwardness. "I don't even have a chance with her, but it wouldn't be right to start seeing you while my heart is in another place." He gathered the courage to look at her then—but her eyes were closed.

He sighed, and went on. "And I hate that. Because you're amazing. You're beautiful, and funny, and warm, and smart, and…bold as hell. You're a woman of your own. You follow your heart wherever it leads you. And what more could a man want in a woman? I wish… I wish…hell, I don't know what I wish exactly because this is all pretty damn confusing. But, if it makes any sense, I wish like hell I wasn't telling you no."

"Me, too," she whispered, the softest of sounds.

And his heart broke a little—for *both* of them.

CHAPTER TWENTY-FOUR

EVERY MUSCLE IN Suzanne's body felt like a lead weight. She'd truly thought this would go her way. She'd told Dahlia she was prepared for any outcome, but she'd been wrong. She'd never have put herself in such a position if she'd really believed he'd turn her down. She'd made the mistake of believing she could have what she wanted, that she could get the hot guy, that she wasn't awkward and romantically clumsy. Only Cal—only Cal had ever really seen past all that.

You have no one to blame but yourself. You ignored the signs and signals. You were the blind, desperate tenth grader too overcome with longing to simply keep it classy and back away. And now she was stuck here, on his couch, holding his hand. Wishing she could hold it forever. Except that it was a handhold of kindness, of letting her down easy. The worst of all known handholds.

And she had no idea what to say, how to gracefully exit the situation she'd so haphazardly created. Then again, she was pretty sure the graceful ship had already sailed. *Now? Now I see it all clearly?*

More winging it. "Thank you for being so nice. And honest. And for the wine—the wine helped. But I should go now."

He looked doubtful. "You don't have to rush away,

Suzanne. Why don't you stay, warm up some more? I could attempt to make us something to eat." He grimaced slightly then, looking doubtful in a way that normally might have made her laugh. "Or we could just talk a while—I'm not much of a cook."

A heart-weary sigh left her. He was trying to *keep* being kind, trying to do the right thing, make her feel less awkward and more normal. But that was actually terrible, because it only made her like him all the more.

And she'd had just enough wine now that she didn't weigh her words as they spilled from her in total candidness. "That's tempting, and sounds nice. But I can't. I'd just end up confiding in you about my life, and then *you'd* confide in *me*, and I'd leave here more infatuated with you than I already am. So the wisest move really seems to be cutting my losses and hoping that by the spring thaw this will all just seem like a distant memory or a bad dream." As she spoke, she pushed up from the couch and sat down on the hearth to put her snow boots back on as swiftly as possible. It allowed her not to even have to try to look at him anymore, and would enable her departure.

"It's a small island," she went on, "so we'll be neighbors for a long time to come, and that will be easier if we never speak of this again and act as if it never happened. And *that* will be easier if I just go."

She was on her feet, reaching for her calf-length parka, which had dried at least a little, for which she was thankful—since she didn't plan to wait around. In fifteen or twenty minutes, she could be back in the privacy of her safe little cottage where she belonged, getting warm and dry for good this time, so a little more wetness seemed minuscule in comparison to her need to get out of Beck's house.

Only as she put the coat on and zipped it up, then reached for her scarf and gloves, she realized there was more she wanted to say. And maybe she shouldn't at this point, given the whole concept of cutting her losses, but wine and cutting losses perhaps worked at cross-purposes.

"I do want to thank you, though," she went on, "for…changing something in me. I didn't think I'd ever…want anything with a man again. After Cal died, I thought that part of me had died along with him. You made me think there could be life after…well, life after death. *His* death. So even if it didn't go anywhere, I'm grateful for that—that shift in myself."

"I'm grateful for it, too, Suzanne. I know you'll find happiness again."

She didn't think so. It had taken five years for a man to truly interest her romantically, and that man didn't want her. Cal had been the only man to ever truly connect with her in a deep way—and the brief hope she'd experienced with Beck, now dashed, reinforced what she'd known all along: Cal was the only man who ever would.

Only when she made a move for the door did Beck say, "Wait."

She stopped, looked up, a last renewed tiny burst of hope blossoming in her chest. Was he changing his mind?

"Let me walk you. Just give me a minute to grab a coat and some boots." Oh. He wanted to walk her home in the storm. Because he was a gentleman. A gentle man. She feared there weren't many of those left in the world, at least not available ones, and it only reminded her even more that she'd lost out here, big-time.

"Thanks, but no," she insisted. "It's terrible out there—no need for both of us to suffer through it, and your walk would be twice as long as mine."

"But—"

"I'll be fine, I promise."

As she headed for the front door, she hoped he heard that in the bigger picture way, as well. *I'll be fine.* And that he believed it. Even if she wasn't so sure herself.

She didn't give him a chance to protest—just opened the door and barreled forward that quickly, back out into the blizzard.

She hadn't even taken the time to bundle herself up properly, so as she hit West Bluff, the street unmarked even by footprints, long since covered by drifting snow, she struggled to pull her hood up, tighten it, get her scarf adjusted, as the wind howled and the snow fell sideways. Dusk had come, dimming her path with flat, fading light, turning her walk back to Mill Street almost otherworldly, as if she traversed a lonely, barren white river.

Tears began to roll down her cheeks as she walked—she pushed her scarf up, using it like a tissue to blot them away. He'd been so nice. And she'd been so…honest. And now felt…foolish. And lonely. As lonely as the wintry desolation of West Bluff Drive at the moment.

Maybe she would forever.

A long lonesome winter loomed. What did she have to look forward to, after all? Sounded like Dahlia would be leaving on this sudden, mysterious trip of hers, a thought which made the isolation feel even worse already. And who knew when the ice would clear enough for Meg to come home. And when she did…well, she had Seth now. Suzanne knew Meg wouldn't abandon their friendship or anything, but it made things different.

She'd thought she'd have all she needed here. All she wanted. Her shop. Books to read, a quaint cottage, a few friends, a simple life. But now she wanted more. And she wasn't sure she'd ever have it. Or how to face that.

Maybe she *shouldn't* have thanked him for reawakening the part of her that yearned for romance. Maybe she'd been better off without it.

Beck had called her a woman of her own. She wasn't even certain exactly what that meant, but it struck her as a supreme compliment. *I want to be that. I'll try to be that.*

Even if the world feels a little more empty to me now.

THE NEXT DAY the snow stopped. But a fresh foot of it lay like a mantel across the island, the sky still white and overcast, and Kentucky felt a world away. And heading home would have indeed been a damn nice distraction from the women weighing on his mind. One who wouldn't forgive him for the way he'd hurt her, and another whom he'd hurt by caring for the first. *Love stinks.*

Beck didn't know how to fix any of his own problems, but maybe he'd feel better if he could fix things for Cade somehow.

He couldn't get the kid home in time for Christmas, of course, any more than he could get himself there—but when he'd checked in with George this morning to make sure they'd survived the storm okay, he'd found out Cade remained inconsolable about this Santa situation.

"I'll try to figure out some way to make it better," he'd promised his neighbor. But now he worried he was just going to let someone else down, too, since he hadn't come up with any great ideas yet.

Tired of TV—he'd watched a lot of it over the past couple days—he turned it off and walked to the dining room, to the Nativity box. And he read.

For longer than on past occasions. Partly because he had time on his hands, and partly because he didn't come across any more sermons that disparaged him. Without that element to get under his skin, he continued to find this unexpected window into his father's soul enlightening and even comforting, when he'd least expected it.

As the afternoon passed, he read more sermons about forgiveness, kindness, and gratitude, but in these he sensed his dad having mellowed over time. The sermons had been placed in the box in chronological order, and it made him happy to read his father's softer take on the world as he'd aged. Turned out Pastor Kenneth Grainger hadn't been such a hard-ass, after all. Though it also made Beck regret all the more having stayed away so much in those later years.

When he reached the end of the stack of papers, the last thing remaining in the box appeared different than most. Each sermon had been a set of folded papers, some handwritten, some typed, some—toward the end—even printed out from a computer, and tossed into the mix had been an occasional letter to a friend or fellow minister that his father had seen fit to make a copy of before sending. But at the bottom of the velvet-lined Nativity box lay an envelope, facedown. And when Beck turned it over, it bore his name.

Huh. He hadn't seen that coming. And he had no idea what to expect. But he opened it, unfolded the sheets of paper inside, and read the letter written in the jagged scrawl of someone who no longer possessed steady hands.

Dear Beck,

I don't know if you'll ever read these words, but either way, it is my deepest wish that you lead a long and joyful life, finding fulfillment in whatever you undertake.

That word has stayed with me lately. Fulfillment. I've led a fulfilling life. I've found fulfillment in my faith, in shepherding a congregation, in giving whatever I can to others. Something happens inside me, Beck, when I give. Maybe not everyone feels it—I can't say. It's a wellspring of rightness and wellbeing that nothing else has ever brought me.

I am an old man, and perhaps stubborn. Maybe I've always been. So it's hard for me to admit when I've been wrong. But in these waning days of my life on this earthly plane, the Lord has delivered to me a revelation. Every time I find myself thinking about you, Beck, and wishing we'd seen more eye to eye, the Lord has brought me a Bible verse. Three distinct times this happened and the verses are these:

Now there are diversities of gifts, but the same Spirit. And there are differences of administrations, but the same Lord. 1 Corinthians 12:4-5.

Let us not therefore judge one another any more: but judge this rather, that no man put a stumbling block or an occasion to fall in his brother's way. Romans 14:13.

A new commandment I give unto you, that ye love one another. John 13:34.

What I realize now, son, is that we are not all the same. I, as a man who has ministered to many, should, above all others, know that. But I suppose it can be a man's weakness to wish for his children to want to emulate him, or at least view life in a similar way. When that didn't happen with you, I pushed against it, tried to bend your heart to my will, and I judged you wrongly for approaching life in a different fashion than I did.

I am proud of you, Beck. I'm proud of the man you've become. I'm proud that you make your way in the world boldly. I'm proud that you've found success. I'm proud that you're generous with your family. I'm proud that you give to the world in your own ways, even if different than mine. That is something I've come to understand late in life—we are all born with different gifts, and we're not all meant to be the same. It shames me, as a pastor, that it's taken me this long to bestow that understanding on you.

Perhaps I should have put this letter on the top of the box, not the bottom. But I am indeed a stubborn old man, and I suppose there is a part of me that just wants you to know my heart, for

*better or worse, whether in agreement or dis-
sension. And my sermons are my heart, so if you
have read them, son, I thank you.*

*I love you, Beck, just as you are.
With love and respect,
Dad*

BECK SAT AT his dining room table staring at the letter
in his hand. He reread it a couple of times. To make
sure he hadn't somehow misinterpreted it.

He'd made his dad proud, after all.

"Why didn't you tell me, old man?" he muttered.
"Before you died." It would have made for one hell of
a happier ending to their story as father and son. But
he supposed it had to do with pride. And that stubbornness his dad mentioned. He supposed he'd inherited a
little of that himself.

His first instinct? Like the last time he'd found a
revelation in this box, he longed to tell Lila about it.

But they'd already said their goodbyes. And even if
they were both stranded here for Christmas, they remained at an impasse.

So he picked up his phone and called his sister instead. "Hey, Em," he said when she answered, "is this
a good time?"

"It is if you're calling to tell me the ferry is running again."

He sighed. "No such luck. Calling for something
else."

"Rats," she said. "Well, I'm just about to head to the
grocery—on the Saturday before Christmas, God help
me. But I've got a few minutes. What's up?"

Okay, so he wouldn't beat around the bush. "I finished reading the stuff from Dad. And at the bottom, there was a letter—to me. And damnedest thing, Em—he told me he was proud of me."

"Of course he was proud of you," she said, like he was a numbskull.

He blinked. "Of course he was? You knew this? Because, I mean, if this is common knowledge, why didn't someone tell *me*? Why on earth do you think I quit coming around?"

"Because he was hard on you and tended to be critical. So I understood why you pulled back and didn't even blame you—you two definitely knocked heads. But in spite of that, I always knew he was proud of you. In the big picture way."

Beck let out a heavy breath. "Well…hell. It's news to me."

"I guess by virtue of not being around, maybe you never got to hear him say it. Or…who knows, maybe he wouldn't have said it if you were there. But *I* knew. And Mom knew. I guess I just assumed you did, too. It would be hard *not* to be proud of you, Beck—you've accomplished a lot and you're a good guy on top of it."

As Beck continued trying to wrap his head around this, he wondered out loud in frustration, "Why can't people just say what they mean? It would make life a hell of a lot easier." The remark left him glad he'd had a frank conversation with Suzanne, even if he'd felt like a jerk doing it, and made him appreciate even more that she'd made her position clear.

Moving on with another sigh, he said, "You guys ready for Christmas down there?"

"It won't be the same without you—or Dad—but

yeah, pretty much. Though I dread seeing our electric bill next month. I was reminiscing, telling Mike and the kids how Dad used to go crazy putting lights up on the rectory when you and I were little. Remember that?"

"Oh. Yeah." Though he hadn't thought about it in years, that had been one of his father's few trivial indulgences—he put a ton of lights on the house back when they were small and still believed in Santa Claus. "I remember him saying it was how Santa would find us."

On the other end, Em laughed. "That's right, he did. Anyway, Mike took it upon himself to go buy a bunch of lights and put them up. And I do mean a bunch. We're the talk of the neighborhood—for better or worse."

Beck chuckled. "Sounds fun. Sorry I won't get to see them."

Emma sighed. "Me, too. We'll send you a picture. But I'd better go—time to get moving. After the grocery, Mike's taking the kids to a holiday parade so I can wrap gifts and hide them. Lots to do to get ready for the big day."

Hanging up, Beck again lamented that he'd not get to see his niece and nephew on Christmas. But he'd be seeing another little boy, who still thought he had a big problem. And...hmm, maybe his dad had unwittingly just given him an idea.

Lights. He was gonna need a hellacious amount of lights.

Phone still in his hand, he dialed George. "George, got any extra Christmas lights? Like...maybe a few thousand?"

FLAT GRAY CLOUDS blanketed the sky and hung heavy in the frigid air the following morning, but that didn't stop Beck from putting on winter gear and setting out toward Harbor Street.

His father had inspired him in more ways than one yesterday, even from the grave. Beck planned to stop by Koester's Market, the only place on the island that would have dependable foot traffic over the next couple of days before Christmas, to put the word out and try to collect the things he needed to give Cade a Christmas miracle. And after that, he intended to take another stab at one for himself, too.

Though his goals with Lila had changed dramatically since the last time he'd hoped for a miracle with her. And maybe that should discourage him—because in comparison, the miracle he sought now was much, much bigger than just getting her to be okay with the development behind the inn by taking her a Christmas tree.

Descending Mill Street, he peered out on Lake Michigan, looking for a miracle there, too. But it teemed with thick, jagged, angry-looking chunks and plates of ice that told him that particular wish would have to be put on hold. And passing by Suzanne's cottage made his heart hurt a little—for her, and for bad timing all around. He hoped she was all right.

Harbor Street was only slightly more traveled with footprints than the others, but lights glowed inside the Skipper's Wheel and the coffee shop. When he stepped into the corner market by Lakeview Park, he found the owner and one cashier on duty, along with Dahlia, who'd apparently stopped in to shop.

"I need to ask for some help from the community,"

he informed them, explaining about little Cade being stuck here for Christmas—then listed the things he needed. "Mini-lights—as many as anyone can spare. And stuff for a five-year-old boy—specifically a bike with training wheels, anything Pokémon-related, and any other toys or things good for a kid his age. Oh, and a stuffed dog of some sort would be great." He couldn't come up with a puppy, but even a facsimile would be welcome under the circumstances. "I hate to ask," Beck concluded, "but my resources are pretty limited at the moment."

"Don't you worry about that," Dahlia was quick to say. "It's darned sweet what you're doing, and we year-rounders stick together when somebody needs a little help."

Indeed, they all promised to spread the word and seemed eager to help, and the owner even offered the store as a collection point. Before Beck knew it, the cashier was on the phone, starting to call various locals, and the owner began hatching a plan with Beck.

"Thanks—I really appreciate it," he told them all. He wasn't sure if he could really pull this off in a convincing way, but he'd give it his best shot, and he left Koester's feeling cautiously optimistic.

From there, he headed west back down the street and through the snow, on a course for the Summerbrook Inn.

His father had finally told Beck how he really felt—but too late for it to give them a better relationship. Suzanne had done the same thing with him, being honest and frank and clear—also too late. Beck had decided he didn't want to be too late with Lila.

Though as he walked up the steps and onto the

porch, the big Victorian looming over him, his chest tightened. It made him admire Suzanne all the more because she'd probably felt yesterday the way he felt today—uneasy, uncertain, hoping like hell for the person on the other side of the door to see things the same way.

He rang the bell, then shifted his weight from one work boot to another, waiting.

When the door opened, Lila stood before him in an oversize sweater, leggings, and fuzzy socks, a skein of purple yarn in her hand. She looked surprised to see him—and maybe…something more. He just couldn't read what that something more in her expression *was*.

"Hi," he said.

"Hi."

"Can I…come in? It's cold."

She didn't answer—just moved back to clear the path through the door. He stepped inside and shut it, vaguely aware of a fire crackling in the next room, then looked back at her. He didn't have a plan. Maybe he should have. He pointed vaguely toward the yarn. "Knitting?"

She nodded. "Trying to knit my troubles away. Some people drink—I knit."

He shrugged. "That's healthier."

She shrugged in return. "Well, *occasionally* I drink. And not that some spiked hot chocolate isn't tempting, mind you. But I guess spiked hot chocolate—" she dropped her gaze, appearing slightly forlorn "—has caused me enough problems since I got here."

Okay, so she considered sex with him a problem. Of course, he knew it was more complicated than that— but all in all, he decided that rather than give her the chance to cut any deeper into his confidence, he'd just forge ahead and speak from the heart.

"Here's the thing," he told her. "I'm in love with you."

CHAPTER TWENTY-FIVE

LILA'S JAW DROPPED. Perhaps understandably. Just like
Suzanne had thrown her affection at him when he'd not
been ready for it, he was doing the exact same thing to
Lila. He only hoped it would turn out better this time.

As he waited for her to form a reply, he noticed her
squeezing the yarn like a stress ball. He could hear
his heartbeat in his ears. Maybe he should say more.
"I thought you should know. That I love you. I never
planned it. I never dreamed when I found you standing
in front of that bulldozer in the snow that you'd turn
out to be someone I can't get off my mind, someone I
want to be with all that time, someone I care for and
admire and want to make happy however I can...but
there it is. I love you."

She peered up at him, her hazel eyes fraught with
emotion. "If you loved me, Beck," she whispered,
"you'd leave the trees alone."

He just blew out a heavy sigh. He'd hoped maybe
love would be the thing that would trump the trees.
No such luck.

"I'm sorry," she said. "I know I sound like a broken record. And I wish like hell I could get past it,
because... I care for you, Beck. More than I want to.
More than makes sense. In fact...okay, I'm pretty sure
I love you, too. I think—perhaps ironically, given the

tree situation—that you're the best man I've ever been with. If I could somehow move past that and the Meg betrayal issue, things would be different between us."

"Different how?" he asked, pushing the issue.

"Maybe… I'd find a reason to come back to the island sooner rather than later. Maybe… I'd find a reason to stay."

Beck's heart warmed as he took all that in. She loved him, too. She really loved him, too. Part of him had been sure she'd deny it—sure he'd end up slinking away heartbroken and defeated, same as Suzanne had less than twenty-four hours earlier. But her words buoyed him, making him feel like anything was possible. Hope burst wide-open in his chest.

He only had to reason with her, make her understand. Maybe there was more he hadn't been clear about. "I wish like hell I could make the tree situation go away, Lila—I'd do it in a heartbeat." He narrowed his gaze on her. "But would it make a difference if I explained that I have investors, people who've entrusted their money to me, that it's not just my own money on the table here? Would it make a difference if you knew that the land has been surveyed, plat maps have been drawn up by engineers, that home plans and permits and builders are all in place? And that literally hundreds of thousands of dollars are involved? It might seem as simple as not bulldozing the trees, but it's a hell of a lot more complicated. And if I could go back in time and choose different property—believe me, I would. But I can't. And who knows—maybe Meg will understand. Maybe Meg wouldn't want you to give up a chance at happiness over this. You haven't even talked to her about it, you know. So this is where we are. I'm in love with you, and I know we could be happy together—but no matter how much I want to, I can't save the woods behind the inn."

He went quiet, having said all he could to convince her. *Please let it be enough. Please don't let a bunch of trees on a hillside come between us. Please find a way to look beyond that.*

He watched as she drew in a deep breath and blew it back out. She set the yarn aside on a table next to the door. Then took his hands in her much warmer ones. Looked down at them. "So cold," she murmured. "And you never wear gloves. I would make you a pair, but that's beyond my current skill level."

He tried to smile—at her concern, at how damn cute she was—but he felt too tense.

Finally, with her dainty fingers still wrapped around his, she lifted her gaze back to his face. "Thank you for telling me all that. It does help me understand better and see where you're coming from.

"But…how could I ever truly be happy with you knowing that each time I'm here, I'd look out that window and see what's not there and know how it hurt my sister and my family and that it was your doing? Maybe some women could. Maybe I should be able to overlook this. Maybe right now I'm just sensitive to…" She stopped, shook her head. "To not wanting to let *any* man take something from me I don't choose to give. But regardless of all that, as soon as the ice clears, I have to figure out how to tell my sister and my parents what's happening to the land, and that I wasn't able to stop it—and it's going to kill me.

"And I've *accepted* that nothing will stop it—but I don't think my heart could ever be completely at peace, completely fulfilled, knowing it was you who changed this place forever and that I just…chose to forget about it, chose to do the easy thing instead of the difficult one. I respect the position you're in, but I just don't think this can be fixed. Because…because…" She sighed, let her gaze drop. "I just want to believe that if something is really right—it won't be this hard, it won't make me feel like I'm doing the wrong thing, it won't make me feel like I'm selfishly betraying my sister, it won't feel like I'm making a concession in my heart." She looked back at him then. "And that's not fair to you—I know it's not. I know it's this…unrealistic, fairy-tale expectation. But regardless of what's fair or even reasonable, it's where my heart is. And that means, for us, everything will *never* be right."

Beck had listened patiently, every muscle in his body going weaker with each word she spoke, until it grew challenging to remain on his feet. When she finished, he could think of only one simple thing to say. "I just thought telling you I love you might change things."

"It does," she told him sadly. "It makes them worse."

A FULL DAY after Beck professed his love, Lila still felt numb. The man of her dreams loved her, but she didn't know how to be happy with him under the circumstances. And Christmas Eve was two days away, and at a time when she longed for her family more than ever, she would spend the holiday without them.

Funny thing—only when she'd found out she'd be stranded here alone did she realize how much she needed to talk to Meg, face-to-face, how much she had to say to her now. About way more than just the trees. And that made it all the harder to know it would have to wait.

"Pull yourself together," she muttered to herself as she trudged up Harbor Street in a bitter wind that made her wonder if she was on the North Pole instead of Summer Island. Dahlia had invited her to Christmas dinner with Mr. Desjardins, Suzanne, and Zack—Meg's ex. It sounded like an awkward group at best—at least two of which had the potential to be unhappy to see her, even if, in Zack's case, only by virtue of family ties. Even so, she'd accepted, and she'd offered to bring cookies. Now she only hoped Koester's had the ingredients she'd need for Gran's butter cookie recipe that she'd found in Meg's well-organized vintage recipe card file.

She was surprised to find Koester's so lively when she walked in—several people bustled about, and Dahlia stood behind a long table heaped with toys, wrapping paper, and a ridiculous amount of Christmas lights. "I don't know if all of them work," she heard Dahlia saying into her cell phone, "but pretty much anyone who had a strand to spare donated a set, and Koester's is donating all the new ones still on their shelves, too."

Next to Dahlia stood a cashier Lila recognized from the market, but instead of manning one of the few registers, she was speaking with Trent Fordham, who Lila knew ran the bike livery and was engaged to Allie from the Knitting Nook. "I'll see if I can come up with some training wheels," he was saying. "Either way, I'll have the bike ready in an hour."

Lila tossed a wave in Dahlia's direction, wondering what the heck was going on, but then went about her business, picking up a shopping basket and making her way to the baking aisle. Fortunately, Meg had flour, sugar, and butter—leaving Lila on the hunt for vanilla, fresh eggs, and cream of tartar. A few minutes later—pay dirt—she had located what she needed, along with a few other groceries to sustain her since she had no idea when she'd get to leave the island.

By the time she'd paid and picked her bags up in mittened hands, ready to face the cold walk home, Dahlia was off the phone. "Lila," she called.

Lila made her way over. "What's all this?" she asked, looking to the table that contained everything from coloring books to toy dump trucks to Lego sets.

"It's for little Cade Walton."

Beck's little friend who she'd met at the tree-lighting. Lila blinked, concerned. "Why? Is something wrong with him?"

Dahlia shook her head. "Oh—no, not at all. He just can't go home for Christmas—like you and a few other folks—so Beck is collecting gifts for Cade to wake up to on Christmas morning. From Santa, you know." She winked behind tiny rectangular, purple-lensed glasses. "The whole island is pulling together, making sure the little boy has a nice holiday. But it's all Beck's doing."

Lila released a wistful sigh. Of course it was Beck's doing. Because he was a wonderful man. Who would make an amazing dad. Not that she even knew for sure if she wanted kids or—God forbid—what kind of mother she'd make. But a man like Beck could inspire a maternal instinct in a woman.

"You seem strangely unhappy to hear this," Dahlia observed.

Lila met her gaze. "No, I'm just strangely unhappy, period. About Beck."

Dahlia tilted her head. "And why is that, my dear?"

Lila saw no reason to mince words. "Because he loves me. And I love him. But…well, you know why we can't be together."

"Because of a few sticks of wood behind the inn?" Dahlia raked a hand down through the air, implying the trees were nothing.

But Lila argued the point. "You know how important they are, for so many reasons. And how much I feel I've let Meg down and put my own selfish wants ahead of her."

"Don't get me wrong—I understand about the trees. It's a situation where no one is at fault and yet no one can see their way clear to give in. But… I'm not sure I understand how falling in love hurts Meg. And he's a good man, Lila. Most would say you're a lucky woman to have his affection. You might want to think long and hard before throwing it away."

Lila drew in a deep breath. Dahlia was preaching to the choir—but both she and Beck made it all sound simpler than it was. "Believe me, I'm aware of all that," she told her new friend. "And…the old me probably would have forgotten all about the trees by this point. But to do that now would feel like…like a betrayal to Meg and my family. And a betrayal to… to the woman inside me who wants to be strong, and loyal, and doesn't think love should be this challenging. Shouldn't it be…perfect? At least closer to perfect?"

"Pretty thoughts," Dahlia said almost dismissively, surprising her. "But sometimes life isn't as picture-perfect as we want it to be. I suspect that making a compromise, for the right man, under certain circumstances, might well be worth it. And I suspect these might be just such circumstances."

Was this Dahlia? It didn't sound like the woman Lila had started getting to know. She'd thought self-sufficient, independent Dahlia would back her up in standing strong, righting wrongs, and not settling for something so much less than perfect. "Who are you and what have you done with Dahlia, the woman who seems not to need a man at all?"

Dahlia stayed quiet for a moment, looking contemplative, like she'd gone somewhere else in her mind. Then she met Lila's gaze and lowered her voice. "I'm going to make a confession to you, but you can never tell another soul."

Lila let her eyes go wide. "I'll take it to the grave," she promised, instantly intrigued.

"In my own perhaps elevated opinion of myself, I don't have a great many large flaws—but I do sometimes wonder if perhaps I hold men to too high a standard. I can be stubborn about it. Independence, on the surface, appears to be a fine trait, but I believe it can, too often, go hand in hand with stubbornness. I have no regrets, but I…sometimes wonder if I should. I sometimes wonder if I've made the right choices with the men in my life."

Lila didn't know what to say. To her, Dahlia was the picture of confidence, of having made a wonderful life for herself that she wouldn't change in any way. Was there more there? Would Dahlia truly be happier with one of her exes? Or… "Is Mr. Desjardins still in the picture?" Lila asked softly.

Dahlia nodded, but looked non-committal. "He is."

"Is this about him?" she went so far as to ask.

"No—this is about you. And Beck. And simply wanting to ensure you make the decision that will bring you the most happiness. What if…what if you just forgave him?" she suggested as merrily and simply as if encouraging Lila to make a healthy choice from a restaurant menu.

Lila blinked. "Forgave him?"

"You could just forgive him. For the situation with the woods. Forgive and forget. Forgiving is a powerful act, Lila."

Lila sighed, thought it through, tried to dissect her emotions. "Maybe I…already *have* forgiven him," she realized aloud, tilting her head slightly. "But it's the forgetting I'm not sure I can do."

When the bell on the market's front door jingled, Lila turned to see Suzanne come in from the cold, toting a cardboard box and announcing to no one in particular, "I gathered up some lights I was using on trees at the shop before they sold." Only as she plopped the box on the floor alongside others also containing strands of mini-bulbs did she notice Dahlia wasn't alone. "Lila," she said then, the greeting decidedly pensive.

"Hi, Suzanne," she replied. And suddenly feeling awkward, she shifted her focus to the piles of lights. "I know what the toys are for, but what about the lights?"

"That we don't know," Dahlia told her. "But Beck said he needed them to pull this off, lots of them, so we're collecting those, as well."

"It's so nice of everyone to contribute," Lila said. "I'll have to see what I can find in the attic."

"Anson is picking up everything here with his sleigh

tomorrow morning and hauling it up to West Bluff.
Going to be a highly sensitive operation—Anson will
call George Walton when he's leaving, and George and
Marie will do something to occupy Cade and keep him
from looking out the window while Beck and Anson
unload the goods at Beck's place. So you have until
then if you want to drop something off."

Lila nodded and thanked her for the information,
then turned to Suzanne, a little more grounded now
and hoping to get past the weirdness. "I'll look forward
to seeing you at Dahlia's on Christmas."

Her sister's best friend smiled—and Lila could see
in her face that she appreciated the gesture. "Likewise—and I'm glad you're coming. I'm... I'm sorry I
haven't been in touch much."

Lila shook her head. "I understand—no biggie. I'm
just...glad we're still friends."

"Of course we are," Suzanne assured her.

LILA DIDN'T REMEMBER ever having visited the inn's attic
as many times in her life as she had in the past few
weeks. But she knew there were lights up there that
hadn't been used on the Christmas tree, and maybe
she could find something else a little boy would enjoy.

Of course, as she climbed the drop-down ladder one
more time, she wanted to kill Beck for being so kind to
Cade. She wanted to kill him for being so adorable and
cute with Cade in front of her at the tree-lighting ceremony. And while she was at it, she wanted to kill him
for being patient and persistent and witty and handsome and sexy and good in bed.

She located the spare lights easily, but finding a
worthy Christmas gift for a five-year-old took a little

more looking. Finally, she spotted a stack of old board games. Most were well used, and God only knew if all the pieces were in the boxes, but two of them appeared to be almost like new: Candy Land and KerPlunk.

She recalled playing both with Gran and Meg when she was small. And part of her wanted to keep them, cherish them. But a bigger part of her remembered Beck learning how one simple gift could change the world, and while she doubted a round of KerPlunk would dramatically alter Cade Walton's life, she still wanted to join in on the project in some way.

So after opening each to confirm the games were in excellent condition on the inside of the box as well as the outside, she carried them downstairs and further tidied them up by putting game pieces in plastic bags that a small child would hopefully never suspect hadn't come from the manufacturer. It felt good to think of Cade opening them on Christmas morning. Once she was satisfied that they looked new other than the lack of being sealed in cellophane, she went so far as to wrap them and plop sticky bows on top, figuring it would save Beck the trouble on at least these two gifts.

Maybe this was how Beck's dad had felt giving things to people. Even if she still thought it wrong to do so much more for strangers than his own children. But maybe Beck would forgive him someday. The way Dahlia was telling her she should forgive Beck. And as she'd told Dahlia, she truly thought she already had. She didn't feel angry anymore. She just didn't know how to be with him under such regretful circumstances.

Yet was Dahlia right? Was she holding him to too high a standard?

Was Simon Alexis part of that, too—was it his fault she wanted to make zero concessions?

Was everyone who'd said she needed to forget about failing Meg right? Was feeling she didn't deserve Beck if it came at her sister's expense holding *herself* to too high a standard?

Was wanting love to be simpler, less fraught with drama, just one more form of selfish immaturity?

She didn't know—she simply didn't know.

But maybe none of that mattered anyway, because even if the answer to all of those questions was yes— she still had no clue how to get her heart on board.

CHAPTER TWENTY-SIX

BECK LABORED IN the Walton's wide front yard, hammering stakes he'd found at Fulton's Hardware, which had opened for him upon special request, down through the snow and ice. Even in frigid temperatures, he was working up a sweat.

But it was worth it when Cade came running out, all wide-eyed under his big winter hat, to ask, "What are you doing, Becker?"

"Making it so Santa can find you tomorrow night," he replied.

The little boy's eyes nearly popped out of his head. *"What? What do you mean? How are you doing that? How will Santa find me?"*

"You just leave that to me," Beck told him on a laugh. He'd known he wouldn't be able to keep his project out here a secret from Cade, but he still wanted the end product to be a surprise.

"What if it doesn't work?" Cade questioned him, turning skeptical.

Beck just shook his head in slow, gentle scolding. "Cade, Cade, Cade. After all we've been through together, don't you trust your good buddy, Becker, to look out for you?"

Cade appeared to think the question over very seriously, finally replying, "I guess so."

"Have no fear, my friend—Santa's going to find you without any problem. Tomorrow night, when it gets dark, I'll come over and show you how it's gonna work. But until then, you have to be patient, and maybe, uh, not look out the window too much. And as long as you can do that—Santa. Deal?" Anson had already delivered all the gifts, but Beck still didn't need Cade being *too* observant.

The little boy nodded. "Deal." Then informed him, "I have to go back inside. Grammy says it's too cold to stay out. But you're supposed to come knock on the door when you want hot chocolate."

"Sounds like a plan. Now get back in there where it's nice and cozy."

An hour later, Beck took Marie up on the offer of hot chocolate and warmed himself by their fire for a few minutes. An hour after that, he had all the stakes in place and began to string the lights around them. Hopefully this part would go faster. And hopefully the lights would stretch as far as he'd calculated.

After he finished outside, he'd work on wrapping gifts. Some had come in gift bags and wrapping paper, and some were already wrapped by virtue of having been purchased for his sister's kids—stuff he could replace for them once the ice cleared. He was grateful to Trent Fordham for donating a bright red child's bike, complete with training wheels, and someone had come up with Pokémon cards, a stuffed Pikachu, and some Pokémon-themed books. According to Anson, Allie Hobbs' mother had kindly donated a stuffed puppy intended for her own grandchild—which he almost hated to take. But thinking of his father, and the joy people experienced in giving, he accepted it in the spirit intended and resolved to thank her personally after Christmas.

All things considered, he thought Cade was going to come out pretty well here. And maybe this wouldn't be such a bad Christmas, after all. He glanced over at the snowman he and Cade had built—still standing, even if lopsided and a little worse for wear after the recent snowstorm. His old hat remained, as well, just buried beneath fresh snowfall now. The sight, and the memory of Lila telling him it was awful, made him grin.

Lila. If things were different with her, this Christmas would be amazing, ice or no ice. As it was, trying to make it amazing for someone else was a welcome distraction from the constant gnawing pain in his gut at remembering her declaration that there was no hope for them. He wanted people to make themselves clear—well, she'd made herself clear. The wind whipping around him suddenly grew a little more bitter at the memory.

Another hour later, he'd wrapped the strings of lights around the many stakes he'd managed to pound into the cold, hard ground. And he was feeling pretty good about how it was coming together—until…damn, turned out he was short on lights, after all. He hadn't quite made it around the *E* in *Cade* when he ran out. Shit.

He weighed options. He could just quit. Would Cade ever really know the *E* was incomplete? But somehow, after all this work, leaving it that way felt wrong. Which meant unwrapping a bunch of the lights and reconfiguring the stakes. Which would suck big-time. He blew out a tired sigh, disgusted by the prospect.

"You really are a good man, Indiana Jones."

He looked up, nearly snow-blind now, but not so much that he didn't see the lovely figure of Lila Sloan coming toward him in a parka and boots, toting large shopping bags in each hand.

Simply the sight of her—her tousled hair, her pretty smile—warmed him up inside right when he'd gone completely cold to the bone. It was easy to smile back. "Just trying to make the little guy's Christmas good despite being stuck here," he told her.

She scanned the yard, taking in the conglomeration of lights strung in lines and curves just above the snow. "I'm not sure what I'm seeing here," she said, "but it's phenomenal." Then she motioned to the bags she carried. "Though maybe I'm too late with the lights."

"No!" he said, letting his eyes widen. "Oh my God—you have no idea how happy I am to hear there are lights in those bags. You're a lifesaver. I just ran out. Only need a few more, but wasn't sure where I was gonna get them. So this is great."

She graced him with another lovely smile. "Good, I'm glad." Then she jiggled one of the bags and said, "Only lights in this one, though. I brought a couple of games, too. They're wrapped, but KerPlunk and Candy Land are from me, and played with joy at the inn as a child, so they come with happy memories."

"Thank you, honey," he said warmly, fighting the inherent desire to lean over and kiss her forehead. That was his natural urge with her now—to kiss her, touch her, get closer to her. Instead he had to settle for adding, "It was sweet of you to walk them all the way up here."

She shrugged, still smiling softly. "I missed the sleigh departure at the market. Late elf."

It made him laugh. Made him want to say *Cute elf*—

but he held back. Flirtation seemed obsolete at this point, like it was too trivial for their circumstances. "Sweet of you to find something for him, too."

Another pleasant shrug from her. "It's bad enough being stranded here for the holiday as an adult—it would be much worse if I worried Santa couldn't find me."

He grinned. "Exactly. I figure we don't *all* have to suffer."

When something in her eyes changed then, he realized she'd heard his words in a way that went beyond being island-bound for Christmas. She was suffering, too, same as him. And he hated it. For both of them.

"All right if I leave these here?" she asked, setting her bags down next to some of his tools.

"Of course—sure."

She lowered them to the snow, then pointed over her shoulder. "Well, I should go."

He nodded acceptingly, wishing he could fix things, not leave them broken, the way his father had. But he didn't know how. Maybe his dad hadn't known how, either.

"Merry Christmas, Lila," he said.

"Merry Christmas, Beck."

"DON'T SUPPOSE THERE'S any change in the ferry situation?" Meg asked Lila on the phone.

Lila lounged in the big easy chair in the nook, stroking Miss Kitty, feeling wistful. "No. And I heard some people looked into the idea of flying out, but the weather has prevented that, too—something about the ceiling being too low, whatever that means."

"Maybe when we hang up," Meg said, "I'll call the

ferry runners. I've known them forever—maybe they can give me some insider information."

"That's a nice idea, but I can't imagine you're suddenly going to get the ferry moving." Although it touched her to know Meg felt as disappointed about this as she did.

"You're right," Meg said evenly, sullenly. "Guess I'm just grasping at straws, trying to fix something that can't be fixed."

Tell me about it. Things that couldn't be fixed were the bane of Lila's existence lately. But… "I guess I just have to look on the bright side here."

"Which is?" Meg inquired.

Damn good question. Lila thought about it for a minute and finally said, "Well, I have a warm house to sleep in, a lovely Christmas tree to look at, a cat to pet, and people to eat dinner with tomorrow—even if I expect Zack to make it awkward."

"You put up a tree?" Meg asked, clearly surprised.

Oh. Lila had momentarily forgotten she hadn't mentioned that. But it had, of course, been for an obvious reason. "Um…yes."

"And…why do you suddenly sound very cryptic about it?"

Lila sighed. "Let's just say I have a lot to tell you when the ice melts." And…maybe by then there would be even *more* to tell.

It was a big maybe.

But she kept thinking about not only forgiving but… forgetting. And stubbornness. And not letting past events determine her future. She still wasn't sure of much, but she was sure Beck was the man she wanted. If only she could figure out how to make it okay to love him.

ON CHRISTMAS EVE, the sun came out for the first time Beck could remember in a while, and the thermostat beside his back door pushed upward of forty degrees.

It was even warm enough out that he and Cade built a new snowman—though this one they constructed in Beck's yard so as not to disturb the complex network of light cords criss-crossing the snow-covered lawn at the Waltons'.

After that came an afternoon spent working jigsaw puzzles with Cade and George—George's idea and George's puzzles, so Beck still didn't know if kids were actually *into* puzzles these days. Marie made them all sandwiches, telling Beck, "We're eating light today to get ready for tomorrow." After the meal, George opened his laptop and pulled up the website that tracked Santa's movements on Christmas Eve—and they determined that Cade would have to go to bed early and be sure to stay there so Santa could come.

When darkness fell, Beck instructed the three Waltons to head upstairs and look out a second floor window. After which he tossed on his coat, went outside, flipped a switch, and lit up West Bluff Drive with a light display that rivaled the best of them.

It had taken several thousand lights, but an enormous illuminated arrow pointed toward the house, along with more lights spelling out the words: SANTA, STOP HERE FOR CADE.

Beck hadn't actually seen it himself yet—he hadn't had the convenience of a test run. But he hoped it looked as good as he intended and assured Cade that Santa wouldn't miss him.

A moment later, the front door burst open and his little friend came running out. "Becker, Becker! Oh my gosh! Santa can find me now! Santa can really find me! You're the best! I love you!" And with that, the little boy threw his arms around Beck's hips and squeezed tight—and Beck bent to hug him back.

Without warning, he suddenly understood what his dad had felt from giving, from helping someone. And he couldn't deny it was pretty awesome.

IT WAS JUST past nine when Beck received a text from George letting him know Cade was fast asleep and it was safe to start bringing over the presents from Santa. It took a lot of trips, but Beck didn't mind. George offered to help, but given the snow and the darkness that had dropped temps a little, he refused to let him, seeing no reason to put the elderly man at risk of slipping and falling when he was able-bodied enough to do it all himself.

George held the door open each time he arrived with a new armload of the gifts the islanders had donated on short notice. The bike, all the wrapped games and toys, the stuffed dog. Turned out there was also a kid's hockey set and a brand new sled—the old-fashioned kind Beck had used as a boy—that he hadn't even seen when he and Anson had been unloading the big sleigh yesterday.

Even though he figured little kids slept pretty soundly, he tried to stay quiet as he came and went. By the time he brought the last few packages over, Marie had arranged all the gifts beneath their Christmas tree in a way that left no doubt Santa Claus had indeed come down the Walton chimney. "This looks great, Marie," he said quietly.

The older lady beamed. "I can't imagine the look

on Cade's face tomorrow morning. He was practically bouncing off the walls all evening after seeing the lights outside—just so excited about Santa being on his way."

Beck hadn't wrapped the stuffed dog from Mrs. Hobbs, and now, though it looked cute enough sitting atop a large wrapped box, Beck couldn't help thinking it needed a little something to jazz it up. Since it wasn't a *real* puppy, he wanted to make the fake one as good as possible. "Marie, do you have any red ribbon?"

"Does she?" George chimed in. "Woman hoards ribbon like a mouse hoards cheese."

Beck chuckled. "Just thinking maybe that dog could use a bow around his neck."

Marie stood back and eyed the stuffed animal. "You're right, Beck. Let's go find just the right one."

Beck wasn't sure it needed to be "just the right one," but was happy enough to indulge Marie in the whim as she led him down the hall and into a craft room, one side of it indeed overflowing with ribbon, thick and thin, fancy and simple, in just about every color, on a large ceiling-to-floor rack against one wall. George hadn't been kidding.

Together, Beck and Marie cut a strip of velvety red ribbon, then returned to the living room where she tied it in a tiny bow around the dog's neck. "What do you think?" she asked after putting the stuffed dog back in place.

"Perfect," Beck told her, grateful to have been able to pull this together for his special little friend. He wouldn't be here to see Cade open it all in the morning, but that was okay—he'd catch up with him afterward.

"Then our work is done," George said, "and we can

enjoy the reward. Have a seat and dig in." He pointed to the plate of cookies Cade had dutifully set out for Santa on the coffee table, a glass of milk beside it.

It surprised Beck to realize he would have enjoyed sitting and talking with his neighbors all night. He wasn't normally *that* gregarious, but the fact that it was Christmas, and a much different, quieter one than he'd expected, left a nagging sort of wistfulness in his belly. He supposed it was just nice to be with other people this time of year.

But it was nearly eleven and he didn't want to overstay his welcome, so after two cookies, he pushed to his feet and announced that he'd better head home. As if he was needed there. As if someone was waiting for him. It was the first time since his divorce that he wished it were true. And maybe it was only because of spending Christmas without his loved ones. Or maybe it was an ache that went deeper.

George walked him to the door—and then surprised Beck by giving him a heartfelt hug. "Thank you for making a little boy's Christmas special. You're a fine man, Beck Grainger."

"And I'm sure Cade will be running over to your house at some point tomorrow morning," Marie told him, "but George and I will expect you for Christmas lunch promptly at one."

The invitation warmed Beck's heart. "That sounds nice," he said with a smile. "I wouldn't miss it."

As he stepped back out into the brisk air, he looked up and realized that, just as with the sun this morning, it was the first night in a week that he'd been able to see any stars. Even with the temporary light pollution he'd added to the area, a million twinkling stars lit the darkness, the universe adding its own Christmas lights up in the sky.

Making his way through the snow down past the stakes and lights, George's words echoed in his ears. People kept telling him what a fine man he was. And he'd always aspired to be a good enough person—but did he feel like *that*, like a *fine man*?

Maybe his doubt was unfounded—maybe it was like Lila beating herself up over things she'd never done wrong. Maybe years of criticism from his father had bored its way into Beck's psyche.

And maybe he thought a *fine man* had to have done more to earn the title: Abraham Lincoln was a *fine man*. Martin Luther King Jr. was a *fine man*.

Or maybe it was simpler. And perhaps his doubt came from someplace closer to home.

Maybe he'd never feel like a fine man until he truly forgave his father, completely, for the rifts between them, and forgave himself for his part in it, too.

Maybe he'd never feel like a fine man until he found a way to make it up to his mother and sister for having been largely absent from their lives for so long.

Maybe he'd never be a fine man until he managed to make the woman he loved happy.

And maybe it was high time he start figuring out how.

CHAPTER TWENTY-SEVEN

Because Dahlia lived on the far side of Lakeview Park, and the rest of her Christmas dinner guests did not, she'd decided to prepare the meal and celebrate the day at the café. Which Suzanne thought just as warm and inviting as anyplace, so it was with a happy heart that she made the short walk there early on Christmas Day to help her friend prepare the feast. Well, as happy as it could be under various circumstances.

Yes, a few days ago she'd hoped that Beck might be part of her holiday, that she might now be in the throes of a fresh, new, exhilarating romance. Yes, her heart ached in a deflating new way for the loss of even the possibility. Sometimes even mere possibility was the spark that ignited a flame in the soul and lifted you up to move forward—and she'd lost that. And she truly didn't relish spending the dinner with the curmudgeonly Zack. She'd always thought him generally selfish and inconsiderate, but losing Meg had pushed him into the curmudgeonly zone. As if the loss wasn't completely his own fault.

But she tried to look on the bright side. The sun was shining again, making the day both merry *and* bright. With just a few words, she'd made amends with Lila—and despite wishing she'd taken the step herself to mend fences with Meg's sister, she was simply relieved that bit of unease would be lifted from the day. She had people to spend the holiday with—and perhaps the combination of Dahlia, Lila, and the debonair Mr. Desjardins would be enough to keep Zack amiable. She had a warm home, and a business she loved, and soon she'd have Meg back, too. And one night soon, after Meg got home and settled, Suzanne intended to steal her away from Seth so they could eat ice cream and watch chick flicks and she could tell Meg everything that had happened—and hadn't happened—with Beck. And Meg, being Meg, would somehow help her be content again.

It was just as she reached the packed snow covering the walkway to the café that she heard a cheerful *toot toot* and looked up to see a ferry boat chugging its way past the South Point Lighthouse toward St. Simon. She blinked to make sure she wasn't imagining it. Nope, still there.

A moment later, she stepped into the café to find Dahlia setting a table near the fireplace, already popping and cracking with a cozy flame. "Merry Christmas," Suzanne said.

Dahlia looked up with a smile, a plate painted with red-nosed reindeers around the rim in her hand. "And the same to you," she replied.

As Suzanne began unwrapping her winter wear by the door, she said, "Did you know the ferry is running?"

Dahlia nodded calmly, lowering the last plate onto the table, centering it just so on a sparkly green placemat. "The ice cleared." Then she lifted her gaze back to Suzanne, her eyes filled with unmistakable sorrow.

"Mr. Desjardins left on the ferry just a few minutes ago."

Oh God. Mr. Desjardins had left? Just like that? With no warning? Dropping the tails of her scarf, abandoning the unwrapping altogether, Suzanne stepped closer to her friend. "I'm so sorry to hear that. He... didn't want to stay?"

"Actually," Dahlia told her softly, brow knit, "he did. But I told him he should go. That he should be with his daughter on Christmas. And that all good things must end."

Suzanne let out a sigh, feeling far less cheerful now, and despite herself, almost angry at Dahlia for pushing away the affections of a worthy man. "Why? Why did you send him away? And on Christmas Day, no less."

Dahlia offered up a tired sort of shrug. "I'm better off on my own, that's all."

Suzanne blinked, chest tight, still frustrated. "Then why do you look so sad?"

"I'm not," Dahlia insisted.

"Are you sure?"

"No," she confessed simply. Then put on a smile that appeared stiff and forced as she came close enough to lock her arm through Suzanne's. "But it's Christmas— I'll deal with everything else another day. Let us make merry, my girl."

BECK AWOKE FEELING more energetic than he had in days—hell, maybe weeks. It was the kind of energy that came from inside—a little nervous, a little excited. He laughed, realizing it wasn't unlike what a kid feels on Christmas morning. He cautiously hoped his Christmas might turn out better than he'd thought it could a mere twelve hours ago when he'd left the Walton house.

He'd wished for quite a few holiday miracles in the last few weeks, and none of them had panned out—so maybe he shouldn't be optimistic. But he was anyway. And even if his plans for the day didn't turn out the way he hoped…well, regardless, he knew his father would be proud of the decision he'd made.

He pushed up from the bed, wondering if Cade had found his presents under the tree yet. And when his phone buzzed the arrival of a text as he made his way down the hall, he wasn't surprised to glance down and see it had come from George. What *did* surprise him was the message itself: Don't know if you've heard, but the ferries are running. We've decided to keep our plans for the day, but pack up this evening and leave tomorrow morning. So Christmas lunch is still on, but we won't hold you to it if you decide to head south.

Hell, it was the last news he'd expected at this point. And part of him felt obligated enough to his family to wonder if he should indeed throw some clothes in a bag and catch the next boat to the mainland. He could drive all day and reach Emma's late tonight.

But he'd still miss the Christmas celebration today. And they'd all still be there tomorrow or the next day. And he felt pretty committed to his plans here.

He wondered briefly if Lila would stay or go. He didn't know her family's holiday plans, but her drive wouldn't be nearly as long as his and she might get to at least enjoy the evening with them.

Before he could form another thought, the doorbell rang. Over and over again. He grinned, suspecting he knew who stood on the other side. Despite being in flannel sleep pants and a T-shirt, he answered—to find a certain little boy beaming up at him excitedly. "Becker, you won't believe it! Santa found me, Santa found me!"

"Of course I believe it," he told Cade a bit smugly. "I'm not surprised at all."

"It was so hard to sleep! I'm pretty sure I heard reindeers!"

Beck smiled, wondering exactly what Cade thought reindeer sounded like.

"Grammy says it's all thanks to you! You have to come see all the stuff I got! There's a really cool bike, and a Pikachu, and a sled, and some LEGOs, and—" He stopped, seeming breathless, then rolled his eyes at the enormity of it all. "Well, you just have to see it all because it's more than I can even remember. So can you get dressed and come over? We can play with stuff until it's time to eat! I wish I could play all day, but Grammy says we have to pack because we can go home now." Then he scrunched up his little face, looking at first sad, then confused. "I thought I wanted to go home, but now I kinda wanna stay."

Beck reached down, ruffling the boy's hair. "I'm sure your Mom and Dad are gonna be excited to see you."

"They will," Cade agreed—before looking sad again. "But I'm gonna miss you."

The words squeezed Beck's heart tight. They'd all been so damn concerned about getting off the island that they hadn't stopped to think about how it would feel when it actually happened. "I'm gonna miss you, too. A lot. But you'll come stay with your grandfolks again, right?"

He sounded glum. "I guess. But not for a long time."

A long time—in little kid world—was probably summer. But at the moment that actually sounded pretty far away to Beck, too. "Well, we'll just have to keep in touch."

"How?"

Good question. Cade probably didn't quite have a cell phone yet, or email. Hell, he probably couldn't quite even read or spell now that Beck thought about it. So Beck said, "I'm gonna give you my number. And your grandpa has it, too. You can call me anytime you want, okay?"

"Okay," he said, appearing a little heartened.

"I'll make sure your grandpa knows that, too, and passes it on to your parents."

Cade nodded, and said "Okay" again. Then tilted his head. "But I hope you won't be lonely for the rest of today after Christmas lunch."

Sweet kid. But Beck rushed to reassure him. "Don't worry—I need to head down into town after that anyway."

"What for?"

"Just have someone I need to wish a merry Christmas to." One more time. Still hoping for miracles.

THE REPEATED RINGING of the doorbell shook Lila from sleep. *Ding dong ding dong ding dong.* Given that she'd been resting better since Beck had come into her life, she'd also started taking advantage of the freedom to sleep in most mornings. As she tumbled out of bed, disoriented, her mind raced. Was she late for dinner at the café? She glanced at a hall clock as she headed for the stairs—but no, that was still a couple hours away.

Ding dong ding dong. She thumped down the stairs and skidded to a stop at the door—vaguely aware that it appeared as if an entire crowd stood on the porch. Was it an angry mob? Villagers with pitchforks? No—that would come later, after she did what she'd decided to do. So, feeling safe for now, she flung open the door—to find her entire family standing on the porch of the Summerbrook Inn.

She almost wondered if they were figments of her imagination. Meg, her parents, Seth, and even an old man she assumed was his grandpa. "What the hell?" she muttered.

"Nice PJs," Meg said.

Lila glanced down to see she wore the purple ones with the snowflakes—which belonged to Meg. "I packed inappropriately," she explained. Then shook her head, beyond confused. "How did you guys get here?"

"I told you—I have friends at the ferry," Meg answered.

Lila squinted at her. "You really got the ferry to run again just because they like you?" Then she blinked. "You're even more amazing than I thought."

Her sister—such a sight for sore eyes—just leaned her head back and laughed. "Well, no. The ice melted. But my ferry friends told me yesterday they were optimistic—so we packed, got up early this morning, called and found out they were going to run, and reached St. Simon about an hour ago."

"We even picked up a turkey on the way!" their dad said, lifting a weighty-looking grocery sack high for Lila to see.

After which Mom jiggled a shopping bag at her side,

adding, "And brought everything else we need to make Christmas dinner."

"If you let us in, that is," Meg said.

And Lila flinched. "Oh!" Then stepped out of the way—still stunned by this sudden turn of events.

"It'll take a while for the turkey to cook," Mom informed her as the group began spilling in the door, all laden with rolling suitcases and bags with wrapped gifts peeking from them, "but we can just open presents and catch up and watch Christmas movies until then."

Lila covered her mouth with her hand, emotion welling inside her. "I can't believe you're really here! You just have no idea...no idea how happy I am to see you guys." Her voice cracked at the end, and she threw one arm around Meg and the other around her Mom before they could even begin to set anything down. Tears snuck out as she buried her face in Meg's shoulder.

"No need to cry, sweetie," Dad said over her shoulder. "We're here now and ready to have a merry Christmas with you."

Lila sniffed back the tears, toughened herself up. Because she was elated. Just emotional. Surprised at *how* emotional. "You're right," she said, wiping her face—and growing sheepish to remember Seth and his grandfather were also witnessing the entire show. She stood up straighter and reached out a hand to the man with the gray mustache. "I'm Lila. And I'm not usually crying or answering the door in pajamas. I'll seem more normal later."

The old man let out a hearty chuckle. "Normal is overrated, and I'm exceedingly pleased to make your acquaintance, young lady."

Then she lifted a small wave in the direction of Meg's off-the-charts-attractive boyfriend who she'd met over Thanksgiving. "Hey, Seth."

"Hey, Lila."

As the crowd dispersed, Mom and Dad heading for the kitchen with groceries and Seth and his granddad carrying gifts to the tree in the parlor, Meg stayed in the foyer and whispered to Lila, "The tears aren't just about Christmas, are they?"

How did Meg know her so well? She shook her head and said, "Lots of things. I'm so glad you're home."

"Me, too." Now that Meg had freed her hands, she gave Lila a hug, which Lila returned tightly.

There was so much to tell her sister.

About Simon, and Whitney.

About the land behind the inn.

And about Beck, too.

All the stuff about Chicago, and the stuff about the trees—well, those would be challenging to talk to her sister about, because they were difficult subjects. But it was when she thought of Beck that her heart hurt the worst.

BECK SAT AT the Waltons' table after a nice lunch that had been followed by two kinds of cookies and some homemade pie. He'd been surprised when George had walked to their Christmas tree and returned with a gift for him. "Just a little something to remind you of home," he said as Beck pulled a bottle of Kentucky bourbon from a tall, thin gift bag. Given the weather and confinement on the island, he suspected it had come from their personal liquor cabinet, and he appreciated the gesture.

"Though maybe you don't need to be reminded of it so badly now," Marie said pleasantly. "Are you headed south, as well?"

"In a day or two," he replied. "Just need to see how some things pan out first."

"I have something for you, too," Cade said. Then produced a hand-drawn picture of Santa Claus with the words *Thank you, Becker! I love you!* scrawled in red crayon.

The sight tugged at Beck's heart as he said, "This is great! I'll cherish it always." And he wasn't even exaggerating—he would truly treasure it. "Come here," he said to Cade then, after which he pulled the little boy into a big bear hug.

They were good people and he was honored to be part of their gathering. But at the same time, he found himself keeping an eye on the clock. Whereas last night he'd welcomed the unhurried visiting time, today he suffered the urge to rush off now that the meal was through. "I know you guys have a lot of packing to do," he began, "so I should let you get to it." He was trying to be considerate of their schedule, but he also worried he'd reach the inn to find Lila gone.

Though as he stood up and they began exchanging goodbyes and Merry Christmases, Beck found himself saying to Marie, "Um, before I go, could I ask you a favor?"

He had a Christmas gift for Lila, but he wanted to make it special. And just as for Cade's stuffed dog, he needed some ribbon.

BEFORE THEIR GRANDMOTHER'S passing, Christmas at the Summerbrook Inn had been a festive, lively affair.

Now, again, the big old Victorian house echoed with laughter, music, the clatter of a large table being set, and good smells wafted from the kitchen all through the house. Cups of hot chocolate and eggnog were sipped by the tree as Gran's old Christmas records spun on the turntable near the hearth.

It seemed to Lila a day of surprises, a day that she felt pushing her toward…well, things she needed to do. And probably should have done before now. But it was Christmas, and maybe that was part of it, too—sometimes Christmas pushed you to just make things right.

And so it was with little forethought or planning that she stole quietly away, upstairs to her bedroom, then pulled out her cell phone and called Whitney.

Her heart beat painfully hard as it began to ring. And maybe Whitney wouldn't even answer, because maybe she'd be afraid Lila was calling to tell her off, to say "I told you so" or something else equally awful. And she was starting to think about whether to leave a voice mail or just give up—when her ex-bestie answered with a timid and cautious, "Hello?"

Lila let out the breath she hadn't realized she was holding, and said, softly, "Merry Christmas."

Whitney's voice sounded a little shaky, nervous, yet still relieved, as she said, "Merry Christmas to you, too. And… I'm sorry, Lila. So, so sorry. I was so wrong."

"It's okay," Lila whispered. And it wasn't really that it was okay, but it was that Lila forgave her.

"I…guess you've seen the news."

"Yes," Lila said. "And I'm sorry, too—that you've had to go through this."

"I should have listened to you, should have believed you."

"It's…hard," Lila said. "When you respect someone so much and then…"

"Then…" Whitney said, and they both let the rest hang in the air, not needing to be said.

"Do you think…we could maybe be friends again?" Lila asked. Not wanting to give Simon one more thought today—wanting instead to focus on what mattered, on her relationships.

"God, yes!" Whitney practically shrilled into the phone. "I've missed you so much."

"I've missed you, too! And I have so much to tell you."

They talked a few minutes longer, agreeing to get together as soon as Lila got back to Chicago, but agreeing that for now, today, they both should just concentrate on enjoying the holiday with their families.

"I'm so glad you called, Lila," Whitney said before they hung up. "Thank you. Thank you so much."

"I'm glad I did, too," Lila told her. Sometimes it wasn't so hard to fix something if you tried. And Lila got off the phone feeling a renewed sense of hope, and also of courage.

When the doorbell rang as she was walking back down the stairs, she opened it to find Dahlia and Suzanne on the other side. "You both came! I'm so happy! Meg will be thrilled!" Then she called down the hall. "Meg? Come see who's here!" She'd texted them both earlier, explaining the unexpected arrivals and that she hoped they would understand why she wouldn't be at dinner. Of course, they did, and she invited them down to surprise her sister.

"Oh my God—it's so good to see you both!" Meg said, rushing to the foyer to greet her friends.

While they exchanged hugs and hellos, Lila squeezed past her father and Seth in the parlor to snatch up her gifts for the two women.

"Thank you both," she said, returning to the entry-way, "for being so welcoming to me, and for becoming my friends."

Suzanne appeared more touched by the gesture than Lila had expected—but perhaps she was just happy to be past the awkwardness about Beck. Still basking in the joy of her phone call with Whitney, Lila remained grateful that Suzanne hadn't held the situation against her—though she hated that Suzanne had gotten hurt, possibly *because* of her.

Both women seemed delighted with their hats, and Dahlia said, "It's true that handmade gifts are the most special."

Which prompted Meg to blink and say, "Who hand made them?"

And Lila answered, "Me. I found my old looms in the attic. I've become quite the loom knitter."

"Oh yes," Dahlia backed her up. "She's joined us for a couple of knitting bees at the Nook. She's a natural."

"Allie Hobbs even offered to sell my work," she bragged, pleased to impress her sister—because she could see that Meg was, indeed, taken aback and admiring the hats.

"These are so great," Meg said, studying at her friends' gifts. "I had no idea you were so talented, Lila."

She shrugged. "Neither did I. I thank Gran. Even if

it took me a while—like twenty years—to really get into the looming thing."

Meg invited her friends to join them for dinner—but Dahlia reminded them why she couldn't. "Thank you for the offer, but I have a ham in the oven for Zack and Suzanne."

Lila raised her eyes to Dahlia. "And for Mr. Desjardins, too?"

Dahlia shook her head. Left it at that. And something in her silence made Lila sad. And reminded her she was pretty sad for herself in a similar way. Maybe she just wanted *someone* to be happy in love, and Dahlia seemed deserving of happiness. At least Meg had Seth now.

"Perhaps we'll come back later this evening if the party is still going on," Dahlia suggested, lightening the mood.

"I suspect it will be," Meg assured her. "So come back whenever you like! I have a feeling we may be at it 'til the wee hours of the morning."

An hour later, the family had all exchanged gifts—and Lila had taken great joy in surprising them all with her knitted goods. Like Meg, her parents were both stunned to hear she'd actually knitted the hats and scarves and potholders they'd opened, and she took a pride in her holiday offerings unlike ever before. At first they'd been made as a distraction from her troubles and a way to fill the time—but they'd also been made with love. A love that had heartened her and given her more strength than she'd realized—lifting her up through all the recent troubles in her life. Of course, she'd had support from other directions, too—like Meg's friends and Beck.

And all in all, somehow it had added up to help-ing her figure out the next steps she needed to make. Not all of them, but at least some. She hadn't planned to talk to Meg and her parents about it all until after Christmas—but suddenly, now, she didn't want to wait.

Up until this moment, she'd seen it as… heavy, too heavy to be in keeping with the holiday spirit. But having her family show up when she'd least expected it, and then making peace with Whitney, all served to remind her that what she had to tell them was actually about strength, and about taking control of her life, and about doing the right thing. That she was taking neg-atives and turning them into positives. Which meant there wasn't really any reason to hold back.

And as for her fears about Meg judging her harshly over this—they'd faded since coming back face-to-face with her. Meg loved her. She'd felt that love practically spilling through the door and all through the house when Meg and the rest of the family had arrived. And if it turned out she was wrong, if it turned out her sis-ter held her responsible in any way…well, she'd deal with it. No more running—from anything.

"That turkey's smelling mighty splendiferous," Seth's grandpa remarked as they all sat in the par-lor, wrapping paper strewn on the floor, Miss Kitty batting around a stray strip of green ribbon near the Christmas tree.

"Another hour or more to go," Mom replied. "We're getting there, though, slowly but surely."

Lila was just about to announce to the room at large that she had something to say—when the doorbell rang again. Someone else must have figured out Meg and Seth were home and stopped by to wish them a merry

Christmas. So instead, Lila held her tongue, pushed up from the sofa with a cup of hot chocolate in her hand, and went to answer.

On the other side of the door stood Beck Grainger, wearing the hat she'd made for him, jaw covered in unshaven stubble, brown eyes warming her up with one glance. He looked good enough to eat—and not just because she was starving. She'd been ready to tell her family how she planned to start the new year, but she'd been on the verge of another big decision, too. Now her heart beat harder at the mere sight of him and she knew, more clearly than ever, what she had to do to give herself a merry Christmas.

CHAPTER TWENTY-EIGHT

"I'M SO GLAD to see you," she told him.

He drew back slightly. "You are?" He raised one eyebrow. "Is this a trick?"

She laughed, drawn back to some of their first meetings and realizing how much had changed between them. "No," she told him. "I was…planning to come see you later, hoping you wouldn't be gone."

"Really?"

She nodded, smiled softly, didn't try to hide the affection she felt for him. "Yes. But now you're here."

"Now I'm here," he said, a small smile unfurling across his handsome face, as well. "Only…is this a good time? I mean…" He leaned in slightly, glanced around. "Seems like you might be having a party."

She let her eyes widen on him. "Guess what—the ferry is running! My family surprised me! They came here for Christmas!"

"Aw, Lila—that's so great! I'm so happy for you."

But then she realized, sadly, that he didn't have the same good fortune. "I'm sorry you don't get to spend the day with yours, though."

"It's okay," he assured her with a quick headshake. "I heard about the ferry, and I'll get there soon enough. Right now, I'm happy to be exactly where I am."

She bit her lip, the promise of joy seeming closer

than it had yesterday as she told him, "Come in. Meet my mom and dad."

"Um, are you sure, Lila, because…"

Oh, the trees. He was worried about the trees. "I haven't told them," she said, "so no one here wants to kill you or anything. At least not yet." She ended with a playful grin.

"Well, that's good," he said, still looking uncertain, "but—"

She used her free hand to reach out and grab onto his arm, pulling him inside. "Just come in already. It's cold."

Shutting the door behind him, she dragged him into the parlor. "Everyone, this is Beck Grainger. He lives up on West Bluff. Beck, these are my parents. And Mr. McNaughton, Seth's grandpa. And of course, you already know Meg and Seth," she ended, motioning toward them.

Greetings were exchanged all around—until Meg said, "Beck, nice to see you. What brings you by?"

Beck appeared unsure. "Um, just stopped in to say merry Christmas."

But Lila didn't like his having to pretend it was a random holiday visit, so she said to Meg, "Beck and I have…gotten to know each other." And letting them know that would also make it seem less insane when she announced her plans in front of him.

"You didn't mention that to me on the phone," Meg said to Lila, brows narrowed as if something very mysterious and intriguing were afoot.

"Well," Lila explained, "it was on my big list of things to talk to you about."

"Oh, I see." Meg smiled slyly now, clearly assuming this was some easy new romance that had come along. Whereas it was actually so much more complicated than Lila would ever be able to put into words.

And yet…in another way, it was getting simpler all the time.

She was going to let herself love him.

She hadn't been completely sure of that until she'd opened the door to find him standing there. But she simply didn't want to let this love go when she thought it might be the best thing that had ever happened to her. So she was going to do her damnedest to forget about the trees and what was easy and what was hard and just love him. And pray Meg could understand. And her parents, too. And her Gran up in heaven.

"And I hope you can stay," she told Beck, "because… I was just about to say something important that I'd like you to hear, too."

From there, Lila took a deep breath and centered herself. And in the most concise and least upsetting manner she could, she told her family what had happened with Simon Alexis at his house in Chicago.

And about her job loss and Whitney's betrayal.

She was succinct and unemotional—her voice didn't even shake. And sure, Seth's grandpa was getting a lot more than he bargained for coming here for Christmas, but she'd just kept this from her family for too long—it was time for it all to come out.

"And I've decided," she went on, "to contact the *Sun-Times* and tell them my story, to back Whitney up. Because one woman can be seen as an aberration, or someone with an ax to grind, or any number of things that doesn't add up to proving his guilt. But two women make the claim be taken a little more seriously. And maybe then a third will come forward. And a fourth.

"I'm not sure what it will involve. And I know I'll be in for a lot of attack and criticism. But I've realized it's as simple as following Whitney's brave example and just saying 'Me, too.' So that's what I'm going to do. Because it feels right to me. And because telling the truth will make me feel stronger." Funny how taking charge of something that had left her so weak was now suddenly making her feel so incredibly capable and strong—this fast.

"And I guess I see it as…a way I can give. Give something to the world. I've been trying to do that more, and it hasn't always worked out well, but I'm trying."

For some reason, her eyes fell on her dad, then. Maybe because she'd feared he'd take what had happened with Simon the hardest. And the glassy look in his eyes told her she was right. "Lila, I…"

"Dad," she said, pointing at him, "don't. Don't get upset. I mean, I know it's upsetting, and I know I'm your little girl—but I'm fine. I'm really fine. I promise."

He spoke through clenched teeth. "I just want to go find this man and hurt him."

"That's pretty much what I said when she told me, too," Beck chimed in.

"He'll get what's coming to him," Lila said stalwartly. "I believe that now. I really do."

"Honey, why didn't you tell us all this at Thanksgiving?" her mom asked, looking forlorn.

Lila gave her head a short shake. "I was still shellshocked, still trying to process it. I just wasn't ready."

She, of course, left out the fear that they'd judge her for it—which seemed crazy to her now—and yet the thought still led her gaze to Meg. What was Meg thinking? Feeling?

And as if on cue, Meg reached out from where she'd been sitting on the arm of the sofa to take Lila's hand. Their eyes met—and Lila felt it again, that overwhelming love. She'd worried for nothing. In fact, she felt awful now for thinking Meg would ever doubt her, no matter *what* kind of sister she'd been most of their lives. Some things went beyond that.

"Lila, I'm so horribly sorry that happened to you." Meg shook her head, looking bereft. "I—I can't even imagine. And you're being so brave." She finished by squeezing Lila's hand.

In response, Lila blew out a breath, and rushed to whisper to her sister, "Can—can I talk to you in private for a minute?"

Despite her low tone, the gravity in her voice had come through loud and clear, and Meg quickly said, "Sure."

With her hand still in her sister's grasp, Lila tugged Meg away from their family, past Beck, through the foyer, and down the hall into the nook. And standing between the built-in bookcases and a tall, frosted windowpane, Lila took Meg's other hand, holding on to both of them now, then looked into her sister's eyes and said, "Meg, I'm so sorry I wasn't there for you. When you had leukemia. And after. And always. I was weak and didn't know how to handle it. But I know that doesn't make it any better. I know I should have been there. I'm sorry if I let you down." Even aware of tears rolling down her cheeks, she worked hard to keep her gaze on Meg's, not back away from this, not let it turn her back into that weaker girl she'd once been.

Meg's face changed, reshaping itself into one Lila seldom saw—jaw clenched slightly, lips pressed tight together, every muscle gone tense. Lila's heart beat faster. Everyone had absolved her. Everyone. But Meg wasn't going to.

"You…you did let me down, Li," she said quietly. "To be honest, it hurt when you weren't there. When you knew what I was going through but you didn't come, didn't call."

"I was young. And weak. And selfish."

"Yes," Meg agreed gently.

Lila's chest tightened—but she had to be tough. "I should have said this a long time ago—but I'm saying it now. I love you and I'm sorry I've been a sucky little sister."

At this, Meg tilted her head, smiled a little. "You're not a sucky little sister." She reached up to wipe away one of Lila's tears with her thumb. "It was a tough time for everyone. And I let go of that hurt a long time ago—I knew it wasn't because you didn't love me. And we all make mistakes."

Lila sniffed, tilted her head inquisitively. "Even you?"

It made Meg laugh. "Yes, of course even me. I came to this tiny island and never left. I isolated myself. I ran away from the life I had before cancer."

Lila gasped. Meg had run from something? Strong, perfect Meg? And yet, it suddenly made sense, seemed clear. Meg had run away from her life. Just like Lila had a few weeks ago.

"Can you forgive me, Meg?" she asked.

"I forgave you years and years ago," her sister said with a soft smile.

"I really, truly want to be a better sister to you, and a better person altogether."

It surprised her when Meg's expression went serious. "You're already a perfectly fine person, Lila." Meg shook her head and said, "Do you know how often I've wished I could be like you in some way?"

Lila drew back, lowered her chin. "Huh?"

"You're so funny, and so fun. I admire that you don't take everything as seriously as I do. I admire your spontaneity, and...even your selfishness, if that makes any sense."

"It doesn't," Lila told her. She'd been feeling so happy there for a minute, but this was confusing.

Meg said, "It took some selfishness for me to figure out, earlier this year, that I wasn't happy with my life. It took some selfishness to make some big changes. A little selfishness can be a good thing. In fact, selfishness is an ugly name for it—it can be about...self-care. And I admire that you know how to give yourself that."

Lila blinked, took that in. Self-care. She'd told Beck he was only taking care of himself when he'd withdrawn from his father. Yet maybe self-care was something *she'd* surrendered recently—she'd tried to run away from her troubles, but at the same time she'd blamed herself for so much, over and over. And so... maybe Meg really *would* understand the decision she'd made about Beck—the decision she *had* to make. That it was bigger than selfishness.

"I'm proud of you, Lila," Meg said. "I'm proud of you for being so brave about this ugly Simon Alexis situation. I'm proud of you for recognizing your faults.

And I'm proud of you for apologizing to me just now. Even if it took a while." She ended on a wink.

Which made Lila clamp her eyes shut in a tiny last bit of self-deprecating embarrassment. But she laughed at the same time—then gave Meg a big hug. "I want to be you when I grow up," she whispered in her sister's ear.

And Meg whispered back, "You already *are* grown-up—and I like you just the way you are, I promise."

When the two women reentered the parlor, Dad asked, "What was *that* about?"

Men—they didn't get that sometimes women just had to say important, private things to each other. Lila let out a sigh and told him, "I just needed to apologize to Meg for something that happened a long time ago." The two sisters exchanged brief looks before Lila went on. "Like I said, I'm trying to learn to be more giving, and sometimes giving can mean apologizing."

"I know you and I don't know each other well," Seth said then, surprising her by speaking up in his Southern drawl, "but if you ask me, I think you're being awful hard on yourself."

Lila felt her eyebrows shoot up. "I am?"

"Well, you seem perfectly giving to me. After all, you gave me and Meg three weeks with my grandpa by coming to stay at the inn and I'm grateful for that. And you gave Meg time away to see someplace new, which she hasn't had very much of."

"When you heard I was collecting stuff for Cade," Beck added, "you took the time to find something you thought he'd like, wrapped it for him, and carried it up to West Bluff in the snow."

"And look at all these amazing hats and gloves and scarves you made for us all," her mom said.

"And you made gifts for Dahlia and Suzanne, too," Meg pointed out.

"You were even kind enough," Seth's grandpa added, "to make one for an old man you don't even know. That's pretty darn giving if you ask me."

"And you've given me," Beck said, more quietly now, turning to look her in the eye, "well, more than you know."

She drew in her breath, replying softly, "Same here." Then she bit her lip. "And just so you know, I've long since forgiven you. About the trees."

"What trees?" her dad asked.

Okay, moment of truth—when she'd least expected it. But it was her own fault for yet another slip of the tongue. Pressing her lips tight together, she tried to gather still more courage as she turned to her sister. "Meg, the thing is—"

Beck's hand clamped down on her arm. "I need to talk to you."

She spun her head back in his direction. "Right now?"

"Sorry, but yes."

She blew out a sigh—then looked back to the rest of the room. "Okay—heavy conversation officially back on hold. Resume your merry-making."

She really wished Beck had just let her finish—now that she'd started barreling through all this hard stuff, she wanted to keep going, get it all out in one big clump while she was feeling all bold and gutsy.

But since he hadn't—well, she had some things to say to him, too. So before they stepped from the room, she snatched up a small package from beneath the tree, then took his hand and led him down the hall and back to the nook.

"Before you say anything, I have something to give you." She held out the gift—the reason she'd originally planned to visit him later today.

"It's urgent I open this?" he asked, sounding impatient. "Because what I have to talk to you about is pretty pressing."

"Yes, and please," she insisted anyway. "Just open it. I'm on a roll here, saying big things, and I need to keep going. And what I need to say next, to you, has to do with what's in the package."

Sighing, he said, "Okay, fine," and ripped into it. Inside lay a pair of knitted gloves, dark gray, with a subtle navy blue snowflake design creating a band around the hand.

"I didn't make these," she informed him before he could say a word. "As I said, gloves are beyond my current skill level. I bought them at the Knitting Nook because you don't have the sense to buy any yourself and I don't like your hands being cold."

"They're nice," he said. "Really nice. And it's damn sweet of you." Then he raised his gaze from the gloves to her. "But...how are they urgent?"

"Look inside them," she instructed.

"Inside them?"

"Dump them out. There's something in one of them."

He did so—and from the right glove dropped the key to the bulldozer, into his other palm. "Oh," he said, looking as if he beheld a rare gem.

"I'm...ready to give it back to you now," she said.

"Even if it pains me, I know it has to be, and I know holding on to it isn't going to stop anything from happening. So I'm making peace with that. And I'm… ready to give us a chance, Beck. A real chance."

He stood up straighter, blinked, looked dumbfounded. And, if she wasn't mistaken, also profoundly happy. "Really, Lila? Are you serious? What changed?"

"I…haven't been able to see the forest for the trees— literally. And you're the forest. I love the trees, but I'm letting them go, and keeping you."

"Oh, honey," he said. "That makes me so damn happy. And hell—that's the most giving thing you could possibly do, because I know how much they mean to you." Then he leaned over and kissed her on the forehead. "But now I have something for you, too."

She looked up. "What is it?" After all, he wasn't carrying any packages or anything.

Taking her hand, he said, "Come with me," and to her surprise, led her to the kitchen, opened the inn's back door, and drew her outside into the backyard by the brook. She stepped carefully—for the first time since her arrival, she'd just come outdoors in leather fashion boots instead of snow boots and she worried for their well-being as they moved through deep, untouched snow.

"Beck, I should probably put on my…"

But when she raised her eyes from her boots and the snow they plodded through, she stopped talking. Because she saw her gift.

Bright red bows dotted the hillside across the brook. Dozens of ribbons had been tied around the trunks of the trees there. The trees stood looking resplendent even while bare, dressed in holiday red.

It was all she could do to stay on her feet as he said, "Merry Christmas, Lila."

"Wh-what's happening?" she managed.

"I'm giving you the land, the hillside behind the inn. I'll have a deed drawn up after the holidays."

"When did you do this?" she asked, shaking her head, still gaping at the beautiful bare winter trees decorated with Christmas ribbon.

"Over the last hour or so. I'm lucky no one glanced out a back window."

Of course, there were much bigger questions. "But... how?" She shook her head once more, confused. "How can you do this? I thought you couldn't."

"I'm...actually not sure yet. But I'm gonna call the surveyors—have them come back out and reconfigure the lots in a way that leaves the hillside alone."

She blinked. "But what about the money?"

"I'll lose some."

"Some?" She peered up at him, wide-eyed, at a loss.

"Okay, a lot actually. But it'll be worth it to make you happy."

She didn't know what to say. Part of her was overjoyed, but another part of her worried. "Beck, I'm not sure I can let you do this."

"You're not?" he asked, drawing back his chin in disbelief. "After the millions of times you asked me to?"

"Well, now that you're doing it," she explained, "I'm concerned. Because you haven't worked out the details and what if it's worse than you think financially?"

"Just trust me to get it figured out, honey. I'll make it happen, one way or another, and it'll be okay. I promise. I want to do this for you. For Meg and your family, too. But mostly for you. I want to make you happy. Whatever it takes."

"Oh, Beck," she said. "You *do* make me happy."

Though despite getting what she'd wanted for all this time, she suddenly found it hard to let go of the concern over his monetary loss here—he'd worked hard for all he had and she didn't want to be the cause of his financial ruin. And yet...he was doing such a kind, amazing, perfect, *giving* thing for her, so maybe she just had to trust him that it would be all right and graciously accept.

"You've made me the happiest woman on the planet right now," she told him. "And it's not just about the trees. I mean, it *is*—it's about the trees. But it's also because...you really love me. Enough to give me what you know is important to me, enough to move heaven and earth for me and my family."

"I'm hoping you'll give me something in return," he said warmly.

"What's that?"

"A yes."

"A yes?" She blinked. "To what?"

Standing next to her in the snow, Beck drew in a deep breath, and for the first time since they'd met, she thought he actually looked nervous. "I know this is going to sound a little crazy, and fast—but it's Christmas, so I'm hoping for a miracle because I want you to marry me." Then he dropped to one knee in the snow. "Will you, Lila? Will you marry me?"

"Yes!" she said. She didn't even have to think about it. And maybe it *was* a little crazy, but it didn't feel that way.

As she threw her arms around his neck to kiss him,

he picked her up off the ground—and she heard Meg say, "You're right—I've missed some things."

They both looked over to see the whole family standing outside the back door in the snow.

"You don't know the half of it," Lila told her, laughing as Beck lowered her back to her feet.

"Um, why are there ribbons on the trees?" Meg asked then, looking even more perplexed.

"We'll tell you everything over dinner," Lila assured her.

Meanwhile, Beck engaged in a quiet little fist pump, whispering to himself, "Yes! Finally got my miracle."

AFTER A CELEBRATION-FILLED Christmas dinner, Beck invited the Waltons down to the inn for pie and games. They'd finished their packing and joined in the party, delighted to hear Beck and Lila's news. Dahlia came back, as well—though Suzanne had chosen to go home early.

The Summerbrook Inn was filled on Christmas night, filled with people and joy and gifts and giving. Looking out over the merry crowd in the parlor, the room awash in the glow of holiday lights, Lila raised a toast. "To Gran. It would make her so happy to see the inn this way."

"Hear, hear," her dad agreed, and glasses and mugs clinked.

After which Meg let out a soft laugh—as she bent to pick up something from the floor.

"What is it?" Lila asked.

"A penny," Meg said. "Sometimes Gran leaves them for me. I have a feeling she's smiling down on us right now."

Lila met her sister's warm gaze, feeling that, too. Then she turned to lift a small, happy kiss to her fiancé's mouth.

"Hey, I thought you said she wasn't your wife," Cade challenged Beck.

"She's not," Beck told the little boy, then glanced lovingly at her. "But she's gonna be."

"Then maybe you can have some little kids for me to play with," Cade suggested.

And though up until that moment Lila hadn't quite been sure how she would feel about that, now, without a doubt she knew. As she looked into Beck's eyes, she smiled and said, "Maybe we will."

After that, the crowd resumed their talking and eating, but Lila stayed wrapped up in the wonder of what had turned out to be the most wonderful Christmas of her life. Turning, she touched her hand to Beck's chest and spoke quietly so that only he could hear. "Thank you," she said. "For the trees. For the laughter. For seeing the good in me even when I can't see it myself. And for the love. *Especially* for the love."

Leaning in to press a kiss to her forehead, he told her, "I'm pretty sure that *all* of those things are love, honey. Just in different ways." Then he added a wink. "And get used to 'em because there's gonna be a lot more where those came from. Well, except for trees. Trees I think we now officially have enough of."

"You're right," she agreed on a light laugh. "But the other stuff I'll take as much of as you can dish out. And the trees I'll cherish forever."

* * * * *